THE DROWNING GROUND

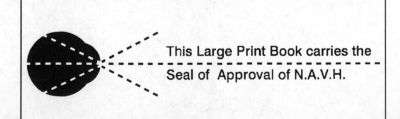

THE DROWNING GROUND

JAMES MARRISON

THORNDIKE PRESS

A part of Gale, Cengage Learning

GALE
CENGAGE Learning·

Farmington Hills, Mich • San Francisco • New York • Waterville, Maine
Meriden, Conn • Mason, Ohio • Chicago

LIBRARY OF CONGRESS CATALOGING-IN-PUBLICATION DATA

Marrison, James.
    The drowning ground / by James Marrison. — Large print edition.
        pages cm. — (Thorndike Press large print crime scene)
    ISBN 978-1-4104-8511-3 (hardcover) — ISBN 1-4104-8511-0 (hardcover)
    1. Police—England—Cotswold Hills—Fiction. 2. Missing children—Investigation—Fiction. 3. Children—Crimes against—Fiction. 4. Large type books. I. Title.
    PR6113.A767D76 2016
    823'.92—dc23   2015031710

Published in 2016 by arrangement with St. Martin's Press, LLC

Printed in Mexico
1 2 3 4 5 6 7 20 19 18 17 16

For Clarisa

The past is a predator.

— Argentinian saying

ACKNOWLEDGEMENTS

I would like to thank first and foremost my agent Helen Heller at the Helen Heller Agency without whose help, guidance and unfailing instincts this book would not have been possible. I would also like to thank Rowland White and Emad Akhtar at Michael Joseph, Hope Dellon at St Martin's Press, Donna Poppy at Penguin Books, and Camilla Ferrier and Jemma McDonagh at the Marsh Agency. Heartfelt thanks and gratitude also to my English and Argentinian families for their continued and unwavering support throughout the writing of this novel.

PROLOGUE

August 1997

Carefully tucked out of view so that it did not ruin the garden's neat symmetry, Frank Hurst's swimming pool was positioned to one side of a raised patio. It was completely surrounded by a tall wooden fence. The sound of our footsteps echoed loudly around the pool's edges as we stepped between a number of blood-stained towels, which were curled up along the granite. Two medics were standing above the body, and when they saw us they moved away so we could have a better look at her. The sun shimmered on the water. A bird called out shrilly and unexpectedly from the fields beyond. It was a hopeless sound somehow.

The housekeeper had managed to pull Sarah Hurst to the shallow end before running inside for the phone. She was face up. The tips of her slender fingers brushed the water as if she were pointing at it. The pages

11

of her magazine fluttered slightly in the wind beneath a deckchair.

Briefly, I looked away. The swimming pool was deep and solid-looking. It was an antique, and it was set away from the house, as if there were something indecent about having a swimming pool there at all. A strong smell of lavender came from a number of borders running along the far side of the fence. Powell had been a smoker back then, and he had lit one as he stared long and hard at the blood coiling on the surface of the pool.

There was a mosaic of a marlin being caught worked into the blue tiles. I started to walk closer to the edge, where there was a large red stain, possibly from Mrs Hurst's having slipped and hit her head.

From beyond the trees, a big car screeched to a halt in the gravel, and within seconds we glimpsed a shadow as Frank Hurst came sprinting across the wide sweep of lawn. Powell stood in his way, barring the gate. Hurst was well muscled and built like a rangy middleweight, and I had to help Powell hold him back when he got his first glimpse of his wife's body lying on the patio beside the pool. Sandy hair cut short. Grey eyes and a moustache severely trimmed along the horrified curve of his mouth.

12

I told Powell to get hold of Brewin and left him by the swimming pool; then I led Hurst back towards the house. There was a smell of freshly cut grass. A light shimmer of heat brushed along the walls of an old shed. It was hot even under the shade of the beech trees. A raised stone platform led to some French windows, which gave a perfect view of the lawn slipping off into the distance below. I led Hurst up the stone stairs and through the French windows to the living room, closing the curtains so he wouldn't have to watch them taking his wife's body across the lawn to the ambulance.

His daughter at some point had come back from school and was with the housekeeper; I could hear her trying to comfort her from deep within the house. A clock struck far off as night slowly fell outside. I asked my questions, and Hurst promptly, and without any hesitation at all, answered them. It was late by the time I left Dashwood Manor. Instead of making Hurst let me out the front door, I simply slipped through the French windows of the living room and headed out across the lawn.

It was still warm. I weaved my way past a large gas barbecue and some garden chairs, which stood stacked high under a green tarpaulin, and then made my way down the sloping lawn. Before I left the garden, I turned to see the house once more.

There was a light on upstairs. Hurst's daughter Rebecca was framed in the yellow light of her bedroom window. She had been about fifteen or sixteen back then. She was pretty, with long black hair and very blue eyes. She was staring at the water of the swimming pool, and when she saw me looking up at her she smiled sweetly. Then she turned away. But you could tell that she'd been crying.

Powell was waiting for me in the car in the gravelled driveway at the front. The ambulance was gone. It was the end of a long, dry summer, and even then, in the growing dark, it was almost as if you could feel the plants waiting for that first thick black drop of rain. Everything was quiet and still. I got in the car and slammed the door, breaking the silence, and we started the drive back to the station.

■ ■ ■ ■

PART ONE:
FIVE YEARS LATER

■ ■ ■ ■

1

December 2002

Graves arrived in Moreton-in-Marsh on the 9.53 train from Oxford. He was surprised to see that it was actually quite busy, and there was a market in full swing. Trellises were laid out all along the centre in uneven but well-spaced lines. Extra plastic chairs, which looked like they must have been commandeered from the village hall, had been placed near the bus stop, and there were three coaches parked along the side of the road. The market seemed to sell just about everything: cheap jewellery, watches, leather goods and bin bags. Brooms. Hats. Bath rugs. Jams. Bags. Cards. Sports clothes were pinned up on hangers with fluorescent signs covered in felt-tip marker: TWO FOR ONE. EVERYTHING FOR A POUND. THREE FOR ONE. SALE!

He threaded his way through the crowds with his luggage, losing his temper a little towards the end of the street as people struggled to get past him, eager to get to the stalls. He heard snatches of conversation as he went by. The accent was different here. Thicker. Friendlier-sounding. Less distant.

He crossed the road quickly. The front door to the police station led to a small waiting room, where a hefty but alert duty sergeant was waiting on the other side of a desk protected by a glass partition. Graves left his bags underneath a bench, and a few minutes later a friendly-looking constable walked in and introduced himself as Burton. A set of heavy keys jangled from the constable's belt as he moved towards the door and pushed it open, allowing Graves to go first. Burton blew his nose loudly into a handkerchief as they walked along a brightly lit but windowless corridor.

'Thought it might be a good idea to show you around before you get settled into work,' Burton said. 'If that's all right, sir. I see you've left your bags out there. You got a place fixed up already, have you?'

'No, not yet. I'm at the hotel up the road. The Manor, I think it's called.'

'Oh, the Manor House,' Burton said, impressed.

'Well, it's only for a few days, until I find

a flat or a room or something. And it was the only one,' Graves said a little defensively. 'I don't suppose you know anywhere? I didn't really have time to look before I came.'

'No, 'fraid not. Always worth asking around, though,' he said. 'One of the lads might have a spare room. Or you can put a notice up in the canteen.'

They walked down the corridor. Along the blue walls were notices pinned on red felt, and to the left a long window looked into the main room of the station itself. As they walked past it, Graves heard the muted murmur of activity through the glass and glimpsed a few figures huddled over computers through the grey blinds.

Burton did not seem to be in any hurry. He led Graves along another corridor and then almost reverently pushed open the door to a small but cosy-looking canteen. Inside, a burly man in a rumpled suit was sitting over the remains of his breakfast and flipping through the pages of a tabloid. It was all very neat and quiet here. Not at all like his old station.

'Who's this, then, Morris?' the man called out over his newspaper.

Burton introduced him.

The man looked at him appraisingly

before going back to his paper. But then he seemed to change his mind and put the paper down. 'Graves,' he said. 'We were expecting you today.'

'Yes.'

'So you'll be old Len's replacement.'

'Len?'

'Powell,' he said impatiently. 'Len Powell.'

'Oh, yes,' Graves said.

The man looked at him with an expression that was hard to read but may well have been concern. Then he smoothed the paper in front of him — indifferent again.

'I'm supposed to be meeting my new chief inspector this morning,' Graves said to Burton as they walked out. 'I was rather hoping that he'd be here to meet me.'

'No, he'll be in later,' Burton said in an offhand way. 'He's off out somewhere as usual. He tends to keep his own hours, and only shows up or phones in when he feels like he has to.' He shrugged. 'Drives her highness mad,' Burton said, looking furtively towards the main room. 'But she has to put up with it and lump it. You'll find out why if you're here long enough.'

Graves spent the rest of the morning organizing his desk, familiarizing himself with the workings of the station and adding a long list of telephone numbers to the contacts in his mobile. At one he found himself back in the canteen. He was joined almost immediately by two men of about his own age who introduced themselves as Edward Irwin and Robert Douglas and placed their trays in front of his. Irwin was narrow-shouldered and slender, with a huge and apparently insatiable appetite. Douglas was more athletic-looking and had a breezy, almost flippant way of talking. He looked at Irwin with a resigned astonishment as Irwin demolished his first course; then he puffed out his cheeks and breathed out again before motioning to the empty plate. Irwin took a long sip of his Coke. When Graves told them who he was going to be working with, there was a short silence. Irwin pushed the tray out in front of him and smoothed back his hair. He smiled broadly while Douglas leant forward in his chair.

Graves tenderly speared a potato with his fork and waited.

'Shotgun,' Douglas said finally.

'What?'

'Shotgun. You're going to be working with Shotgun.'

'Who's Shotgun?'

'Downes, of course.' Irwin laughed and lowered his voice. 'That's what we call him 'round here. Not to his face, mind.'

'Strange nickname,' Graves said quietly, not liking it all that much. 'What did he do? Shoot someone?' he added a little nervously.

Douglas shrugged. 'Don't know,' he said thoughtfully. 'He could have.' He laughed. 'You wouldn't know with 'im. Not in a million years. Keeps himself to himself and there's no telling. Not like most of them 'round here,' he said loudly, looking around the canteen. 'But that's what we call him. For as long as I can remember anyway.'

'You reckon he'll last long?' Irwin said, peering at Graves.

'Hard to tell,' Douglas said and smiled again.

'Last?' Graves said.

'You're his third since Len got sick,' Irwin announced. 'And Len's only been sick for . . . what is it? Two months now, is it?'

'Three.'

'He got rid of them,' Graves said. 'But why?'

Irwin shrugged. 'Pretty good lads as well. Good laugh that Mark fella was anyway, wasn't he?'

'Oh, he was all right,' Douglas said without enthusiasm.

'I didn't know,' Graves said quietly and immediately on edge. 'No one told me.' He put his fork down on his plate. Suddenly not hungry. Almost straightaway he started to think of Oxford. Of course, the super must have known when he had called him into his office. This wasn't a lifeline at all.

When Graves's superintendent back in Oxford had told him that he would be working with another senior officer, elsewhere, in just two weeks' time, he had been waiting for it. All the same, the news had surprised him, because it had happened so fast. Officially they couldn't get rid of him. He hadn't done anything wrong. The contemptuous backward glances of his old colleagues in Oxford had lost none of their sting as he remembered the long walk back to his desk from the super's office.

Graves smiled despite himself and shook his head. His own exile had been handled so smoothly that you couldn't help but admire it in a way. If this Downes got rid of him as well, then . . . well, it was all over, wasn't it? He'd probably be looking at demotion at the very least, or they'd find another way to get him out.

'Okay,' Graves said, deciding suddenly to try the direct approach, 'is there anything I should know, so that I don't end up like the other two?'

There was a pause. Irwin leant back in his chair and seemed to study him. 'Well,' he

23

said finally, 'he's quite formal. Polite. But he can go absolutely bananas when he feels like it . . . he's . . . I don't know. Keeps to himself, like I said. Never comes in here much,' he said, looking at the small queue by the till. 'And he used to be famous.'

'Famous?' Graves said.

'Oh, come off it,' Douglas said. 'Hardly. Well known maybe.'

'Up in London,' Irwin said. 'But that was before he came here, of course.'

'But you must know already,' Douglas said, 'that he's not from around here, right?'

'Well, I did hear something,' Graves said.

'He's from over in South America somewhere,' Douglas said vaguely. 'He's an Argie, ain't he,' he said without malice. 'One of them Argies.'

'Argentina?'

'Yes, yes, Argentina,' Douglas said impatiently.

'But how on earth did he end up here? Here in —'

'The middle of nowhere, you mean,' Douglas said, but he did not seem remotely offended. 'No idea.'

'He can be a sly old bugger when he feels like it.' Irwin reached for his jacket on the back of his chair. 'You know what that lot are like. Just look at that Maradona fella.'

'Cheating bastard,' Douglas said automatically.

Well, actually, Graves thought, he didn't know what they were like at all, and he had never had the slightest interest in football. Not even during the World Cup. Argentina: he tried to conjure up some kind of mental image, but his mind remained almost completely blank. Aside from the Falkland Islands and a few stray chords of tango from a film he had forgotten, there wasn't much at all.

After lunch, he was at his desk once more, familiarizing himself with timetables, duty rosters, expenses forms and punching in more phone numbers, including the coroner's office in Cheltenham, the victim support unit, hospitals and the forensic laboratory. At 4.00, he was still waiting to meet his new DCI. In the absence of anything more to do, he slid along past his own desk, until he was behind the desk in front of his.

It was cluttered with files and papers, and there was an old Styrofoam cup half filled with strong-looking black coffee. Most of the desks had a scattering of personal items pinned to the sides of the panelled walls or to the shelves. The desk opposite his own had no such bits and pieces. Or at least it didn't seem that way at first. Graves began to look more closely. Pinned neatly to the partition between the desks was a photo. The picture was in colour and quite large, and looked like it had once been the front page of an old magazine. A lithe and unmistakably foreign football player wearing a red-and-white shirt and black shorts was jumping with a great deal of grace over another player's outstretched legs. His eyes were fixed intently on the ball at his feet. The pitch itself seemed to be covered in white confetti, and streamers covered the touchline. Around the pitch was a seething cauldron of caged violence. Half the fans were gleefully spinning their shirts in the air above them, while standing before them was a line of tough-looking policemen carrying guns. Hanging on to the top of the tall metal fence that separated them was a lean, young man. His legs swung nonchalantly from the ten-foot drop on either side. Smoke from flares was everywhere. Reddish flames pushed liquidly outwards, spraying the shoulders of the crowd with sparks.

The headline was in the same shade of dark red as the stripes on the player's shirt, and there were a few other headlines at the side of the page in yellow. They were all written in Spanish. Graves tried to read them as best he could. He tried to say the words out loud but stumbled over them. *La revancha esperada,* or something like that. Whatever that meant. He tried again. It sounded even worse this time around.

' "The anticipated rematch",' came a quiet voice from behind him.

Graves closed his eyes for a second, wincing like the defender in the picture, and then turned around. The man looked amused. He motioned to the picture and pointed with his index finger at the headline.

'That's what it means.' His finger moved down towards the striker. 'And this player here. You know who he is?' he said hopefully. 'You recognize him maybe?'

'I'm afraid not,' Graves said.

'That's Enzo Francescoli. The Prince, they call him. He won five league titles and the Copa Libertadores in 1996 for River Plate football club,' he said, and nodded in deep satisfaction.

'Oh,' Graves said. 'Right.' He tried to look suitably impressed. 'The Copa —'

'Libertadores,' the man finished for him.

Graves looked at him. The first thing he noticed was the scar. It began at the very top of his forehead and ran deep and white almost straight beneath his thick but closely cropped black hair. Must have needed a lot of stitches, Graves thought, trying not to look at it and wondering how he'd got it. He was very brown despite the cold. He was around forty or forty-one years old and taller than Graves by a couple of inches, which put him at six foot one.

He pointed to the picture again. 'You see this,' he said, touching a flag that looked like it had been made of enough sheets to supply a small hospital. On it was written *Los Borrachos del Tablón.* '*Barra brava.* Hooligans,' he said with the faintest trace of what could have been fondness in his voice.

With some regret, he turned away from the picture and stared directly at Graves. In a moment his expression had changed to one of businesslike neutrality. There was a distant and detached look in his eye. It happened so quickly that Graves had the sudden feeling that he was gazing at a mask.

The man put out his hand. 'I'm Downes,' he said.

2

It was cold outside and as usual I was freezing. As I walked along the side of the village green, towards the welcoming lights of the pub, I saw a big old American car: a Falcon, by the looks of it. I hadn't seen one like it for years. I'd been thinking about my new sergeant, but the moment I saw the car I forgot all about him and about everything else too. A sleek outline to begin with and then an almost luminous flash of silver. It nosed its way through the night, fumes rising into the air from its exhaust. I stood still.

Yes, it was a Ford Falcon. Its huge engine let out a throaty roar as it went sliding along; its back fins sliced through the wintery air. It passed me by, and then it drew to a languorous stop at the traffic lights near the empty shops. There were two men sitting in front, though I could not make out their faces. The long, sleek bonnet of the car shook slightly. The pace of my heartbeat quickened as I watched it. My fists opened and closed, clenched and squeezed the air. I blinked and rubbed the back of my neck.

The traffic lights changed and, ever so slowly, it moved off. I held my breath and didn't move a muscle until the car had finally disappeared from view. I grunted, and my lips drew down in a hard angular line. Then I climbed the steps of the pub, hearing the familiar, happy, muffled murmur of the people inside, and ran my fingers through my hair.

The usual suspects were sitting in a far corner near the pool table. Their coats and scarves were piled up on a bench near the dartboard. I waved to them in a distracted kind of way, and then I weaved my way around the tables, heading straight for the fireplace in the middle near the windows.

For a while I stared at the fire licking against the throat of the chimney. My mind drifted, and I began to think about that car again. It had been a while since I'd seen one of those. I still felt slightly on edge. I started thinking about home again, and about the Falcon nosing its way along the streets as it had searched for me all those years ago.

With some effort, I stopped thinking about it and the image of the car slowly faded as I warmed up. I moved stiffly away from the fire towards the bar and, finally feeling warm, let out a contented sigh and shook off my coat. I ordered a pint, chatted for a while with Des the barman, bought him a drink and then headed over to the three men gathered around the table.

'So we were thinking next Thursday night,' said Richard in his usual hesitant murmur as I drew up a chair. 'Think you can swing it, William? Be round your place around 7.00, 7.30.'

For a moment my mind was completely blank, and it must have shown on my face, but then Gavin cut in. 'Nice try, Richard, but he won't fall for it. No one goes into that house; not even the postman gets in there.'

'He's got his very own harem tucked away, that's why,' Henry said from the head of the table and winked lewdly. 'Ain't that right, Will?'

I smiled and changed the subject. After all, they were used to me by now. When I owed someone a dinner, I took them out to a restaurant. I'm not a good cook. They seem to take my lack of domestic hospitality in their stride. Sometimes I'm absolutely convinced that whenever they think of me, they imagine me doing a tango with a rose clutched firmly in my teeth. But then that's not even tango; it's flamenco. And there's nothing quaint about tango. Tango was born in the slums of my ancestors. It was born in the bars around the docks, amidst the pandemonium and brawls of the old city. It isn't quaint at all.

I sat looking at my friends. I wondered how long they'd survive back home. Or what they would really think of it. Actually, I think that it would drive them mad after a while. Out here, in the quaint ceaseless calm of an English village, it is hard to imagine a life beyond. From the outside, everything seems to make sense. Everything has its place.

My friends are open and unsuspecting. There is none of the natural suspicion of the Argentinian. It was almost the first thing I noticed about them: the feeling that you are going to get ripped off, robbed or walked over unless you are careful is almost entirely absent. For me, it's unbelievable in a way. Here, if things don't work out, you shrug and come back later. If something doesn't work back home, there is almost always a riot. People start shouting and knocking on office doors. You have to make a lot of noise if you're to have any hope of getting anything done or getting what you want. It took me years before I stopped thinking someone was lurking near my front door, trying to get in. Years before I stopped rolling up cash and stuffing it deep down inside my pockets for fear of pickpockets. Habits like that are a pleasure to leave behind, but it's hard for me to keep a level of restrained indifference when things go wrong, or when someone gets in my way. I want to go for the jugular and cause a fuss. Mix things up a bit and let off a bit of steam in a public place.

There is a word for it back home. For the sense of constant chaos. *Un quilombo.* It translates literally as 'A brothel!' But it really means the mess arising from a disaster. An unsolvable problem. *¡Que quilombo!* 'What a mess!' It's an old expression and used almost constantly. A personal disaster. A political scandal. Hyper-inflation. The lights go out. *¡Que quilombo!*

The Argentinian knows from experience that things will go wrong. He does not trust the mechanic, the builder, the plumber, the electrician, the politician, the policeman, the judge or the accountant. He expects to get ripped off. It is the natural way of things. Police are the worst criminal gang in the world. Better off with a robber than a policeman. Never trust a policeman. Never let one in your house unless you can help it. They are *coimeros:* bribe-takers in league with gangsters and sometimes killers. And as for the politicians: they make the police look like little children when it comes to stealing.

I picked up my pint and took a large gulp, quite content to watch my friends talk. Pubs are one of my favourite things about England. We don't really get them back home. Not like this anyway.

One of the locals, a skinny old farmer, bent down, picked up a log, threw it roughly on the fire and then kicked it once with the toe of his boot, so that it rested more firmly in the back of the grate. The log, flickering and spluttering, caught fire. Outside, the branches of the trees stirred restlessly in the growing darkness, as the wind picked up and raced along the ancient walls of the pub.

3

The phone woke me the next morning, and, shivering, I reached for it and stared through the gap in the curtains. Frost clung stubbornly to the edges of the windows, and the sullen silence out in the woods was so deep that you could almost reach out and touch it. I mumbled into the phone, wrote down the address, changed quickly, grabbed a coffee and then drove straight to Lower Quinton.

It was a short drive, but it took me a while to find the entrance to the field, spotting it only when I saw the blue lights of the ambulance spinning above the treetops. I slowed down and parked my car behind one of two unmarked transit vans. I stepped out, opened the boot, got my wellington boots and then hurriedly put them on before moving quickly along the muddy path.

Light was just beginning to push through the mass of cloud above, and there was a stiff breeze blowing. The whole village was still asleep. I walked quickly through the gate and stopped when I reached the ambulance. Its back doors were open, and there was a thin old lady perched on the edge of a stretcher. She was clutching forlornly at a green overcoat in her lap, and a thin trickle of blood was crawling its way down her forehead and towards her left eye. Without thinking, I stepped forward to help her, then stopped when I saw that a medic was already rummaging about for a bandage in the back.

All the same, I peered in. Yes, it was a nasty cut all right. You could see it underneath the grey hair. She was going to need stitches, and quite a few by the looks of it.

I put my head inside. 'Are you all right?' I asked her.

She looked at me as if noticing me for the first time, smiled and didn't say anything. Poor dear, I thought. She must be going slightly batty. But then the smile slowly turned into an impatient and sarcastic grimace as it drew slowly back along her teeth.

'Well, of course I'm not all right, am I?' she said. 'Do I look all right to you? I'm cold and I'm wet and all I want to do is go home,' she said, and emphasized the word 'home' by nodding her head forward, which only made the blood flow faster towards her eye. 'But this horrible little man,' she said, glaring at the medic, 'won't let me and now I don't know where my Jacky is.'

'Your what?' I said, wondering if it might be a brand of hearing aid or perhaps a type of English walking stick that I had never heard of.

She looked at me as if I had just said the most stupid thing she had ever heard in her entire life. 'My Jacky. My dog, man. My dog.'

But I was already backing out. 'I'm sure your dog's fine,' I said a little meekly, turning on my heel and moving towards the gate. Old bag, I thought, and then at almost exactly the same time my mind moved as if of its own accord to search for the Argentinian equivalent: *Vieja Bruja* — 'Old Witch'.

By the gate I saw that the old woman's dog was being taken care of by a young police constable called Varley. There were plenty of words in English and Spanish for Varley — none-too-flattering ones — but I tried not to think of them. The dog, I noticed without much surprise, was already causing him trouble.

Varley was patting the dog behind the ears and trying to settle it. But that didn't seem to be working, so he got down on his haunches and tried to make it sit and stay there by pressing its back legs down on to the ground, imploring it all the while to calm down. But the dog, a rakish and very young-looking fox terrier, seemed hell-bent on racing back up the hill. It hopped forward on its two hind legs, straining against the lead, whining in its desperation to examine the strange and exciting phenomenon it had just seen up on Meon Hill.

Varley looked up when he heard me approach and momentarily lost concentration, letting slip his grip on the lead. The dog suddenly pulled away, and the lead slipped out of Varley's hands. Varley stumbled and then fell over into the mud, fumbling for the lead but missing it by the very tips of his fingers as the dog began to crawl under the gate.

But by then I was already speeding up towards him. I took a few quick strides and stamped on the dog's lead, stopping it dead in its tracks. I reeled the creature in like a fish before tying the lead to the gate. Varley looked like I was about to give him a bollocking. But it was too early, and I was too cold and still half asleep. Instead, I looked with some admiration at the woman's dog and patted it around the ears while Varley brushed his jacket off as best he could.

The dog at last seemed to calm down, and, now knowing that there was no chance of getting back up the hill, it looked wistfully upwards towards it from time to time, sometimes gazing at me and then Varley in a friendly sort of way.

'This little bugger belongs to the lady in the ambulance, I presume,' I said. 'The lady who called it in.'

'Yes, sir.'

'She looks pretty banged up,' I said, already feeling guilty about calling her an old bag even if I hadn't actually said it out loud.

'I think she's all right, sir. The cut's not as bad as it looks. But they're going to have to take her to A & E and do a head scan just in case. She fell over when she tried to climb the stile and hit her head. She was in a bit of a hurry to get to a phone, y'see.'

'Yes,' I said. 'I can imagine. Just walking along minding your own business and suddenly that.'

'Well, yes, sir,' Varley said, as if I had just said something rather insensitive. 'I know I'm not going to forget it in a hurry.'

'You've been up there, then?' I said, surprised.

'Yes, sir. I was first on the scene, and, as

the lady wasn't making much sense, I thought I'd better check. She kept going on about a dog or something. About how she knew who it was up there because she recognized his dog.'

'His dog?' I said. 'So his dog must still be on the hill.'

'I guess it must be,' Varley said, as if realizing this for the first time. 'Must have run off, though, because I didn't see it.' He looked baffled; then his face brightened. 'But I did see a body — there's definitely a body up there. The old lady's dog found it. She told me that the moment she let her dog off his lead, he went racing up the hill like a demon. He must have sniffed out the body. And when she got to the top, Jacky was there, wagging his tail like mad and sniffing at it.' Varley shot the dog an indignant look.

I wrapped my coat more tightly round my body before glancing up at the hill rising in the distance beyond the gate. 'Apart from Dr Brewin and his team, anybody else been up and tried to get in?'

'Only a couple. Villagers with their dogs. The hill's a popular run for them, so I told them there had been an accident. And sent them home.'

'Good,' I said. 'Keep on telling them that.'

At the far end of a garden, by the side of the path, was a neat-looking cottage. It was very cold outside. I looked at Varley. His jacket was splattered with mud. He had a long day ahead of him; we all did.

'Dr Brewin probably told you this already,' I said, watching Varley carefully. 'But I'm going to tell you again just in case. No one is to go past that gate without his say so. No one. It's his crime scene for now, and he decides who comes in and who doesn't. So you radio in every time anyone tries to get access. And I mean anyone. Okay?'

'Yes, sir,' Varley said. 'But your . . .' He paused before saying, 'Well . . . your sergeant asked me to tell you to enter the field from the garden over there.' Varley pointed to the garden that ran along the side of the path. 'He's informed the owner and he's given orders that everyone is to go through that way, sir, so as not to disturb the path into the field.'

There was a brief moment of confusion. In my mind the image that flashed before me was of Powell. But then I remembered. Powell was sick. Really sick.

'Oh. He has, has he?' I said, my eyes looking towards the small field on the other side.

'Yes, sir.'

'And I'm to take the other way, am I?'

'That's what he said.'

I grunted and looked down the path. A member of the forensic team was getting some pictures of the mud just below the bottom of the stile at the other end. Nearby was a sign erected by the field's ungracious owner that read: THE FIELD IS NOT HERE FOR THE BENEFIT OF WALKERS. Someone, probably the village wag, had crossed out the word 'not' with a felt-tip pen.

I patted the dog one more time and strode towards the garden, sensing eyes watching me. I looked right, beyond the small neat garden and into the kitchen of the cottage, where a pale-looking boy, still dressed in his Spider-Man pyjamas, was staring at me. I gave him a wave and, as if against his better judgement, he waved back.

4

Meon Hill had once been the site of an Iron Age settlement, and wide, corrugated ridges undulated all the way across it. Black hedgerows surrounded the fields, and at the top a handful of ancient oak trees clustered around the hill's crest. I had glimpsed the hill rising on the horizon from time to time from my car, but I had never actually been there before. It was quiet and empty and somehow mournful too.

I trudged across the ridges of the field; the mud clung to my boots in large wet clumps. I dug my gloved hands deeper into my pockets as I walked, already dreaming of warmer climes. The cold is something that I have never been able to get used to. It reaches deep into my bones, and, no matter how many layers of clothing I put on, the wind slips beneath them. Scarves, mittens, gloves and hats seem to serve no purpose at all for me. The cold shakes and rattles the teeth in my head so badly that sometimes I can hardly think or even breathe, and every winter without fail I always end up in bed with a damned lousy cold or flu for a week, no use to anyone. And in the winter it is always so dark out here in the country. You'd think I'd be used to it by now. But I'm not.

I looked up. Dr Brewin had fixed yellow police tape around the oak trees at the top of the hill, and my step quickened when I saw it. For a moment the cold was forgotten, and I was suddenly eager to get on with it. But when I glanced up again a few moments later I saw Graves coming down the hill towards me. I stopped in my tracks and waited for him.

Graves's blond hair was just visible underneath a knitted hat, which he pulled firmly over his ears in a sudden gesture as he caught sight of me. Around his neck was a matching grey scarf, which he had tucked very precisely into the collar of his overcoat. He was wearing a suit. On anybody else the woolly hat with the black suit would have been ridiculous, but on Graves the combination seemed somehow to work, creating an impression that was elegant and yet roguish at the same time. Unable to help myself, I gazed down critically at my now rather threadbare trench coat and straightened my tie. Graves seemed immaculate and, I couldn't help but think, kind of brand-new-looking too.

'Good morning, Graves,' I said. It was an apt name for a policeman. I'd thought it the first time I'd seen it on his file.

'Morning, sir. We already know who the victim is,' Graves said, a little out of breath but obviously pleased with himself. 'Dr Brewin recognized him. Apparently he owns this field. He's called Frank. Frank Hurst.'

The moment, the very moment I heard that name, I thought of a swimming pool in summer and of a dead woman lying face up on its surface.

'Apparently he lives on the other side of this hill,' Graves said, looking around.

'Frank Hurst. Jesus. What happened to him?'

'Someone's rammed a pitchfork into his throat,' Graves said, looking as if he wished that there had been a nicer way to say it.

'Jesus,' I said again.

'You knew him?'

'You could say that,' I said grimly. I paused, thinking, and gave him a long look. Graves had turned a little pale and was trembling inside his coat, though he was trying very hard to cover it up — not because of the cold but because of whatever it was he had seen at the top of the hill. You tried to prepare yourself for what was waiting for you, but sometimes it wasn't enough.

'Well, you'd better send someone to his house,' I said a little doubtfully. 'And you'd better try to get as many PCs as they can spare. We're going to need them. You can do that for me, can't you, Graves?' I said hesitantly. 'Set all that up?'

Graves smiled. 'Oh, I'm sure I'll manage.'

I nodded. 'All right, then.'

I moved up the hill. Frank Hurst. I turned around suddenly. Graves was already nearing the gate.

'Graves!' I yelled.

He turned around and trotted back up the hill.

'He has a daughter,' I said. 'She may still live there — in the house — and there's a housekeeper or at least there used to be. She might be there too. If she isn't, you should try to find her — be worth talking to her, I think. Lives locally, if I remember rightly. But find his daughter first — be good if we can let her know before the papers get wind of it and she learns the hard way.'

Graves nodded and immediately started down the steep incline. I watched critically for a few moments, until he disappeared beyond the hedgerow. Graves looked more than a little rattled. I turned around and started to walk, feeling oddly out of place all of a sudden. Sometimes the strangeness of the countryside hits me. And it struck me right then like a cold wet slap as I trudged alone under the moving shadows of the clouds and up the hill. To me, for a moment, the hill seemed completely unreal, as if the earth before me had split into a thousand cracks and one more step would see me flung straight into the abyss. Maybe it was the cold that was making my head spin or the remnants of the dream of home, which now seemed to be following me as I shuffled up the hill. I tried to shake it off. But it was no good.

It happens to me more and more as I get older. This feeling that I'm in two places at once. Or should be somewhere else. How did I end up here, so far from home? For a moment the very idea that I was standing here, on this hill, in winter, seemed absurd.

It is a strange, unsettling feeling, which is hard to shake off once it takes hold. Like the cold in a way. The Spanish voice inside my head is becoming louder and more insistent. It will not be bullied and it will not be crowded out. It would be summer in

Buenos Aires now. The usual writhing delirium of heat and noise. So hot you could literally fry an egg on the pavement. In truth, I was lucky to be away from it. Power cuts. Protests. The buses rammed solid with people. Tempers flaring out of hand. Random senseless acts of violence spreading in points of light and fury around the city, quenched only to rise again amongst the network of never-ending streets. The streets that would quite happily swallow you up if you didn't know your way about. I stared around me at the gathering cold. Not like here at all. A snatch of an old tango from home came to me as I walked. Precise and insistent. Cheerful despite the cynicism.

He who does not cry does not get fed,
and he who does not steal is an idiot.
Go ahead! Keep it up!
We'll all meet again in hell.
Don't think about it any more,
Sit to one side.
Nobody cares
if you were born honourable.

I smiled and then put it out of my mind as I finished my journey up the hill. Or tried to.

Two figures were sharply outlined at the

48

top. Taped police barricades encircled the crime scene. With some effort, I pulled myself back into this life. The cold morning sun edged the contours of the trees, sharpening the reality both of the morning and of what awaited me beyond the barricades.

Dr Brewin was crouched over the body. He had been a pretty handy prop forward in his day, but now, in his early fifties, he was running to fat. Despite this, he still looked tough. He was broad-shouldered with a flat nose, and his big, meaty hands seemed specifically designed for pushing someone's face straight into the mud. But there was a daintiness to his movements right now as he searched for trace evidence, picking away at the corpse's neck, the side of its face, its overcoat. Dressed in white overalls, Brewin looked, as always, happy to be at work.

Next to him, kneeling by the side of the body, Brewin's assistant, Fiona, smiled sweetly up at me before going back to her task: cutting off the dead man's fingernails and collecting them in an evidence bag. Brewin noticed the smile, and finally turned around.

'Morning, Shotgun,' he said cheerfully.

I nodded. I have known Brewin for a very long time. Brewin sometimes ironically imitates the graveyard humour that coroners use on television, the ones that eat egg sandwiches while they sever heads on mortuary slabs, and then offer squeamish policemen a bite of their lunch. So what he said next did not surprise me all that much.

'Ten pesos if you guess the cause of death?' Brewin finally stood aside and gestured in a theatrical way, as if he were welcoming me into a circus tent displaying the corpse.

Of course, the first thing I noticed was the pitchfork sticking out of the dead man's neck. It had been driven in with such force that two of the four metal prongs had passed all the way through the neck and embedded themselves in the mud on the other side. The overall effect was that the man's throat had been slashed almost all the way across. It had taken an enormous amount of force. The horrendous, irregularly shaped gash revealed cartilage and bone, and, I realized with some horror, that I could even see earth at the back of the wound, beyond a final white shock of shattered bone.

The pitchfork was new by the looks of it. It had a bright-yellow plastic handle, and the wooden wishbone shaft tapered inwards, met by the stainless-steel-pronged fork at the bottom. It was wedged in deep. Really deep. I looked at the pitchfork, thinking of my walled garden at home in the summer. I thought of water hitting the roses in the borders of my garden and ricocheting into the grass. I blinked, suddenly seeing the body and smelling its dampness. I became aware of the sound of the wind rustling in the branches of the trees.

'You know what,' Brewin said, 'I thought we were going to have to order another stretcher for . . . old . . . what's his name.'

'Graves,' I said absently.

'The man turned green, didn't he, Fiona?'

'Ah, don't be too hard on him,' Fiona said and sighed a little dreamily. 'Poor thing.'

An admirer already, I thought. I thrust my hands deep into my pockets and stood there indecisively for a moment before looking once more at the body. A surprisingly large bunch of keys, along with a few pound coins, had spilled out of the man's pocket and lay on the grass. By a log on the ground were the remains of his last-ever meal.

Hurst had possessed the typical voracious farmer's appetite. There was an apple core, the plastic wrapping from a whole pack of mini pork pies and two empty packets of budget-brand crisps. The inside of a chocolate-bar wrapper shone dully in the grey early-morning light. Next to it was a small carton: a dancing cartoon orange wearing a bowler hat and carrying a cane stared out at me. The orange juice was unopened, with the straw fixed tightly to its back. A ragged piece of bread had been trodden underfoot and ground hard into the earth.

Frank Hurst was still lean-looking. His head, with its grey closely cropped hair, was tilted at a slight angle, and he was staring upwards at the sky. For a moment a cloud reflected in his eyes and was gone.

'Jesus Christ,' I heard myself saying. 'It really is Frank Hurst, isn't it?'

Brewin nodded.

I looked at Frank Hurst's screaming mouth, and, as I did so, a trace of a late-summer day came back to me. With well-practised precision I remembered Frank's wife lying face up in the water. Her blood had coiled along the surface. It was Hurst's blood that was now flowing into the mud. Hers had meandered gently in the blue water of their swimming pool, drifting in small eddies towards the tiled edges. Water and mud. Mud and water. Blood and the smell of chlorine and that smell of lavender. But why lavender? I remembered now that there had been banks and banks of it lining the fence surrounding their swimming pool. The smell had been overpowering, unpleasant.

'He's been here all night,' Brewin said. 'No one spotted him till this morning, so I'm guessing that whoever did this must have done it just as it was getting dark and he was packing up to go home.'

Hurst's other tools were stacked up by the log: shears, a spade, a few coils of brand-new barbed wire. Pliers. It looked as if Hurst had been doing some general maintenance on his field. Clearing the ditches. Cutting back the hedgerows. Fixing the fences. He would have had a clear vantage of the entire hill from here. So whoever had killed him must have crept all the way here and sneaked up from behind. Perhaps they grabbed the pitchfork from where the other tools were lying near the log. Unless Hurst had known them, seen them coming and waited.

Brewin ran his gloved fingers along the bottom of his jaw and straightened up. 'I'll tell you what I think I know,' Brewin said. 'Though we can't be certain until I examine the body properly. But, so far, it looks like he didn't have time to put up much of a struggle. There are no defensive wounds on his arms and none on his hands either. So whoever did this was strong and fairly quick too. Knocked him to the ground' — Brewin lifted both hands up, as if he were holding the pitchfork — 'and then in.'

Fiona had stopped what she was doing and was listening. She nodded and smiled all the while as Brewin talked. Hurst's left hand was still clutched in her own as if she were giving him a manicure.

It sounded about right. It was nasty but, generally speaking, not all that different to the majority of homicides I have investigated. A messy, nasty and sordid business, but then that's killing for you. I learnt very quickly that the people who murder hardly ever seem to plan it. Sometimes I can't help but feel that every time I look at a murdered corpse, somehow something has been taken away from me.

I said, 'What about the dog? The old lady down there said something about his dog.'

'It's over there.' Brewin pointed to a clearing in the trees past the body. For some reason Brewin suddenly seemed angry.

I strolled away from the crime scene and went further into the woods, weaving my way between the trees. As I walked towards the clearing, I caught a glimpse of Frank Hurst's big old house through a gap in the hedgerow. It lay at the bottom of the other side of the hill and appeared dark and isolated in the hill's shadow. A strange place to build a house, I had always thought. The hill seemed to take away all the brightness of the morning light and leave only grey, so that from here the house seemed like an institution of some sort: an old people's home maybe, or even a hospital. I could see the tiled roof above and the grounds sweeping away from it; and I could just make out the swimming pool at the back.

I turned away and continued to the clearing and then stopped in my tracks. From one of the trees hung something dark and heavy. A strange odd shape suspended from a low thick branch. The trees seemed to be crowding round the pitiful sight before them like witnesses to a senseless accident.

Hanging by its neck was a large black Labrador. It had been strung up on a tree branch. Its choke chain had embedded itself deeply into the black fur around its neck. Its tongue, still wet with saliva, looked black as it lolled out of the blood-flecked mouth. The dog swayed in the breeze amongst the creaking branches, and its long shadow spilled out, slowly dancing and twisting beneath it. Despite the appalling way it must have died, it still looked ferocious and big and menacing in death.

The air had got much colder, and suddenly there was a flurry of snow. I gazed down the hill at the sloping roofs of the village. Word would soon be out there. Some would be saying that Frank Hurst had got what he deserved. I knew that. Unable to see what had happened to him, to see its truly horrifying nature up close, they would be pleased as they drank their tea, and ate their huge fried breakfasts and pushed their half-asleep kids out of the door to school. Yes, the villagers would be happy that he was finally gone from their midst. Some of them anyway.

Standing in the cold, I started to remember other things. A girl's flower hairpin, bent out of shape and slightly rusty, glinting in the sunshine in the palm of my hand. My fist closing. Thinking. Wondering, as I stood beside Hurst's pool with his house tall and silent behind me in the early morning.

I walked back towards Brewin, imagining the brief and silent struggle as the life drained away from Hurst and his eyes slowly dimming. It was the absurdity of a dead body that always got to me the most. And its ugliness: Frank Hurst in death forever nailed to the top of Meon Hill. His whole life would now be defined by this moment. This is how he would be remembered.

You were remembered if you were murdered.

5

The PCs, along with Douglas and Irwin and a few other officers Graves did not recognize, stood by their vehicles, which were parked along the line of shops opposite the village green. Snow had begun to fall. The shadows of the cars formed wide strips on the road. A lorry-driver noisily unloaded pallets of food and drink wrapped in cellophane to a small supermarket, while at the post office next door a matronly woman stared at them fiercely in disapproval. Already the villagers seemed tense and on edge. Lights blazed from the cottages and houses. Children, who would normally be agitated by the snow, seemed cautious and subdued as their parents drew them hastily up the street to the small school at the edge of the village.

Graves stood leaning on his car, which he had parked near the old telephone box, watching the traffic pass along the street.

The man who had quizzed him in the canteen the morning before, a sergeant, got out of his car and stood next to Douglas, as a narrow door opened across the road, and a morose old man gazed in stunned silence at the activity on the green. One of the PCs called out and made a signal for a light, but for the most part the men were silent and, like the children being led along the road, strangely subdued.

Downes was already making his way towards them on the pavement. The hollow sound of his footsteps echoed off the houses. He glanced up and, seeing the men before him, seemed to shake off the cold; his step became more authoritative. The men shuffled their feet and drew more closely together. A constable sidled up towards Graves and his hesitant, wary gaze fixed on Downes.

'Oh, Christ,' he said, and shook his head.

Graves looked at the PC. He was near retirement age but sturdy. He winced and wiped a snowflake from the top of his broad skull.

'You'll be his new sergeant, then. That's what the boys are saying.'

Graves said that he was.

'I'm Drayton,' he said, and gave Graves a look of unmistakable pity. Then he turned away. 'And on your first day this,' he said, running the palm of his hand along the top of Graves's new car as if he owned it. 'We're going to be stuck out here for days, you know that, don't you? Traipsing round in the blooming cold. And Christmas. You can forget about Christmas an' all. Christmas,' he proclaimed, 'is cancelled until this is all over.'

Graves shrugged. Christmas had never bothered him much either way.

A look of resigned annoyance crossed Drayton's face as Downes stood before them, motionless, yet still managing to appear like someone slowly uncoiling from the cold.

'Bloody Shotgun,' Drayton said very quietly but with vehemence. 'He's on the warpath, all right. The lads knew he would be,' he said,

'Of course he's on the warpath,' Graves said, and motioned to the hill rising beyond the village. 'What do you expect?'

Drayton didn't say anything for a moment. Then: 'It's Frank Hurst, though, ain't it?'

'You knew him?'

'Knew *of* him,' Drayton said, looking away.

Downes scanned the upturned and expectant faces, and for a moment his gaze settled on Graves in what might have been a slight nod of encouragement before moving on. Graves pushed himself off the car, leaving Drayton behind. In the cold, Downes seemed white beneath his brown skin, and the scar appeared more pronounced. He undid the top of his coat. His imposing height and bulk made him resemble one of those old Hollywood actors of the forties or fifties. But the scar gave him a slightly menacing air. Perhaps it was Downes's undeniable strangeness that had prompted Graves to think of another time. He didn't belong here in this small village, standing in the snow. Yesterday he had seemed calm and at ease; now he looked extraordinarily alert. Some of the men before him appeared reluctant to return his gaze.

Downes waited impatiently while a run-down old jeep passed on the road and then said, 'For those who don't already know, this is Sergeant Graves.'

Graves suddenly found that all eyes were on him.

'He's new here, but an extremely experienced officer and we're lucky to have him. So I would ask you all to do exactly what he says and I mean *exactly*. Understood?'

Silence.

61

'Because he'll be reporting back to me. Now Graves will fill you all in properly later. But for now we're looking for dog-walkers,' he said. 'Looks like half the village uses that field to walk their dogs. And there could be others too. From further afield. We'll need to find them and interview them as well. But we need to know if anyone saw anything up on that hill. Anyone leaving the village in a hurry. Any strangers hanging about. People usually notice in a small place like this, as you all well know. And ask about a white van. It looks like there was one parked near the bottom of the hill. And a man was seen having some kind of argument with Hurst up there: a couple saw them. Sometime in the afternoon, we think. Around 3.00. We don't have a good description of him yet. And we don't know what they were arguing about. So far, that's all we've got.'

Graves listened, but he was still really thinking about the pitchfork and the dead man on the hill. It wasn't his first dead body by a long shot. But the poor man's neck. It had looked like some animal had got to him and literally tried to tear out his throat. The image of the body, lying pale in the wet field, blazed vividly before him.

He shifted in the snow and gazed over the shoulders of the other policemen, who were all listening intently to what Downes had to say. When Downes spoke, he was somehow more animated and involved than other policemen of the same rank, and this made him seem energetic, younger even. His hands moved up and down as if of their own free will, and sometimes when he appeared unhappy or dissatisfied his shoulders would draw in and he would point to himself with the tips of his thumbs touching the tips of his index fingers and the wrists of both hands angled towards his chest. It was a disconcerting gesture, and, though the men seemed to expect it, they nonetheless shrank from it.

Downes finished, nodded curtly in Graves's direction and turned away. As the men looked on, Graves marched up to his car and pulled a map from the front seat, then closed the door. He laid it on the bonnet of his car and carefully placed a stone on each corner to stop it flapping in the wind. The men at once huddled around him.

Graves had just had time to scout out the village, along with Douglas and Irwin; and with their help he had drawn this rough map of the village and where he wanted the men to start conducting interviews. He'd also got an Ordinance Survey map of some of the nearby villages: there were an awful lot of them dotted about, some barely more than a bunch of houses lining a road. And they had strange, ancient-sounding names.

Graves began to divide the men up into pairs, and when a few moments later he looked up, Downes was gone.

6

Standing outside in the late-afternoon dark, snow falling heavily all around me, I stamped my feet and checked my notes, just to make sure that I had the right address. I pressed the doorbell again and waited; a light flicked on, a figure shuffled towards the glass porch, slowly fiddled with the locks and began to undo the latch. The door opened as far as the chain would allow, and an old man's face was suddenly glaring out at me through the crack.

'Yes?' the man said.

'Mr Fernsby?'

'Yes?'

'I'm here to talk to you about Frank Hurst,' I said. 'You saw him yesterday out on Meon Hill, I hear.'

Fernsby, without saying another word, nodded, closed the door and began to unlatch it. We walked through the glass porch and the hall, emerging into the stifling heat of his living room. He picked up the remote control from the coffee table and snapped off the TV in a childishly exaggerated gesture before lowering himself fussily into his armchair.

Fernsby's living room was immaculate, but it did smell faintly of Vicks, wet dog and stale cigarette smoke. Lying sprawled out in front of the red bars of the electric fire was the fattest golden retriever I had ever seen in my life. I sniffed the air and frowned when I got an unpleasant smell of burning. The dog seemed to get a whiff of it too, and it lifted its head off its huge paws and leisurely sniffed the air, unaware that a coiling plume of bluish smoke was now rising from its fur. Fernsby saw the smoke as well, but it did not seem to surprise him. He sighed, pulled himself out of his chair, grabbed the dog by the collar and dragged it roughly across the rug.

'He keeps on doing that,' he said, patting at the fur.

I noticed that tied around the palm of Fernsby's left hand was a bandage. It looked fairly new. And wrapped around his neck was a grey scarf, despite the heat. For some reason Fernsby, looking at me through thick black spectacles, reminded me of a cartoon turtle. The thin scarf exaggerated the length of his wrinkled neck; the bald head; the sunken chin.

'Would you like a tea or anything?' Fernsby said halfheartedly. 'A coffee perhaps?'

I shook my head as I took off my overcoat and put it in my lap. I had been politely refusing cups of tea all day. Just as all day I had been intruding upon the carefully maintained rituals of the elderly. I glanced outside: it was completely dark now, and the cul-de-sac was very quiet. Hard to believe that only a few streets away police-men were still banging on every door amongst the worried, peering faces. Like an occupying army under the command of my sergeant, the uniformed mobs had swept through the village. They were trampling over the village green and the flowerbeds, and rapping loudly on windows when there was no reply, while their radios cracked and shrieked in the gathering cold. But here, at least, the invasion seemed far away, and in its place was a strange hush, now made deeper by the falling snow.

'So what's going on?' Fernsby demanded, before primly straightening out the creases in his trousers.

According to Graves's notes, Alistair Fernsby used to be a teacher at the local prep school in Stratford, and there was still something of the querulous schoolmaster about him as he waited almost crossly for me to get on with it and state my business.

'You told one of my constables that you saw Frank Hurst yesterday evening — is that right?'

'Yes, that's right. And?'

'And he's dead,' I said simply. 'Murdered, actually.'

Fernsby leant forward in his chair, reaching for a cigarette. He didn't seem all that surprised. Of course, word had got round hours ago.

'Murdered. Murdered how?' he said cautiously.

I ignored him. 'You told the police constable that you arrived in the field on Meon Hill at around 4.30 — is that right?'

'Yes, around that time, yes.'

'Are you sure?'

'Yes, of course I'm sure. I'm almost always the last up there. Jumbo isn't all that keen on other dogs. He's got a nasty tendency to go for them,' Fernsby said, looking fondly at his dog. 'Don't you, Jumbo, you big ugly sod.'

Jumbo, on hearing his name, wearily lifted his head with a pained expression, then promptly seemed to go to sleep.

68

'I have to keep him on the lead,' Fernsby explained almost guiltily. 'If there are other dogs on the hill. Not much fun for him if he can't run about, so I'm almost always the last one up there. Just before it gets dark. That way I can let him off the lead, and he can have a nice long run. We don't bother anyone else that way. But Frank was there with his dog, so I couldn't very well let Jumbo off. We weren't there for long. Felt like I was trespassing with him up — although' — Fernsby wagged his finger in the air at me as if I were about to contradict him — 'Frank's got absolutely no right to stop us walking on that hill.'

For some reason Fernsby started to laugh. It was a hearty laugh, or at least it was to begin with. But it brought on an alarming and drawn-out coughing fit, which ended in an ominously wet rattle. When it was all over, Fernsby, somewhat defiantly, lit his cigarette with a plastic lighter, breathed in and let it hang jauntily from his lower lip.

'Of course,' he said, 'I did make sure I stuck to the path. You saw that charming sign he put up, I suppose?'

'Yes,' I said, 'pretty hard to miss.'

'He absolutely hated our walking on his field. Resented it. He tried for years to keep us off. Ploughed over the footpath. Padlocked the gate shut. Knocked down the stile one year, even put a bull in another year to scare us off. Mean bugger it was too,' Fernsby said with some admiration before adding, 'Didn't do him an ounce of good, though. Public right of way on Meon Hill, and the people round here know it. We set the council on him in the end.' Fernsby said this almost as if he regretted it.

'And you saw nobody else? No other dog-walkers. Nobody at all in the field? It was just you and Frank Hurst?'

'Yes.'

'And when you went first into the field — when you crossed the stile — did you see a van parked out there? A white van?'

Fernsby shook his head. 'A white van. Why?'

'A man was seen arguing with Hurst up on the field. Around 3.00, we think. But you're saying that by the time you walked into the field the man was gone? And there was no sign of this van?'

'There was no van,' Fernsby said firmly. 'And there was nobody else up there either. It was just Frank up there. And me.'

'All right, so when you saw him up there working, did you give him a wave perhaps? Go to say hello?'

Fernsby snorted as if I had said something

70

ridiculous. 'No, I certainly did not.'

That was about right. Hurst had kept pretty much to himself. I couldn't say that I blamed him. The majority of people who had seen him working in his field yesterday afternoon had taken him for some lowly odd-job man sent by the council to clean the place up on their behalf. Almost all of the dog-walkers who regularly used Meon Hill, and there were a surprisingly large number of them, had a strange tendency to talk about the place as if they owned it or as if it were part of a state-run park and not just a right of way through someone else's private property. All day I had rather pointlessly, I realized, been feeling increasingly indignant on the dead man's behalf.

Fernsby was watching me with a sly smile, as if he had just remembered something amusing. 'You ever meet him?' he asked.

I nodded. 'Yes, I met him. Around five years ago.'

'So you'll know all about his wife. It was the second one he buried, you know?'

'Yes,' I said quickly. 'I know all about that.'

Fernsby was still smiling at me; I wondered if he expected me to go into all the grisly details for him. His sudden streak of cheery sadism was unexpected and unsettling. 'I know exactly what happened to his second wife, Mr Fernsby, and to his first one too,' I said coldly. 'But how did Frank Hurst look to you yesterday?'

Fernsby's smile vanished. 'What do you mean, how did he look?'

'Well,' I said, 'did he look nervous, perhaps, or anxious? Did he seem to be looking for someone, or did he seem to be waiting for someone?'

Fernsby thought it over. 'It was a bit of a surprise to see him there, actually. I hadn't seen him for years. I don't know' — Fernsby stared at the floor — 'two years. Maybe more. And I can't even remember where that was. He didn't go out much, you know. Who could blame him, after what happened? But I used to see him from time to time in the village shop, getting his groceries, bombing about in his jeep, driving too fast down the road. Mostly, he kept to himself up in that big old house of his. Yesterday, he looked' — Fernsby paused, searching for the right word — 'he looked grim.' Fernsby's face fell, dissatisfied. 'But then, of course, he always looked grim. Not speaking to anyone. Glaring at people with their dogs all afternoon, because he hadn't anything better to do.

'But there is something else,' he said finally. 'It was more than that.' He put out his cigarette.

I waited.

'He looked . . . well, to be perfectly honest, he didn't look quite all there. He was talking to himself, for one thing. I thought he was talking to the dog at first. The dog was tied to one of the trees. I couldn't really hear what he was saying, but it sounded like silly stuff. Stuff like what he had to do when he got back home. Odd jobs he had to do. What he was going to have for his tea. Felt a bit sorry for him, really. But then I had always felt a bit sorry for him. He never seemed to get over it. You know, after what happened to his wife.'

'His wife drowned, didn't she?' I said, finally giving in.

'That's right,' Fernsby said, quite cheerful again. 'Cracked her head against the side of her swimming pool and drowned. Lot of nasty gossip about it at the time, as I'm sure you're aware.'

I nodded. I had believed some of it at the time. I folded my coat tighter on my lap, remembering.

'God, he was a stubborn sod,' Fernsby said. 'Anyone else would have shut up shop, sold the place and never come back, but not Hurst. You been up there? To the house?'

'No. Not yet.'

73

Fernsby shook his head in disgust. 'Let the whole place go, by the looks of it. His daughter walked out on him. Can't say I blame her.'

'Actually,' I said, 'I wanted to ask you about her. We've been trying to reach her all day. She went away years ago, that's what we're hearing.'

'Rebecca,' Fernsby said. 'Rebecca Hurst. She moved. But don't ask me where. Ran off with some fella.' Fernsby now looked taken aback. 'Hold on. So you didn't find him in his house?'

'No,' I said, 'we didn't. We think he was killed around 5.00 yesterday afternoon. And near the place where you said you were out walking your dog. In fact,' I added a little cruelly, 'you may well have been the last one to see him alive.'

I had not really intended to shock the old man or worry him all that much. He seemed far too self-assured for that anyway. But my words seemed to shake him. He started feeling along the bandage on his hand.

'What?' I said. 'What is it?'

'Well, it was his dog,' Fernsby said. 'I told you he had tied it to a tree. I think it might have even been asleep.' Fernsby paused. 'Can't really remember now. Sorry. But as we were on our way back across the field

74

towards home, it started barking. I thought it might have been at us to begin with. But it definitely wasn't us it was interested in. It was something on the other side of the hill. A fox or a rabbit, I suppose. It seemed to want to go after it, but of course it couldn't. It just ran along the lead — back and forth, barking.'

'Barking towards the house — in the direction of Hurst's house? Is that what you're saying?'

Fernsby folded his arms over his chest and nodded. 'Yes.'

I leant forward in my chair. 'And did you see what the dog was barking at, Mr Fernsby? Did you see anyone cutting across the back of the hill? Not a dog-walker — someone else?'

Fernsby paused, thinking. 'No,' he said.

'Perhaps you remember something else?' I asked. 'Anything at all? Doesn't matter if it seems of no consequence. Like the dog. When did it start barking? Can you remember? Are you sure it only started to bark later?'

Fernsby's eyes dimmed, and he sat back, thinking harder, worrying at the edges of his memory. 'No, it was definitely later,' Fernsby said finally. 'As I was on my way back across the field — on my way back home. Frank lost his patience with it. He started shouting and gave it a wallop. But it didn't seem to do any good. The dog just got more and more worked up.' Fernsby pushed himself further back in his chair.

'But there's something else, though, isn't there?' I said, pushing him, albeit gently for now. 'Something was wrong, wasn't there? There was something else you didn't like about yesterday's walk.'

Fernsby nodded reluctantly. He reached for another cigarette, thought better of it and closed his eyes for a moment. 'Well, as I was nearing the end of the walk . . . it was funny, I kept on looking up at Hurst, because I was sure he was staring at me. You know I could feel . . . well, it was like I could feel him staring at me. But he wasn't: he was bent over, working. He wasn't paying attention to me at all. It's silly but . . .' Fernsby shrugged, too embarrassed to go on.

'You felt as if you were being watched,' I said. 'Didn't you?'

'Yes — I suppose that's it,' Fernsby said, relieved that I had said it for him. 'You have to try to understand,' he said. 'It was getting dark and . . . well . . . I suppose I got a bit jumpy. Jumbo seemed to want to go home as well. It was like he was dragging me away from there — probably just desperate for his tea — practically pulled me out of that field, didn't you, Jumbo?'

Jumbo, I noticed, had moved much closer to the fire and was on the verge of once more setting himself alight. But maybe Jumbo wasn't quite as dumb as he looked.

'I could hear Frank raving to himself on the top of the hill, talking to himself. That, and his dog barking like mad. It was getting dark after all, so I suppose I was really glad to get out of there.' Fernsby laughed half-heartedly. 'Fell over when I climbed over the stile,' he said, lifting up his bandaged hand and showing it to me.

Yes, I could just imagine Fernsby and his dog moving through the growing darkness, the animal pulling his master's frail frame along the path and towards the gate. An old man made worried by the sudden eeriness of the hill, but not really wanting to admit it to himself. And, once back amongst the re-assuring lights of the village, Fernsby would have no doubt reprimanded himself for having got all worked up over nothing. Finally in the safety of his home. On goes the latch.

The sound of the wind blowing through the trees on Meon Hill came back to me, and with it a memory of the damp, used-up smell of Hurst's corpse. I imagined someone moving quickly and silently towards Frank Hurst as he worked in his field. I thought of the hill; imagined a blurred shadow peeling itself away from the darkness of the trees. For a moment, in the darkening light, I seemed to see Hurst's hunched-over back, and then his panic-stricken face as he turned.

I looked up. The old boy was staring at me again. Another cigarette in his mouth.

'Downes,' Fernsby said thoughtfully. 'The name — it's English, isn't it? But you're not from here, are you?'

I sighed and stood up. I get this a lot. 'No,' I said, 'I'm not.'

7

It was a relief to be out of Fernsby's stuffy living room and into the falling snow. Away from self-igniting golden retrievers and worried old men. I strode past the other homes in the cul-de-sac. It was starting to snow even more heavily now, and the December air felt raw. I turned up the collar of my coat, although it seemed to do me no good at all, and as I did so I caught a glimpse of television light reflecting against a windowpane in one of the houses.

On the TV was a children's programme, though it was playing to an empty room: the children were off somewhere, probably having their tea. The screen showed a crowd of plastic penguins dancing in circles around an iceberg. There was something compelling about the image, hypnotic even, and I found myself, almost against my will, watching the penguins sliding around and around, and then suddenly skidding off the ice and tumbling into a pale blue papery sea. I came to myself as soon as they hit the water and began to walk towards the car waiting for me at the end of the road. Graves looked pretty anxious as I approached, which pleased me. He leant across the front-passenger seat, pushed open the car door, and I looked in.

'Any luck with those house keys?' I said.

'I'm afraid not, sir. There was blood on them, and forensics need to confirm whether it belongs to Hurst or to his attacker. No results until tomorrow and,' Graves added nervously, 'that's at the very earliest.'

This really wasn't all that unexpected, but I was annoyed nonetheless. It was already dark, and, drumming my fingers loudly on the roof of the car, I began to consider what to do next. Should we try to break in now or was it better to wait until the morning? For a moment I just couldn't decide. It would be easier in the morning — but, then again, I had been waiting a very long time to get back into that old house.

'I don't suppose you know the way?' I said, more gruffly than I had intended.

'To where, sir?' Graves said.

'The house,' I said. 'Hurst's house.'

'But why? We can't get in without the keys?'

'We'll just have to find another way in, then. Shouldn't be too difficult for a young fellow like you,' I said, before clambering into the car and out of the snow.

I gave him the directions. Graves made a face, shrugged and switched on the engine, and the flashy Peugeot estate nosed cautiously out of the narrow street and towards the village green. I had a quick look at him and shook my head. He was certainly no Powell, and I was stuck with him.

I stared out at the water of the pond beyond the green as we drifted alongside the low wooden railings towards the pub, thinking about Powell lying in the stark surroundings of the hospital ward before his doctors decided to send him home. The Christmas lights, strung loosely along the branches of the trees, were mirrored dimly in the water, so that the water went to yellow and then to black again.

I stared out at the pond: muddy and grey-banked, it glimmered darkly at the far edge of the village, ignored and forgotten. Lower Quinton hadn't really changed much over the years. The pub was still there, of course, near the pond on the other side of the green.

It seemed to be doing a good trade. A

small party was heading towards the doors. The men, dressed in dinner jackets, all looked pleased with themselves, while some of the women seemed a little out of breath, as if they had squeezed themselves too tightly into their dresses. A Christmas office party, by the looks of it, and one that had got off to an early start. When the doors opened, laughter burst out, muffled by the closed windows of the car.

'We've found a few more dog-walkers, sir,' Graves said, as we turned a corner and left the pub behind, 'but it seems as if there's more than one place where people walk their dogs around here. Some take them up on Meon Hill. Others take them along to a village called Mickleton or to another nearby village called Ilmington.'

'And anyone else see the argument?' I said. 'No one recognized the man he was arguing with up on the hill?'

'No, only the young couple saw them arguing. They've just moved in, sir, and they didn't know who the other man was. But it looked like Hurst and this man were really getting into it. They saw the van before they crossed the gate.'

'Well, it looks like the van was gone by 5.00 and the man along with it. And, according to the old boy I've just been talking to, Hurst was still alive then.'

'Maybe he came back.'

I nodded. 'Could be. And you got a description?'

'Yes. Short and thin-looking. Around thirty. Black hair, kind of spiky. Bit odd for a man his age. Wearing a black coat. Leather, they think, and white trousers.'

'Not much, is it?'

'No, sir. I'm afraid not.'

'And they can't recall the number plate?'

'No.'

'And no one noticed anything else out of place in the village?'

Graves shook his head.

'You sure?' I said, surprised. 'No strangers hanging about? Nothing at all?'

'No, sir. Nothing. But we haven't been able to talk to everyone. A lot of people just aren't back from work yet. Probably be quite a few of them later, though.'

Graves was talking about the Lower Quinton commuters, who take the train from the nearby village of Moreton-in-Marsh direct to Paddington. I scowled to myself as we drove past some of the bigger houses sedately tucked away behind well-manicured hedges. London commuters had swooped en masse into small villages like this all over the Cotswolds and bought up all the best houses. For a second, I was almost glad of the murder on their doorstep, hoping that it would knock off a bit of the old Cotswolds charm.

'We'll have to try them again,' Graves said. 'But we're nearly done. Just two more streets, sir: Fairfield Road and Bourton Close, and then a few houses at the back of the pub.'

'The pub'd be a good place to try as well,' I said. 'Wait till it gets really busy and send a few fellows in to have a chat with the locals.' Then I added drily, 'That's if there are any locals left.'

We were leaving the village now. The road curved past a small housing estate and then finally took us beyond a few hardy-looking labourers' cottages that clung stubbornly to the edges of the village. After that, there was no sign of anyone.

Graves put his foot down, and we gathered speed. The black road began to race beneath us, and the snow danced frantically in the beams of the headlights. The outline of the village behind us loomed out of the darkness. The hill rose stark upon the horizon and then sloped away again, until it was lost amongst the smaller, greyer contours of the surrounding hills.

Graves tapped the steering wheel, glancing from time to time at the countryside behind him in the rear-view mirror. It seemed as if he wanted to say something but was unsure as to whether he should go on.

'There has been an awful lot of talk, though,' he said finally.

I had been expecting that.

'It all seems odd to me,' Graves said, shifting in his seat. 'I mean, the poor guy's been murdered. But nobody really seems to care. Okay, so the chap likes to keep a low profile. Keeps himself to himself. But so what? He doesn't like the villagers walking all over his field, but who can blame him for that? It's like the whole village seems to think that the field is there for their own benefit,' Graves said, clearly remembering the sign by the gate. 'But was he really all that bad? Why do they seem to have hated him so much? One of the old dears I talked to this morning literally came out and said she was glad he was dead, and that he deserved it. I couldn't believe it. Wouldn't tell me why either. Just flat out refused. The sweetest old granny you're ever likely to see as well.' Graves swallowed as if he had just tasted something unpleasant. 'It was a bit creepy, in truth,' he said.

I let out a long sigh. 'I imagine it's because

they all think he murdered his wife.' It came out as almost flippant. But I was actually horrified by the way the gossip had been festering for the past five years.

'But it was an accident, wasn't it?' Graves said indignantly. 'She drowned in the swimming pool. That's what you told me.'

'It was an accident all right.'

Graves looked vaguely disappointed.

'His second wife used to go swimming most days in the summer,' I explained. 'They had a big outside pool. And one day she just fell in. Simple as that. Happens all the time, apparently. Slipped as she was walking back towards the house and smacked the back of her head before she hit the water. It was the housekeeper . . . Nancy Williams . . . who saw her and called the ambulance. But she was dead by the time they got there.' I folded my arms. 'You managed to talk to her yet?'

'Only on the phone. She's moved . . . to Brighton. Said she hasn't heard from him in years. Didn't seem all that bothered, when I told her.'

That didn't surprise me either. I watched the snow swirling out over the grey horizon, remembering Hurst slumped on a sofa in the grand surroundings of his house, and the fading sun slanting through the French windows. It had been the first of many visits to Dashwood Manor.

Graves still looked confused. 'But if it was an accident, why do they automatically assume that he killed her? It doesn't make sense. Shouldn't they all be feeling sorry for him?'

'Believe me,' I said, 'Hurst was not the kind of man who invited pity. And for some reason he seems to have locked himself away in his house and turned recluse. Villagers probably took it for a sure sign of a guilty conscience.' I lowered my voice, as if I were just about to impart a juicy piece of village gossip myself. 'The thing is, it was his second wife, like I said. Villagers never thought much of her. Thought she'd set her sights on him for his money, and in the end she proved them right. It didn't take her long either. Ended up having an affair with some chap.' I frowned. 'God, I can't remember who now. Lived locally, I think. A builder. She wasn't exactly discreet about it. Used to meet him before she picked up her kid from school. She was late the whole time — you know, keeping the poor kid waiting.

'Somebody must have tipped Hurst off about it. Hurst tracked him down and made a big scene in a pub. Beat him up pretty badly and threatened to do it all over again and a lot worse. And he could have done, if he'd wanted to: Hurst was no walk in the park, believe me. A few weeks later, and she's lying face up in the swimming pool. So now you can see how it all looked.'

'But you checked it?' Graves said, with a great deal of caution. 'His alibi checked out, sir?'

I nodded. I had checked it all right. 'He was out buying a pony for his daughter. His foreman on the farm went along with him to help him choose the right one — big old guy called Sam Griffin. It might be worth talking to him too.'

We drove on. The farther we went, the narrower the lanes became, and they took us deeper and deeper into the folds of the fields.

'A lot of the newer villagers don't even know who he is,' Graves said. 'And one of them told me he'd gone round to Hurst's house and the old man had set the dog on him.'

'One of the commuters, you mean?'

'An advertising exec from London. Didn't know any better. Wanted to buy the house.'

I grinned happily in the warm darkness of the car and crossed my arms, liking Frank Hurst for that and hoping that Hurst's dog had bitten the advertising executive, no doubt a commuter and yuppie of the first order, right in the arse. Then my eyes caught what looked to be a lane branching off to the right through the falling snow.

Graves drew to a stop by the sign, which stood by the side of a battered-looking wooden gate. Etched into a tall column of grey limestone were the words DASHWOOD MANOR.

Graves undid his seatbelt, ran out into the snow and dragged open the wooden gate. It snagged on a stone, and he had to lift it up; then he drew it back and left it snug against some bushes. We drove on.

Branches arched across the lane, forming a long, dark tunnel. There were no longer any points of light visible on the horizon; ahead of us lay a solid darkness, broken only occasionally by the flashing lights of cars glimpsed through the woods. The village suddenly seemed very far away, as the lane led us inevitably to the house that could now be seen rising above the tops of the trees.

'You know what I think,' Graves said, 'I think we need to talk to everyone who was around when Hurst's wife died — those who think that he murdered his wife and got away with it.'

'So you think it was revenge, then,' I said, interested. 'Revenge for his dead wife.'

'Well, maybe. But I don't think it really went like that.'

'So how did it happen?'

Graves paused, uncertain. For a moment it looked as if he had changed his mind, and he slowed down as we drew close to a steep bend in the lane. 'Well, okay,' he began a little sheepishly, 'let's say I'm one of the villagers, right, and I'm out walking my dog — just as I do every afternoon — and there right in front of me is our man Hurst. I haven't seen him for years and years, and suddenly there he is. And, as I'm walking my mutt along that field, I start thinking about Hurst's dead wife, and this big old house of his, and all the fields he owns, and the way people like him always seem to get away with it. So I decide to have a little word with him now that I've got the chance — let him know that people like him don't fool me. So I go and tell him — tell him I know what he's done.'

'You tell him he's a murderer?' I said bluntly.

'Yes, right to his face. Hurst obviously doesn't like that and so —'

'And so there's a fight. Our indignant villager finds he's on the losing end, grabs the pitchfork, panics and heads for the hills.'

'Yes. That would make sense, wouldn't it? And it doesn't even have to be a dog-walker. Word might easily have got round the village that Hurst was out in that field. Someone getting their groceries in the village shop overhears a conversation. Or it could even be a dog-walker's husband,' Graves said, gaining enthusiasm. 'The missus gets back home and she's like, "You'll never guess who I just saw." Killed because of stupid gossip,' Graves said, before adding, without much sincerity, 'tragic really.'

I didn't say anything for a while. I had considered this myself. 'I'm afraid you're forgetting about the dog,' I said, not unkindly. 'Whoever killed Hurst seems to have strung the poor thing up. Why do something like that?'

'Oh,' Graves said, put out.

I gave him a hard sideways look and said, 'But you might not be that far off. There's something else. Something the village doesn't know about.'

There was a patrol car standing in front of the black wrought-iron gates that led to the gravelled driveway. It had slipped my mind that I had ordered a squad car to be sent out here first thing that morning, and for a second I wondered what the hell it was doing there. Then I remembered. The inside lights of the car were on, and, with automatic annoyance, I recognized a PC called Cleaver. Cleaver was slumped in the front seat, drinking out of a flask as if he had happened upon the house and had stopped to admire the view. When Cleaver saw our car, he got out and cupped his hand over his face, peering at us through the snow.

I stared at the house rising in front of us. 'A long time ago,' I said, 'Hurst might have been involved in something else. Nothing was ever proven, mind, and we had to keep it to ourselves in case anybody got wind of it.'

'Got wind of what, sir?'

'Well, it was a lot, lot worse than a dead wife.' I paused and then said very quietly, 'Two girls went missing.'

'What? Around here?'

'Yes,' I said.

Graves swung around in his seat.

'Two of them,' I said. 'In just two weeks and in broad daylight too.'

'Jesus,' Graves said.

It seemed to take a while for it to sink in, because a few seconds later Graves drew to a sudden stop: the gravel flew up in the air, and I was pitched forward in my seat.

'But you didn't say anything about any missing girls,' Graves said.

I smiled. Of course Graves had an absolute right to be angry. I should have told him, but had quite deliberately decided not to. I took another long look at him, very carefully gauging his reaction. He didn't look bored or resentful any more. No, Graves was furious. Good.

'I wanted to wait until we'd got to the house,' I said. 'You'll know why when you get a better look at it. Anyway, they were both local, like I say. Names were Gail Foster and Elise Pennington.'

'Runaways?'

'No,' I said. 'Too young.'

'How young?'

'Gail was thirteen. Elise was even younger. Twelve.'

'And they never found them?'

I shook my head. 'No. Whoever did it was quick, and they didn't leave a single trace. Did it twice and never again.'

'That's unusual,' Graves said thoughtfully. 'Hurst?'

I undid my seatbelt and took a long look up at the house before opening the car door. I didn't answer straightaway.

'But what did Hurst have to do with it?' Graves repeated.

'I'm not sure,' I said. 'Tell Cleaver over there that we're going to have a look inside. Then I'll tell you what I think I know.'

8

Dashwood Manor had been built in the eighteenth century, and the tiles on the roof now looked grey under the wide sweep of dark sky. Its neoclassical design was unusual around here: most of the larger manor houses were often hundreds of years older and characterized by the yellow Cotswold stone of the walls and roofs. The façade of Dashwood Manor was a very dark grey interspersed with patches of rust-coloured brown, especially near the windows of the upper floor. Leaves had piled up along the base of the stone walls on either side of the driveway, and there was an earthy smell of rotting vegetation together with the smell of smoke. Someone, somewhere, must have tried to light a bonfire despite the snow.

Though the house was not vast, by English country-house standards, it was big enough; neat and compact and nearly symmetrical, it seemed to cower behind the guard of two enormous yew trees, which stood on either side of its grey limestone front. Dwarfed by Meon Hill, the house almost seemed to be receding towards it, as if merging with the hill's overpowering mass.

It cast a long, cold shadow on the gravel driveway. Hurst's old, battered and apparently immortal Land Rover was parked at the front, which meant, as I had thought, that yesterday Hurst had simply hopped over his garden wall at the back and then climbed up the hill to the other side.

I turned away and walked towards the gates, where Cleaver and Graves were looking through the bars. Cleaver was gesturing to the house as if he owned it, but it was Graves — younger, aristocratic-looking — who appeared more in keeping with the sedate surroundings of Dashwood Manor.

Graves moved his head closer, so that his forehead was touching the flaking black-painted metal bars, and squinted as he tried to look further in at the house. 'I still can't see what you're talking about,' he was saying. 'And I really don't see why you just can't tell me, Cleaver.'

Cleaver was in his mid-forties, wiry and ruddy-faced, and at the best of times surly and bad-tempered. I always had the impression that the moment I told Cleaver to do something, he'd be rolling his eyes like a teenager in disgust behind my back. But Cleaver seemed relatively cooperative right now and even eager to please, despite the peculiar guessing game he appeared to be playing with Graves.

'There,' he said, putting his hand as far as it would go through the bars, 'and there,' he said, pointing to the bottom of the house. Then he slowly moved his finger upwards towards the second floor. 'And there,' he said finally.

'Oh, for Christ's sake, Cleaver,' Graves said, losing patience, 'will you stop playing silly buggers and bloody well tell me or . . .' Graves stopped and began to press his face even closer to the bars of the gate. 'All of them, you say?'

Cleaver nodded and poured out a cup of something hot from his flask and offered it to Graves as if he had just won a prize. Graves took it, looking doubtful while Cleaver wasn't watching, but then taking a polite sip when Cleaver turned towards him.

'What is it?' I said. 'What's the big deal about the house?'

Cleaver wisely did not play the same guessing game with me. 'Hurst's only gone and barred all the windows, sir. All of 'em. Noticed it first thing this morning.'

97

I looked. I hadn't noticed either on first inspection. But now that Cleaver had pointed it out, I realized immediately that he was right. Thick black bars spanned every single window. The original front door also appeared to be barred from the outside.

'How very odd,' Graves said quietly.

'Maybe this isn't going to be so easy after all,' I said. 'Maybe we could try round the back?'

'I don't think that's going to help much, sir,' Cleaver said, sounding pleased with himself.

'What do you mean?'

'Well, when they sent me out this morning' — Cleaver looked vaguely resentful at the thought — 'to guard the house, I had to check to see if there was any sign of a break-in, didn't I? So of course I had to go round the back. You're not going to believe this, but he's only gone and bricked up some of the windows in the back and put bars on all the others. Looks bloody horrible.'

'Bricked some of them in?'

Cleaver nodded. 'He's bricked in the big old French windows at the back, and he's barred all the others. Didn't do a great job of it either. It looks sturdy enough, but there's cement everywhere.'

I briefly considered this. 'Does it look

recent?' I asked.

Cleaver scratched at the back of his neck. 'Hard to tell, really. But no. Looks like it's been that way for a while — few years at any rate.'

'What is it, sir?' Graves said quickly.

'Well,' I said, not all that sure myself yet, 'the only place where you can get a glimpse of the back of the house is from the top of that hill over there. We've been hearing all day about how much he hated people rambling through his field.'

'So you think he wasn't really bothered about the field at all?'

I shrugged. 'Maybe he just didn't want people to know what he'd done to the back of his house.'

'Yes,' Graves said, 'there must be laws against that kind of thing. You can't just do whatever you want to a house, even if you do own it.'

Cleaver said bitterly, 'Took a year before the council gave me permission to build a conservatory for the missus.'

'I bet it looks absolutely horrendous,' Graves said, before adding politely, 'Hurst's house, Cleaver, not your wife's conservatory.'

'Bloody terrible job,' he said. Ironically, Cleaver himself had the look of one of those cowboy builders who knock on your door and tell you cheerfully that your roof is about to cave in.

'He must have really lost it,' Graves said in awe. 'Wonder what else he's done to the place.'

'Looks like we're about to find out,' I said, suddenly in a hurry to get going. 'If we can find a way in, that is. You got a couple of torches in that car of yours, Cleaver?'

Together, Graves and I walked towards the gates as Cleaver rummaged loudly in his patrol car for a couple of torches. Then, after handing them over, he switched on the car's headlights so that they were shining through the bars of the gates towards the house. Dashwood Manor probably still looked all right by daylight, but now, in the dark, I could only think: Christ Almighty, but it's grim. The barred front door was like a big yawning mouth full of teeth. You could see the signs of slow decay: the wet, crumbling stone lintel above the front door; the roof patchy where the tiles had slipped off; the gutters blocked by fallen tiles and God knew what else. Ivy had crept along the walls of the house and wrapped itself around the windowsills. There had been flowerbeds on each side of the driveway, but the weeds had taken over and smothered them, while large clumps of grass had managed to find a foothold in the driveway's gravel.

And through the bars you could just make out dark piles of what looked to be newspapers, as if Hurst had piled stacks and stacks of them behind the windowpanes. It was all wrong somehow. The bars made it wrong, of course, but there was something else too, apart from its strange and unsettling remoteness. But right now I didn't know what that was.

Less than a mile away were homes and shops and cars and people. There were televisions and radios and houses and people buying stuff in supermarkets. I thought of the pub on the green. I thought of families in their homes, gathered round comforting pools of light. I thought of plastic penguins tumbling into a pale blue papery sea and disappearing beneath the water. All of it seemed very far away now and somehow unreal.

It was as if we had stumbled upon something that had stood here for years, silent and watchful but yet unnoticed as it had slowly deteriorated in its isolation. I suddenly seemed to see both myself and Graves as if from above: two small figures preparing for a long journey to a place where neither of us particularly wanted to go.

101

'Are you ready?' I said.

Graves nodded, but now he too looked tense and uncertain. Cleaver pushed open the gates for us, and we set out on the gravelled driveway towards the house.

9

Near the front door we slipped a little, almost colliding with Hurst's Land Rover. Then we took the narrow path at the side of the house, leading to the garden at the back.

I used Cleaver's torch to get a good, long look at the garden. There was a kind of carefully maintained ruggedness to it, and Hurst had, with some sustained determination, kept it up. This was rather surprising, given the general air of abandonment that pervaded the rest of the place, and it pleased me now to see that Hurst had not let it go completely to ruin.

I lifted the torch higher and its strong beam revealed the low wall on the other side of the garden and a handful of stone steps.

'So what happened to them?' Graves asked impatiently. 'The girls that went missing. Gail . . . and Elise. They just disappeared you said, sir?'

'Surprised you never heard the names before. Couldn't be more than, I don't know, around seven years now.'

'Seven years? I was just finishing school then,' Graves said.

'It was everywhere for a while. All over the television. In the newspapers. You sure you never heard the names?'

Graves slowed down a little. 'I'm not sure now,' he said, a little flustered. 'Maybe I have. I don't know.'

'Well, you won't get much out of the villagers. They won't talk about it even now, if they can help it. They'll speak about it amongst themselves, but not to us and definitely not to any outsiders. Gail Foster went missing from Quinton. The village never really got over it. Never will either, until she's found one way or the other. She's there, though.'

'Where?' Graves said.

'Out in the village,' I said simply. 'You can feel her, ever since she vanished. The village kind of . . . drew in on itself and shut up shop. But it's waiting — waiting for her to come back.'

Graves looked at me doubtfully. 'But she's never coming back, is she?' he said finally.

'No,' I said, 'she's not. It's been far too long for that.'

'And nothing's been heard of the other girl either. Nothing at all?'

'There are still appeals every so often, and every now and again something will turn up and lead nowhere.' I gestured vaguely at the black fields and ridges. 'But someone got their hooks into those two little girls, and one day we'll find what's left of them and then we'll know for sure.'

'But what do *you* think happened to them?'

I didn't answer straightaway. The horror of it all was coming back far too quickly, now that I was at Hurst's house again. But then the horror really hadn't gone away. It didn't matter where I was or what I was doing. Sometimes it would hit me almost like a physical force. I could be driving, sitting in my house, reading about how River Plate were faring in the Apertura tournament, preparing my dinner, standing over the boiling saucepans, and I would suddenly remember them both. A cold sickness would run over my body.

I would remember their pictures: removed with great care from scrapbooks by parents with shaking hands. Childish grins staring up at me that became branded in my memory forever. But perhaps all that really remained of them were ashes and fragments of burnt and shattered bone.

For a while longer we carried on in silence. I ducked under the branches of an old silver birch and let Graves go on ahead, then caught up with him again.

'Sir? I said what happened to them?'

'They were abducted,' I said finally. 'Elise lived in Chipping Norton, a few miles away from Quinton. She was out in the garden. Just got home from the school they have over there, and she was messing about in her garden, playing. She was supposed to be inside doing her homework, and her older brother was supposed to be making sure she was doing it. But he had some friends round, and they went to play football out the front. When he came back she was gone. He looked for her up and down the street. He thought she might have been hiding or playing a game. So he waited until his mother came home from work. She was a GP, and on Tuesdays she always arrived late. But Elise was gone.

'Their house backed on to a little lane, and the lane overlooked the rear gardens of some of the houses. We think someone waited. Saw her brother leave, or maybe saw him messing about with his mates. So they went round the back and somehow coaxed her out of her garden and into the lane.

Then they took her.'

'And Gail?'

'She went missing almost exactly a week after Elise, and at roughly the same time. Just after school at around 4.00. A teacher saw her leaving the school and heading back home. He didn't give it a second thought. The kids had been warned by then, of course, told to watch out and stick together. But her mother's house was in the middle of a small street that practically backed on to the school playground. Later, a few neighbours remembered seeing her walking towards her house in the lane that the locals use as a shortcut to the shops. They knew her, you see, and they remembered her. But she never got beyond that lane.'

'So someone was waiting for her?'

'Looks like it. They talked her into coming with them. Had a car waiting, maybe, and just took her. And the same goes for Elise. That's what we think anyway.'

'Someone she knew, then?' Graves said.

'Yes. Someone who knew she'd be walking home at that time. Was aware of her routine. Probably local. It was almost . . . it was almost, I don't know, instinctive somehow. I always thought of it that way.'

'And no one remembered seeing a car hanging about, or Gail waiting for anyone near the shops?'

'No. She just . . . well . . . she just vanished. Of course we checked the lane. Looked for tyre tracks and any evidence on the scene. We interviewed absolutely everyone — rounded up all the local sex offenders, but there was nothing.'

'God, their poor parents,' Graves said, echoing my own thoughts exactly. 'Imagine not knowing like that.'

'They moved,' I said.

We carried on walking. The path skirted past wild-looking bushes, and as we drew closer to the house the vegetation on either side became increasingly thick. Tendrils from weeds coiled along the grass and reached out towards the edges of the path. It was almost as if you could see Hurst purposefully letting go of control of the garden at this specific point, with this wilder space marking the boundary between the determined order of the garden and the strange disorder of the house itself.

'It's something truly terrible to make someone disappear,' I said. 'You have to try to imagine it, if you can, Graves. To make someone simply vanish, so that no one knows where they are or what happened to them. It's even worse than murder. Because the family never know, you see. There's hope, but such hope is worse than despair. It's poison.'

I had already said too much and knew it. Graves looked at me, baffled again, and waited for me to go on, but I didn't. I stopped walking.

Through the trees I had glimpsed a collection of small outbuildings by the side of a far wall: a battered-looking old shed, a small garage, and, next to that, as if slumped against the shed, a small greenhouse. Beyond these was the black fence surrounding the swimming pool.

'We're going to need something to break our way in,' I said, looking closely at the barred windows. 'Go see if there's something over there in that shed, will you?'

'We're going to break in?' Graves said. He sounded genuinely shocked. 'We can't do that, sir. What about Rebecca — his daughter? What if she comes back and sees that we've smashed her door down?' Graves laughed. 'We can't just break in. First we need to . . .'

I looked at him, really wondering. So far today Graves had seemed efficient but a little limited. Lacking in imagination. Maybe he lacked guts as well. Again, I thought of Powell. But it was no good thinking about all that now.

'I do think we should come back tomorrow, once we've got the keys,' Graves said a little nervously.

I kept on looking at him and wishing Powell was with me instead. Was Graves going to slow things down? Be a burden to me? If so, I might have to get rid of him somehow, like the others. I didn't like doing it, but there it was. We might get in a little trouble for the door. But so what? It was only a door. But then I remembered. Graves was already on thin ice.

I kept on looking at him, then I said, 'I didn't come all the way out here in the cold just to admire his garden. Hurst isn't going to mind either way, and I couldn't care less about his daughter.' Involuntarily my shoulders hunched; I lifted my right hand into the air, brought it down very quickly to my waist and looked directly at him. 'I'm going into that house. So do what I tell you and go find me something in that shed of his.'

Graves stood very still. He seemed disconcerted. This was a moment in which things could go either way, and that would be it. Both of us were perfectly aware of this. For a second I was sure that Graves was going to refuse, and I would be seeing the back of him. Then very suddenly Graves made up his mind.

He nodded. 'Yes, of course, sir.'

Together we strode off the path and through the trees. Graves trotted ahead, towards the shed's open doors. His torch flickered through the gaps in the shed's wooden frame, and a few minutes later he emerged carrying a rusty old pickaxe broken halfway along the wooden shaft.

Graves lifted it in the air and examined it. 'Sorry, sir, but that's all there was.'

I shrugged. 'It'll do.'

We reached the back of the house. Stretching all along the back of it stood a raised stone platform surrounded on either side by balustrades topped at the crest by globes of moss-covered stone. Five years ago I had led Hurst along this platform to the French windows in his living room. Now it looked dark and the stone stairs leading up to it slippery and treacherous.

Breaking the platform into two was another, far less grand flight of stairs, which led downwards. A servants' entrance by the looks of it. Graves headed straight towards it and disappeared, while I shone my torch along the house, scanning the upper walls.

At the top, near the roof, were large patches of old grime, as if the black rain from the roof had slowly stained the stone over the years. Then I caught a dark, sunken shape like a sightless eye in the round, yellow beam of light.

It caught me completely by surprise. I had forgotten about the windows. I swung the torch back to a far corner of the patio, taking in the ugly dripping gouts of cement that smeared the house and staring in astonishment at the grey-streaked walls.

Cleaver had been right. Hurst had bricked in the French windows and barred all the other windows. The bricked-in French windows somehow distorted the whole sense of the house; the delicate balance of the design was gone. And Cleaver had been right about something else: Hurst had done a lousy job, and it looked like he had done it in a hurry.

In the far corner of the patio, and half buried amongst a clump of shrubs, was a large mound of cement and a bucket lying in an old bag of lime. Gaps where Hurst had misjudged the angle of the window-frame were everywhere, and whenever he had made a mistake he had simply chipped off pieces of brick and squeezed in the small pieces. The bricks lay unevenly in large, unsightly clots of excess mortar.

'Sir!' Graves shouted, his voice muffled at the bottom of the stairwell.

I strode down the steps and peered at the door.

'It's definitely locked,' Graves said.

'Are you sure? Give it another shove.'

Graves pushed it again. 'It's locked, all right.'

'Well, you'd better get on with it, then,' I said.

Graves took off his coat and handed it to me; then I went up the stairs to get out of the way. He picked up the pickaxe and started to smash at the door. I stared entranced at the odd effect of the bricked-in windows as I listened to Graves working. It struck me that I hadn't been all that pleasant to him since he arrived.

But every time I saw Graves I thought of Powell lying in that damned hospital in Warwick. I couldn't help it. Couldn't help thinking of those monitors reflected in the windows along the ward, and the strange and heavy machinery standing by his bed. The blood began to pulse in my ears and I felt a sudden futile panic. I pushed the thought away and again listened to Graves working away at the door. Then came a hesitant thud, followed by a much louder bang.

10

With a sudden loud crack the side of the door split away from the locks. Graves had made short work of it. I passed him his coat. Graves took it with his left hand and with his right pushed at the door. It wouldn't budge. So he tried again, leaning his whole weight against it and giving it a good hard shove and then another.

The door opened outwards into the bottom of the stairwell and sagged against its hinges. Graves disappeared inside. Suddenly light began to pour into the stairwell from the hallway on the other side. I went down the stairs and peered in. The corridor was wide, solid and surprisingly grand for what had once been the servants' entrance. Shoved roughly to one side by the door was a coat rack, beneath which was a pile of boots and shoes and the grass-stained end of an umbrella. Halfway along the carpeted hallway were a few stone steps leading up to another door.

A long time ago, by the looks of it, Hurst had started to paint the corridor olive-green. But the paint ended around three quarters of the way along, as if he'd just got bored one day and given up. And where the green paint ended a more general sense of disorder seemed to descend. Amongst a stacked pile of empty bags of dog food, which for some reason Hurst had felt compelled to keep, was a black bucket and an old grey Hoover, which looked like it had been standing there for years. Woven amongst the bags were long lengths of blue string, and on the floor lay a cracked jam jar full of nails and screws. Graves was staring at the mess.

'Was it always like this?' he asked wearily.

'I'm not really sure. I never entered this way before. I went through the French windows with Hurst after his wife had her accident. And after that it was always the front door.'

'So you were here more than once,' Graves said, surprised.

'I'm afraid I didn't really believe him to begin with,' I explained. 'So I kept on coming back.'

'I bet he didn't like that,' Graves said.

'Made a formal complaint. Brewin had

already ruled it as an accidental death.' I shrugged. 'But he was lying about something. Hurst was old money.' I let this hang in the air for a minute, as if it accounted for everything. 'He was used to getting his own way, and he wasn't used to being pushed around by the likes of me. So he started pushing back. Lot of good it did him. Well, not to begin with anyway. His second wife, well . . . she had smoothed away some of the rougher edges, but deep down he hadn't changed at all. She was very beautiful, you know. He worshipped her.'

'So he totally lost the plot when she died,' Graves said flippantly, looking at the corridor. 'Fell to pieces. Grieving widower loses mind,' he said, almost as if he were reading out a headline in a tabloid newspaper.

I said, 'It would look that way, wouldn't it, unless it really was a guilty conscience. But, like I said, his alibi checked out.'

'But old money?' Graves said. 'You know, that doesn't fit with the idea I have of him. I mean, doing his own labouring up there on that field — I can't put it together with his background. Usually people who own houses like this get other people to do everything for them. From what I've gathered in the village, he doesn't sound . . . all that well-to-do, to be honest.'

116

'His family have owned land round here for a long, long time. And none of them have ever ventured far away. Although they've had money, they've worked the land themselves forever. Frank never seemed much interested in anything else. I imagine his parents shipped him off to public school, but I think after that it was an agricultural college or perhaps straight back here. He seemed perfectly content. Sent his daughter to the village school. And his first wife was a local girl.'

'So the place was a working farm until he sold up?'

'Yes. Frank ran it along with a foreman. Used to be a big employer round here and a lot of people lost their jobs when he decided to sell up. But the family's always had plenty of money, even before he sold off the land. He must have made a fortune selling that land to developers.'

'What about his first wife?' Graves said. 'She was local, you say.'

'She died when she was pretty young. Not nearly as glamorous as the second wife. Used to work in one of the pubs. That's where Frank met her.' I stooped suddenly. 'Now that. That I've seen somewhere before.'

Lying propped against the wall near the

door was a painting. It was far too valuable to be shoved back here, where no one would ever see it but Hurst. But then maybe that was the point. It was almost as if on impulse he had gone and fetched it from somewhere else in the house and put it here, so he might see it as he went about his everyday business. Part of a half-hearted attempt to brighten the place up perhaps.

I did not know who the artist was, but in the painting ships were being hurled from the top of waves and crashed against black jagged rocks; sailors clung to shattered pieces of timber amongst the churning sea. But the dim light in the hallway dulled the power of the painting, and the sea in the picture seemed restless and dreary, the fate of the drowning sailors of little consequence.

I said to myself: your wife drowns in your very own swimming pool, right in your back garden, and that's what you choose to hang on the wall. Pictures of drowning men.

It didn't make sense. Or did it? Remorse, punishment, guilt, I thought in quick succession. Or was it something else? A message, perhaps subconsciously chosen and thrown out on to the walls of the hallway: something about Hurst's own predicament. I looked again at the survivors in the painting as they clung to the wreckage and watched helplessly as those around them drowned in dark turmoil.

'More locks,' Graves said.

The bolts, one at the top of the door, the other at the bottom, were thick, black and squared-edged, and double the size of the ornate brass locks you usually see in manor houses. They were well oiled and slid easily across before making a sharp dry crack.

Graves went ahead and found the light switch. The kitchen, after the bleakness of the exterior of the house, looked almost cosy, or at least it did until you noticed the bars lining the windows. Even then the bars weren't quite enough to make a difference to the overall determined cheeriness of the room, and thanks to a dark green Aga in the corner it was fairly warm too.

'But what,' Graves said, his voice sounding loud in the silence, 'what had Hurst got to do with Gail Foster and Elise Pennington?'

I paused before answering. 'A hairpin. Probably not even that.'

'A hairpin?'

I took a few steps towards the table, thinking. The kitchen, while not exactly spotless, was clean enough, but there was an underlying sense of male disorder to the place, and some of the things Hurst had added to it seemed random and absent-minded. There was a handful of red shotgun shells lying at the bottom of a large fruit bowl on a sideboard, a screwdriver on a microwave, and an old broken kettle on the floor. By the radiator under the window was an old dog basket: it was lined with a dirty white rug, and a huge red rubber bone lay beside it on the floor.

'When Hurst's wife drowned, I got them to drain the pool,' I said finally. 'Just a feeling I had at the time. I didn't really expect to find anything. Certainly nothing at all to do with those girls. Hurst never really struck me as the type. And anyway they'd been gone for over two years by then. But something down there had got caught in one of the drains. It was all rusty and bent out of shape, and you could hardly see what it was to begin with. But . . . well, it turned out to be a hairpin. A kid's hairpin. One of the constables left it lying there at the side of the pool after they drained it. And when I saw it I remembered. I remembered the girls.'

Absently, I ran my finger along the edge of the table and squinted for a moment in the light. 'It had a little plastic daisy stuck on to it, though one had fallen off. We never found that one. Gail had been wearing a hairpin in the shape of a flower when she went missing. That's one of the things her mother remembered. Of course, the thing is, they're pretty common — hairpins with flowers on them. And, as it turns out, there're quite a lot of different ones all with different types of flowers stuck to them. You wouldn't believe how many, Graves. Her mother couldn't be sure what type of flower it was. So we couldn't be sure either.' I sighed heavily. 'Of course I had to let O'Donnell know straightaway.'

'O'Donnell?'

'Our super back then,' I said. 'I didn't really feel like doing it, but there you go. I had to tell him. Very nearly didn't bother, because I wanted this whole house searched, and I was all for doing it on my own if I had to. But . . . well, he said no, of course. He said there wasn't nearly enough to go on and it was a waste of time.' I shrugged. 'Maybe he was right. There was only the hairpin, and that probably belonged to Hurst's daughter anyway.'

'And did it? Did it belong to her?'

'No, she didn't recognize it, but then that didn't really mean anything. It was so broken. She said it might have belonged to her when she was younger but she wasn't sure.'

I took a step forward to the table and winced when I remembered. 'And then there was the press,' I said. 'If the press had got wind of it, well, it would have been the end of Hurst and probably all for nothing. You must know what they're like. And Hurst would have been right up their street. Wealthy landowner. Glamorous wife just died tragically. Big old house. They'd have been camping outside his gates for weeks.'

'Yes, sir,' Graves said quietly.

I noticed that he had become very still.

'I can understand that, but surely that wasn't enough to prevent a proper search.'

'You have to try to understand . . .' I said quickly, wanting to get it over and done with, but then I stopped myself. Why justify myself to Graves? I hardly knew him.

'But you let it go?' Graves said, incredulous. 'Just as easy as that? You didn't think it was worth trying just a little bit harder? I know it's not all that much. Certainly not enough to get a search warrant. But we're talking about two little girls here.'

Once again I had another good look at Graves. It was like I was beginning to see him for the first time. Although I had absolutely no intention of explaining my actions to him, or to anyone else for that matter, Graves had, and to my great surprise, just gone up a lot in my estimation. He seemed to have a temper on him as well as a big mouth. That could be a good thing. I waited, curious to see just how far he would take it.

'Sir,' Graves said. He seemed to be trying to keep a lid on it. It wasn't working. 'I said you waited all this time to come back. Just because you and your super didn't want to ruin . . . to ruin Hurst's reputation, in case you were wrong.' His lips turned down in distaste. 'Because you were afraid of what the press would do to him. So you wait until someone sticks him with a pitchfork to come back and have a good nose around this house. What if you were right? What if he really did kill those two little girls?'

I nodded in a distracted kind of way and then continued to explore the kitchen.

'Sir, I said —'

'I know what you said, Graves,' I replied, and then forgot all about him.

The ceiling at the far side of the kitchen sloped down slightly, creating a cosy alcove. Hurst had converted that section into a kind of living room, and it looked like he had raided the other rooms in the house for the pieces of furniture he'd liked best, just as he had raided the painting and put it in the hall. In the middle of the alcove was a

Persian rug. And in front of an armchair and directly behind the television was another door with two sets of industrial-style bolts.

I moved towards the bars on the window, my interest momentarily divided between the kitchen and the snow falling outside. There was a glass cabinet standing in a far corner near the windows. Inside, at the back, nestled amongst the glasses and tankards, was a small framed photograph: a much younger Frank Hurst peered out at me through the dust. Gently, I opened the cabinet doors and took out the photo.

Hurst was surrounded by other young men, all of them wearing their cricket whites and posing together in front of a pavilion. Hurst was kneeling at the front and grinning. He had a wavy, foppish mop of hair, his teeth were slightly crooked, and his trousers red-stained. He looked quite handsome in the photo. The transformation to the broken-down and hated recluse had happened so completely that it was difficult to believe it was him. I put the photo back. There were no pictures of his wives or daughter. There was just that one summer's day looking out at me from the middle shelf of the cabinet.

From outside, I could just make out the

sound of the wind rushing through the branches of the trees. Cleaver still had his lights on, and I was momentarily glad for it. They were like a beacon in the blackness of the forest outside.

'Idiot's going to run the batteries out if he isn't careful,' Graves muttered behind me.

At that exact moment, as if Cleaver had somehow heard him through the glass, the lights of the squad car went out. The snow glittered faintly in the light spilling out from the kitchen window.

'Sir,' Graves said suddenly.

I turned around. Graves was standing on the Persian rug and looking fiercely at something on the other side of the armchair.

Resting against the far side of the chair, its barrels pointing up towards the ceiling, was a shotgun. I quickly walked towards it, then gingerly picked it up. It was a sportsman's double-barrelled model, and not the kind of practical and more powerful gaming rifle I would have expected to see in a manor house like this one. I examined the shotgun, feeling its coolness. It was surprisingly light and, in its own way, beautiful.

The receiver at the top was engraved. 'Beretta EELL Classic. Made in Italy,' I read out loud. I turned the gun in my hands and checked the safety before cracking open the

chamber. The gun was not all that powerful, but it would do the trick if some unexpected intruder came bursting in. The shot
would spread out, making it impossible to
miss. And there was something very pur-
poseful about the way it had been put at
the side of the armchair, within easy reach.

'Safety wasn't even on,' I said.

'Maybe he went out shooting for his
supper,' Graves said without much convic-
tion. 'Meant to lock it up when he got back.'

In the chamber were two red cartridges. I
pulled them out. For a while I stood there,
undecided as to what I should do with
them. Then I put them in my coat pocket. I
left the chamber open and, carrying it
crooked under my arm, placed it on top of
the kitchen table.

'So what do you make of it all?' I said,
looking around the kitchen.

'It's a bloody shambles, I'd say, and it's
against the law to have a loaded gun that's
not locked up.'

With a weary patience I said, 'I know it's
a bloody shambles, Graves, but what do you
think Hurst was doing?'

Finding himself on the spot, Graves
seemed to grow tight with worry as he gazed
around the kitchen. His eyes finally rested
near to where I was standing motionless,

my hands on the back of the armchair, as if I were involuntarily offering him up some sort of clue. Graves paused, frowning, glancing from the armchair to the window, and back again. For a moment, he looked pleased with himself, but then his face clouded over with doubt, as if he suspected some trap.

'Well, obviously he was afraid of something,' Graves said. 'But the question is who?'

I nodded. 'And if he did have something to do with those girls after all?'

'And someone found out?' Graves said. He turned around and stared anxiously out of the window, as if he half expected to see some face staring at them through the bars. 'God, it's all pretty grim,' he said.

I didn't reply. I stared at the gun now lying on the kitchen table, not sure if I should take it with me. Instead I left it, and Graves followed me down the hallway.

11

Graves started trying all the doors, while a clock chimed out gloomily from somewhere far away in the front of the house. The hallway light cast only a single yellow glare on to the dusty carpet. Shoved hastily against one wall was a row of battered green filing cabinets. Some of the drawers had fallen open, and what looked to be years of correspondence, bills and invoices spilt out and lay in piles on the floor.

I walked towards the stairs and looked up. The sense of cold and permanent decay was even worse here. Things had obviously got bad and very quickly. Actually, I couldn't believe how bad things had got. All the doors save one at the end of the hallway were locked. Graves opened it, searched for the light and flicked it on. I recognized the living room as we stepped inside. My eyes were immediately drawn to the two large brown curtains at the far side of the room; I knew the French windows would be behind them. Like a butler briskly performing his morning duties, Graves was already striding across the floor towards them; he drew the curtains open wide. But on the other side only the cement-smeared bricks could be seen. Graves looked shocked to see them.

A fine, round oak table occupied the centre of the room. Next to the open curtains was a dainty-looking writing desk, and beside that were more filing cabinets. Yet, unlike those in the hall, they were well organized, and no paper spilt from outstretched drawers. They looked new and solid and were painted a uniform gunmetal-grey.

'What a mess,' Graves said, wincing, 'and what's that awful smell?'

'Radiator's leaked somewhere, I imagine.'

Graves drew his hand slowly along the glass of the French windows, tracing the pattern of the bricks on the other side. 'What was the old man playing at?' he said, staring with disapproval at his now-black fingertips and looking to me, for an instant, exactly like a school prefect examining a dorm room.

'Go and check those cabinets.'

Graves crouched down and opened the nearest one. 'Empty,' he said.

'Try the others. Look in all of them, and if they're locked break them open as well.'

I turned and looked around. There was just too much stuff crammed into the living room. A lot of it crockery and wine glasses and boxes full of junk. I headed towards the writing desk. 'Used to be a nice room, if I remember rightly,' I said, sitting down. 'Nice view of the garden anyway.'

I started to search the top drawers. There was nothing of any interest. I sighed, then pulled out a bottom drawer as far as possible before delving my hand in deep at the back of it. Dust, coloured writing paper and then something light at the back: just an old newspaper. I tossed it back towards the oak table. Of course it missed and the pages lay spread out on the carpet.

Absently, I began to pick at a loose thread on the corner of my shirt while glancing at a big brown leather armchair shoved into a corner of the room. Graves was once again staring at the huge bricked-in French windows, and I found that I was now doing the same thing, half expecting to see the snow falling outside.

Annoyed, and not at all sure what we were looking for, I stood with my hands at my sides, thinking vaguely that I might have a quick look upstairs. Graves opened another drawer. I wandered back towards the table and, without thinking, picked up the newspaper pages one by one and laid them on the table. I tensed when I saw the picture in the middle.

I quickly reassembled the paper into its right order. It was an old copy of the *Cotswold Herald* dated 14 December 1994. I pulled the torch from my coat pocket and shone it on to the pages at the back.

A black-and-white photograph took up almost half of one of the back pages. There had once been a lengthy column of text at the side of the photo and more text beneath it. But that text had been deliberately cut out.

The photo showed around thirty to forty schoolchildren posing and smiling into the camera. A school photo taken, by the looks of it, on the stage in a gym, which, I imagined, doubled as the assembly room. White rings had been drawn around the heads of two of the children, so that they seemed to have large halos behind their heads: boys of about twelve or thirteen, standing next to each other. They looked similar: both seemed rowdy-looking and one, the smaller of the pair, was pulling a cheeky face. I guessed that the photo had been taken to celebrate some prize awarded to a local school somewhere, and that the editor had had some purpose in picking out these two children for his readers. The only text that remained was a caption attached to the bottom of the photo. Two names: Ned and Owen Taylor.

They didn't mean anything to me. I stared long and hard at the photo, and it wasn't until a few minutes later that I realized that I was seeing someone I knew, or at least someone whom I thought I knew.

She was staring out at me from the bottom-right-hand corner of the page. She had a thin, pretty face. Hurst's daughter? I couldn't be entirely sure. If it was her, she would have been almost three years younger than when I'd seen her last. Like the majority of the faces in the picture, hers was not highlighted. I looked a little longer, thinking. There were bound to be other photos of her in the house. But so far I hadn't seen any.

I left the newspaper where it was. As Graves continued to search the filing cabinets, I came out of the living room and trudged upstairs.

From somewhere far off, water started to hiss and spit as the rickety old boiler began to heat up. I found the corridor's light switch and flicked it on: luminous strips along the ceiling, like those of a hospital ward, flickered on the length of the hallway. Hurst must have had them installed at some point as another security measure. Perhaps in case someone managed to get into his house and make their way up the stairs.

On my right I passed a door that was open: Hurst's bedroom. I felt along the inside of the door and, as I expected, found two more sets of locks exactly like the ones in the kitchen. I found the light switch and discovered that Hurst had also felt it necessary to bar the windows of his own bedroom, so that his room looked like a cell.

The corridor dipped left and curved along towards the front of the house. I walked on, passing yet another barred-in window, wondering if Hurst had really 'lost the plot', as Graves had put it. I could only imagine what it must have been like to patrol these dark corridors night after night.

But, despite what was before my own eyes, I did not think Hurst had lost his mind. The bricked-in windows, the bars and the gun, although strange, had a logic to them and, combined, showed a definite sense of purpose. After all, Hurst's paranoia had proved right in the end. Whoever was after him had waited ever so patiently, and the moment he left the safety of this place they had got him.

I had arrived at the far end of the house. I moved closer and saw that there was a much narrower corridor here, leading to a thick brown curtain. I stepped in and snapped on a light switch on the side of the wall. This hall was much cleaner than the rest of the house, and the reddish carpet that lined the floor felt thick and almost new. On the wallpaper, pink roses coiled gently towards the curtain. I walked along the corridor and pushed the curtain aside. Behind it was an immaculate white staircase, which curved right and out of view. I found that I couldn't find the light to the stairs. So I took the torch out of my coat pocket again, switched it on and headed straight up.

There was a pale blue door at the top of the stairs. I pushed the handle and peeked through. For a moment the only thing I could see was what seemed to be an electric alarm clock somewhere at the back, giving out a narrow strip of light. Then the clouds outside the window cleared for a moment, and moonlight slowly began to fill the room.

I stared in. Objects in the room slowly took shape. A rocking chair beside an electric heater. Books stacked in neat piles on the floor. A snowglobe: a plastic cottage encased in a plastic dome.

Down below, I could hear Graves on the move. He walked through the corridor, pushed the curtain aside and walked up the steps. I turned around and shone the torch in his direction. In the sudden warmth of the narrow stairwell Graves took off his scarf and put it in his pocket. He had some files wedged under his other arm.

'What's up here, sir?'

With both of us now squeezed tightly in the narrow stairwell, I felt a sudden sense of claustrophobia and nearly told Graves to go back down. Instead I said, 'His daughter's room, I think.' And, gently opening the door wider, I added, 'He's kept it just as she left it.'

'God, how weird. Whatever for?'

I didn't say anything. It didn't seem to bother Graves that Hurst's daughter had abandoned him, and that Hurst had no doubt died an appallingly violent death just hours ago. It was the disruption to the order of things that seemed to bother Graves the most. All this mess. The barred-in windows. Hurst's failure to keep a gun safely secured in a gun cabinet as the law demanded.

I sighed. 'So there *was* something in those cabinets?' I said, looking at the files.

'Yes, sir. Not in all of them, though. He kept letters and correspondence and loads of old bills. Never seems to have chucked anything out. Ever. Supermarket receipts, petrol receipts. All of it is really muddled up. These, though, were all together in one file, and there was a bunch of old videotapes on top of them.'

'Videotapes?'

'Yep.'

'Were they locked up?'

'Yes, sir.'

'And the files?'

'Stuff from some kind of agency. A detective agency, I think. Looks like his daughter really ran out on him for good. And so he spent a packet on trying to find out where she had got to.'

I gestured towards the files and took them. Then I opened them up. There were three pale grey files and in all of them without exception the notes at the back had been written by the same hand. There were also several typewritten sheaves of paper bearing signatures in the same handwriting, along with invoices attached neatly with paper-clips.

'You want me to get any more? There're loads of files like these downstairs.'

'No, that's probably enough for one day,' I said, making up my mind. 'We'll take the tapes as well. And they definitely were locked up, you say?'

'Yes,' Graves said. 'A boxful of them at least.'

'He must have locked them up for a reason. We'll come back tomorrow for the rest of it.'

I stayed where I was for a while longer. Disappointed. But what had I really expected to find here? I had been waiting a long time to have a proper look at Hurst's house without O'Donnell interfering, and now I'd had the chance it seemed there was nothing in it. Caged darkness and locked doors. That's all there was, really. That, and Hurst's lingering presence.

We could have a better look tomorrow. All the same, it had been a mistake coming here in the dark and so late, and I knew it. Graves had been right. But I didn't leave straightaway. Instead I stepped inside the room and found the light switch.

Hurst had clearly been at pains to keep his daughter's room clean, and actually Graves was right about the room too: it *was* weird the way he had kept it as if frozen in time.

The space had obviously once been an attic and had, in fact, been turned into a suite of rooms that ran some distance through the top of the house. There was a bedroom, a small separate living room and beyond that a spacious bathroom. There were no bars on the window.

I took another few steps and my hair touched the upside-down V of the ceiling. The room was very neat. The bed had been made, and ornaments had been carefully arranged on a writing desk. Graves warily followed me in and the door closed behind him. For a moment he stood at the threshold, taking it all in. Like me, he had to crouch a little to avoid the ceiling as he moved across the sheepskin rug by the side of the bed.

I looked out of the single large window and stared at the snow-capped hill in the distance, stretching across the horizon in a solid sloping arc.

Outside, the snow was falling even faster, and after the dug-in darkness it was a relief to see the sky. Beyond, I could just make out a car inching its way along the curve of Meon Hill. A moth started beating against the window, its wings fluttering uselessly against the glass. I reached for the window and opened it: a stone fell and went tumbling down over the roof, and the moth flew outside. I had a sense of time stretching out. But that was really all that now remained in this room: time past. And then, as if to mark

it, a clock began to chime from somewhere
down below.

12

As usual, my house was very warm, with the radiators already blazing away by the time I got home. The moment I enter my house I always feel greatly at ease: my arms hang more loosely at my sides, and the English voice and aloofness inside my head slowly fade. The tension leaves my body. It's as if I'm shedding my English skin as I take off my coat and hang it in the porch.

There was a knocked-about parcel from Carlos, wrapped in yellowish paper, waiting for me on the table of my porch. My brother has been sending me parcels just like it ever since I arrived in England over twenty years ago. I switched on the lights in the hall with my elbow and left the box of videotapes and files by the telephone at the bottom of the stairs. I picked up the parcel and walked to the kitchen to fix myself a drink.

I took a lemon out of the fridge, tossed it into the air and then cut it very neatly into quarters. I put one of the quarters into a long glass and poured myself a Fernet-Branca, a syrupy and very bitter Italian aperitif, which looks like engine oil and tastes like it until you get used to it.

Apart from the occasional plumber, builder or electrician, no one ever stepped inside this house apart from Powell. Certainly no women. None of that ever lasts for long anyway. They soon get fed up with me, and I can't say I blame them.

I become more animated when I'm at home. If I'm watching football on television, I angrily curse and berate the players on the screen. I shout and scream; clutch my hands in horror when I watch them lose. I cajole and tease the cat. I pace more. Slam doors. Stalk through rooms. I drink *mate* out on my patio and cook huge *asados,* which keep me going in meat for about a week. I write long letters to my brother. I monitor the news back home via his letters and feel the same level of indignation and despair as my fellow Argentinians when my country lurches from one crisis to the next.

At home I'm more prone to sudden outbursts. I'm less reserved, and I'm far more direct. At work I know that I can sometimes seem flippant and detached. I'm careful not to give myself away. For years I told myself that this reserve of mine came from my English father and the occasional bouts of recklessness from my Argentinian mother. The theory had a nice feel to it, and I clung to it for a while. But it's something else — something that runs much more deeply than that. From here, inside this environment, I have made impulsive decisions that trouble me later.

Sometimes, it's as if a part of me has stubbornly refused to adapt. As if the young man who came here all those years ago is still essentially the same. And, strangely, I'm becoming more Argentinian as I get older. The longer I stay here, the less English I become. It's a very Argentinian trait, this homesickness. It gives Buenos Aires its mournful appeal: the homesickness of the emigrant who can never go back is etched into the very fabric of the city itself. And it's here, right here in this house as well.

I finished my drink, went upstairs, had a shower and changed into jeans and a thick, navy-blue jumper and then lit the fire in my study. I leant against my desk for a while, thinking about Hurst, then went downstairs and had another drink before making dinner. I opened my brother's parcel while the water boiled and hissed, splashing a little on the hob.

The house on the inside does not look like any of the other houses around here. If you had asked me years ago whether I missed home and wanted to go back, I would have told you very firmly absolutely not. But the house of course tells a different story. It's something about the light perhaps. There're the green metal shutters I had installed on some of the windows years ago, which give the house a heavy, almost resentful silence, as if it somehow pines for boisterous noise from outside. And then there're the thick-leaved tropical plants that stand in large pots in many of the rooms and line the hallway. There's the very dark wood of the furniture that I've chosen and the faded rugs that cover the tiled floor of my down-stairs hallway, giving it an almost rustic air. Upstairs, I stripped out most of the wall-to-wall carpets years ago to reveal the old wood beneath, which adds to the overall oaken darkness of the house.

I began to cook, listening to some old tango CDs. I hummed along, feeling quite cosy in the alcove of my kitchen. I took another sip of my drink. Enzo, my cat, was outside, scrabbling at the window above the sideboard, leaving muddy marks. For a while I ignored him, and then with a sigh I let him in and quickly closed the window.

The cat, whose full name is (of course) Enzo Francescoli, dropped silently down from the sideboard to the floor and went straight towards the food bowl by the washing machine.

I tore away the paper from my brother's package. First off the prized *yerba mate* — a drink like tea but much stronger. I held up the *mate* for a moment as if it were a trophy and felt its weight. Satisfied, I put it in the cupboard and threw out the old packet. Then came the usual articles that had been meticulously cut out of the local papers. As always, Carlos had included news of my old football club, which had gone up against Boca Juniors, their arch-enemy, the previous week and lost.

I read Carlos's letter. First came the usual cheery heartfelt complaints about the economy (rising inflation across the board), corrupt politicians and increasing crime, which had culminated in a number of high-speed kidnappings that the press were now calling *secuestro express.* There was also another, new type of kidnapping called *secuestro virtual,* or virtual kidnapping, which was a sophisticated con being run by inmates out of local prisons in Buenos Aires. My brother is interested in that kind of thing, being a born conman himself.

144

I read the articles. More tales of political woe and unrestrained chaos. The country always seemed to be hovering on the brink of the abyss, especially since the devaluation of the peso last December and the run on the banks. Burning tyres blocking roads. Protests still everywhere. The subway workers on strike again. It was oddly reassuring in a way. A tango played. Astor Piazzolla. Quicker than the last. Absently, I began to go through some more of the clippings and froze when I came to the last one. It was an article cut out of *El Correo* showing a photo of an old man in the street, his arm trying to shield his face from the glare of a dozen cameras.

'General Jorge Rafael Videla.' I said the name out loud in the silence of my kitchen. Then I regretted saying it in the sanctity of my own home. I looked more closely at the photo: the old man seemed to be trying to get into an apartment building on the other side of the road. It was late at night, and that made sense if you thought about it. Surrounding him was a mob being kept at bay by a couple of tough-looking policemen. The old man, as he tried to push his way through the street, appeared furious and indignant. Someone had painted ASESINO right in the middle of the street in

145

bright red letters.

I pushed away my plate, suddenly not hungry. I saw the General in person once but from far off. It had been during the World Cup in Buenos Aires in 1978. I had been seventeen years old. Videla had been out of his general's uniform for a change and was wearing a blue suit. As President it had fallen to him to present the cup to the Argentinian captain, Daniel Passarella, who had looked as if he wasn't sure whether he wanted to take it from him. Much later, I had learnt that, less than a mile away from the stadium, hundreds of Argentinian citizens, hooded and handcuffed to beds in clandestine detention centres, were listening to the match along with their captors on the radio.

To me the old General had always seemed a little bit like an untrustworthy and seedy-looking accountant. One who had just been caught cooking the books. And he still had that absurd Adolf Hitler moustache.

I slammed my fist hard on the table, so that Enzo jumped and scurried off, and my knife fell off the table. The bastard was supposed to be in jail. I read the article, remembering now in growing dismay. The courts had decided to let him serve out the rest of his sentence from the comfort of his own home back in 1998. According to the article, Videla had a history of heart problems, and a few weeks ago the authorities had bundled him out in the middle of the night to see his doctors and run some tests. The relatives of those whom he had made disappear while he had been in power had got word of it and been ready for him when he got back.

I was glad of the reception he had received, but the article had made me angry, and I knew I was going to start thinking about home again and raking it all up. Thinking about what happened is useless, and with a great effort of will I blocked it out. I imagined the past as something small and black and inconsequential and crushed it beneath my heel, and, just to make sure it wouldn't come back, before I went to bed I settled down to some more work. I took the box of files and tapes into my study and emptied them out on to my desk. As I went through them, I thought not of home and people like Videla but of Hurst lying stone cold on a mortuary slab and that horrible gashing wound in his neck. I thought of Hurst's house standing there, dark and impenetrable like some kind of bunker.

I thought of those dark corridors at night and of the elegant gun clutched in Hurst's hands. In my mind, Hurst, as he had patrolled those corridors, was a man white-faced and afraid. The dog, sensing his fear, was at his heels, its ears pressed tight against its head. Then I thought of all those empty rooms gathering dust, and of his daughter's room kept so immaculate that it must look exactly as it had the day she ran out on him. Hurst had definitely been trying to find her.

The last letter in the third file was dated April 2001 and had an invoice attached. Bray's Detective Agency was embossed on the head of each typed sheet, along with an address in Warwick. I didn't recognize the name or the address. It looked as if Hurst believed she had been in London, and that's where he had sent Bray to find her.

Bray had personally carried out the investigation himself. Visits to hotels and youth hostels. Inquiries made at employment agencies where Hurst's daughter might have applied for work. Bars and restaurants and letting agencies. Possible leads, and where he had planned to look for her next. A thorough job. But he had not been able to find her. I went through the files a second time, and then I went to bed, leaving the box locked up in a filing cabinet in my study.

I closed my eyes, and after what seemed a very long time I was able to think about something other than Frank Hurst and the weird emptiness of his house. I began to remember a holiday with my parents a few years before they'd had their accident. I remembered swimming towards a big black rock in the sea.

My father, an engineer for the railways, had been granted an entire month's holiday from the British company where he worked. I remembered my mother, brown and slender, lying in the sun. I couldn't be sure now where it had been. Mar de las Pampas or perhaps Mar del Plata. Somewhere along the Atlantic coast. The water had been very cold. I remembered reaching the rock and suddenly becoming frightened by what lay waiting for me, because I couldn't see the bottom any more. I had swum out too far.

I had waved to my father on the beach for reassurance, but my father, indifferent as usual, with his head buried deep in the paper or a book, hadn't seen me. And it was while I was thinking of my father and mother and of the cold water that I finally started to drift off to sleep. My mind fixed on one random object after the other; images flickered and vanished. And then I began to dream.

I dreamt that I was back at Hurst's house. In my dream it was winter, but I was sitting on a deckchair in front of Hurst's swimming pool. Hurst was with me, and, past his shoulder, young girls dressed identically in school uniforms were lining up near the metal stairs that led to the pool on the far side. They were all wearing hairpins in the shape of broken flowers. One after the other, they jumped into the swimming pool in the cold, frosty afternoon. But the pool was dirty and dark and full of rotting leaves and rubbish. Bottles and plastic shopping bags floated on its white, scum-covered surface, while oily black branches bobbed and were churned by some strange current below. But the children did not seem to notice. They disappeared one by one beneath the surface and did not come back up.

In my dream, there was something dark in the water — something below the surface, sliding about, waiting for the children to jump in. I wanted to stop them, but found that I could not. I wanted to scream out, warn them against whatever terrible fate was down there.

But in my dream Hurst grabbed me and wouldn't let me go. I looked into his deep-set blue eyes in his suntanned weathered face. I stared down at his checked work-shirt, the sleeves rolled up over his strong

150

sinewy forearms. I looked beyond his shoulder. I couldn't take my eyes off the foaming waters and the grinning children; I couldn't pull myself out of the nightmare.

'Downes,' Hurst was saying. 'There's something I have to tell you. Something I should have . . .'

I leant forward, trying to make out what he had to say, but Hurst's words were torn away from me and lost in the wind.

On my bedside table the phone was ringing. I could hear it in my sleep. It sounded as if it were coming from under water. I tried to wake up, but I couldn't. I tried to pull myself out of the dream, but it was as if a current seethed all around me and held me down. I was in the back of the Falcon again. Trying to open the window. But the window wouldn't open. And then, as the water finally pulled me under, I woke up. I reached for the phone.

'So sorry, sir,' Graves's polite voice said on the line. 'But I've just got word from the station. Something's up.'

I shifted my feet to the floor and stared mournfully at my legs poking out of my pyjamas. 'Up?'

'Over at Hurst's place,' Graves said.

'What's happened?'

'It's the house.'

'The house,' I said immediately, awake now. 'What's wrong with it?'

'Well, it's on fire,' Graves said.

13

Even though I had already been told what was happening over the police radio, I was not prepared for the enormity of the blaze when I got there. The rolling flames filled the entire windscreen as I approached the house, and when I got out of the car the raw power of it hit me like a wave. Even from the other side of the front gates, I could sense its urgency, and its desire to keep on going until all the trees and the surrounding fields had been laid to waste.

As I stared at the house, a narrow stick of timber beneath the tiles hit the guttering at the top and landed on one of the great yew trees standing by the side of the house. It remained lodged stubbornly in the crook of a branch, and then ever so slowly the branch caught fire. As if in triumph, the fire raging inside the house rose higher, its bright flames piercing the smoke that seemed to envelop the sky.

A sudden wave of heat hit me across the gravelled driveway, and a chimney pot fell from the roof to the ground. Its image, set against the dark walls of the house, stayed with me for a moment when I blinked: a shaft of light framed against the blackness of my eyes.

It crashed into the flowerbeds beneath the kitchen window and burnt at the base of the house. The weeds and flowers, the forgotten ornamental trees and the tough old roses all started to burn and crackle while the water from the fire engines cascaded down in fountains and formed glistening puddles in the driveway.

I took a few wary steps forward, shielding my eyes from the blaze. Already a long, cold line of sweat was dripping from my neck and crawling the entire way down my back. There were two fire engines. And, as I watched, a third, this one a truck with an extra supply of water, came hurtling along the lane, through the gates and straight on to the driveway, shuddering to a halt just outside the front door. A series of groans came from deep within the house, followed by a low wail from somewhere far off. I feared that the noise signified some fundamental and appalling shift in the building's structure. The roof began to slump further in on itself.

From the very depths of the house came another groan and then an ominous ricocheting bang, as something had finally given way. There was a moment when everything seemed very still. The firemen tensed. The captain yelled out an order above the din, and the men surprisingly quickly, but with their hoses still trained on the blaze, moved back. They had already been pushed back as far as the gates.

I stepped back too and looked up. There was a huge crack as the whole of the eastern section of the roof imploded and fell in on itself. As it did so a massive ball of flame shot up into the sky. Both teams immediately closed in again on the fire, shifting in tandem in the gravel, leaning into the weight of the water jetting out of the hoses.

Although mesmerized by the blaze and all the activity around it, I finally turned away and moved towards an ambulance. There was no sign of Graves, but his car was parked amongst the trees on the other side of the lane. Cleaver was leaning nonchalantly against the bonnet. A medic was wrapping his arm with a bandage. As if he hadn't breathed in enough smoke already, Cleaver was puffing away on a thick roll-up.

'Anyone hurt?' I asked.

'Yes, sir,' Cleaver said. 'A bloke got trapped for a while, breathed in a ton of smoke.'

'Who? One of the firemen?'

'No, sir. A passer-by. Came along and saw the fire before they got there. He ran inside before I could stop him.'

'A passer-by,' I said, genuinely horrified. 'How the hell did he manage to do that?'

'I told him to stay put. It all went up so fast. I didn't know it was even on fire to begin with, because of all the bricked-in windows and them bars. It was only when I got to the back that I saw it and smelt it. Petrol.'

'Petrol? Are you sure?'

'Yes,' Cleaver said. 'Then I saw the smoke. And then the whole place just went up.' Cleaver moved both hands in the air. 'Whoosh,' he said. 'You never seen anything like it. The next thing I know this fella's leggin' it straight past me and right towards the house. I couldn't stop him.'

'He going to be all right?'

'Yes, sir. I got to him in time. Near thing, though.' Incredibly, Cleaver sounded immensely pleased with himself.

I walked round to the back of the ambulance, peered in and saw through the back window the blurred shape of a large man sitting with his head forward, breathing into a mask. He took the mask off and pushed it weakly away, while a second medic urged him to replace it. I moved a little closer. There was something immediately familiar about him, although I could not figure out exactly what it was.

'Breathed in a lot of smoke,' Cleaver said again, appearing beside me. 'Thought he was a goner. But I managed to pull him out of there in the end. He were in a right old state. Poor bugger kept on passing out by the time I got to him. You shoulda seen 'im. Looked like he was pissed or something.' Cleaver laughed.

I took a long deep breath and looked beyond the ambulance at the fire rising up above the tops of the trees. Then I said with a great deal of restraint, 'Did you see anyone else, Cleaver?'

Cleaver shook his head.

I looked past his shoulder, thinking that if there really had been any more evidence in the house, it had literally gone up in smoke.

Graves came round the back of the ambulance. 'They can't control it, sir,' he said. 'Called in for backup. Looks like the whole place is finished. They might have to let it just burn itself out.' Graves paused when he saw Cleaver and said, with a nasty glint in his eye, 'Good job, Cleaver.'

Cleaver didn't say anything. Graves turned on his heel and disappeared.

'I reckon whoever started it must have come over the back, through the fields,' Cleaver said. 'If he'd have come round the front, I woulda seen him.'

'You mean you would have seen him if you'd been awake, Cleaver. It was a passer-by, wasn't it?' I said. 'A passer-by who saw the smoke from the road, ran down the lane, rapped on the window and woke you up. That's what happened, wasn't it? And by the time you'd woken up he was already halfway round the back, and it was too late to stop him.'

Cleaver sighed and gave in. 'I tried to catch up with him. But the next thing I know he's running towards the house. Christ knows why — but he went straight down those steps. The whole thing nearly fell right on top of him.'

I looked through the ambulance window again. The injured man was sitting upright on the stretcher. The tips of his fingers looked red and swollen, and there were grazes along the sides of his hands as well as thick gouges of broken skin along his arms. He had lost a boot, and the wet imprint of his right foot inside his sock

158

stood out clearly in the fluorescent light.

'Sir,' Graves said.

I turned around.

'They've found something,' Graves said breathlessly. 'Round the back. You'd better come and have a look.'

There was a fireman standing beside him. He took off his helmet, ran his hand through his hair and put the helmet on again, leaving it cocked at an angle on his head. The visor was streaked with what looked like black oil.

'We're playing it a bit by ear here,' Graves said, 'because apparently nothing like this has ever happened before. And I mean ever. They think you might not get another chance to look at it. Looks like the whole thing is going to go up any minute, and they may never get it out.'

'Get what out?' I said impatiently. 'Come on, Graves. What is it?'

'A body.'

'What?'

'They were checking to see if anyone was still alive in there as they put the fire out. So they got as close as they could to the blaze. They didn't know that no one was living here, so they assumed that there were people trapped inside. They couldn't get that close, but they saw something. Deep down. There's a body beneath the house. Round the back. It looks like it might have been there for a very long time.'

We all started to run towards the gates. Then I turned round so suddenly that Graves nearly ran straight into me.

'Graves, I need you to start a search right now,' I said. 'Get everyone you can and tell them to start looking all around the fields, and the roads too. Looks like whoever started the fire probably came from across the fields. They'll be trying to change their clothes, because they torched the place with petrol. Stop any cars coming out of the village too.'

Graves nodded and took off towards the car. The fireman was waiting for me, looking anxiously towards the house.

My God, I thought, as I began to follow him. Another body. That made two within twenty-four hours. A record. I wondered grimly if there would be a third.

14

I followed the fireman through the gates and on to the fire engines. The din beyond the gates was unbelievable. The fireman handed me a thick coat exactly like his own; I pulled off my coat and left it on top of one of the tool boxes inside the fire engine. The fireman, despite the heat and noise, felt compelled to introduce himself as Fred Turner and shook my hand.

'We can't hang about,' Turner said. 'When we get to the side, wait for me to give the all-clear, then we're going to have to peg it. Once we're through, we should be all right for a few minutes.'

Turner was surprisingly young but big and built like a farmer. He rummaged around in the fire truck, found a helmet and passed it to me. Then he took off his own, threw it carelessly inside, grabbed another one and put it on before sliding the visor down his face and gesturing for me to do the same.

He shot off, and I followed, breaking into a run, leaping over pieces of broken glass and chunks of burning wood, until we reached the side of the house. Ignoring the path, Turner ran straight across the garden, following the thick hose snaking its way across the lawn, to the raised stone platform that straddled the bottom of the house. The hose cut thick swathes into the snow.

One of the men was using a pike to tear away at the bricks on the French windows. He had already cleared a gaping hole, through which another fireman was directing water at the flames inside, but the platform looked as if it could give at any moment. The fireman with the hose suddenly drew well back and changed his position to the edge of the lawn. The globes of stone on the balustrades rose up before us as we drew closer. *Una fila de tumbas,* I thought when I saw them: they looked just like a row of tombs.

The house continued to wail like a stricken animal from deep inside its centre. Another almighty cloud of dust and debris came hurtling towards us. The cloud spread, obscuring the firemen in a billowing mass of splintered glass, shattered timber and shards of brick. The whole side of the house seemed to sag, and then what was left of the eastern section of roof above the living room finally came tumbling down. Fire shot out through the broken bricks of the French windows, but was immediately quenched by tonnes of falling tiles.

'Jeeeesus,' Turner said, stunned.

The fireman watched the fire for a moment longer, and then grabbed me roughly by the arm and marched me straight towards the raised platform and the French windows. Turner pointed beneath the broken steps. I got on my haunches and peered into the darkness below.

A massive-looking piece of timber, perhaps one of the main joists, had fallen from somewhere high upstairs and smashed right through the raised platform. The paving stones had shattered outwards in splintery pieces and lay all around the edges of the hole. One end of the thick, very straight piece of wood now lay at an angle and was visible through the steps, which were also shattered and covered with rubble and ash.

Turner was pointing at the hole beneath the steps. I pulled up the visor of the helmet, wiped my eyes and leant in. The heat was unbelievable.

'There!' Turner yelled above the din. 'Can you see it?'

I looked. The piece of wood had not only

broken through the platform but had also pounded its way some distance into the ground beneath it. There was something poking out from amongst the dirt, dust and debris. A flap of something. It was difficult to make out what it was. An overcoat? A blanket? I couldn't be sure.

I wiped at my eyes with a corner of the heavy coat. The smoke cleared for an instant, and I finally saw what it was. Just visible was the corner of a groundsheet. Green tarpaulin covered in earth and dust. I took another step.

Gail Foster. Elise Pennington. Which one was it? Unless they were both buried here, perhaps their bodies entwined together. Down here all this time. Hurst, the bastard, must have buried them really deep. And what sort of room was this? A cellar? I could just make out other objects in the space below.

What had he done to them? I felt a surge of despair as I stared at the fire. Now the flames would take what was left.

I crouched down a little further, looking up anxiously from time to time at the house burning above me. There was so much smoke I was already out of breath.

The other fireman was still spraying water from the edge of the lawn. The stream rose above me, so that water hit my back and fell in tinny thumps on my helmet like rain. The visor was making it hard to see, so I stood and lifted it up again.

I got on my haunches once again and stared in. Smoke filled the space beneath the stone steps, and I could no longer see anything. I raised my arm to my mouth and peered through the gaps in the smashed-in stairs.

Suddenly I felt a hand grabbing me by the shoulder. I wheeled around, furious. It was Turner. The yellow bands around the sleeves of his uniform shone in the light of the flames. Turner shouted out something; I couldn't hear him. I shook him away. He reached for me again and then, giving up, gestured to the visor. As a concession, I reluctantly put it down and pushed first my head and then my neck and shoulders through the narrow space.

For a moment everything seemed almost calm, like being at the bottom of a raging sea. But once again a hand grabbed me by the shoulder, and this time I pushed it roughly away. I saw the edge of something frail near the groundsheet. I breathed in sharply when I saw it. It was a hand. Beyond it lay something smooth, along with a mass of clumped, dirty-looking hair.

165

The platform was going to go at any second. The whole house shook. Something landed hard near me, sending a shower of dust into the narrow space. But I was already pushing my way through the hole. I crept along the narrow passageway, coughing up dust and smoke. The huge piece of wood wedged in the centre shifted slightly, the floor rattled and a burning rock fell through and hit hard against my knuckles.

I kept moving, inching ever closer to the body. Fear rose. I tried to push it away. With each inch of progress I was certain that the ceiling would collapse. My fists clenched and unclenched. The dread of each step reverberated off the memory of the last, so that I became increasingly fearful and hesitant. Instinct screamed at me to turn around and get out while I still had the chance. For a few moments my mind went mercifully blank, and I took in nothing but the sound of the fire raging all around me.

I took another hesitant step. The tarpaulin was the type gardeners used to collect weeds or mounds of grass. It had a metal eyelet in one corner, the sort that allowed you to put a rope through it. The metal was something cheap, possibly tin. The edge of the tarpaulin had been buried in the earth.

Once again the floor rattled and something

landed with a shattering bang above. Another avalanche of stone cascaded down, and a piece of rock hit my helmet so hard it was as if my head had been driven into my neck. My ears rang. I held my breath and shut my eyes. But, for the moment, the ceiling by some miracle still held.

I reached for the tarpaulin. It was covered in a layer of very dry earth, but poking up from the surface was the smooth, rounding curve of a skull, and her hand. It looked as if she were trying to pull herself out of the earth.

A noise came behind me, muffled in the roar of the fire. A shout. I looked back. Turner was crouching in the opening of the space, gesturing wildly for me to get out. I had never seen anyone so angry or so scared. I ignored him and concentrated on the body in front of me. They would never find her again if the house collapsed. She had been down here long enough.

I started scrabbling away at the earth with my hands, scraping out handful after handful. The joist had smashed through the earth and jolted the body from its resting place, shifting the earth upwards. She came away with surprising ease: she could not have been buried very deeply. The tips of my fingers suddenly touched something buried beneath her. The other end of the ground-sheet. I pressed the flat of my hand upon its uneven surface and dug around it. My own fear seemed to rise again, wavering and flickering. My whole body was trembling beneath the heavy fireman's coat.

I moved my fingers in the earth, again and again, digging around the edges of the groundsheet, until I was able to clutch the base of the tarpaulin at both ends with both hands. I gave a hesitant pull and then another more insistent tug. The earth began to give.

There was another more furious yell from behind me. Turner had pushed himself through the hole beneath the steps and was making his way towards me. He looked like he wanted to kill me. I couldn't blame him. For some reason I laughed. It came out wrong, though, and I didn't like the sound of it. I shut my mouth and kept digging, fixed on the idea that there could be another body.

I moved away more earth. All around me was a steady, cackling roar. I could hardly see or breathe.

I thought of the girls lying down here for all these years, and then I thought of their parents. Moved away. Gone forever. And, as I dug, I felt from time to time the smooth fragile contour of her bones and the soft crumbling fabric of her clothes. My fingers dug into something soft yet very dry. I tried not to think about it.

I cleared away more dirt; I gave it another pull.

It still wouldn't give entirely. Were there two of them down here? Had to be. I looked down. No, definitely just the one body. I caught a look at her from the corner of my eye. She had been down here for a long while, but there was still some flesh on her bones and on her face. But she was unrecognizable.

I pulled, and the tarpaulin flew out in one go from under her, but she remained where she was, down in the hole. I swore very loudly in Spanish, cursing the dead girl and the groundsheet roundly. Then I clambered across, leant down, picked her up as gently as I could and put her back on the groundsheet. Then I began to drag her out.

Turner was suddenly beside me. There was hardly any room for the two of us, but, when he saw the girl, he reached for the other corner of the groundsheet without a word and we both began to pull her out and back towards the steps.

We moved quickly. A huge chunk of masonry exploded through the floor in front of us. We covered our heads. Dust and smoke everywhere. Turner grabbed my arm, motioning for me to stop, and we waited for the dust to settle. The large timber in front of us had caught fire and was now surrounded by burning pieces of wood and more rubble. We shook off the dust and the burning rocks and moved back the way we had come.

I could now recognize the discarded and forgotten objects lodged down here: stacks upon stacks of bottles in plastic crates. Unidentifiable pieces of machinery. An old tyre. A kid's mountain bike. Ancient newspapers.

The ceiling of the space was on fire, expanding in ever-widening pools of flame. Turner grabbed me hard by the arm, and we shuffled our way along, past the burning timber, dragging the groundsheet behind us.

I didn't know where I was suddenly. What direction to take. I desperately waved at the smoke. My breath was harsh and ragged. Fear, cold and sharp, rose in the pit of my stomach, freezing me for a moment. I kept going. The thumping in my head grew louder. Turner was moving forward, pushing through the rubble with his fists, searching in the darkness for the way out. I grabbed the groundsheet again and pulled myself after him, weaving our way out.

A vicious orange glow rose up as the enormous piece of timber shifted and fell, thundering against the floor. I could not believe just how quickly the fire had spread down here. The sound of it raged inside the narrow space, emanated from every corner.

Masonry was falling; stone creaked and shifted and fell on to the floor and on to our backs. Ash covered our faces, while plaster dropped in clumps all around us. The smoke thickened, whirring and twisting in the air, choking us.

I started to cough again, and found that this time I couldn't stop. Turner was doing the same. Fear had in a matter of seconds become a grinding panic. The old newspapers that had been dumped here burst eagerly into flame. A thick sheaf of paper was lifted and held briefly by the rising currents like a bat.

All around us fell sparks of impossibly bright and dazzling flame. The fire was marauding its way through the narrow space. Cinders and chunks of wood burnt my face and arms. The blackness rose up, and with it a whirling nausea. I blinked and the darkness went away, but not for long.

Turner grabbed me and pulled me along

and shouted something. By some miracle, we had reached the steps at the entrance to the hole. I looked up. The stone platform was sagging and beginning to crack, a thin long line suddenly racing across it. Another, larger crack followed, spreading quickly along the length of stone. Turner was trying to smash through the rubble blocking the exit at the steps. But it looked hopeless. We had become lost in the din and the smoke and the debris, and there was no way out.

I still clung to the groundsheet. An ember landed in the girl's hair and it suddenly caught fire. I stared in a kind of numb horror as a burning smell rose off her. Withered old burning flesh and bone. But it wasn't just her: what remained of her clothes had also caught alight. Then came a smell of melting plastic. The groundsheet.

I could feel the flames once more beginning to rise at my back. But I crouched there for a moment with a dazed fascination, unable to tear my eyes away as the fire burnt relentlessly into the girl's body. Her smile seemed to get much wider; she was grinning up at me as the orange flames curled up towards her cheek. The fire reached out and burnt the back of my coat; it clutched at me from all sides.

I realized that the girl was melting. Right

in front of me. Melting. Melting. Melting. Like the wicked witch in that old film. The name came to me in Spanish in an instant: *El mago de oz — The Wizard of Oz*. And for a moment all I could think about was the old witch in that old film disappearing inside her coat and the pointy hat lying on the floor while the silly little dog Totó went running around in circles. Then the horror rose again, and the smell of her burning filled my consciousness.

A voice — tentative at first — now screamed so loudly and so clearly that it eclipsed even the din of the fire. *Tengo que salir de acá. ¡Déjala! ¡Por ¡Dios! ¡Déjala!* I had to get out. I had to leave her here. I had to help Turner and get out. I lurched to my feet and stood as high as I could and ripped off the heavy coat. Then I placed it over her, smothering the fire.

Turner was now smashing his whole body against the solid weight of the rubble. Everything was getting dark. A shifting darkness that came and went. It was hard to breathe and impossible to think. I felt light-headed, sick and weaker than a child.

I glanced backwards and looked on helplessly as the fire began to sweep its way towards us. I was now coughing almost all the time. Again, everything went momen-

173

tarily black, but it was a different type of darkness this time — more insistent. A heavy kind of light-headedness that became something far more serious. I was passing out. I could feel the whole place falling away. I saw the back of the steps towering above me, and as the blood rushed and pounded in my head I began to topple over. Everything went blank. And then, a second later, Turner was reaching for me and screaming. I got to my knees, coughing, struggling for breath.

In the gathering smoke, I grabbed a broken rock and crouched next to Turner. As he pounded away with his shoulder, I smashed at the rubble with the rock. The fire was billowing along the walls with a relentless and steady purpose. We hammered at the stone.

Then I saw Turner freeze. I heard something else above the rumble of the fire. It was coming from the other side of the rubble. It was like a scream coming from under water.

Men's voices on the other side of the debris. A voice I recognized: Graves's. A shout again, which fell abruptly to a murmur. I looked up and saw some of the rubble above me shudder and then shift. Turner was starting to yell through the widening gap. One of the rocks above him gave way and landed hard against his shoulder. The edge of a long metal pole came through, and the rubble began to fall away. Turner was shouting and motioning for me to get back. I collapsed backwards and lay there helplessly as more rubble shifted and moved and fell.

A face appeared. A fireman. Mule-faced and squinting. I got to my knees and staggered towards him in disbelief. The fireman and Turner started to pull away at the rubble. I got a glimpse of men on the other side. More hands were suddenly there helping. Bricks and rocks tumbled at my feet. Air was rushing in. Turner's hand shot forward and grabbed me roughly by the shoulder, trying to pull me out. Another hand dug deep into my flesh, pulling me, dragging me through the hole. But I shook them off. I reached behind me, and with the last of my strength grabbed the body wrapped in my coat and thrust it out towards the waiting hands. The hands took it and disappeared. Then I moved forward. In seconds I was pulled through the gap.

My head hit something hard. Turner had already emerged from the hole. The smoke, drawn towards the oxygen of the only exit, poured out and choked us both as we flailed about like hooked fish in the open air.

The whole world was on fire. It rose above the manor's roof in a gigantic ball of flame that lit up the sky. Two firemen began to drag me away from what was left of the raised stone platform, past the broken balustrades and down the shattered steps. From behind me, I could see Graves. Shouting all the time, it seemed.

I wanted to stay exactly where I was; to breathe in the cold air and cough out the smoke still deep in my lungs. I wanted them to leave me alone. But the damned hands wouldn't let me go. I was being dragged down mossy slippery steps, then across the grass. The hands released me for a split second, only to redouble their grip.

When the fireman finally let me go, I fell straight on to my back. I found myself next to an old wheelbarrow. Its red wheels were buried in snow. I turned over, and got to my knees. I leant on the wheelbarrow for support and tried to stand up. But the wheelbarrow collapsed on its side and out spilt a bunch of old weeds.

They'd got the girl out. They had placed her gently in the centre of the lawn. Graves was now standing above the groundsheet, protecting her. I tried to stand up again, and couldn't. It didn't surprise me all that

much. So I lay back down on the cold grass
and let everything go black.

PART TWO

15

Frank Hurst's funeral was held five days later, on a cold Monday afternoon. It had stopped snowing, but many of the smaller roads were still impassable. I arrived late, because of the pills the doctor had put me on the moment I left the hospital. They were bright yellow and there were too many *z*'s on the labels, and they all made me feel weak and slow on my feet. I parked my car on the green. For a moment I stayed where I was and glanced across my seat at the open copy of the *Cotswold Herald* beside me. UNIDENTIFIED BODY LINKED TO PITCHFORK MURDER CASE ran the headline. Thankfully, as yet no mention of the girls. I scrunched up the newspaper and threw it in a nearby bin as I left the car. Then I stalked up the hill and pushed open the wooden gate to the church. I began to thread my way as quickly as I could through the oblong tombs and crosses of the graveyard.

Halfway along by the wall a cherub's face looked up at me above an open bible. I patted the cherub on the head and, although not particularly religious, prayed to whoever was up there and gave heartfelt thanks for my safe delivery from the fire. I picked up speed when I glimpsed the small funeral procession through the trees, on the other side of the churchyard. There were only a few mourners, and as soon as the rector left the others followed. All apart from Simon Hurst.

Last time I had seen him he had been sitting in the back of the ambulance at Dashwood Manor. He had heard about the murder on Meon Hill on the radio and, after being unable to contact his brother, had gone rushing off to his house to see if he was all right. Of course the first thing he had seen was Cleaver fast asleep in the squad car and his brother's house on fire; he then unwisely tried to rush in and put it out. He had made a quick recovery, all things considered. But even here, in the bright morning light of the graveyard, there was a nervous and restless quality to him. The resemblance to Frank was unmistakable, though he looked like a watered-down version: less intense and somehow not all there. There was a weakness and a petulance to his mouth that he seemed unable to conceal. Seeing me looking at him, he nodded curtly and slunk off.

I waited a while longer and then stepped through the arching darkness of the rugged yews; the outlines of the final rows of tombs emerged. I stood for a few moments in front of the overturned earth. Other Hursts were buried out here in the family plot. Next to where they would later place Hurst's headstone was one of polished marble. I knelt down and looked more closely, brushing away the snow and reading the name.

Sarah Hurst.

Frank's second wife. Her name stood out clearly in gold leaf. Still, even after all these years, her gravestone looked almost new. There were some withered flowers half buried in the snow on top of her grave; I looked around and, seeing no one about, very gently picked them up. Six roses. They were dry and brittle, but they looked as if they had been put there quite recently. I replaced them neatly on top of the disturbed snow.

I walked towards the church. At the side of the building Hurst's old foreman on the farm, Sam Griffin, and his wife were talking to Frank's old housekeeper, Nancy Williams. Williams lifted her hand, nodded and moved off. I followed and caught up with her near the church gate.

Nancy looked up at me with the same shrewd expression that she'd had the first time we met. She'd aged over the past five years of course: her chin and neck were fleshier; her eyes were more watchful. Heavy gold rings dug into her fingers. She was wearing a simple black skirt, a white blouse, a heavy fawn coat and a lot of make-up; her high-heeled shoes looked unsuitable for the weather. There was a dry sweetish smell of perfume. Gardenias.

'Hello, Nancy. You remember me, don't you?' I said. But I found that my voice came out in a harsh, inaudible whisper. I swallowed and tried again.

She seemed to hesitate a moment and then nodded. 'Mrs Hurst's accident,' she said. 'The swimming pool. Yes, I remember.'

'I hear you're living over in Brighton nowadays,' I said.

'Yes,' Nancy said. 'I run a guest house there.'

'Sounds all right. So you thought you'd come and pay your respects, did you?'

Nancy shrugged. 'Thought I'd come and see my sister as well. While I'm at it.'

'You're staying with her?'

'Yes, over in Lower Slaughter.'

'Quite a long way to come for an ex-boss,' I said. 'I heard you weren't all that upset about it when you found out.'

Nancy shrugged. 'He were always all right to me. I've had a lot worse.'

'He had to let you go in the end, though, didn't he?'

'Well,' Nancy said reasonably, 'there wasn't much point me hanging round. It was just him alone in that house after Rebecca took off. Said he didn't really need me any more. He were pretty nice about it, though. Made sure I had time to get another job lined up before I left.'

A deep silence had fallen in the graveyard. There was a sharp, clear smell of moss-spattered stone. Nancy tightened her coat around her shoulders. Her eyes turned up towards me. I reached for the bottle of pills in my pocket and unscrewed the top. Nancy watched me.

'I suppose you know by now that we're doing some digging down there?' I said, tipping a pill into the palm of my hand.

'Yes, I heard.' She seemed curiously detached.

'Do you know what was down there, under the house?' I asked. 'There seemed to be some kind of space beneath those big old French windows at the back, underneath the steps.'

'So that's where you found the little girl?' Nancy said quietly.

'Yes.'

Nancy shivered. 'We used it to dump stuff sometimes.' She grimaced at the expression. 'Or put things we thought might come in handy later. Crates and such like. You could get under there round the side of the house.'

'And you never noticed anything?' I said. 'Nothing was moved or seemed out of place?'

Nancy shook her head. 'I hardly ever went down there.'

'And who else knew about the space under the house, apart from you and Frank?'

'Quite a lot of people, I expect. It weren't all that difficult to miss. The gardeners, when they came, they used it as a kind of extra shed when they needed to do any work near the house, and Mr Hurst used it to dump old things he didn't want any more. Bottles. Bits and pieces.'

I waited. Then, making up my mind, I said quietly, 'But you know that there might be another girl down there, Nancy. Under Frank's house.'

She became very still. Her heels dug deep

into the gravel beneath the snow. She didn't say anything.

I decided to change tack. 'I was hoping that maybe Rebecca might have shown up,' I said, looking around. 'Have you heard from her since all this started? She ran off, didn't she?'

'They kicked her out of boarding school,' Nancy said. 'She was too much for 'em to handle. Thought they might knock some sense into her and do her some good. But it was no use. She walked all over him and he let her.'

'But where is she? All we know is that she might be in London somewhere. Used to send him letters every now and again. That's what we're hearing.' I motioned towards the car park. 'That's what his brother told me anyway.'

'No, not letters. Rebecca never'd take the time to write him a letter. Too selfish. Just postcards.'

'Postcards. And they ever have an address?'

Nancy shrugged.

'And how often did she send them?'

'Not often,' Nancy said crisply, and plucked at the collar of her blouse. 'Mr Hurst spoilt that girl rotten. But that's how she paid him back. She walked out on him

187

without any kind of warning. No apology. Nothing.'

Behind us the bells from the clock on the church tolled out into the cold morning air. As the last echoes of the bells rang out, I said, 'You know he locked himself in. Barred all the windows.'

Nancy nodded. 'I heard. But it was after I'd gone. He wasn't always like that. He never used to be afraid of anyone. It was only later, after she left, that he really started to change. He kind of . . .' Nancy paused. 'Well, he kind of lost it. When Rebecca left he kind of . . . he took it pretty hard. Kind of gave up. He couldn't understand it. Blamed himself, I guess.'

'But *why* did she leave, Nancy? Was there a fella, maybe, who she might have run off with? A friend from the village? Someone who left around the same time that she did?'

'She didn't have any friends,' Nancy said. 'Not in the village, and she stayed at home most of the time. Of course, her dad didn't like her coming out here to the village.'

'Why not?'

'Because of what happened down there of course.' Nancy gestured impatiently down the hill, towards the green. 'He didn't want her thinking about it. He wanted her to forget it.'

'Forget what?'

'Her *accident,*' Nancy said, and sighed loudly. 'Out on the pond.'

'What accident?'

'Some policeman you are. He nearly lost her.'

'Lost her?'

'When she were little. She and her mates were playing silly buggers. Out on the ice. She went in and nearly drowned. The other two weren't so lucky. They all went to the same school.'

'Ned and Owen Taylor,' I said quickly, remembering the picture in Hurst's house.

'That's right. Brothers. She managed to pull herself out. But they couldn't. Drowned. Both of 'em.'

I took a step back and involuntarily looked at the graves, wondering if the two boys were buried here as well. Nancy was looking across the wall and towards the pond. From up here you got a clear view of it: it was surrounded by an ugly chainlink fence. At its far end, amongst huge clumps of dogwood, was a crumbling wall.

'And you were there? The day she left?' I said finally.

'No. I came back the next morning and Mr Hurst told me she'd gone. She'd taken all her stuff. No note. Nothing like that.'

'But she sent him these postcards. I guess that was to put his mind at rest, I suppose. Can you remember what they said? The postcards. Where they were from?'

'They were from London, like you said. Can't remember much about them. He went to see her there once, though. She arranged to see him. Got his hopes up like that and then never even bothered showing up.'

'But what happened?' I said.

'All I know is that he took the train up there,' Nancy said impatiently. 'That's what he told me. He arrived early because he didn't want to miss her. They were going to meet at a café. Somewhere public, in case he made a big fuss. But she stood him up. He waited there all day long. That was just like her, you know. Bloody selfish. When she didn't make an appearance he got the last train home. He was hoping that maybe she'd phoned and left a message.' Nancy paused and took a half-step backwards. 'And that's when he saw someone had broken into his house,' she said. 'They'd broken through one of the windows at the back. But nothing had been taken or even touched. Or that's what he thought to begin with. But then he thought that maybe she'd got him to go to London, so she could sneak back in and get some of her old things. Or perhaps she was after some of his money. But there was no money missing.'

'So he checked her room?'

'Yes, someone had been in there. He thought it was Rebecca — that she'd come back.'

'And had anything been taken? Taken from her room, I mean?'

'No, not as far as he could tell. But it had been turned inside out. The whole thing was a mess. I should know because I had to spend the following week clearing it up, didn't I? The bedding and her clothes were all over the floor. Drawers turned out. Even the mattress had been torn open.'

'And did he report it to the police?'

'He didn't think much of the police,' Nancy said pointedly.

'And did he ever hear from her again?'

'Don't think so.'

'And you never heard from her. You never saw her again?'

'No. Never.'

16

I got back in my car, and, although there wasn't much light left, I drove straight to what remained of Hurst's house. The air still stank of burnt wood and acrid plastic and burnt foam. The immensity of the blaze hit me and not for the first time. Where there had been something, there was nothing now.

The constables whom Graves had commandeered for the huge task of removing the debris from the back of the house were all gone. The rubble they had been able to move stood piled in stacks in the centre of the lawn. Ten new-looking wheelbarrows and a neat line of equally new-looking spades stood propped against the wall. Graves had done a pretty good job. It couldn't have been easy telling all those police constables what to do. They wouldn't have liked taking orders from him, but it looked as if he had whipped them into shape, and quickly too.

The whole back section of the house had been removed, so that where the raised platform had once stood there was now the semblance of order. Indeed, the chaos of the ruin stopped abruptly exactly where Graves had ordered the removal to begin. A cleared, oblong black space, around twice as long and twice as wide as the central strip of a cricket field, lay behind the charred ruin of the house, with two telescopic lights shining down directly on to it. The lamps were powered by two generators, which filled the air with a repetitive fairground hum.

Graves cut a forlorn figure as he picked his way along the edge of the cleared space, making demarcation lines with police tape. His shoulders were stooped as he stared into the blackened ground before him, like an old farmer working in a field. The only other person there was a police constable called Drayton, who was busy arranging something inside the white tent that had been erected at the side of the garden. He was getting on a bit, but could still be useful when he had a mind to be.

Long tracks of hard, overturned mud stretched across the lawn, marking the path taken by the two work crews with their wheelbarrows full of shattered pieces of tile, masonry and glass. The rest of the house rose behind, black and filthy-looking in the winter sunlight.

I waved to Graves to let him know I was here and then walked towards the house. All around us the blackness of the evening gathered, and the wind began to rise. I stared in awe at the jagged wreckage juddering in the cold wind, its rippling shadows cast upon the flowerbeds and the lawn. I started thinking about the girl I had dragged out just inches from where I now stood. Only a few days ago I had seen her in the morgue beneath Cheltenham General Hospital, with Brewin standing in stony silence beside me. It hadn't been just the sudden bright horror of her. That she had been buried down here like an animal was what somehow made it worse than anything else. Even worse than the terrible way in which she may have died.

For a moment longer I stood there, remembering. Brewin had admitted straightaway that it could take weeks, even months, before they would be able to determine age and even gender for sure. He was already arranging the transfer of the remains to the forensic anthropology lab in Oxford. He had also collected DNA samples from the body, which he would compare to those of both sets of parents. When the girls had disappeared, DNA for forensic profiling had been in its infancy. But two years ago Brewin wisely, and with my approval, had collected DNA from the girls' parents, so that we would be able to make comparisons should the need arise.

Brewin had placed the groundsheet on the side of the room on a stretcher. It had been laid flat, but the corners draped over the edges. It was burnt and torn in places, and the tin eyelets in the corners were bent or broken. At first, I hadn't been able to make out what it was. In fact, none of it had seemed to make any sense to begin with. Then, ever so slowly, she had begun to take form.

A mass of crumpled and charred bones. Some fragments of clothing but not many. Jeans? A dress? A school uniform? I couldn't be sure. Tarry-looking flesh clung to the bones here and there. Repulsively withered and hardened. A strand of hair. Her face had been burnt away, and there were whole parts of her missing or, worse, torn in two. Bone poked through jagged pieces of wet material. A forearm stood alone, separated from the upper arm, so that you could see the shining polished metal of the trolley beneath it. A piece of backbone. The spine curved upwards towards the neck and then the skull. The upper jaw and mandible yawning wide open as if in laughter.

I stood before the house a while longer. Glad in a way that someone had felt fit to torch it. Ash poured black and thick from the ruins and swirled in the wind amongst the snow. Within seconds, the rising wind had blown pieces of feathery black grime out and across the fields towards Meon Hill. I thought of the girls again. Which one was still buried in the blackened ground? The images of both, here, in this place, would be stamped indelibly in my mind.

17

I got home just after dark. Although I wasn't supposed to drink at all with the bright yellow pills, I made myself a drink anyway and then had a quick shower.

Hurst's videotapes were still locked in my study, along with the three pale grey files from the detective agency, which I'd been meaning to call all day. So, after I got changed, I decided to start there.

I lugged my old video player out of storage and hooked it up to the portable television in the kitchen. Then I hauled the crate of tapes on to the table.

I reached in for a tape and slid it out of its box. The white label running along the front read: '1 May 2000'.

I ended up emptying the crate of tapes on to the thick carpet in front of the electric fire, then I arranged them in date order, starting with February 2000 and finishing with March 2001. Two tapes a month to

start. Then once a month or so, and sometimes less frequently as time went on. Then
once every two months. Then every now
and again, until they petered out altogether.

They had all been labelled with the same
elegant hand. I went back upstairs and
fetched the three files from my study. There
was no doubt about it. The handwritten
notes at the back of the files matched the
handwriting on the tapes.

I walked quickly downstairs, grabbed one
of the tapes at random from the middle of
the row, slotted it in and pressed 'play'. To
begin with nothing happened. There was
just white static and a blank screen. I
pressed 'fast-forward'. Again, nothing happened. The tape was empty.

I reached for another tape and then another, starting on the left of the pile this
time and moving slowly along the row. But
they all seemed to be blank. I would have to
go through them sooner or later, so I fast-
forwarded through the tapes, beginning at
the latest one first, as I prepared myself a
huge steak. I flipped the meat and when I
turned round I saw that something had
come into focus on the screen. I turned
down the heat on the pan. Then I reached
for the remote, rewound the tape and
pressed 'play'.

I looked more closely at the television screen and saw the dim interior of a car. The footage had been taken by a camera that was propped up on the dashboard on the passenger side; concealing it was a blue coat or sweater that was getting in the way of the top of the picture. Outside the car window it was night. Yellow lights and cars lined both sides of a narrow, curving street. Sitting with its mouth open on the driver's side of the dashboard was a half-empty packet of Benson & Hedges. After a few moments a podgy male hand reached for the gold packet and removed one. There was the sound of a window being wound down and then of a lighter being clicked open and then snapped shut. Grey smoke filled part of the screen.

Smoke, I now realized, was filling my own kitchen, so I moved quickly to retrieve my steak from the hob and open the kitchen windows. With the remote still in my hand, I again looked closely at the television. It looked as if the camera was pointing very purposefully to a house about three quarters of the way along the street. It was more run down than the other properties. There was a new-looking white van parked in the driveway.

I turned up the volume on the television.

There was a rustling sound of someone shifting restlessly in their seat. Someone in the car sighed loudly. The car radio was on in the background. Pop music. But very faint. The camera stayed steady and focused on the house. A man's voice started humming tunelessly along with the song.

I did not recognize the street. I wondered if it might be London. Maybe that detective fella — what was his name? — Bray had found Rebecca after all. Perhaps there had been other files in Hurst's house that had gone up in smoke. But it didn't look like London to me.

What *was* he up to? I picked up the penultimate tape and looked at it before inserting it into the slot. November 2000. Around four months before the last tape. This time something flickered on to the screen almost immediately. The same view from the dashboard. The camera was still concealed by a blue sweater or a jacket, and the cigarette packet had been crushed into a tight ball beside it. The windscreen looked slightly dirtier. But this was a different house, and it was daytime. Yet the same white van was sitting outside in the driveway.

This street was more affluent than the last and stood somewhere in the middle of a small village. The warm yellow Cotswold stone was unmistakable, as were the grey, sloping roofs. I didn't recognize the village, though. It looked sunny but cold, and leaves were falling on to the green and on to the small lane in front of the house and on to the roof of the white van.

The camera stayed where it was. There was more impatient shuffling. A cough. Then ever so suddenly more light fell on to the dashboard as the car door opened. The car rose a bit as the occupant climbed out, and the man could then be seen through the windscreen of his car. And there, in a perfectly framed shot, stood, I assumed, Mr James Bray of the Bray Detective Agency.

Bray stared at the house and ran his fingers through his long but thinning brown hair. Then, with his head straining forward, he took a few tentative steps towards the van. He pushed his hands deep into the pockets of his old leather jacket and moved in the direction of the house next door. He stood behind a rhododendron bush for camouflage.

I paused the tape. Bray was in his midforties with soft brown eyes behind thickrimmed black glasses. He was big, stocky and powerful, but he didn't look all that light on his feet. The old leather jacket didn't quite go with the old-man spectacles and newish-looking trainers either. I pressed 'play' and saw Bray throw a cigarette to the ground and stamp it out with the toe of his shoe, then stare at the sky in exasperation. His hands fell to his sides. Then he returned wearily to the car, which once more rocked under his weight. His hand seemed to reach automatically for the cigarette packet, but, as it was empty, he only threw it back and sighed loudly.

I waited, then pressed 'forward' and 'play'. A few minutes later the front door of the house opened and someone approached the white van from the side. A hand reached for the camera and the focus shifted to the outline of the van. A man approached the back doors. He had a relaxed, swaggering gait. It was too far away to see his face, but there was a glimpse of black hair, white overalls and trainers as he swung the doors open wide.

The man disappeared inside the house and returned carrying a metal ladder, which he slid into the van's roof rack. Once more he disappeared into the house. He came back a minute later, carrying large heavy bundles of yellowish cloth, which he hurled into the back of the van. He slammed the doors shut and waved in the direction of the front door, where a woman was standing; he seemed to be making some sort of joke to her. Then he got in the van and reversed out of the drive.

Bray scrabbled and grabbed the camera and placed it on the seat beside him; then came a blurred hunched shoulder and the sound of fabric rubbing against a leather seat — Bray ducking down, out of sight. The dim roar of a car passing nearby and very fast. The car shook. The camera was jolted as Bray reversed and began his pursuit.

The camera rolled dangerously close to the edge of the brown leather seat covers from time to time. Both Bray and the white van must have been going at quite a clip by the sound of it. Bray's hand reached for the gear stick as the car surged forward; and then suddenly he braked. The camera rolled and fell to the floor. Bray absently reached for it. His face appeared for a second in the camera, filling the screen. Then it went dark.

I waited.

Bray's wide, anxious-looking face reappeared. He placed the camera carefully once more on the dashboard and gently covered it with the sweater. And there it was: the white van. Parked halfway up on the pavement of a busy road on the outskirts

of a village or small town. It looked as if
Bray had tucked away his own car at the
end of a side street. The straight outlines of
the van could only just be made out in the
growing darkness, which meant that some
time had passed — though it was difficult
to know how much. I could also see some
kind of car park and a big square building:
a sports centre perhaps. I could see the
blue-green of a swimming pool in a large
window at the side. And next to it there was
something else: another, much larger building. It sprawled out on to the grey tarmac.
Figures were pouring out of all the buildings. I froze, watching, listening. Children
were screaming and laughing as they left
the gates of a school.

18

'*No lo puedo creer,*' I mumbled to myself in the warmth of my kitchen.

The doors of the white van suddenly opened, the man got out and slammed the door. He had changed out of his overalls and was wearing jeans and a heavy-looking donkey jacket. I could see the smudge of a pale face above the blue upturned collar of his jacket.

Bray reached for the camera and placed it firmly in the bottom of what looked like a thick brown satchel or sports bag. The camera was pushed forward until its lens was facing into a small neat hole cut into the bag's front.

Almost immediately, the camera was swung round and hung from Bray's right shoulder. There was the sound of the car door opening and then being closed with some care. For a few moments there were shots of nothing but the pavement and the road along with a stretch of grey afternoon. Then a glimpse of grass on the other side of the pavement. Then children.

They were laughing and talking excitedly to each other as they passed by Bray, giggling and shouting out as they headed on home. One of the boys dropped a blue schoolbook, picked it up and frowned as he wiped the mud from the front with the sleeve of his coat. Another boy punched him in the arm. The boy's face screwed up in an exaggeration of pain. More small knots of children unravelling as Bray's hulking shadow walked through their midst in the direction of the school.

But Bray didn't go to the school. Instead, the camera paused as he waited to cross the road. Then came another lane with houses on either side, and then a much quieter suburban-looking street — at the end of which was a dilapidated fence and a muddy path leading to a small grassy slope and a park. The man's figure trudged ahead of the camera on the wet grass.

Bray crested the top of the rise, and he could be heard to be breathing heavily. For a few moments everything was still. But Bray, obviously realizing he had become exposed to view, ducked into the cover of a small copse of trees at the top of the rise.

He moved towards the brown slats of an old wooden fence; I could hear the sound of undergrowth slapping against the sides of the camera bag. The camera stayed where it was for the moment, while Bray caught his breath.

Bray placed the bag on to the ground — I could see fallen twigs and leaves — and took out the camera. He crept forward to the edge of the trees and zoomed in on the scene below.

At the near end of a wet field stood an old cricket pavilion and leading up to it was a crumbling whitish mass of concrete that, I supposed, once might have been steps. Suddenly, the camera moved forward as Bray, no doubt on his haunches, pushed himself through the undergrowth and to the edge of the trees. The camera zoomed in. There were kids, around five or six of them, gathered on the broken steps. A handful of girls and a few lads. The boys were around fifteen. Maybe sixteen years old. The girls looked around the same age.

They were wearing their school uniforms. Some were smoking, holding the cigarettes in their hands and making a big deal about offering each other a drag and playing with their lighters.

The man Bray was following was already

nearly amongst them. He had taken off his jacket and it now lay draped across his shoulder. They seemed to be expecting him. He approached them and started talking. His swagger became more exaggerated, stagy. The boys laughed, pleased to see him. They had a football, and they began to kick it around. The man kicked the ball between one of the boy's legs, raised his arms in the air and ran in a circle.

'Goal!'

I watched. The man stood in goal for a while, and then they switched positions. The ball slid along the grass and landed near the foot of the pavilion, where three of the girls were sitting on the remains of the stone steps. One of the girls stood up and kicked back the ball. The boys laughed again.

Sitting away from the others, on her own, was a thin girl, perched on the edge of a broken-down bench, staring at her knees. Bray zoomed the camera on to her and kept it there. She was pale, with thick brown hair and an elfin face. She looked a little bemused, as if she wasn't sure what she was doing there. Although it didn't seem all that cold, she seemed to be shivering.

She was, I realized, the only one not watching the boys play. In fact, she seemed to be very purposefully not looking in their direction at all.

The football game stopped abruptly. The man picked up his jacket and sauntered off towards the pavilion. He passed the girls sitting on the steps. The girl sitting on the broken bench seemed to shrink in on herself. She clutched the blazer in her lap more tightly. But the man sat next to her on the bench. He reached for her and put his arm around her. The girl flinched, but she seemed frozen, unable to move. Then he turned his face towards her, trying to kiss her. This seemed to snap her out of it, because she sidled away from him. He let her go with a laugh. I felt sick to my stomach. The camera tracked outwards, as Bray steadied his grip, and then finally zoomed in on the man's face as he stood up.

When I saw that face, my stomach gave another nauseated lurch and my thoughts went straight into Spanish, then English, and then Spanish and English at the same time, until I couldn't think at all. I breathed in and then out came a long, uninterrupted stream of profanity. Then, still not able to believe what I was seeing, I said all of it over again, only more loudly. I reached for the remote and pressed 'pause'.

I carried on staring at the screen, trying to calm down. I sat at my kitchen table, resting my chin on my upraised fist. Well, it was pretty obvious what he was doing there. Just like old times. There was no doubt about it. The son of a bitch hadn't changed a bit.

19

I decided to call Bray straightaway and used the mobile telephone number at the top of the agency's invoice. Bray answered the phone in mid-sentence. In the background were sounds of brittle laughter, clinking glasses. A pub or a busy restaurant. The voice at the other end of the line was very direct and underpinned with a fading London accent. As soon as I mentioned Frank Hurst, Bray asked me politely to please wait and took the phone outside. I could hear a door swinging open and then footsteps in gravel. I wasn't quite sure where to begin. With Rebecca or with the man Bray had been following? I suppose that I was still a little shocked by the ordinariness of it all. By the slightly damp Wednesday-afternoon feel of the footage on the videotape. By how easily that man had got so close and with such apparent ease to those teenagers. And in the open too. The video was still paused.

Seen in profile, the man's nose was aquiline. His arm was draped around the girl's thin shoulders. I had to turn away, so that I was staring at the cold night gathering outside my kitchen windows.

'You were working for Frank Hurst then, Mr Bray,' I said, deciding finally to begin with Rebecca. 'He first got in contact with your agency because he was trying to find his daughter?'

'Yes, well, agency,' Bray said sheepishly. 'We're a pretty small outfit. It's just me, really, most of the time. All of the time, actually. After Rebecca went walkabout, Hurst called me and asked me to try to find her.'

'But why didn't he try the police?'

'He had a pretty low opinion of the police, I'm afraid. Besides, she was seventeen or eighteen by then, so she was old enough to do whatever she liked. And there wasn't much he could do about it. He'd had a go himself, but realized it was no use, so he thought he'd let me have a try. More or less gave me a blank cheque to find her. But she'd gone — disappeared. I told him I thought she must have moved away from London. Probably shacked up with some fella somewhere. Told him she could be anywhere. He wouldn't have that, of course.

But I'd have found her if she'd still been in London.' He paused. 'So she hasn't come forward, then?'

'No. Not yet,' I said a little uneasily, but I didn't know why. I leant against the edge of the worktop in the kitchen and forced myself to stare hard at the television in front of me. 'But there's something else I need to talk to you about,' I said. 'He got you to do some other work for him as well, didn't he? Another job, after you'd finished looking for Rebecca.'

'How do you know?' Bray said sharply, and then, realizing, said, 'The files. Hurst kept them.'

'Yes, and some videotapes.'

'Well, like I said, I couldn't find her. But he was happy with the work I'd done for him. He said he was pleased with the way I'd kept him up to date and informed. He said he trusted me.' Bray sounded quite proud about it. 'So he phoned me later on and asked me to do something else for him, if I could do with the extra work. I didn't really understand any of it to begin with. I asked him to explain but he wouldn't. He just wanted to know what they were up to.'

'They?' I said.

'Yes. Some men.'

'So it wasn't just Gardner?'

'So you know him?' Bray said, taken aback.

'Yes. But there were others, you say. He asked you to follow more than just one man?'

'Yes, but that was only part of it. What he really wanted to know was what they were up to.'

'Up to?'

'Yes. He wanted to know where they were and what they were doing. And he wanted me to keep an eye on them. Check up on 'em. That was all. And, of course, if they moved he wanted to know about that too.'

'So these men — they were all local?'

'Yes.'

'How many?'

'Three.'

'Three,' I said quietly.

'Yes.'

'And who were they?'

'God, I can't remember the name of the first one. Not off the top of my head. It'll be in the file. Anyway he'd moved. Gone to Canada. Ontario. No. Hold on. Actually Vancouver, I think it was. Had family over there, and the neighbours said he'd got a job out there and wasn't coming back. Gone for good. And they were all glad to see the back of him, which I thought was a bit funny to begin with. So I told Hurst and he said all right and then he gave me another name.'

'Edward Secoy,' I said softly. 'That was the name of the first man, wasn't it?'

'Yes, that's it. Well, of course, as a DCI, you'd know what was happening on your patch. And I bet you can name the next one too.'

'Another local?'

'Yep. From over in Broadway.'

'Ben Tanner,' I said straightaway. 'But he was dead, right?'

'Yeah, that one was even easier. Croaked in his sleep.'

'Heart attack.'

'Yep. Full marks again. So I phone Hurst and tell him. All right, he says, and then he gives me the last name.'

'Christopher,' I said. 'Christopher Gardner.'

'Yeah. A decorator. I had to follow him all over the place.'

'Anything else?' I said. 'Anything more specific he may have wanted you to look out for?'

There was a pause. 'Yes,' Bray said finally. 'He wanted to know if there was a place they often went to — a storeroom or an old warehouse. A place out of the way and that

215

no one else knew about. A secret place. That's what Frank called it. Sounded a bit silly. It was like something out of a book for little kiddies. I asked him if he could be a bit more specific. Of course, I didn't really know what I was getting myself into then. He said he didn't know. Could even be really out of the way, like. A field. A wood. Anything. And if there was, I was to tell him straightaway. But I could pretty much do as I saw fit. As long as I kept him posted, kept an eye on 'em and billed him for the hours I put in, that was fine by him.'

'But you must have made the connection between the three men eventually.'

'Yeah. Didn't take long. You know — the looks I got when I started asking about 'em.'

'But you didn't tell him?'

'No — wasn't my job to. I just did what he asked me to do and kept an eye on this Gardner fella. I followed him on and off a few times a month for about a year, I think. Then, after a while, he seemed to lose interest, so I stopped.'

'Even when you followed him to a school?'

'God. You saw that?' Bray said thinly.

'Yes.'

'Hurst didn't seem all that bothered. He asked me for Gardner's telephone number when I sent him the tape. And I gave it to

216

him along with his address. He was going a bit loopy by then, I think. I went to see him. Like I said, I'd twigged what it all meant by then. I was angry. I didn't want to get involved in any of that. And seeing Gardner with those kids . . . well . . . it was just fucking awful. But Hurst wouldn't even let me through the front door.'

'You didn't consider contacting the police when you saw Gardner with that girl?'

There was a long pause on the other end of the line. 'If I'd gone to the police, they'd have asked me why I was following Gardner. So no. But I did have a long chat with that girl when Gardner was gone. He . . . well, he tried to kiss her. You saw that. She swore that it was the first time. I said I'd be watching, and that if I saw anything like it again I'd report it to her school. And for good measure I told all her mates that if I caught any of them hanging out with Gardner, they'd have me to deal with.'

'All right. And after Hurst got you to keep an eye on these three men, he never asked about Rebecca. You were to abandon that altogether?'

'Yes. He'd pretty much given up on her by then.'

'And you were to concentrate on Gardner?'

'Yes. But it wasn't a full-time gig or anything like that. It was . . . well, he said it was at my own convenience. So, to prove I wasn't wasting his money and I was on the job, I videoed some of it and sent the tapes to him along with reports on what I'd found.'

'So did you write reports on Gardner?'

'Yes.'

'All right,' I said, thinking that we must have left those in Hurst's house. 'And is there any way you might have been seen? Do you think Gardner realized that Hurst had set you on to him?'

'I don't know,' Bray said thoughtfully. 'I was pretty careful. He just might have known someone was following him, but I don't know how. And I never really got that impression. Anyway, even if he had known, how would he have been able to link me to Hurst?'

On the other end of the line I could hear Bray's feet crunching in the gravel as he moved back towards the pub. I asked him to get me Gardner's last-known address and phone me as soon as he had it; then I thanked him and hung up.

20

Early the next morning Graves was reading a well-known tabloid that Drayton had left in the warmth of the tent in Frank Hurst's garden. He turned the page and almost did a double-take. There, at the top of the page, was a picture of the tent he was now standing in and the charred remains of Hurst's house right next to it. Beyond the rubble, collapsed walls leading to stretches of broken, jagged brick could be seen. Some stone stairs in the middle of the house spiralled up, collapsed and led nowhere — the stairs that Graves had climbed only a few days ago. The photographer had captured the desolate air of the place very well.

Graves shook his head. They must have come last night, when no one else was around. Beneath the photo was a lurid account of the discovery of Hurst's body at the top of the hill. Then the story went on to recount the tale of the two missing girls and the police's failure to find them. He almost decided to phone Downes and tell him straightaway about the article, but Downes would find out soon enough. If he didn't know already.

Graves left the tent and resolved to forget about it. He began to search through the charred rubble while Drayton threw the heavier rocks and pieces of debris into a wheelbarrow, then carted them away. The ruins had a damp, muddy and spongy feel to them as he made his way over their surface. He marked each area that he had covered with police tape fixed to spikes. Then he started all over again somewhere else.

It was long, painstaking and dull work. To begin with, there had been a very real dread every time he dug his hands into the ground. Perhaps he would feel the soft curve of a skull. The hem of a dress. A bone. But, as the days had worn on, he thought about this less and less, to the point where now he no longer thought about it at all. So far, he had come up with nothing of interest. A piece of old foam. Something broken and unrecognizable. A smooth-shaped rock that he threw to one side.

He looked up and massaged his eye with the back of a cold hand. Despite what he was searching for, it was still difficult to believe that anything dreadful could really happen in these far-off and remote hills. They were almost like a picture postcard, with all the snow. But already they seemed darker now. They held the potential for violence.

After a while his hands seemed to dig and search almost of their own accord. He kept at it, and by 11.00 a good portion of the place where the raised platform had once stood was covered with lines of fluttering police tape. He worked in silence as the cold deepened. So isolated did he feel that time out here seemed to be slowing down. Occasionally, leaves from the trees at the far end of the garden drifted down in the wind. The trees glistened. The clouds pushed over the fields. He kept searching.

21

Powell's son lived in a small, neat semi on the outskirts of Stratford-upon-Avon, near the river. He seemed to be holding up pretty well, all things considered. His gentle but weary face brightened when he saw me framed in the door, and with his usual disconcerting familiarity he took me gently by the elbow and led me through the hallway and into the living room.

'The old sod's had a good day so far,' Alex said in a hushed voice as we walked up the stairs to the bedroom. 'Better than yesterday anyway. Just glad to get out of hospital for now. So that's cheered him up. Sometimes he's completely out of it, though. So, Will, do me a huge favour and try not to keep him up too long if you can help it?'

Alex was in his late thirties. Slim and good-looking, he moved gracefully and quickly up the stairs, knocked on the bedroom door and then without waiting for an answer pushed it open, while a dog yapped from somewhere else in the house.

Powell was sitting upright in an armchair by the bed, sneering over a paper as usual. Alex gave me a quick and grateful glance, gently nudged me farther inside the room and shut the door behind him when he left.

I had seen Powell when the illness had first taken him, and even then the speed of it had surprised me. But this . . . this was different. Powell had aged years in weeks. His once lean but full frame had been replaced by fragile bones. His shaggy, messy mop of black hair hung in damp-looking strands. His lips were bloodless, and his eyes were two glowing sparks beneath his eyebrows.

I stood rooted to the spot. Powell's high-browed and elongated face tilted towards me in malicious amusement, enjoying, in his usual perverse way, my discomfort. He waved the red top in the air as I walked in. I smiled lightly and stood there a little longer.

'I've seen it,' I said. 'Super was on the phone first thing this morning. Furious, of course.' I shrugged.

'Who leaked it?'

'We don't know. Could be anyone. We had around a dozen men out there clearing out the rubble to begin with. Could have been any one of them or someone they talked to down the pub. A fireman even.'

'But it's true, is it? You've found one of 'em. Over at Frank's house. Buried down there? And you still don't know which one, do you? It doesn't say here.'

'No. We don't know. Not for sure. There's no way of knowing yet. We've had to send the remains to the forensics lab in Oxford, and Brewin is comparing the DNA profile with the samples we took from Gail's and Elise's parents. There wasn't much left of her to begin with, and the fire got the rest. But it's possible — possible that it could be one of the girls. We'll know either way in a couple of days.'

Powell sat very still, studying me. He said, without much interest, 'You look bloody awful.'

'Well, I had to get her out.'

'Oh, bloody hell, Will,' Powell said in despair. '*You* got her out? You know that's what they've got firemen for. Why didn't you let one of them do it?'

'They wouldn't go in. They were just standing there, looking at her, to begin with,' I said, a little unfairly.

Powell shook his head in disappointment. 'Christ. You never learn. The times I've told

224

you . . . The times I've tried to . . .' He let out a gloomy sigh and, knowing it was no use, gave up.

'I didn't have much choice, you know. There was —'

Wearily, Powell put up his hand, not wanting to hear it. 'So if it is one of the girls under there, it means that we were right all along,' Powell said, and placed the newspaper in his lap. 'After all these years. I suppose that's why the bastard never sold up and moved. That way he could be sure no one'd find them. And I suppose you're blaming yourself as usual,' Powell said and grunted.

I wandered over and sat on the edge of the bed. 'A bit. The thing is, I can't help thinking that we should have tried harder. You know, back when we really had the chance. I don't know why we listened to O'Donnell. We should have taken that place apart or leaked it to the papers. Now we might never find the other girl at all. You haven't been out there yet, Len. But she was buried really deep.'

'We didn't have much choice. But, Christ, did he have a fit. When he found out.' Powell smiled in grim satisfaction. 'One of his worst.'

I nodded, remembering the superintendent's look of stunned rage when he learnt that Powell and I had been snooping around Hurst's garden weeks after we had discovered the hairpin. Both of us nearly lost our jobs when Hurst, incensed, phoned the station and made a formal complaint. It was my second reprimand in as many weeks.

'But at least we might find out what happened to those little girls now,' Powell continued. 'It could be that while we were running around like a couple of headless chickens, they were under his feet the whole time.'

'Did you think Hurst was lying?' I said.

Powell shrugged. 'You never could tell with him. Anyway, what the hell does any of that matter now? The thing is, you were right. And you kept your eye on him. Nobody asked you to do that either.'

'I couldn't keep my eye on him all the time.' I stared for a moment at the carpet. 'Look, I need to see what you make of something,' I said. 'Turns out that Hurst was keeping his eye on a couple of fellas himself. Some fellas we used to know quite well.'

I drew out the first two names very deliberately. It took a few moments for them to register. Powell repeated the names twice in a low voice. His face, lit by the yellow lamp by his side, contorted suddenly in recognition. His heavy eyelids opened wider.

'Edward Secoy,' I said.

'Moved to Canada.'

'Ben Tanner.'

'Heart attack,' Powell said straightaway. 'Neighbours found him two weeks later, dead in bed. And good riddance too.' Powell threw the newspaper on to the table next to him. 'Both of them had a thing for little kiddies,' he said. 'We found that out when we looked at all the local sex offenders who could have been around at the time of one or both disappearances. And we listened very carefully for any rumours flying around about any of the local weirdos. We were able to rule them out as well.'

'Secoy. Nothing ever proved about him, just a few nasty rumours,' I said. 'A co-worker came forward with his name when the second girl went missing. But there wasn't much in it as far as we could see. Papers got hold of his name, though. And Tanner's as well. And Tanner had a definite track record, if you remember. Was in jail twice, for sexual assaults on girls. Each man was near one of the scenes when Elise and Gail went missing. And both had access to a vehicle.'

Powell nodded and reached for a glass of

water. Downstairs, I could hear Alex busying himself in the kitchen. A tap being turned off and on. Plates clinking in the sink.

'And there was a third one. You remember Christopher Gardner?'

Powell's mouth turned down in disgust. 'He'd gone to jail as well — molested a teenager. He was in his early twenties; she was just fifteen. Her old man had got wind of it and called in the police.' Powell became thoughtful. 'There had been rumours about him for a while before he was arrested. Rumours that he liked getting all pally with teenage girls — earned him a busted jaw once, if I remember rightly. The little prick deserved it no doubt. He was doing a decorating job just outside the village when the girls went missing, wasn't he? Or something like that. Christ, I can't remember now.'

I nodded. 'Gail's mother spotted him in a van around an hour after Gail was seen for the last time.'

'And so Frank was keeping an eye on Gardner,' he said. 'But whatever for?' He paused, thinking, and looked up. 'I don't get it,' he said. 'You've already found one of the girls under Frank's house by the looks of it. That proves that these men were innocent all along. It was just a coincidence that they were in the area at the time. I mean, we ruled them out pretty quickly. Especially Gardner. So why the hell would Hurst have the remotest interest in these three men, unless . . .' Powell said, and then stopped abruptly, as the realization sank in. He looked away. 'Oh, no,' he said so quietly that I could hardly hear him. 'He was watching them himself, you say?'

'No.' And then I told him about Bray. 'He knew that Tanner was dead and that Secoy had emigrated. But he was still interested in Gardner. Wanted to know what he was up to. I think that could be the reason . . . the reason why we weren't able to tie anyone — any *one* — person to the disappearances. We'd always thought it was someone working alone. Someone who had been watching these girls for some time. But what if it was more than one person?'

'Four men with a shared interest,' Powell said, his voice harsh all of a sudden. 'All of them working together. Three of them we were aware of, but Hurst . . . And that house of his,' Powell said, catching his breath sharply.

I nodded. My forehead suddenly felt hot. I forced myself to say what I was thinking out loud. 'The house would have been ideal for their . . . well . . . for their purposes. If they had wanted to draw things out. If they were working together, one of them could drive the girl to where, say, Hurst was waiting in his car. He takes her back to the house, and the other one goes back to whatever he was doing. So he's gone for only a matter of minutes. Then they meet later in the house. Far away from the village, where nobody can see them. To that big old house in the middle of nowhere. And there'd be plenty of time to get rid of the bodies afterwards. They decide to do it twice and then never again — which is really unusual, because these pricks can't seem to help themselves once they get started. And they choose both of the girls well in advance. They take great care over that.

'We were able to tie Gardner to Gail but only vaguely. He was in the area. But not to Elise at all. Secoy was in the area when Gail went missing, but when Elise was taken, he wasn't even in the same county. And the same goes for Tanner. There was never more than a vague connection between them and the girls. Hurst we didn't even know about then.'

'Until later,' Powell reminded me. 'I did a bit of checking when we found the hairpin, remember? He was out working most of the time. Out on his farm. Usually alone. But he could have easily taken off in that Land Rover.'

'They may have been kept alive . . . for some time out there,' I said. I could sense the horror of what had happened clawing at me, though I did not want to think about it. For years the fate of the two girls had been like a constant presence, eyeing me patiently from somewhere deep within my mind. Now it was as if I could actually see them. First Elise and then Gail. I imagined footsteps; the door opening. The long shadow of one of the four men. Perhaps Hurst himself. And with that image the old anger came tearing through. Pure and clear and undiminished by the years.

I remembered Gail's mother sitting slumped and helpless in her kitchen as I asked her as gently as I could about her daughter. Where had she last seen Gail? Did she have any idea where she may have gone? She'd tried all her friends? Had there been any kind of trouble at home? She was recently divorced, I understood. Might that have caused Gail to change her behaviour? Had she been late home before? Had there been an argument, anything like that? Something that might make her stay away from home?

She had answered as best she could. She was in a daze. Her house was full of strangers — police — but it was as if she didn't know who had let them in. Radio static screeched from somewhere far out in her garden. They had been searching the fields beyond her gates. I promised her that I would find her daughter, no matter what it took.

'Hurst wasn't married then,' Powell was saying. 'So he could have just sent his kid off somewhere — off to some relative for the night.'

I nodded in agreement. It was good, sound logic, and it was what I had come to expect from Powell over the years. Powell glanced away and stared in silence at the carpet. Then there was a hesitant look in his eye. 'You always seem to know,' he said almost angrily. 'You knew it with Hurst. I couldn't understand why you kept on going on and on about him. Needling him like that, even though we'd just pulled his wife out of the swimming pool. Most of us would have backed off just a little bit. But not you, Will. You had it in for him right from the start. But you never told me why.'

I didn't say anything. He was right of course.

'You might not like it,' he said. 'But I want

to understand. If I can. Humour me.' Powell grinned, but his eyes betrayed a keen curiosity. 'It's not just Hurst. I've seen you do it more times than I care to remember. You get an idea inside your head and —'

'It's not hard to know when someone's lying to you,' I said, cutting him off quickly. 'You know that better than anyone.

'Anyway, there's still no sign of Rebecca. She didn't even show up to his funeral. Just sends him postcards when she feels like it. That's what Nancy said.'

'You spoke to her?'

'A couple of days ago. At the funeral.'

'At his funeral,' Powell said sharply. 'Not much love lost between those two. She's up to something, Will, you mark my words. Girl like Nancy. She's smarter than she lets on.'

Powell was silent for a moment. 'So he was having 'em looked into. But why? You reckon that Hurst wanted to make sure that none of them would ever do anything like that again and put them all in danger? Is that it? If another little girl went missing, all four would be in the spotlight again. That's why he was having them followed. The moment this fella . . . this detective seemed to be on to something with Gardner, Hurst told him to stop. Didn't he, Will? Told him to leave it alone.'

'Yes,' I said.

'So of course it works the other way too.'

'Hurst was a risk to the others, you mean?' I said.

'Exactly. Maybe Hurst was up to his old tricks again — planning something else — and Gardner got wind of it. Or what if Gardner found out that Hurst was having him followed?'

'And he can't get to Hurst because of what he's done to the house,' I said quietly. 'But the moment he does leave the house —'

'Somebody gets to him,' Powell said. 'They act fast and they nail him to the top of that hill.'

22

Graves continued to search, as the afternoon wore slowly on and the light began to fade. In a few hours it would be dark and they'd have to call it a day. His lower back was driving him mad. He stared up at the patch of cleared rubble and briefly closed his eyes in cold despair. It seemed to be taking them forever. They would never find anything else out here: he had known that from the very beginning. If the other girl had been buried here, the fire must have destroyed every trace of her.

He stood up, sorely tempted to warm up for a while in the tent. Drayton seemed to have had enough for one day as well. He was pouring himself a cup of hot soup from a flask and watching Graves through the flap of the tent as if he were sorry for him. Graves had kept Drayton there in case he needed help with anything. Graves swore loudly and then crouched back down again.

His lower back, for what must have been the hundredth time that day, screamed out at him in pain, as he made his way along the ground, searching painstakingly beneath the burnt rubble and clutching at his back from time to time like an old woman.

He kept working, looking up every now and then to make sure no one was taking his photograph. To his dismay, more journalists had arrived just after lunch — so many, in fact, that he'd had to call in someone with a little more natural authority than Drayton to keep them out. He thought about journalists and wondered how they lived with themselves as he searched. Then he stopped. All of them forgotten. He began to gently push away the stones and rubble with the palms of his hands, until he had created a small hole.

He plucked out a long shard of mud-streaked glass and threw it to the side. His hands slipped down further. There was a shifting, shuffling sound. Another piece of glass. Smaller this time. And, after that, a piece of old plastic and then the shattered remains of some piping or guttering. Something gave, and dust and black stone poured off a surface. There was something down there all right, though it was impossible to see what it was. There was no longer enough light. He made himself stop and take his time. He breathed in deeply and stood up.

Graves strode off towards the two rugged generators. Then he hoisted up both lights so that they were fixed exactly on the point of interest. There in front of him, within the widened hole, was a blackish material of some kind. Clothes? A coat? A jacket? Another groundsheet perhaps. Impossible to tell. He stood looking down and then knelt on the rubble.

He dug a little deeper clearing a larger space around the sides of the object and feeling along its sides before reaching in. More dust came off the top. Earth went spiralling down into the darkness below. He reached in again, then changed his mind.

'Drayton!' he yelled. 'Come over here.' More quietly he added: 'Might have something.'

Drayton appeared beside him.

'Get Shotgun on the phone and have him come over here quick.' Graves reached for his mobile from his inside pocket and passed it to Drayton. 'His number's in there. You'd better warn him about all those fucking journalists as well.'

As Drayton scanned the contacts list, Graves dug further around the object. A glimpse of something else now. A string or a cord. Something plastic. A buckle perhaps? No, he couldn't see.

'He's not answering,' Drayton said.

'All right,' Graves said. 'Keep trying.'

Graves moved his hands around the object and reached further in. He yanked. The material shifted once more and rose a few inches higher into the white light. Then, finally, with infinite care, Graves pulled and brought a rucksack out into the open air.

23

The press had left their cars and vans parked along the side of the lane. I slowed down when I saw them. They were crowded together, joking, laughing, smoking their cigarettes, but when they saw my car all camaraderie instantly vanished in the mad scramble to get at their gear. A wily and alert-looking police officer was keeping them at bay; he nodded when he saw me and waved me through. But in seconds they were on my car. Bulbs flashed. A scrum of microphones and telephones. One of them banged the car window. A man who had been eating a pork pie hurled it to the ground and took what appeared like a hundred pictures of my car. I beeped my horn until they got out of the way, then watched them through my rear-view mirror as the constable closed the gates behind me.

Graves was waiting for me outside the large white tent.

'You managed to get through them all right?' he said sheepishly.

'Just,' I said.

'You saw the story, then?'

I nodded.

'They must have come last night after we'd left and got their pictures. I'm really sorry, sir.'

'It's all right, Graves,' I said. 'Not your fault. They were going to be here sooner or later.'

Graves held open the flap of the tent and we walked inside. Despite the cold, the air was close and oppressive. There were two arc lights powered by generators. It was the smell that hit me first: rotting vegetation and ancient mud and something deep within the smell. Something ripe and over-sweet. Something that shouldn't be there at all, coiling its way through.

'So it was out there, you say. By the house?'

'Yes,' Graves said. 'It was around ten to twelve feet in under the stone platform, and then I'd say five feet to the left of the stone steps. Not all that far away from the girl, in fact. I very nearly missed it. It was buried rather deep.'

I looked over his shoulder. Inside the tent were a long trestle table and a single chair. I could see a broken, muddy strap hanging over the table's edge. Clots of mud lay on the crumpled grass.

'All right,' I said. 'Let's have a look at it.'

Graves pulled the plastic disposable gloves tighter over his fingers before taking a few steps towards the table. Very gently, as if he were lifting a sleeping puppy, he set it upright. He undid the cord at the top. The rucksack was still intact, although it had been crushed almost flat. It was lime green and black and covered in chalky dust and mud. On the top were pieces of broken mortar and stone, and it seemed to have been stained with something that looked like black tar. At the top and around the sides it was brushed with reddish, broken streaks of brick dust. There was black webbing at the front, and just beneath a front pocket was a logo: a red tent and a pine tree. GLOBALHIKE was written in simple black lettering above the symbol.

'What was it buried under?' I said. 'Was there another groundsheet?'

'No, sir. Don't think so. As I said, it was near the place where you found the girl.' Graves turned once more to the rucksack.

It was so crushed that he had to pull hard at its neck to get at the remaining contents. He pulled out, first, a blue polo-neck sweater. Two pairs of jeans. Levis. With holes in. A green anorak bunched up into a tight ball, and something that looked like it had once been a pamphlet. The clothes were damp, and the pages of the pamphlet stained and curled at the edges. There were a few pairs of woollen socks, some musty-smelling T-shirts, a yellow skirt and a thin red sweater.

It was not at all what I had expected to see. Standing closer to the rucksack, I now noticed that it was giving off a deep smell of sour earth. Again, I remembered the mortuary and the girl lying on the slab. It was the same smell somehow. Graves was, I realized, looking at me, curious to see how I was reacting. The mud around the bag was black and thick. The rucksack looked permanently tainted now that I could smell it.

Lodged near the bottom of the bag was a daisy-patterned washbag containing a broken toothbrush, toothpaste, a broken shampoo bottle, two bars of damp soap along with a pair of small bent scissors. Graves placed all of these objects beside the washbag. There was also a thick black hairbrush.

Very carefully, Graves pulled away a number of hairs. They were too thin for me to be able to discern their exact colour, but they looked opaque and greyish in the strong artificial light. Graves placed the hairs into a small Ziploc evidence bag.

Next came several pairs of women's tights, a neat black blouse, jogging pants and various bits of women's underwear, which had been rolled into a ball. Also, wrapped in a green mud-smeared towel was a make-up bag. Inside were two shades of cracked lipstick, nail varnish, a shattered nail file and a bottle of inexpensive-looking perfume, the contents of which had long since evaporated.

Graves started to explore the side pockets. An old novel was bent double and had been stuffed inside the largest pocket at the side. Beneath it was a plastic Bic lighter without a flint. In the other side pocket were a cracked biro and a box of crushed and wet-looking Marlboro Lights as well as a half-finished faded packet of Juicy Fruit chewing gum.

Graves laid the rucksack on its back, unzipped the front pocket and pulled out an old and faded bus ticket. He put it on the table and I peered at it. But the destination was so faint that it was impossible to read. Then he reached once more into the pocket and this time drew out a few pound coins along with a single folded five-pound note, which he laid on the table.

'Gail Foster was only thirteen when she went missing,' I said quietly, 'and Elise was only twelve. All this stuff belongs to someone else. Someone a lot older.'

'But who?' Graves said. 'Maybe Hurst put more of them down there than we thought,' he ventured. 'Maybe she was a hitchhiker he picked up.'

I lifted up my hand. 'Let's not get carried away just yet. You sound like one of those journalists. They'd just love that. There's no identification in there? Nothing like that?'

Graves began to recheck all of the pockets on the bag a second time and then looked inside again. But all of its contents were now neatly laid in a row on the table. Graves took off his gloves, rolled them into a ball and put them in his pocket. I looked at the bag again.

I crossed my arms. I'd left the files Graves had found in Hurst's house in my kitchen along with the videotapes; and, thinking that, I realized with some shock that they were the only things that remained extant from Hurst's house. Everything else was gone.

24

I told Graves to bag and label the contents of the rucksack and to take it back to the station. After he was gone, I drove there myself. On my way to my office, I waved absently through the open door to the dispatcher, Terry, who was sitting slumped on a high red office chair behind a monitor.

'They're bringing him in now, sir,' Terry said when he saw me, his head a little to one side. 'Shouldn't be long.'

'Who? Bringing who in?'

I turned around to face the super. My face expressionless. 'A suspect,' I said in a vague way.

'Already.'

I nodded.

She looked at me suspiciously for a moment and then turned around and motioned for me to follow, and of course I followed. Emma Collinson had a large mane of red hair. She was possessed of a cold, austere and almost intimidating kind of beauty, of which she seemed utterly aware without seeming vain. Not an easy trick to pull off. I had thought that the first time I saw her. She carried an air of adult disapproval with her everywhere, and, though I was older than her, it was particularly acute in all her dealings with me.

'I hope you're right, Downes,' she said. 'About the other girl. That sounds awful, but it will be better . . . better for the families if we're able to find her . . . and they know for sure. How long do you think it will take?'

'I'm not sure. A lot depends on Graves,' I said. 'He's in charge there now.'

Collinson's heels clicked loudly along the corridor as we walked. 'How are you two getting along?'

I shrugged. 'He seems all right, I suppose. Better than the other two you lumbered me with. But young, you know.'

'And he's not Powell,' she said, looking straight at me, coolly and appraisingly as always.

I didn't say anything straightaway. 'What did he do in Oxford?' I said. 'He got himself in some kind of trouble over there, didn't he?'

'He hasn't told you?'

I shook my head.

'Well, nothing really wrong. It's in his file if you're interested. You haven't looked at it yet?' she said, surprised.

'No.' Collinson had picked Graves out for me. I knew that Powell was never coming back. But reading Graves's file would have somehow made it real.

'A woman was assaulted outside a pub. It was pretty nasty. She had to go to hospital. She didn't see her attacker, who came up from behind and took her bag. But someone saw it.'

'Who?'

'A taxi driver reported it, and two officers took his statement. The description of her assailant matched a known suspect — he'd been involved in a number of similar incidents over the years. So it all looked straightforward to begin with. But then later the taxi driver came back to the station and signed a retraction. Said he couldn't be so sure now. The two officers who'd originally taken his statement had been out, so Graves dealt with it.

'Anyway, according to what Graves said later, the cab driver had felt uncomfortable and under pressure when he'd been interviewed. Graves took down his retraction — and then a few days later it simply disappeared.'

'All right. So what did he do?'

'Apparently Graves, when he saw it had gone missing, went straight to the Independent Police Complaints Commission, instead of going to his super, who could have dealt with it more tactfully.'

'But perhaps he did go to the super.'

'Yes. Reading between the lines, I think he may have tried the super or another superior officer and got nowhere. Maybe he'd been told to keep a lid on it.'

'And he wouldn't?'

'No.'

'So he opened that big mouth of his.'

Collinson nodded. 'Yes. He made it official. Took some guts. Those two officers could well be out of a job. Could even go to jail. We don't know yet. They're on suspension right now. But a lot of people wanted Graves out of there for good. They would have found a way to get rid of him sooner or later. And when they saw that there was a job open here —'

'They sent him to the middle of nowhere.'

Collinson smiled. She paused by the doorway to her office. 'Actually, it's rather fortunate that I ran into you,' she said, changing tack suddenly, 'because now we're going to account for why Frank Hurst's house was never searched properly. I'm not blaming you, Downes. Far from it. I understand that permission was denied. But what I don't understand is why my predecessor was so adamant about it. You made the request on more than one occasion, I gather. Is that right?'

'Yes,' I said. 'That's right.'

'Go on.'

'O'Donnell was afraid of what the newspapers would do with it if they found out. And the timing was all wrong too.'

'Timing?'

'The papers had just named a suspect and harassed him so badly that he ended up trying to kill himself. Front-page news everywhere and on the TV too. Turns out he was innocent.'

'A murder case?'

I nodded. 'And when it was all over he sued the police for invasion of privacy because someone leaked it.'

'Good for him. And so I suppose they didn't want the same thing happening with Hurst?' Collinson said thoughtfully. 'Yes, I can understand that.' She pushed a stray strand of hair behind her ear. 'Look, there's something else I better tell you.' She lowered her voice. 'That article in the paper this morning . . .' She paused and glared around the station. 'When I find out who leaked it I'm going to bloody well . . . well, we'll deal with that later. Anyway, the phone hasn't stopped ringing, as you can imagine. I called Elise Pennington's parents first thing. Told them we'd keep them informed as much as possible. But I got a call from Gail Foster's mother before I could even reach her. She's here now.'

'Here?'

'Yes. As soon as she saw the paper she drove straight here. She moved you know?'

'Yes,' I said. 'I know.'

'Of course, I told her that she should go home and we'd be in touch as soon as we knew anything, but she's booked herself into the B & B. She wants to talk to you.'

'When?'

'As soon as you're free.'

I sighed. 'I'm pretty busy,' I said. 'And what am I going to tell her? We don't even know which one we pulled out yet, do we? And we're no closer to finding the other one. We might not ever find her now.'

Collinson looked as if she were about to say something, but the doors swung open and in walked Christopher Gardner, bound in handcuffs. On either side of him were two police constables: Varley and an older man called Russell with an absurd walrus moustache.

I put my hands in my pockets and sauntered down the corridor towards them. There had obviously been some kind of scuffle. Russell's uniform was stained with foliage, and his boots and trousers were caked in mud. Gardner had a small bandage on his hand. He looked slightly wild, and there was a large smear of dirt along his left cheek and a long, thin cut on his neck.

'He tried to make a run for it,' Russell explained. 'Ran out the back door and legged it across the fields. Led us all over the fucking place, didn't you, Gardner, you pointless shit.' Then, noticing Collinson, he said, 'Oh, I mean you . . . er, you, er, led us a right merry dance, didn't you?'

I smiled, amused. Gardner winced when he saw me and closed his eyes. His head slumped forward. His hands moved inside his cuffs. 'I want a brief,' he said.

25

The interview room consisted of four soft office chairs, a tape recorder and a table. The walls were beige and the blue carpet was thick; on the wall facing me was a plastic clock. After Gardner had consulted with Mark Baxter, his solicitor, we all sat down and I began the interview.

'I'm wondering why you ran off like that,' I said, as if out of friendly curiosity. 'Why did you run when the boys went to your house to pick you up?'

'I'm not sure I have to answer that,' Gardner said. 'Looks like I don't have to answer anything if I don't want to.'

The man next to him nodded curtly. He was wearing a red bow tie, which was slightly crooked but suited him, and he sat bored in his chair, waiting.

I gave Gardner another long look. I had forgotten just how grating and annoying he was.

'All right,' I said. 'Where's your van? You lent it to some friend maybe? Or left it in a lock-up somewhere? They tell me there was no van when they went to pick you up just now.'

It seemed to take a moment for Gardner to gather his thoughts, as if the question surprised him. 'Van?' Gardner said.

'The one you use for work. Why isn't it out front, where it normally is?'

'A busted brake light. It's in the shop. You can —'

'Shut up,' I snapped wearily. 'You were seen and you damned well know it. And that's why you tried to run just now, and that's why you got rid of the van. A couple saw it and then you up on Meon Hill. Lanky fellow, they said. Spiky black hair — just like yours. They said you and Frank Hurst were arguing about something. Couldn't make out what it was, though. Two hours later, and Hurst's staring at the sky with a pitchfork rammed into his throat.'

'I don't know what he's on about,' Gardner said to Baxter, and crossed his arms. 'I don't even know who this . . . who this Hurst bloke is.'

I watched him very closely. I smiled and held the smile a little while. Up close, Gardner's attempt to appear youthful looked absurd. His hair was styled so that sculpted rows of it jutted out from the front and from the sides. He leant further back in his chair so that it was sitting on its back legs.

'I think you were doing a job nearby, and somehow you found out that Frank Hurst was up on Meon Hill. You hadn't been able to see him before, because he'd locked himself up in that big house of his, but you needed to talk to him in person. So the moment you heard he was out there, you got in your van, and you drove to Quinton. You had it out with him on that hill, and then you went back to work. But you were still angry about something. So you went back when no one else was there, just after dark. Maybe things got out of hand,' I said reasonably. 'I can understand that. Maybe Hurst attacked you. His temper had got him into trouble before.'

'Mr Gardner,' Baxter said in prim tones, 'has already informed you that he does not know this . . . this Frank Hurst and denies he was ever there. And there are lots of vans around, and plenty of people who could just as easily fit Mr Gardner's description. Have you even bothered to check, Chief Inspector?'

'You needed to talk to him about the girls,

didn't you, Gardner?' I said, ignoring Baxter.

'Girls?' Gardner said. 'What girls?'

'The two girls who went missing seven years ago. Gail Foster and Elise Pennington.'

At the mention of the girls, Gardner visibly tensed. He gulped and seemed uncharacteristically at a loss for words.

I pushed on as quickly as I could. 'You were in the village when Gail went missing. Gail's mother remembered seeing you out there. You know what I think happened. Somehow you found out that Hurst was having you followed and keeping tabs on you. And you didn't like it. Was he a threat to you? Had he wanted you to stop following around young girls, because if you were caught he'd also be exposed? Still quite a hobby for you, though.'

Baxter put his hand on Gardner's forearm, urging him not to answer. But Gardner was making a very good attempt at seeming indignant and said, 'I don't know what you're talking about. I'm not like that. Never have been. It's just bloody gossip, that's all it is. People have got it in for me. They always have. And that bitch who got me sent to prison — she was lying. I never had anything to do with all that.'

'Jealous of your youthful good looks no

doubt,' I said, before changing tack. 'Or perhaps he was the one loose end that could tie you to their disappearance.'

Gardner opened his mouth and then shut it when Baxter, stirring eagerly into life, intervened on his behalf. 'Now that's enough, Downes. Quite enough. You're beyond belief sometimes, you really are.' Baxter raised his hands in the air and then let them fall, so that his fingers hit the edge of the table. 'We've been through this a thousand times. My client had already served his sentence well before you dragged his name through the mud a second time and tried to link him to those two missing girls. Tell me you're not digging all that up again. Because if you are,' he said, and let the words hang in the air, 'if you are, Mr Gardner needs to be formally read the police caution. That's a separate case. I suppose you think that it's perfectly all right to blindside us like this.'

I waited and glanced at the plastic clock with a bland look in my eye. It was almost 5.00. It would be dark outside by now.

'All you had back then was a very tenuous connection between my client and your case. All you could ever prove was that he was somewhere in the general vicinity when one of the girls went missing.' Baxter went on, 'And let me say, Chief Inspector, this is a case that should have been cleared up years ago by this department. By you, in fact.'

'She's been found,' I said in a neutral voice, watching Gardner closely.

'Who?' Gardner said and laughed. 'Who's been found? What're you talking about, Downes?'

'The fire was a mistake,' I said. 'You wanted to destroy what was left of them for good and to make sure that anything linking you to Hurst was gone as well. Things like videotapes.' Again, I looked very closely across the table. There was no reaction at all. Gardner didn't even blink. He had been a pretty cool customer back then, if I remembered rightly. He hadn't changed.

'Now listen, I —' Baxter said.

I moved forward in my chair. 'One of the girls was down there. We don't know which one yet, but when we find the other one we'll tie them both right back to you and Hurst.'

'That's enough,' Baxter said. 'I won't sit here and let you ambush my client like this.'

Gardner looked boldly right back at me with his arms crossed like a belligerent teenager. He put the front legs of his chair back on the floor and stared at the ceiling.

'Are you going to charge my client or not?' Baxter said.

Gardner was grinning at me. I was sorely tempted to outline the contents of the videotape and very nearly did so just to wipe the grin off his face. But it was much too soon for that. For now, Gardner looked pleased. He reached for his jacket on the back of his chair.

For a few moments longer, I watched him, collecting my thoughts. The room was silent. The other two men looked at me, impatient to leave. The interview had gone pretty much exactly as I had expected. Of course, Baxter was right. I had no case against Gardner.

I stood up finally and informed them that Gardner would have to make himself available for a police line-up as soon as one could be arranged. I also asked for the make and model of Gardner's van along with the registration number. I looked at the clock, read the time and date into the tape recorder and switched it off.

26

There was only one B & B in Moreton-in-Marsh, and I walked to it through town. I'd called ahead, so I knew that Emily Foster would be waiting for me in the small lobby. A lot of the villagers had moved away after Gail disappeared, but Emily had stayed as long as she could stand it. I had admired her a great deal at the time. Still did. I remembered passing her house much later, when all the trails leading to Gail had finally run cold — when the summer was almost over, and the first traces of autumn were making their presence felt, and frustration and despair were starting to reach out for me.

The last time I had been to her house the street had looked cold and dark, almost uninhabited, although there were cars in the driveways on both sides of the street. Now I wondered how many of her neighbours — the ones who had been crowding outside her house during that seemingly endless night — were still in the village, perhaps sitting even now in their front rooms, their own children grown up and gone away. I wondered, with Hurst dead, whether they were talking about Gail and that hot, dry summer when she had disappeared.

I remembered Emily Foster staring at the road from her daughter's window. She had still been waiting for her to come home; she had still half expected Gail to turn round the bend in the road with her schoolbag slung over her shoulder as if nothing had happened. She had not seen me watching her. Her eyes had been vacant and glazed. Pop stars on the walls had been grinning at her in the half-darkness of Gail's room. But of course Gail was never coming back.

Now Emily was waiting for me in a quiet corner of the B & B with a pot of tea getting cold in front of her. She had to be in her mid-forties. But she looked much older. Frail, nervous and diminished, as if only there at all by sheer force of will. She smiled faintly when she saw me and stood up and we shook hands.

I had made it my business over the years to keep both families personally informed. Elise's parents had moved to London a long time ago. They were still together. But Emily lived alone in Redditch near Birmingham. She had divorced her husband just before Gail went missing and had not remarried.

'So,' I said, sitting down, 'you saw it in the paper, then.'

She nodded. 'Joan, my sister, rang. Told me she'd seen it.'

'I wish she hadn't. I would have liked to have waited a little longer. Until we were sure. There's not really much that I can tell you.'

She crouched forward in her chair. 'But you have found something? Something in that man's house?'

'Yes,' I said.

'A body, that's what the paper says. But is it . . . is it Gail's body?'

'I don't know. I'm sorry. You know there was a fire out there?' I said gently.

'But you think it might be her?' She gazed desperately across the table. 'You think that you might have found her? You think she might have been there all this time?'

'We don't know,' I said quickly. 'There's no way to be sure for now.'

'So the hairpin. It *was* Gail's all along. The one you found in his swimming pool.'

I sighed. 'We don't know that. We're still

261

very much in the dark. I'm sorry, but it might turn out that it's all got nothing to do with Gail at all. So you really shouldn't be here. It's far too early on, and it won't do you any good being back here. You must know that. It's only going to make things worse.'

'I can't help that,' she said coldly. 'And how can things be any worse than they are already? All I want to know is what happened to Gail. And I want to know why you didn't search his house. You had the hairpin. What else did you need?'

'But we couldn't be sure, remember. You couldn't be sure if it was hers at the time. You know we went through all that. It was bent. And rusty. That's all we had. And even if we had searched his house, there's no guarantee we would have found anything. None at all.'

'But you should have searched,' Emily said. 'You should have searched his house. Why didn't you?'

I didn't say anything. I looked outside, aware that I was just making excuses. She was right, of course. Why hadn't I ignored O'Donnell and taken the place apart? Seven years she'd been waiting for news, and it was all my fault. I couldn't believe how badly I'd let her down. For a few moments

I struggled against the enormity of my own error. Hurst was gone, and it was possible that we would never know what had happened out there. All that time under his house. And what had I done about it? Nothing.

'Look,' I said finally, turning towards her, 'you're right. We should have searched it. I wanted to, but . . . well, all I can tell you is that the fire . . . the fire destroyed the whole house. There's nothing left of it at all. And if it hadn't been for the fire, I don't think we would ever have found . . . found what was out there.' I paused. 'There was this huge joist. It fell straight through the house and crashed down into the ground.'

Emily didn't say anything for a while. In fact, she didn't even seem to be listening. Finally, she said, 'But she's been out there. All this time. And you did nothing. You swore to me that you would find her for me. You remember that?'

'Yes. I'm sorry.' I stood up. There was nothing else to say.

27

In the end, I decided to take Graves along with me to Lower Slaughter to see Nancy. I let him drive. The trees and bushes rushed past us as the road uncoiled beneath our wheels. We plunged further into the growing darkness while the names of small villages whipped past us and we were enveloped by the falling snow.

'What did Brewin say?' I said. 'Did the samples he took from the body match the missing girls?'

'The results aren't in yet. He'll know tomorrow.'

'And what about the forensics lab? He phoned them?'

'Yes. They don't want to say too much until they're sure. But they say that they might be able to extrapolate, or at least get some idea of the age from one of the bones. They're going to have to try to make their best guess from a single bone once the biological profile is complete. The femur is almost intact. But all they can confirm so far is that the body is female.'

'That's not much to go on, is it? Nothing else at all?'

Graves shook his head.

The houses looked empty and silent. There was a trampled path of frozen sludge leading towards Number 5 Patch Close, a small semi at the end of the road. A grey Nissan was in the driveway, and a woman with her back to us was lifting bags of shopping out of the boot. She whirled round when she saw us looming out of the darkness towards her.

'We're looking for Nancy,' I said. 'You're her sister, right? She told me she'd be staying with you for a bit. While she was here for her old boss's funeral. Frank Hurst.'

'Yes,' she said. 'Who are you?'

She was a little older than her sister; tall but with a rounder face. She was looking at me with the bags weighing heavy in her hands, and the plastic digging into her fingers. She slumped slightly and let the bags rest on the ground in the snow.

'I'm Detective Chief Inspector Downes,' I said. 'I'd like to talk to her. Do you know where she is? In the village perhaps?'

'No. She's out.'

'Out where?'

'She's gone to Cheltenham. Took the bus.'

'When?'

'Oh, about an hour ago.'

'What for?'

Miss Williams looked worried. 'Well, she's meeting someone, I think. She wouldn't say.'

'Who?'

'A man, I think.'

'A man. Okay,' I said. 'Do you know him? Has he ever been to the house to see her?'

'No. I've never seen him.'

'Local?'

She shrugged.

'He's phoned the house? You ever talked to him?'

'No. He always calls on her mobile or she phones him on hers. They were on the phone this morning.'

'What's wrong, Miss Williams? Are you all right?'

'I don't know. I've been worried about it all day. Look, I don't want to get her in any trouble, but . . . I don't know. I phoned her from work and told her not to go out — not in this weather — but she was adamant about it. We had a bit of an argument. Looks like she might get stuck out there now.' She looked up at the sky. 'Must be serious for her to go out in this weather. Wish she

266

hadn't, not with all this snow forecast. She's going to take a train home after.'

'Miss Williams — what happened? You had an argument with your sister. What was it about?'

'I heard her talking. I didn't mean to,' she said quickly. 'This morning, before I went off to work. But I'd forgotten my purse so I had to let myself back in. And I heard her talking on the phone. She was angry with this fella. I thought it was just some man she'd met while she was down here, but they were talking about that girl, which didn't make any sense.'

'What girl?'

'I didn't hear all that much, because she hung up after a few minutes. And then she came running down the stairs. Asked me what I thought I was doing, eavesdropping on her like that. She's got a terrible temper on her. And I said I hadn't heard anything. But she was furious. I didn't tell her what I'd heard. But she was talking about that girl, the one who ran off years ago. Stuck-up bitch, that's what Nancy always said. Hurst's daughter.'

'Rebecca Hurst?'

'Yes.'

'Can you remember anything else at all?'

'No. I just heard the name Rebecca Hurst.

She was saying something about her running away or something; I couldn't hear the rest. And then I asked her.'

'Asked her what? About Rebecca Hurst?'

'No. I asked her what she was really doing down here. Back home.'

'But she was here for Frank Hurst's funeral,' I said, surprised.

'But why would she go to his funeral? She couldn't stand him. Frank Hurst sacked her. No warning, nothing, and she'd been working like a dog for him for years and years. So when he sacked her she went off to Brighton, because she'd always wanted to live by the sea. But she's just a chambermaid now.'

'A chambermaid. But when I saw her at the funeral she told me she ran a guest house.'

'She doesn't. She's a chambermaid in a hotel.'

'And so you're worried about her because you thought she might be up to something — that she was here for a reason other than Hurst's funeral.'

'Yes. She was furious. Told me to mind my own business and keep out of it. So I said it was her life and she could do what she wanted and that was fine with me. And I went off to work. Went off in a huff. Then

I phoned her to see if we could make up before she left. But I couldn't stop her from going to Cheltenham or change her mind.'

'All right,' I said. 'She's gone to meet this man before she goes home to Brighton on the train. And you think it might have something to do with Rebecca Hurst.'

'I think it might. But I don't understand what it can all be about. I don't want to get her in any trouble,' she said helplessly. 'But Nancy — she's just so damned stubborn sometimes.'

'Her number,' I said, clicking my fingers. 'Try her number. If she knows it's you, she might answer. Quickly.'

She seemed uncertain in the muted light of the porch. Graves took her shopping bags and placed them gently on the doorstep. It seemed to reassure her.

'All right,' she said. She opened the car door and reached for her bag on the passenger's side. She searched her handbag, pulling out a lipstick, a packet of tissues and a large fat purse. It seemed to be taking a long time. I gave Graves a pained look over the roof of the car, and Graves rolled his eyes. Finally, she had the phone. She backed out of the car, peered at it and dialled. We watched.

She shook her head and looked up. 'No.

She's not answering,' she said, sounding a little puzzled. 'Straight to voicemail.'

'Leave her a message,' I said. 'Tell her to call DCI Downes if she gets the message. I'll give you my number. She knows me. Tell her to call me and I'll meet her in Cheltenham. She's not to get on that train before she speaks to me. All right?'

'She's not in any trouble, is she?'

I shook my head, uncertain. 'No. But you're sure you don't know who this man is?'

'No, I don't.'

'And can you think of where she might go in town? A place where she might meet this person?'

She paused, thinking. 'Well, not off the top of my head. But . . .' She reached into her bag for her front door keys and gripped them in the palm of her hand. 'Hold on. Yes,' she said. 'There is. There's a café near that daft old clock they've got there.'

'Clock?'

'Yeah, you know the one. You must have seen it. It's in that shopping centre. It's like a duck or something. It's for the kiddies. It's not really a clock at all.'

'You don't know it, do you, Graves?'

Graves shook his head. ' 'Fraid not. Never been to Cheltenham,' he said. 'Haven't had time yet.'

'It's in the arcade. Off the high street, at the top. She goes there for a cup of tea sometimes before she takes her train.'

28

I let Graves drive again. It was less than twenty miles to Cheltenham, and the roads leading there were quicker than the winding lanes that had taken us to Lower Slaughter. Every now and again I would reach for the phone and dial Nancy. But there was no reply. I didn't really know what to make of it. Only that I didn't like it. Nancy was smart, like Powell had said. She'd acted quickly when Sarah Hurst had had her accident by the pool. But now that we knew she hadn't come here for Hurst's funeral at all it changed everything. She was here for another reason — and that reason sounded like it had something to do with Hurst's daughter. But what could Rebecca have to do with any of it?

We made good time, despite the bad weather, and we soon left the tiny villages far behind us. Within half an hour we were in the town. We stopped the car and parked it high on a kerb outside a guest house.

I didn't know the clock Nancy's sister had mentioned. But I knew where the shopping centre was and that the only way to it was through a great quantity of people. At the bottom of the rise, the high street stretched out before us, cutting a thick swathe all the way across the bottom of the hill. A huge splintering crowd streamed across the road in both directions. We headed quickly down the slope.

What had from above seemed to be a solid wall of people now turned into individual faces and shapes. The melted snow had left the walkways shining. Laughing and giggling, people pushed past us and became indistinguishable from the other moving bodies. It was nearly 9.00, but most of the shops were still open because it was almost Christmas.

We strode on, leaving puzzled and annoyed faces in our wake as we barged through the Christmas shoppers. Grim-faced people rushed from shop to shop like soldiers jumping from trench to trench, emerging with yet more bags clutched in their hands or sometimes unbelievingly empty-handed. In minutes we had reached the high street. Here the throngs moved and swayed in a mass. They poured into the shopping centre, calling out to one another in the gathering cold.

'She told me she ran a guest house, but she was lying,' I said over my shoulder to Graves.

Graves picked up speed. His face was tucked into the collar of his coat. His thick brogues rang out on to the street.

'She's here for another reason — something to do with Rebecca.'

'But what?'

'I don't know.'

'And this man she's meeting — she's chosen a very public place, hasn't she?'

'Yes,' I said. 'Could be because she's scared of him.'

For a moment Graves lapsed into silence and gazed mournfully at all the shoppers.

'And why all the secrecy?' I asked. 'Why hide it from her sister?'

'I don't know, sir.' Graves shrugged. 'But, to be honest, I don't like it either: her just showing up like this for a funeral of someone she couldn't stand.

We walked on towards the shopping centre. Heavy Christmas lights and bulky decorations, stars and branches of holly, shone out above us. We passed the heavy brass doors of a department store. I stood for a while watching the rolling tide of people pouring forward. Graves pushed himself across the road and headed towards the shopping centre. I reached for the phone inside my pocket and dialled Nancy's number, staring at the crowds and hoping I might hear it ring out. But there was nothing. Half the people in the street seemed to be talking into their telephones. I stepped back into the moving mass and headed inside the centre.

Fewer people here. Piped music reverberating around the walls. A constant echoing murmur of footsteps and people. A video-game shop was packed full of kids vying for the controls. A fountain with blue water. Heavy potted plants grew along some of the walls.

In the middle of the shopping centre more people were gathered, looking up towards the ceiling. I pushed past a group of teenagers. All of them were looking up. Waiting.

There above me was the clock. Nancy's sister had been right. It was absurd. At the top of the clock face was a white wooden duck and beneath it a wooden fish. The whole contraption began to spin. This was what the crowd had been waiting for. I looked at my watch. It was 9.00 exactly. The duck laid what looked like a wooden egg, and the egg went spiralling down a red chute. A second later, the fish began to flap its fins and spin round. Bubbles floated out of the fish's open mouth. A tinkling piano; a voice ringing out a tune I vaguely recognized, 'I'm Forever Blowing Bubbles'.

I watched it for a moment, transfixed like the others. Then it stopped spinning. Graves moved off first. I followed, and we climbed up the escalators. Bubbles were floating along the upper floor and towards the glass-domed roof of the shopping centre. Some of the children were trying to catch them. The tune still followed us as we strode through the upper floor.

There was a single small café tucked away at the end of a small hall at the far end of the shopping centre. Graves pushed open the door and we walked into the centre of the room, staring at the customers. We checked all of the booths and tables. An employee was on the other side of the counter at the back, shaking used coffee granules into a plastic bin and looking at us warily. 'I'm looking for someone,' I said quickly. 'A woman. Mid-thirties. Would have been carrying a bag. A suitcase with her maybe.'

He looked blank and shrugged his shoulders. He was tall and rather self-conscious.

'She was with someone. A man,' I said. 'Would have been here . . . I don't know.

Not long ago. Half an hour maybe.'

The man shrugged and rubbed his hands on a cloth. 'We've been pretty busy,' he said, and looked at the crowds surging outside the window.

'She comes here quite a lot,' I said as calmly as I could. 'Is there a shortcut to the station near here?'

'Yes,' he said, already losing interest and turning back to his espresso machine. 'Down the bottom there. You take the exit by the jeweller's and then cut out through Fox Towns Lane at the back of the shops and past the church.'

We stalked out. I took off my coat and clutched it under my arm. I felt the first hard jab of real fear. A low ache right in my gut. I stood at the railing and peered down over the edge. The clock on the ceiling, now nearly at eye level, was still again. But I couldn't get the damned silly tune out of my head. My forehead was beaded with sweat, and my hands were fidgeting nervously by my sides. I wiped the sleeve of my coat hard against my forehead. I pushed myself off the rail.

'Let's try that shortcut,' I said.

We kept on going. We headed down the escalator, went straight to the back and out a side entrance. The door rattled on its hinges. A shoe shop. The jeweller's. A car park. The cold hit me straightaway, and a few moments later we were back in the never-ending crowds.

It was less well lit here at the back, and the further we went the smaller the shops became and gradually there were fewer people. Within minutes the shops had all but petered out. The noise of the crowd subsided into a distant murmur, while the town shed its quaint Georgian charm and became rugged and sparse. We found and then followed Fox Towns Lane towards the station.

Walls were smeared with graffiti. Squat windows were ringed with dirt. From far off came an announcement in neutral tones from a speaker. A single train rattled across a bridge, cutting the horizon in two. Its heavy rumble echoed off the reddish walls.

We had almost reached the station. There was a shadowy patch of wall. Some old garages. We turned a corner.

Graves saw her first, because he picked up speed and began to run. The first thing I noticed was the shoes. The same ones she had been wearing for Hurst's funeral. The blood began to pulse in my ears. My mind snapped, as if recoiling from what was in front of me. I let out a kind of hiss through my teeth.

My feet pounded along the path. Graves, ahead of me, leapt over an old mattress. A very small green suitcase was lying by her side.

Graves hovered over her. Then he darted off down the lane. He disappeared from view as he headed towards the orange lights of the train station. I stopped and stood over her.

Chubby ankles poked out of high-heeled shoes. Her face was pressed against the mud and slush. Mud brushed her teeth. A splattering of saliva and blood came from the corner of her mouth, and blood was spattered on the dirty snow. I knelt beside her. A large thick flap of jagged skin hung loosely on her forehead. Her eyes were wide open, just like Hurst's had been. It was as if she were staring at me from the darkness and saying it had all been my fault. And maybe it was.

29

A few hours later, I was sitting in my car and looking at Gardner's scrawny silhouette through the top window of his house. As I watched Gardner, I thought of Nancy, and of Brewin standing over her body in the arc lamps. Then policemen blocking the path and the sudden chaos in that quiet, sordid back alley. Graves had come back empty-handed. Whoever it was, they could have blended into the masses of people at the train station or made their way to the high street in seconds. The sing-song old-fashioned crooning voice kept on coming back to me. It had sounded cheerful back in the shopping centre. Now it seemed mocking. Cruel even. I saw the egg falling down that long chute and the bubbles rising to the ceiling. I saw Nancy lying dead in the dirt.

I closed my eyes and then stepped out of the car, thinking that I had been wrong about Gardner all along, but I wouldn't know for sure until I had talked to him again, and this time without his lawyer. On my way over, I had thought about those tapes. So what had Hurst really wanted Bray to find out about those men? A secret spot. An out-of-the-way place, which they may have visited and which no one else knew about. That's what he'd asked Bray to look at specifically when he'd hired him. But why? What had Hurst really been after? If I were right, it meant that Gardner, despite his taste for younger girls, was innocent when it came to Gail and Elise.

I moved quickly across the front garden and round to the back of Gardner's house. I looked in through the kitchen window, beyond the overloaded dirty sink and towards the living room. I tried the cold metal handle of the kitchen door. It made a small, tentative squeak as I pushed against it and stepped into the flat light of his kitchen. I waited. Then I closed the door, turned the key in the lock and slipped it into my coat pocket. I could hear Gardner talking on the phone upstairs.

Very quietly, I moved across the lino of the kitchen, past the grease-splattered oven and towards the hallway, still listening. I planted myself very firmly at the bottom of the narrow, dusty stairs and waited for him.

Gardner was laughing ingratiatingly into the telephone. He hung up quite suddenly. A door opened and a few moments later a toilet flushed. Then Gardner started to move along the landing and down the stairs, looking at his feet as he padded down in his trainers. He rubbed his hands together, pleased with himself. He was halfway down when he seemed to sense that something wasn't quite right. He paused abruptly, the toe of his shoe about to touch the next step, when he looked down and saw me, and froze.

I stared up. Gardner's face was sun-salon brown, but the tan was fading in the hard Cotswold winter, and it went almost completely white when he realized who was staring at him from the darkness of his stairwell. His eyes became much wider, and his bottom lip turned down, revealing a row of crooked teeth. He took a step back and actually clutched his heart like an old woman in a black-and-white melodrama. I almost hoped I'd given the bastard a heart attack.

But Gardner seemed to recover quickly. His face screwed up. His cockiness instantly returned. I moved away from the stairwell with my right hand resting on the banister.

Gardner looked to the front door. He took another step forward and glanced towards the kitchen. He licked his bottom lip and turned his head towards the kitchen again. I watched, amused that Gardner had to consider the same thing twice. I reached into my coat pocket and waggled the back door key at him.

'What? What do you want?' he said. 'Give me my key. You can't just come in here like this, Downes. This is private property. It's breaking and . . .'

Gardner stared uncertainly at the rush mats by the front door, and then, suddenly resigned to my presence, walked down the stairs, pushed past me and wandered into the living room. He fell into a sagging brown sofa, picked up a can of beer from the coffee table and started to open it. Then, thinking better of it, he put it back on the table. I switched off the television and moved closer.

'All right,' Gardner said, finally looking up. 'What is it? I told you I know nothing about any of this. Why can't you people just leave me alone? I'll be on the phone to Baxter as soon as you're out the door. Or maybe I should call him now.'

'You don't know a woman called Nancy, Nancy Williams, do you?'

Gardner shook his head.

'Hurst's old housekeeper.'

'No. Never heard of her.'

'Didn't think so. Been here all night, have you?'

Gardner nodded towards the remains of a takeaway. 'Yeah. Having a quiet one.'

'You know something, Chris,' I said, 'I got it all wrong. I was wrong about you and Hurst.'

'I know,' Gardner said. 'I told you, didn't I? So I suppose you've come all this way to offer me an apology. All right, apology accepted. Now please fuck off and give me my fucking key before you go.'

I stood still for a moment, hovering over him. 'You knew him, though,' I said. 'But not as well as I thought you did.'

Although I didn't relish the prospect, I moved in until I was standing just inches away from him. Up close, I could see the wrinkles beneath his eyes and his thinning scalp. 'I've got a tape of you hanging around schoolchildren. Little kids,' I said, almost conversationally. 'What do you think of that, Gardner?'

Gardner's body twitched.

'What tape? What are you talking about?'

'Hurst had it. It was in his house. Locked up with a bunch of other stuff in a drawer.

284

Didn't know I had it, did you?'

'What?' Gardner said.

'I watched it last night,' I said, ignoring him, 'while I was cooking my dinner. Of course, I wasn't very hungry after that.'

'What tape?' he almost pleaded. 'What are you talking about?'

'It showed you hanging about an old cricket pavilion with a bunch of kids.'

When I mentioned the cricket pavilion, Gardner breathed in very sharply. There was a look of furtive panic on his face, which he immediately tried to conceal. It was very quiet in the living room, with the snow falling outside. Peaceful even.

'I'm going to bury you,' I said. 'You understand that, Christopher? I'm going to bury you with that tape. I know you've been in a lot of trouble over that kind of thing before. But it will be nothing compared to what will happen as soon as I hand over that tape to my supervisor. It's proof that you've been trying to molest a minor.'

'But what tape? I . . . For Christ's sake, I don't know what you're talking about.'

'You don't know?' I said, surprised.

'Know what? Come on.'

'Hurst was having you followed.'

'Followed?'

I nodded.

'But who? Who by?'

'Hurst hired someone to follow you.'

'Oh, Christ,' Gardner said. 'So that's how he knew.'

'Yes,' I said. 'Look, I know now that you didn't have anything to do with those two girls. I got it wrong. You're in the clear on that one. But I'm dealing with two murders in just one week and I've got you on tape hanging about outside a school. I'm not sure how far it went. But if it went as far as I think it did —'

'But nothing happened,' Gardner interrupted quickly. 'Nothing happened, I swear.'

Gardner's forehead was shiny with perspiration. He held out for a moment longer, then said, 'All right, all right. I was there. There on the hill with Hurst. I knew you'd be on to me sooner or later, but I didn't know what to do. I suppose I panicked when I heard. When I heard what had happened to him.'

'You heard Hurst was dead on the news?'

'Yeah, on the radio on the way to work. I heard some bloke had been found up there. Dead. I thought it could have been him or it might have been a walker — but there was no way of knowing. Not to begin with. I nearly shit myself when I heard it were him.' Gardner cleared his throat. 'Look, I very nearly came forward when I found out. You have to believe me about that. But then I thought, what's the point? I didn't see anything, and why get into trouble over a silly argument. And it was nothing more than that. I'm telling you that right now.'

'That's not what the people who saw you up there say.'

Gardner looked at his hands and shrugged. 'Well, I can't help that,' he said shortly.

'Let's go back a bit,' I said. 'Frank Hurst was up on Meon Hill. He was working there when you decided to go to see him. Am I right?'

'Yes. He was fixing some old fences, by the looks of it. I don't know farmer stuff. Hardly noticed I was there to begin with. Even though his dog was barking like mad. Stupid sod.' Gardner laughed.

'So his dog was already tied up when you arrived? Tied to a tree.'

'Cujo you mean? Yeah, otherwise I wouldn't have bothered.'

'And you went over there to speak to him because you were angry with him. But you didn't know about the tapes. You didn't know that he was having you followed.'

Gardner's shoulders hunched. He looked at me balefully.

287

'You must have found out somehow, though,' I said. 'Somehow you found out that he was having you looked into. That's why you went to confront him when you heard he was up on his field.'

'I got a phone call,' Gardner said quietly. 'A few months ago he called me straight out of the blue. Just as I got home from work. I didn't even know who it was to begin with. All I heard was this breathing and then this scary, creepy old man's voice on the other end. That and his bloody dog barking in the background. He started telling me that I'd better watch my step. I honestly didn't know what the hell he was talking about.'

'But he accused you of something. Must have come as quite a shock, considering you'd been so careful.'

Gardner swallowed and his voice rose. As he had done back at the station, he made a good attempt at seeming indignant. He was rather skilled at it. 'Well, none of it was true,' he said. 'I'm not like that. Like I said, it's just a lot of talk, and I was innocent the last time. And I told him so and all. Told him to mind his own fucking business. Nothing happened out there.'

'But he phoned you. That's what you're saying? Frank Hurst phoned you one night at home and he gave you a warning. He told you to stay away.'

Gardner opened his mouth as if to protest some more, but, when he could see I was grinning at him, he shut it again with a loud, wet slap. He pushed his head against the soft corded fabric of the sofa. 'He told me to . . . he told me to stay away . . .' Gardner's voice trailed off. His eyes became woeful. He didn't seem able to say it.

'He told you to stay away from kids,' I said bluntly. 'He told you to stop hanging about schoolyards.'

'Yes,' Gardner said and sighed. 'I asked him where he'd heard it. He wouldn't say. Jesus, the guy was really . . . the guy was really crazy.' Gardner laughed a little desperately. With an abrupt movement he shifted forward and then stood up.

'I don't even know how he got my number.' He fell silent and smoothed back his hair. A tuft of it sprang back up almost immediately.

'So what happened?' I said.

'I got fed up with it.'

'He phoned you more than once?'

'Yeah. Told me his name and said if he ever heard . . . if he heard I was doing anything like that with kids, he'd come looking for me. He threatened me. Said he'd break my neck. Or worse. Well, no one can talk to me like that. I did some asking around and found out where he lived, and I went round his house to tell him to leave off.' Gardner's voice had become hoarse all of a sudden.

'But you couldn't get anywhere near him.'

'No. Bloody dog comes tearing round the front as soon as I get outside the car. Got all these bars and all. Like Fort Knox it was.'

'So you could never have it out with him,' I said, almost sympathetically. 'Not in person. Until that day you heard he was up in his field.'

Gardner looked down at his knees. 'Yeah,' he said.

'And you were doing a job nearby, I suppose.'

'Over in Bampton. The owner told me. She said she'd just seen Hurst. She couldn't believe how' — Gardner's voice became high and upper-class — 'how that awful man dared to show his face. Not after what he'd done to his poor wife. She got in a big huff about it. Daft cow.'

'And so off you went?'

Gardner nodded. 'Said I had run out of paint and I went on over there.'

'In your van?'

'Yes.'

'And you had it out with him?'

'No, I *told* you. I just wanted to tell him to mind his own business. He just stood there and took it. Didn't seem to care one way or the other. Didn't even seem to be listening. He just stood there staring at me and then he went back to work. Like talking to a fucking zombie, it was, and so I walked back down the hill and went straight back to work. I was gone less than half an hour.'

'I suppose you can prove that?'

'Just ask her. She'll tell you. One of them posh new cottages in Bampton, like I said.' Gardner grinned a little, getting back his confidence again.

'But who's to say you didn't go back there,' I said. 'When Hurst was leaving the field and there was no one else about.'

The grin vanished.

'Where did you go after the job?' I said.

'Home. I went home.'

'You didn't go out? See anyone?'

'No. I was knackered.'

'What did you do?'

'Had a few beers. Watched the telly.'

'Talk to anyone?'

'I can't remember. Might have. But only on the phone.'

'And there's no one who can back that up?'

'No,' Gardner said miserably. 'There isn't.'

'And the first time you ever spoke to Hurst was when he phoned you out of the blue.'

'Yes,' Gardner said.

'And so how did he know who you were? Why you? Didn't you wonder about that?'

'My name was all over the papers, if you remember. One of your lot must have leaked my name when those two girls went missing. Those journalists made my life hell for a while. People still give me dirty looks about it. Hurst must have just found out where I lived and got my number. Had nothing better to do.'

'And you've been here all night?'

'Yes,' Gardner said.

'All right,' I said. I took out the key from my pocket and chucked it on the table. Then I crossed the living room, relieved to be heading outside and into the fresh air.

'So that's it? You believe me, then?' Gardner shouted after me. 'You believe me about Hurst?'

'Yes,' I said, and turned around. 'I do.'

'And the tape? The tape Hurst had of me.'

'Oh, that. I suppose I'll be handing over the tapes first thing tomorrow to my superintendent,' I said breezily. 'She often takes a dim view of things like that. So I imagine there'll be a full-scale investigation.'

I watched and waited. Suddenly there was a look in the corner of Gardner's eye. He licked his bottom lip. Then he bounded across the room.

'You fucking foreign bastard!' Gardner shouted. 'You think you can come in here, into my own home and . . .' And then he did exactly what I had hoped he would do all along. He threw an awkward and un-practised cross, which missed me by a mile. I punched low and hard at the base of Gardner's gut, driving the fist in hard.

Spittle flew out of Gardner's mouth. He slumped to the floor. He pawed at his stomach, looking wildly around in panic as he tried to catch his breath. I looked at him in a detached kind of way, wondering if he were going to be sick. Then, almost gently, I picked him up, led him to the sofa and sat him down. I sat next to him. I took the key from the table and put it firmly in the palm of his hand and closed his fingers around it. Then I let myself out the front door.

30

Graves watched the lights of the ambulance fade. Nancy's body had been taken away, and there was nothing else he could do here. The crime-scene manager had placed a number of evidence markers in the sludge where her body had lain, and the whole area by the garages was cordoned off with yellow police tape. They had not been able to find the murder weapon. Graves turned away from the sharp glare of the arc lights and let the forensic team take their pictures and get on with it.

He walked along the side street towards town. He glimpsed the backs of ill-kept gardens. There was a shopping trolley lying on its side and an old car seat with a few ripped black bins surrounding it. In a few minutes he had left the alley behind. The shops had closed hours ago, and the lights were more diffuse, making the core of the town leaner somehow. But there were a lot of pubs and restaurants still open on the main street, and the town was busy with Christmas drinkers huddled together, walking in the cold.

Graves knitted his hands behind his head as he walked. He'd have to get a lift back to the station, as Downes had taken the car. It didn't matter. The last hours since they had found Nancy had passed in a blur. When he had returned from his search of the train station, Downes was already on the phone to Collinson. Then things had really started to move. Graves nodded his head in approval as he walked, still impressed by the speed of the operation.

Collinson had talked first to the assistant chief constable of Gloucestershire and then the divisional commander, whose area of responsibility encompassed both Cheltenham and Tewkesbury. This message had been instantly relayed to all officers currently in the area, while a further handful of officers, who could be spared, had been dispatched immediately to the alley to cordon off the crime scene. Nearly all the police officers now on duty in the town were canvassing the pubs, cafés and restaurants using the concise description of Nancy that Downes had provided for them. But so far none of it had done any good. No one in the café near the clock remembered seeing her. So Nancy must have met up with the man somewhere else, but where was anyone's guess; neither Nancy nor anyone else had been seen entering or leaving the alley.

At the other side of the street, near an electronics shop, Graves saw two police officers making their way along. A man and a woman around the same age. They moved lithely through the small crowds on either side of the high street. The male officer disappeared inside a pub and reappeared a few moments later, while his partner continued to search outside, looking round an empty side street. Another policeman was cutting through a small group of people farther up the street.

Graves wandered towards the male and female officers, who waited for him when they saw him approach. 'Nothing, sir,' the female officer said. 'I'm afraid no one seems to have seen her.'

Graves knew deep down it was hopeless. Her killer had disappeared into the shifting crowds hours ago.

'All right,' he said. 'Keep trying and let me know the moment you hear something. All right?'

They nodded and went straight back to work. He needed to think, so he walked on, leaving the shopping centre behind and heading up the slope towards the Georgian houses at the top of the rise. It was much quieter up here. Soon the pubs and restaurants would close, the town would be completely deserted, and they would have to call it quits. He moved quickly past the grey walls of a bank. He peered through the windows of an Italian restaurant and then went in. But some constables had already paid them a visit and none of the staff had seen Nancy.

For a moment, he stood on the steps of the restaurant, thinking. It was impossible to know if the man she had been meeting had gone down that darkened alley with her, or if he had been waiting for her amongst those old garages all along. He might also have followed her. Graves put his hands in his pockets. Since he'd arrived he'd seen the results of three murders up close: Hurst; the girl under his house; and now Nancy. And he'd been here less than a week.

He tried to unravel the events of the last few days and to make some sense of them, but it all seemed to merge. Hurst's lying dead on the hill. His house standing cold and dark on the other side. The fire leaping into the dark. The girl wrapped in the dirty folds of the groundsheet. The broken lines

of her body exposed to the merciless on-
slaught of the fire. And now this.

Shotgun's face, when he had seen Nancy
lying on the ground, had been difficult to
read. Almost expressionless. But his eyes
had glimmered. Anger, perhaps, darkening
his face like a cloud. Or horror. His own
face, Graves was sure, had betrayed his
shock. He pushed the image away and
turned back towards the centre of town,
determined to make as early a start as possible the next day. Somebody must have
seen something. He rang Downes on his
mobile, but there was no reply.

31

As promised, early the next morning, I took the tapes and the files into the station and handed them over to Collinson. I marked Gardner's tape with a felt-tip pen and made sure it was on the top of the pile. Graves came with me.

I didn't begin with Nancy. Instead, I began with Gardner, and after I finished talking there was a long silence. Collinson moved forward in her chair and leant across her desk.

'But if it's not . . .' She stopped and let the sentence hang in the air. She nodded to herself several times.

'But who the hell is it?' Graves said suddenly, and then looked taken aback by his outburst. 'If it's not Elise Pennington down there and it's not Gail Foster,' he said more quietly, 'whose body have we got in the morgue?'

Graves hunched in his chair and blinked.

He looked worried. 'Are you sure you don't want me to start searching, sir? Some of the other men and I,' he said, motioning outside the glass walls of the office, 'we can make a start on it right now and try to get some kind of match. Female. A hitchhiker or a runaway maybe. Someone who never came back. I . . .'

'Thank you, Graves,' I interrupted politely, 'but it's not going to be necessary.'

'But why, sir? How do you know that there aren't more down there? We haven't finished searching yet. And how can you be sure that one of the girls isn't down there just because of the rucksack? The DNA will tell us that once Brewin's done the comparison anyway.'

I didn't reply immediately. On the other side of the wall one of the officers tried to throw a paper ball into the bin and missed. There was a dry sarcastic round of applause.

'When Hurst found out that Gardner was hanging around that school, he warned him off,' I said finally. 'He told him, and in no uncertain terms, that he'd go round there and break his neck if he ever found out that Gardner was up to his old tricks. Hurst was getting on a bit, but he was perfectly capable of doing something like that if he felt like it.

I thought that it was because of a link between the two. That Hurst was afraid they'd all be exposed. It made sense, considering he's got a dead body under his house. But, according to Gardner, the first time he came into contact with Hurst was when Hurst called him completely out of the blue and told him he'd better watch his step.'

'You believe him?' Collinson said.

'Yes,' I said. 'Actually, I do. Gardner hadn't even known he was being followed. But Hurst warned him. He phoned him up and told him to stay away from little kids or else. And to Gardner, Hurst was a total stranger. Which of course changes everything.'

I looked at Collinson and then at Graves. 'It means that Hurst wasn't acting to protect his own interests. He was genuinely concerned about the well-being of those children. He wanted to protect them.'

'But,' Graves almost cried out, unable to contain himself, 'that doesn't make any sense at all. I'm sorry, but why would he care about a bunch of kids? The man was a bloody paedophile. He's got a dead schoolgirl buried under his house, for God's sake.'

'There was never any schoolgirl,' I said. 'I was wrong.'

'What?'

I glanced across at Graves. Graves looked shocked and indignant, as if I had just pulled a trick on him to make him look stupid. Graves looked at Collinson, embarrassed at his outburst.

'The private detective whom Hurst had hired was given instructions,' I said. 'Hurst didn't just want these men monitored. He was after something more specific than that. He wanted to know if there were any places where they kept going back to. Out-of-the-way spots. Spots out in the country or isolated buildings, that kind of thing. He called it a "secret place", a place that only these men knew about. Bray told me that he thought it all sounded a bit silly. Childish even. But Hurst was very serious about it.'

'So what was he looking for?' Collinson said.

'A burial ground,' I said. 'He was looking for a place where Elise and Gail may have been buried, or where they might have been taken and then disposed of.

'If one of these men kept returning to a specific place, it's possible that's where they had taken the girls after they'd been abducted. But it wasn't those two girls Hurst was really concerned about. What he really wanted to know was what had happened to his daughter. Rebecca.'

'But he knew perfectly well what happened to her. She left home,' Graves said.

'But why hasn't she come forward?' I said. 'It's been on the news and in all the papers. She must know by now. So where is she? None of the villagers seem to have seen her, have they?'

'No,' Graves said. 'Well, no one ever mentioned seeing her again. And anyway that doesn't necessarily mean she hasn't been back. She could have been back loads of times and just gone to the house and not bothered with the village.'

'No, she didn't come back,' I said. 'Bray would have told me if she'd come back. Because that's what Hurst hired him for in the first place. He hired him to find his daughter. But what do we really know about her?'

I waited. Neither answered, but I had a feeling Collinson had a pretty good idea. So I said, 'All we really know is that Hurst came back one day and she was gone. Bags packed. Her room empty. She went . . .' I paused, trying to remember the unusual expression Bray had used, 'she went walkabout. That's what the villagers are saying. One summer she just took off with all her things, and she never came back.'

'Yes,' Graves said. 'And?'

'And how old was she when she left?'

'Seventeen or eighteen.'

'So more than three years ago,' I said. 'And around four years after the girls went missing.'

'About that, yes,' Graves said.

'And no one has seen her since. Absolutely no one. In all that time. No sign of her. Nothing. Think about what was in the rucksack, Graves. You saw what was in it. Make-up. A young woman's clothes. Cigarettes. Chewing gum. A pamphlet in there, if I remember. Too old to see what it was after all these years, of course. A timetable? A train timetable? What if,' I said, 'what if she never left at all? What if she never got the chance?'

Inside the room there was another short silence. Graves looked like he was about to say something, then hesitated. He surveyed the room beyond the glass.

I sat back in the chair, and my left hand hovered above my chest for a moment before resting on the plastic arm of the chair. 'This is how I think it went,' I said. 'Hurst comes back from work one day and Rebecca's gone. Probably he goes tearing off in that Land Rover of his to try to stop her. Maybe gets to the train station. But of course it's too late. She's gone. If she was planning on leaving, she would have given herself a good head start. And it would have been a day when the housekeeper wasn't there either. So he comes back. And of course her room's empty. She's packed up her things, and she's done exactly what she had been threatening to do. Maybe she left him a note.

'Now there's nothing particularly out of the ordinary about that. Rebecca was old enough to leave and to take care of herself, and it happens all the time. Especially in villages like Quinton. Kids get bored out of their minds. You know how it is. Now he was worried about her of course,' I said. 'What parent wouldn't be? But then he gets something in the post. A postcard. From London. It's from Rebecca. And she says she'll be in touch as soon as she's settled. And every now and again he'd get another one. Not very often, but it's enough to put his mind at ease. To begin with anyway. And not a letter. A postcard. She wasn't really the type to take the time to write a whole letter. The girl was too selfish, by the sound of it, so it fits in with her personality as well.'

'And a postcard is easier to fake,' Graves said, staring at me, 'isn't it?'

I nodded. 'Now Nancy told me that after

305

a while Hurst wouldn't even read them any more. And Nancy told me that one day he went up to London to see Rebecca and she never showed up. And when he gets home her room and some parts of the house have been turned upside down.

'He might have told himself that Rebecca had got him to come to London so she could come back to find something in her room. Something that she had forgotten or needed. Or maybe she was after some cash in the house. But I think deep down he must have known. Known that something was very wrong and had been wrong for a very long time.'

Both Graves and Collinson were watching me almost warily. I took a deep breath and ran my hand along the back of my neck.

'So what does he do?' I continued after a short pause. 'He hires Bray to go looking for her. Now, Bray told me that if she'd been in London he would have found her. But there's no sign of her. No sign of her ever having arrived in London at all. So now her old man really must know that something isn't right.'

'Oh, I don't know, sir,' Graves said in a more careful tone of voice than before. 'It seems like a bit of a leap. Really, there's no way of knowing for sure that Rebecca's still not alive somewhere. She could have changed her name. Might have got married since then. I mean Bray might have only done a half-assed job of it. She could easily have moved abroad. And if Hurst really did have something to do with those two girls, the same kind of thing might have been happening at home. So why *would* she come back? There's literally nothing here for her to come back to now.'

'All right,' I said. 'But let's assume Bray was right. Right or wrong, Hurst seems to have believed him. So what does Hurst really know about what happened to his daughter? All he knows for sure is that she's disappeared,' I said and looked across the desk at Collinson. 'And she's not the first girl to disappear from Quinton.'

Graves shifted forward in his seat. 'So he begins looking at the original cases,' he said quietly.

'Yes. Maybe he does some digging on his own and discovers that there were three men. Three men that we'd looked at really closely. And he gets them looked into too. Maybe he can find something . . . something that we missed. Of course, he doesn't come to me after what I put him through.' I shrugged. 'But he has them looked into all the same.' I fell silent and tapped my fingers twice on the chair.

'Well, even if you're right,' Graves said, 'and it is her down there, Hurst could still be guilty. Maybe Hurst caught her. Walked in as she was on the way out the door and went ballistic. Killed her and buried her with all her stuff.'

'I don't think so,' I said. 'Why hire a detective agency to try to find her if he knew she was already dead? And you saw her room, Graves. Looked like a shrine. He was waiting. He was waiting for her to come back.'

'Covering his tracks?' Graves suggested.

'No,' I said more firmly this time. 'He was obviously worried about her, though, and wanted her back. But I think after a while . . . he must have realized that she was never coming home.'

Graves looked as if he were about to object when Collinson intervened. 'Because she was there the whole time. The whole time he was looking for her she was under his feet, and he didn't even know it. That's what you think now?'

'Yes,' I said.

Collinson swivelled on her chair so that she was peering through the walls of her office. 'If it's true, that means whoever killed her did it just at the point when Rebecca was leaving,' Collinson said thoughtfully.

'Killed her when she was packing up and getting ready to go. She couldn't be allowed to leave the village. She might have seen something when she was younger. Maybe she saw something but hadn't realized its importance. Too young perhaps.'

'Maybe,' I said. 'And I think that's why her old man was killed too. Whoever killed Hurst must have known that he was getting close. Close to the truth of what happened to those two little girls and his daughter.'

She gave me a long, hard look. 'So it means we're still looking for a local,' she said finally. 'Only a local would have known Hurst was up there on that hill.'

I nodded.

'And Nancy?'

I looked at Graves.

'Nothing much,' he said. 'We might have had a sighting of her in a café. A greasy spoon on the edge of town. But we're not sure yet. That came through this morning. It was closed by the time we started asking around last night. If it was her, she seemed to be waiting for someone. But whoever it was didn't show up. So she paid and left. There're lots of trains to London. Around one an hour to Paddington. None direct to Brighton. But she could have changed easily enough once she was in London. She just decided to take the shortcut to the station.'

Collinson nodded. 'So she knew something,' she said.

'Yes,' I said. 'That's why she returned home. She must have seen something when she was working in that house. Something she never told anyone about, and it's something to do with Hurst's daughter, because she mentioned Rebecca on the phone to the man she was meeting. And when she found out Hurst was dead, she must have realized that what she had seen was important. And she came back here and contacted this man.'

'And her phone, Graves?'

'We're checking that now.'

'So I suppose you want to change direction on this thing,' Collinson said, studying my face keenly. 'You think that if we can find out what happened to Rebecca, we'll find out what happened to those girls. And it all ties in with Hurst.'

'Yes,' I said. 'But there's nothing certain. There's still no word from forensics in Oxford about the age of the victim, and so we can't completely rule out that it's not Gail or Elise. Not yet anyway. I mean I could be wrong. There still could be another body down there for all we know. But I don't think we're going to have to wait long.

Brewin should have his DNA results later on today. So we'll know for sure one way or another if the body we found down there was Elise's or Gail's.'

In the small glass office there was a sudden air of expectancy. The idea that it could be Rebecca seemed to hover uncertainly in the air. There was another silence while I, knowing that I needed Collinson's approval, waited anxiously for her to make up her mind.

She stared across the desk at me. 'Downes, I sincerely wish you'd come to this conclusion before the bloody papers got wind of it,' she said coldly. 'Because we're going to have to tell the poor girls' parents.' She sighed and rubbed her forehead, glaring at me with a hard look in her eye. 'Now I'm going to have to . . .' It took her a few moments to put her anger to one side. 'All right,' she said and picked up a pencil. 'Well, we hardly know a thing about this girl . . . Rebecca,' she said. 'Let's assume you're right, Downes. And if you are, of course it changes the whole direction of everything. So the first thing we'll need is another DNA sample to make sure. Not Frank Hurst's. His funeral was days ago, wasn't it?'

'His brother,' Graves suggested. 'We can get a sample from his brother and see if that matches.'

I nodded. 'The lab in Oxford might come up with something in the meantime. But I think we'll probably have to wait for the results we get from Hurst's brother to see if they match the body. And if they match, it's Rebecca.'

'So what do you propose we do?' Collinson said.

'We need to find out as much as we can about her as quickly as possible,' I said. 'All I know is that Hurst sent her off to some boarding school somewhere. His brother will probably know which one. You can get the address for me when you get that sample, Graves. But get on the phone to the forensics lab in Oxford first or get Brewin to do it. Find out if they've got anything on the age of the body. After you've talked to them, I need you to go into the village and ask questions about Rebecca. Take Irwin and Douglas with you. And canvas the whole place. Ask about close friends. Boyfriends. Any talk at all. We need to try to get a good picture of the type of person she was.'

'So the postcards,' Graves said. 'Who was sending the postcards?'

'Her killer,' I said and stood up.

■ ■ ■ ■

PART THREE

■ ■ ■ ■

32

Graves paid a quick visit to Simon Hurst and then delivered the DNA sample to Brewin. Next he took Douglas and Irwin with him to knock on doors in Quinton.

By 11.00 he found himself walking along the green. Although they had no constables at their disposal, they were interested only in villagers who had been around when Rebecca was still living there, so there were relatively few people to interview. Douglas took the small lanes and the cul-de-sacs on the north of the village; Irwin took those on the south; both moved inwards while Graves worked outwards from the centre.

Graves asked his questions and noted down the answers when there were any. When he finished with the houses, he tried the shops. At 2.00 they met in the centre and went for lunch in the pub near the green. They talked about Rebecca. There wasn't much.

When the food came, they put their notes away and started eating. Hoping to get Irwin off guard, Graves put his sandwich down on to his plate and said as lightly as he could manage, 'You said he was famous. Shotgun, I mean. You remember, the other day. Back in the canteen. You said he was famous up in London. I was wondering what you meant.'

Irwin shrugged. 'I might have been exaggerating a little bit.'

Graves said, 'Well, is it true? Drayton said he nearly killed someone. Did you guys ever hear anything like that?'

Douglas nodded. 'I heard something. While back, that was. But that's all.'

'Only that it happened in London?'

'Yes. Think so.'

'You really want to know, don't you?' Douglas laughed. 'Driving you mad. Not knowing.'

Graves shrugged. 'Wouldn't you want to know if you were working with him every day? I just can't figure him out at all. I tried him on Google. There's plenty of stuff about his work around here, but there's nothing about him in London.'

'Ed knows,' Douglas said. 'Don't you, Ed?'

'Thanks,' Irwin said. 'Really. Thanks a lot. If Shotgun finds out I've been talking about

316

him behind his back, I'll be in the shit.'

'So there is something,' Graves said. 'I knew it.' Graves took a bite out of his sandwich and sat back so that the chair rocked on its back legs.

Irwin looked worried. 'What did Drayton tell you?'

'That he nearly killed someone and that he won't ever get in the back seat of a car. Hence the nickname. Is that true?'

'That's what they say,' Douglas said.

'Come on,' Graves said. 'I won't tell him.'

'Yes, come on, Ed.' Douglas seemed to be enjoying himself.

'Well, I heard something a while back.'

'Who was it anyway?' said Graves. 'One of the old boys at the station?'

Irwin eyed him warily over his plate. 'No. Someone else. He's retired now, I imagine. Maybe you should know. So you know what you might be up against.'

'Up against?' Graves said, surprised.

'All right, throw in a curry in town tonight and I'll think about it. But if I do tell you — you didn't hear it from me, all right?'

'All right,' Graves said. 'Done.'

They finished their lunch and left the pub.

'We don't have nearly enough,' Graves said, and slipped his notebook back into his pocket.

'We could try some of those old cottages,' Douglas said. 'The ones we saw coming in. And there're old farmhouses near Hurst's house. And the secondary school. Could try the shops again maybe.'

Graves nodded. 'All right,' he said.

They stood there a little longer before heading back to the car. The church stood against the grey sky on the top of the rise overlooking the pond. The village was very quiet. Graves waited while the other two automatically reached for cigarettes. Far above the yellowish roofs of the houses, a ragged blackbird flew and was buffeted by the wind and then faded finally out of sight.

33

Rebecca Hurst's old boarding school was over in Banbury. It didn't take me long to find it. Her old housemistress, Ms Walker, told me what little she knew, while the headmaster, a toadyish-looking man, hovered and huffed around impatiently, then ushered me without a word straight outside and off the premises. There wasn't much. A strikingly pretty girl who kept to herself before they had to exclude her. No boyfriends as far as they were aware and just one friend. A girl called Alice Hunt.

There was one other thing. A psychologist called Victor Lang used to come to see her at school on Frank's orders. They didn't know much about it, but they gave me his phone number and they had an address for Alice Hunt's parents on file as well. I would need a court order to talk to Lang about Rebecca, so I asked Collinson if we could get one rushed through; she thought it would be possible if we outlined our suspicions that Rebecca could well be dead and linked her death to the disappearance of Gail and Elise. Then, having got Hunt's new address from her parents, I called her. She said that I could come over and see her.

She was in her third year at Oxford studying chemistry, and was living in Cowley in a modern-looking building that was attached to the far end of the dorm rooms for the other students. Her study window looked out on to some frozen and sullen-looking hockey fields.

She was plump, and pretty. Her hair was tied back severely in a ponytail held in place with a blue ribbon. As I took off my coat, I glanced quickly around her study. But the study was, like its owner, cold and detached and gave no sign of a personal life at all.

'So you think that Rebecca might have run away? After she left school?'

'We don't really know,' I said. 'We're just trying to find out where she is. She hasn't shown up yet and we need to speak to her. You know what's happened? To her father?'

She nodded. 'It was in the papers.'

'And you've not heard anything from her?'

'No. Not for years now. Not since school.'

'You were friends, right?'

'Well, yes, kind of. But we weren't friends

for long. She wasn't at the school for that long and when she left I never heard from her again.'

'So how close were you?'

'Well, we were friends for a while. But not really close friends.'

'What about anyone else from school? Was there someone else she might have confided in? Or maybe been in touch with?'

'I can't think of anyone at all. She was a very quiet girl, and she didn't really have friends apart from me.'

'But why you?'

'I suppose I felt sorry for her.'

'Sorry for her?'

'It's a bit hard to explain. The thing is, she came to the school relatively late. When she was fifteen or sixteen, I think it must have been. The other girls kind of ganged up on her. Well, some of the more popular girls did, and the others just ignored her.'

'But why?'

'Most of the girls were already pally by the time Rebecca arrived. We'd all formed our little groups and cliques, and we'd been living there a good while together. Since we were twelve or thirteen, most of us. Rebecca came halfway through term.'

'But is it usually such a big deal — starting late at the school?' I asked, quite shocked.

'Well,' she said thoughtfully, 'the school kind of advertises itself as a friendly place to the parents. But it's not really like that at all, once you're in the thick of things. You have to try your best to settle in. None of the girls really tried to make Rebecca feel welcome.'

'So she was bullied?'

'Yes, a little bit. Nothing physical. But, yes, teased. Teased quite a lot.'

'And how did she take it?'

'She tried to make friends and then I think she just gave up. It was a bit pathetic. After that she never seemed to take to anyone or anything at all apart from me, really, and I think that's because I was the only one who would give her the time of day. Her house-mistress asked me to try to take her under my wing, which, of course, I did. But she simply preferred her own company, and I think she kept everything to herself. She liked writing in her diary, going for walks round the grounds. Reading. That sort of thing.'

'She kept a diary?' I said quickly. 'We didn't find a diary with her things.'

'Yes, she was very attached to it. After a while she just seemed to fade into the background. We got used to her being there.

I did try to be nice. Tried to make an effort with her.'

'And she responded to that?'

'Yes, and she could be sweet when you got to know her. But I was a little surprised when she invited me over during the holidays. I mean, we weren't close friends, as I said.'

'She invited you over?'

'Just the once. For a weekend in the summer holidays. That was it.'

'Did you go?'

'Yes. It was just a weekend.'

'And what did you make of it? The set-up, I mean, in her house.'

'Well, her father simply adored her. And she was like a different person back home. The house was really beautiful. And she was much more confident. More herself. But she'd been through a lot, you know. Her stepmother died over there. There was an accident.'

'She told you about that, did she?'

'Yes.'

'And her father. Frank Hurst. What did you make of him?'

'He adored her, like I say. He got their housekeeper to cook us big meals. Took us out for the day to some big old stately home. He seemed very happy to have her back home. Spoilt her a little bit, I think.'

'And there was a doctor who came to see her every now and again at the school. Do you know anything about that?'

'We all knew she saw someone from time to time. Someone from out of school. Her father arranged it — I think. But she never talked about it. It was always after dinner, while everyone else was at prep.'

'He was a psychologist. Did you know that?'

'No,' she said.

I paused. 'Look, I hate to have to say this, but was there anything . . . I mean, did you sense anything wrong with their relationship? Her and her father. Something not quite right when you were there?'

'Sexual you mean,' Alice Hunt said with surprising directness. 'No. Nothing at all. It all seemed perfectly normal.'

'All right, then. But what about any local boys? Any boys in her village she might have talked about? Or any boys near the school she might have mentioned?'

'No, and there was nothing at the school either. We were strongly discouraged from going into town and fraternizing with the locals — especially boys. Not that that stopped most of the girls from doing it whenever they got the chance. But to be honest,' she said, 'I personally didn't see anything of that sort. Rebecca could have taken her pick if she'd wanted. She was extremely pretty. She just didn't seem all that interested.'

'So no one? She never mentioned any boys. She never talked about anyone. Anyone she might have met?'

'No. Not that I can remember.'

'All right. And she didn't last long at the school? She was expelled, right?'

'Academically speaking she was very bright indeed. I got the impression that the teachers thought she'd sail through her A levels.'

'But she was gone before then. That's what her housemistress said. They expelled her.'

'I don't think they had much choice.' She smiled. She had surprisingly white teeth. 'It was unexpected. Some money disappeared. It went missing from the bursar's office. You know about that?'

'Yes, I know. Her housemistress didn't like talking about it much.'

'Rebecca refused to admit it. One of the other housemistresses came forward and said that they'd seen Rebecca sneaking out of the dorm room the night the money went missing.'

'And they informed the police straightaway?'

'No. They decided that it would be better to keep it all in house, I think. And I don't think they wanted the publicity. But Rebecca refused point blank to hand over the money.'

'How much money?'

'Almost eight hundred pounds. That's what I heard.'

For a moment I stared out of the window, thinking. 'She was already planning on leaving,' I said quietly.

'What?' Alice Hunt said.

'It was so she could leave,' I said. 'She took the money because she was already planning on leaving. And it got her expelled too. It was her going-away money.'

She didn't say anything.

'Just to be completely sure,' I said. 'Are you positive she never mentioned anyone? Someone she could have been planning on running away with? A man maybe? Or someone your age? Someone from her village.'

'No,' she said. 'I'm sure of it.'

I phoned Graves from the car.

'Looks like you're right, sir,' Graves said. 'The samples Brewin compared with Gail's and Elise's parents. They don't match. He's just got the results. He's going to compare Simon Hurst's DNA with the samples he collected from the body under the house right now, but it will be a few more days before we get the results on that. But I've been talking to the lab in Oxford. They'll never be able to confirm that it's Rebecca, because so little was left of the body. But it's their opinion that the body was older. Older than we thought by at least five years. So, whoever it was, they were around seventeen to twenty-five and female. That's their best estimate.'

'So older than we first thought?'

'Yes.'

'So it could be her? It really could be Rebecca?'

'Looks like it.'

'And how long has she been down there, if it is her?'

'They still don't know, sir. But there's one thing. We might have got lucky. We started asking around some of the old cottages outside the village. A couple remembered Rebecca. Used to know the family quite well. Remember you said that her step-mother, Sarah, was having an affair and Frank Hurst got wind of it?'

'Yes.'

'Well,' Graves said, 'do you know how he found out about it?'

'No,' I said, interested.

'Rebecca,' Graves said. 'Apparently, Rebecca knew about it all along. She'd seen them together or she'd become suspicious. The couple were extremely discreet and nobody else knew about it.'

'That's good stuff,' I said. 'So Rebecca was the one who told. She must have been fairly young.'

'Fifteen or sixteen,' Graves said.

'Do we know who this fellow was?' I said, trying to remember. 'It was a local, I think. A builder or something.'

'Yes, we got a name for him,' said Graves, pleased. 'A fella called Brad Hooper. He's on a job over in Woodstock. Hurst gave him a good kicking when he found out about the affair, like you said. Some of the locals are still talking about it even now. Happened in a pub in a nearby village. Hooper had to be taken to hospital.'

'Yes, I remember,' I said. 'Hurst got the pool done up for Sarah after they were married, and had some other things fixed, and Hooper was in the house for a while working. That's how they met. He was a stone mason back then. Big old thing, it was. The pool, I mean. Hurst let the house go after his first wife passed away. Not sure how serious it all was, though. More of a fling.'

I stared out of the car window. 'All right. Leave Irwin and Douglas in the village. Hooper can be quite tricky, so push him if you have to. It won't take you long to get to Woodstock and then as soon as you've talked to him call me back.'

34

The court order from Cheltenham Magistrates' Court came through just after 5.00. I picked it up from the station and drove straight to Dr Lang's house. He lived in one of the many smaller villages tucked away deep in the Cotswold hills. His cottage was set off from the road at the back of a long straight front garden, and his was the last house before the road curved and dipped farther into the snow-covered fields. I left my car in the driveway, behind a very old Volvo estate, and rang the bell.

The door opened after what seemed like ages, and a big brown dog appeared from nowhere and bounded outside. It barked and ran around in circles and then, losing interest, it raced off and started furiously digging a hole in the snow.

'Bloody dog,' Dr Lang said without much enthusiasm. He looked over my shoulder at the dog with a kind of resigned despair, while the dog looked quizzically at him and then went back to digging with renewed vigour.

'Jeeeesus,' Dr Lang said, drawing the word out. 'You'd think it was doing it on purpose.'

Lang was in his mid-fifties, shabby and overweight. He was wearing an old grey cardigan and faded jeans. But, while his grey hair was thinning, there was a hard evenness of features beneath the flesh. He was holding a pair of smeared black spectacles in his right hand, and he looked ever so slightly dazed and sleepy, as if I had just woken him from a nap.

Lang ushered me inside and shut the door, and I followed him past the kitchen and into his study, which was set away in a far corner of the house and looked out on to a small wild patch of garden at the side.

'Don't mind all those books. Take a seat,' he said and yawned.

I weaved my way through the piles of books on the floor, removed a few magazines from a chair and sat down, while Lang sat behind his desk.

I showed him the court order. He read it carefully and handed it back.

'I thought Rebecca was in London.'

I explained.

'So you think it's her. You think she's

been . . . dead all these years?' he said after I had finished.

'No,' I said. 'Not for sure. All we think is that it might be her. There's been no sign of her for some time. That's all we know for now. We're just trying to find out where she might be or get an idea of what she's like. We need to talk to her or at least find her, and we need to know more about her.'

Lang still looked shocked. He swivelled his chair around and stared out of the window. I could hear the dog scratching and pawing at the front door. Lang ignored it. Still staring outside, he said softly, 'You'll have to forgive me. But I did know her for quite a while, if it is her you've found out there. And it was someone at her school, then, who gave you this address?'

'Yes,' I said. 'You went to see Rebecca at the school, they tell me. Hurst's orders.'

Lang nodded and placed his glasses neatly near a picture frame on the desk. He rubbed his eyes.

'Yes. But I'd started to see her before she was sent to school. Frank asked me to continue after she started there.'

'But what happened?'

'She'd had a bit of a scare.' Lang smiled grimly. 'That's how Frank described it. A bit of a scare,' he repeated. 'That was classic Frank, by the way.'

'So you knew him? You two were friends?'

Lang paused while he considered the question. 'Not really. We got on well enough, I suppose, and we got to know each other pretty well later. We used to play county cricket together back in the day, and we had a good run of it. But we hadn't seen each other for years, and to be honest when he did call it took me a while to remember who he was. He needed some help with Rebecca.'

'What kind of help?'

'I'm a psychologist. Though back then I didn't really advertise it all that much. Kind of viewed with suspicion round here, or was then. Just told everyone I was a medical consultant. Things haven't really picked up all that much.' Lang gestured sheepishly at his office. 'He wanted me to go over straightaway. So off I went to that big house in Quinton. First time I'd ever been there. He said she'd been playing up a bit. He wouldn't say much else.'

'Something was wrong with her?'

Lang nodded. 'Nothing major. But she needed help. When I got there, Frank told me that Rebecca had been having trouble sleeping at night. She'd been having bad dreams. And when she woke up she couldn't remember what they were about. She was keeping them both up at night. Him and Sarah. His new wife.'

'And how old would she have been then? Just a girl, wasn't she?'

'Fourteen, I think. Maybe fifteen.'

'They'd always been pretty close,' I said. 'That's what I heard. He seems to have spoilt her a bit.'

'Oh, he did. Especially after her mother died. Rebecca was very young when she died. Cancer.'

'How old?'

'Around five.'

'And how did she get on with her new stepmother? Did she take to her when he remarried?'

'They got on very well. But she could act out when she felt like it. But that wasn't the problem. It was something else, and actually it was Nancy, the housekeeper, who told me what it was.'

'Nancy told you?' I said.

'Yes. Well, she pointed me in the right direction anyway. Soon after I started to see Rebecca . . . oh, I don't know, around six months later . . . Nancy spotted Rebecca's bike in the village, out on the green. Rebecca hadn't really been making all that much progress, to be perfectly honest. She was still having these bad dreams and she was very unwilling to talk to me about them. But when Nancy went to the pond she saw Rebecca. Somehow she'd managed to get through the fence they'd put round it. She was just staring at the pond. And that's when Frank told me all about it. About Rebecca's accident. He thought it was irrelevant. He thought she'd put it behind her.'

'What exactly happened?'

'She very nearly drowned,' Lang said. 'One day, just after school broke up for Christmas, it started snowing. And it was even colder then than it is now. So three of them — her and her two friends — had the great idea of going ice skating on the village pond in Quinton, near that awful pub they have over there. They were really young — only twelve or thirteen, I think, so I suppose they didn't know any better. It was just a silly game. They waited till dark, and sneaked out when their parents were asleep. They met on the village green.

'Afterwards, she said she had told them not to. That she had changed her mind. That's why she didn't go out too far — it looked dangerous. But they just kept on daring her, and as soon as she stepped on the ice she felt it shift beneath her feet. Then the whole thing just cracked. The boys drowned. She went in too.'

'They were brothers, weren't they?' I said.

'Yes,' Lang said. 'She said she could see them both down there . . . You know, struggling. She wouldn't say anything else about it, though.'

My eyes strayed momentarily outside. It was already getting dark and the drive back to the station was going to be a long one in the snow.

'So what you're saying is that the memory had come back to . . . to haunt her?' I said.

Lang grimaced at the expression. 'Well, I suppose you could say that. It'll do for now anyway. But what really happened was that the trauma had finally begun to manifest itself. The experience had been lying dormant, because when the traumatic event occurred she had been too young to fully take on board what she'd seen out there.'

'So the nightmares were all part of it?'

'Yes. And when she woke up she could never really remember what the dreams were about.'

Someone had let the dog in. From outside the study door the dog let out a low whimper. 'Bloody dog,' Lang said again with a deep sigh.

'She was grieving too, I suppose,' I said. 'They were her best friends after all.'

Lang nodded. 'And so I treated her.'

'At her home?'

'Yes, and then later at the school.'

'But it didn't seem to be working,' I said. 'It seems like she was still a handful at school. Got expelled in the end. Stole some money.'

'Yes, and I never saw her again. She refused to see me, and Frank blamed me. It had been my idea to send her to the school. Away from the village.'

'She kept a diary,' I said. 'Spent a lot of time writing in it; that's what one of her friends told me. We didn't find it. Any idea where it could be?'

'That was my idea,' Lang said.

'She seemed quite attached to it.'

Lang shrugged. The phone rang from deep inside the house, and a female voice answered it. Lang looked furtively at his watch.

'This won't take much longer,' I said. 'But do you know of anyone? Someone she might have gone to meet? Or might have planned to run away with to London? A boyfriend or a man in the village? She was a very pretty girl, that's what I'm hearing. We know she wanted to leave home. She'd talked about it openly.'

'I imagine she was going to go alone. But

she never mentioned it to me. And there were no boyfriends, or at least none that she ever told me about. It was Frank who phoned and told me she'd finally gone. Wanted to know if I had some idea of her whereabouts, but I hadn't the faintest. He told me that she'd packed all her stuff and taken off.'

'And I don't suppose you know why she wanted to go? I mean, the pond and how it affected her,' I said as tactfully as I could manage, 'well . . . it's helpful to a degree. It gives me a sense of who she was. But I'm really after something much more concrete than that. After all, she must have confided in you. Did you ever get the impression that there might have been something else? Something other than her accident by the pond that might have been giving her these nightmares? Were there any signs that she had been in contact with an older man when she was younger? That an older man had befriended her? That someone perhaps had got to . . . got to her sexually at an early age?'

'Oh, no,' Lang said quickly. 'I didn't see anything like that. There was nothing like that at all. I would have known,' Lang said.

'All right,' I said. 'And nothing. Nothing like that happening at home?'

'Oh, no, definitely not,' Lang said. 'And Frank was absolutely devastated when she left.'

35

Graves sat gazing at the chubby, sullen-looking man standing beneath the scaffolding. Brad Hooper had been described to him by the owner of the building company in less than glowing terms on the telephone. He had a puffy face and beady eyes. There was a sly watchfulness to him. A drinker's face, Graves thought. Hooper hawked and spat loudly into the bushes. He must have let himself go since his affair with Sarah Hurst, Graves thought, because Sarah Hurst had been a looker. Hooper was out of shape and seemed incredibly bored. Graves stepped out of the car and stared across the tree-lined road. Apart from the sounds of the workmen the street was very quiet. Hooper wiped his hands on his shirt and looked at Graves as he crossed the road. He did not seem nervous or afraid.

'I suppose you've been expecting me,' Graves said.

Hooper stared at him boldly. 'Yes,' he said. 'I heard someone was looking for me.'

'Anywhere we can talk?'

'We can talk right here if you like,' Hooper said, motioning to the low wall that surrounded the property. 'If you go any further in, you'll have to wear a silly hat just like this one and we ain't got any spare.'

Hooper paused and stared upwards at the wooden walkways at the top. 'It's about Frank Hurst, isn't it?' he said.

'So you know what happened?'

'I heard.' Hooper shrugged. 'Stabbed, I think. Someone said he'd been stabbed.'

'Actually, someone drove a pitchfork into his throat,' Graves said. 'While he was working in one of his fields. Where were you Monday afternoon?'

'Why?'

'Monday afternoon,' Graves said. 'Where were you?'

'What time?'

'From 4.00 until late.'

'I was here. We all finished up here at around 5.00 and then I went home. One of the boys dropped me off.'

'And after that?'

'I stayed at home.'

'You married, Brad?' Graves asked.

He grinned. 'No,' he said. 'I'm not

married.'

'Shacked up with anyone?'

'No.'

'So after 6.00 you've got no one who can say where you were. Is that what you're saying?'

'I think I might have gone to the pub. What day did you say it was again?'

'Monday.'

'I can't remember. Though I probably went to the pub.'

'When's the last time you saw him?' Graves said.

'Frank Hurst?'

'Yes.'

'Years ago,' Hooper said. 'I hadn't seen him in years.'

'Where?'

'In a pub.'

'What pub?'

'The Horse and Jockey.'

'That's where Hurst assaulted you, isn't it?'

'That's right.'

'You never pressed charges.'

'He had a good reason.'

'So no hard feelings then,' Graves said a little sarcastically. 'The locals still remember it even now. They say they had to carry you off in an ambulance. Blood everywhere.

Your blood, Brad. Not Frank Hurst's.'

Hooper smiled ruefully. He reached into his pocket, pulled out a pouch of tobacco and papers and started to roll a cigarette. 'Assault,' Hooper said thoughtfully. 'You're right. That's exactly what it was. I suppose I should have pressed charges. You think I could have got some money out of him for it?'

'Probably. Or put him in jail for a while. So what happened?'

'He beat the shit out of me,' Hooper said with remarkable good nature. 'No one knew what it was all about to begin with.'

'He found you in there drinking?'

'I didn't know he knew who I was. There was just this big bloody awful silence. The place was packed, and all of a sudden there he is. Big guy. Well, not big. But tough. He walked straight up to me. I thought it was something about the job we'd done over at his house to begin with. Then bam. There was no warning,' Hooper said in an offhand way. 'Wham, right in the face. Broke my fucking nose straight off the bat. And the next thing I knew I was tits up on the floor. He let me get up, and I thought he were going to call it quits. But then the bastard had another pop at me, and the next thing I knew I was flat on my arse again. They had to drag him off me in the end. Someone had called the coppers by then. Lot of fucking good they were.'

'Sounds like he gave you a good pasting,' Graves said happily.

'Doctors in A & E said I nearly lost an eye. I was fucking bleeding everywhere. Hurst never gave me a chance.'

'Seems to me he gave you lots of chances,' Graves said.

'It was like something out of a fucking film,' Hooper said as if he hadn't heard him. 'Told me I had to leave. He said that if he ever saw me again he'd kill me.'

'And what did you think about that?' Graves said.

'I believed him,' Hooper said, looking straight at Graves.

'But did you see him after that?' Graves asked. 'You never ran into him again?'

Hooper nodded. 'Once was enough, thanks very much.'

'And his wife. You stayed well clear of her too?'

Hooper was silent for a moment.

'You never saw her again?' Graves said.

Hooper shifted a little on his feet. He seemed undecided about something, and he glanced back towards the building site as if he were suddenly eager to get back to work.

'If there's something you're not telling me, now's the time to give it up,' Graves said. 'Frank Hurst's dead and his daughter too. She's been buried down there beneath his house for years maybe. And you've got motive for both of them and maybe no alibi.'

'His daughter?' Hooper said quickly. 'But she was just a kid. What the hell would I have against a little kid like that? And I told you I never saw Frank Hurst again. Not after that time in the pub.'

'Who told?' Graves said, ignoring him. 'Who told Frank Hurst that you were having an affair with his wife?'

Hooper shrugged and pouted sulkily. 'One of the locals I suppose.'

'So you weren't all that discreet,' Graves said. 'You sure you didn't tell any of your mates about the affair? Boast about it.'

'No. Why would I? I'd have got sacked if the foreman found out I was having it off with one of the client's wives, and I'm not like those other blokes. I don't go round showing off about things like that. And anyway, it was just a few times. Bit of fun, that's all it was. We both knew that.'

'She was the one who tipped him off,' Graves said. 'It was his daughter, Rebecca. Don't tell me you never knew that.'

'No,' Hooper murmured. 'I thought it

345

must have been one of the locals. Someone with a grudge.'

'But who? Who would have it in for a nice fella like you? Another angry husband? I reckon you knew,' Graves said, moving in much closer. 'You knew it was her all along. Or maybe you found out later. She was the only one who could have known, because you were both so discreet. You blamed her for the beating. Her old man gave you a hiding in a room full of people. And,' he added, 'they were all your mates. And maybe you'd done it before, Hooper. Maybe you'd made somebody vanish before. Maybe your taste extends to little kids.'

Graves paused. Hooper looked terrified.

'So I think that you waited and one day,' Graves said, 'you decided to pay her a visit when you knew her dad would be out. Maybe you'd had a bit to drink. Things might have got out of hand. You knew the house because you'd worked there, and when it was all over you buried her.'

Hooper was shaking his head. He had paled.

'And then much later maybe you heard that Hurst was up on that field, working all alone,' Graves said. 'And I think you decided it was time to get even with him too. Maybe you saw the pitchfork and decided to use it.'

'No,' Hooper said, his voice rising. 'That's not true. I never had anything to do with his daughter, and I was afraid of Hurst. I told you I never wanted to go anywhere near him after what he did to me.'

'But he was an old man,' Graves pointed out. 'Maybe you thought it was time to give him a pasting just like the one he gave you.'

Hooper shook his head, more vigorously this time. He dragged on his cigarette quite savagely, and then threw it at his feet, pushed past Graves and started to walk towards the house. 'Look, it all happened years ago. I couldn't care less about what happened to Hurst. And I was here all day anyway. Ask any of the boys. And how the hell would I know if Hurst was out there on his field? And her . . . Didn't even know she was dead until now. Jesus Christ. Do I look like the kind of person who could do something like that — and to a kid too?'

Graves shrugged. 'But there is something, Brad,' he said, walking after him. 'There's something you're not telling me, isn't there?'

Hooper stopped and turned around. For a moment, he looked utterly dejected. Then he seemed to rally. He plunged his hands deeper into his pockets and stared down at the floor. He kicked at a cigarette butt with his muddy boots. Then he looked up.

'I'm going to ask you one more time,' Graves said. 'Did you ever see her again? Did you ever see Sarah after Hurst gave you that beating?'

His hands fell to his sides. There was a sense of cold and sudden anger. 'Yes,' he said finally and with a great deal of reluctance. 'Yes, all right, I saw Sarah again.'

'How many times?'

'Once,' Hooper said quickly. 'Just the once and I didn't say a single word to her.'

'When?'

Hooper spoke fast, as if trying to get it over and done with. 'I saw her on that day. The day she had her accident by the pool.'

'The day she died?' Graves said.

Hooper closed his eyes briefly and took a deep breath. A look of real worry came over his face. 'I thought it might have been her,' he said. 'I thought it might have been Sarah who had told Hurst about us. That perhaps she'd felt all guilty about it and spilled the beans. Got me into trouble. And I wanted to know why. It was the housekeeper's afternoon off, so I just went round the back. And there she was. By the swimming pool.

'She was lying by the side of the water. Sunbathing as usual. Vain cow. She never saw me. She could have been asleep for all I know. And then, when I was halfway across the lawn, I bottled it. Went back the way I came.'

'But why? What stopped you?' Graves said.

'Because someone else was there,' Hooper said angrily. 'She was there. I saw her up in her room.'

'Who?'

'The girl.'

'Rebecca?'

'Christ, I don't know. I never knew her name. His daughter. I thought she was supposed to be at school.'

'But she was,' Graves said surprised. 'It was a school day.'

'Well, she was there,' Hooper said firmly. 'She must have been skiving or ill. She didn't see me, but I got a glimpse of her up in her room. I thought she might tell her old man if she saw me hanging about. So I chickened out. Slipped back out over the lawn. Next thing I knew someone was telling me that Sarah was dead. That she'd slipped and drowned in her swimming pool.'

Graves took a deep breath. 'And you didn't think to tell us?' he said with as much patience as he could manage, which right then wasn't much. 'You didn't think it might have been a good idea to tell the police that you'd been there the day she died.'

'It was an accident,' Hooper said, his shoulders hunched. 'That's what everyone said. What was the point of me getting involved? She just fell in and smacked her head.'

Graves pushed himself off the wall and stood so he was facing Hooper. Hooper looked petulant and defiant now that it was over.

'And are you sure she was there? Hurst's daughter. She was there in the house when you walked round the back? You saw her? That's what you're telling me?'

Hooper coughed. His yellow builder's helmet was resting on top of the wall. Someone, perhaps for a joke or out of boredom, had sawed a very thin line through the top of it. 'Yes,' Hooper said, reaching for his hat. 'She was there. Up in her room.'

36

I told Graves to meet me at Hurst's house straightaway. It would take him a while to get there from Woodstock, so on the way I decided to have another quick talk with Frank's brother over in Shipston.

Simon Hurst was in his late fifties, big, tough and physically very strong, like his brother, and the cream-coloured chair in which he was sitting looked like it might break under his weight. He had his grand-daughter staying with him for the Christmas holidays. The girl was around nine or ten, and she stared at me insolently from the back of a wicker chair. With a certain regal air, she had walked into the living room a few moments ago and since then had calmly, and as if it were a matter of course, ignored her grandfather's entreaties to go back to the kitchen to her grandmother. Hurst looked at the girl a little helplessly, then gave up, let out a low sigh, pulled himself out of the chair and called out for his wife through the open doorway. She seemed to appear instantly and led the girl away without a word.

'I know one of my men came to see you earlier and you've gone through this all before,' I said, 'but —'

'But here you are,' Hurst said. 'That officer said you needed my DNA for something. But what? He refused to say. I don't understand any of it. And what on earth is a dead girl doing underneath Frank's house? The papers are saying they found a body under there and there could be another one.' Hurst looked utterly miserable. 'And, God, if it is one of them down there . . .' Hurst lapsed into silence.

'Look, we don't know who it is,' I said. 'Not yet. We're trying to find out and we're still in the dark about most of it. And you know what the papers are like. I just want to go through everything with you again to make sure I've got everything right. Tell me, how did you hear about what had happened to your brother?'

'All right.' Hurst sighed. 'I heard about it from Susan. My wife. She said there was something on the radio about the police being over in Quinton. Something about them finding a body out there. I was out most of the day: I have a foreman to run the farm but I needed to talk to him and check up on things,' Hurst said.

'Let me get something straight: you inherited part of the farm?'

'Frank got the lion's share, including the house, but some of the land went to me. Frank sold up years ago. But I kept my part as it was — as a working farm,' he said proudly.

'So you went to check up on things at the farm — and then what?'

'Then I had to go off into town and buy a Christmas tree.'

'So what did you do when you got back? When you heard about the body?'

'I phoned up Frank to see if he knew anything about it. I was curious more than anything else. But he didn't answer the phone, which was unusual for him — because he hardly ever went out if he could help it. He was a bit funny like that.' Hurst took a sip of his tea. 'So I waited. I didn't think any more about it. Not to begin with anyway. I had my supper — watched the television for a while. There was nothing on as usual. But then I suppose it started to really, well . . . prey on my mind a bit. So I phoned again, and when there still wasn't any answer I became worried, I suppose. So

I kept on ringing him. It wasn't like Frank at all to be out — especially at that time of night.

'Susan told me I was getting in a state and making a fuss over nothing as usual. But I couldn't stop thinking about him and the radio wasn't much help either. Actually, it just made everything worse. They started talking about suspicious circumstances. And we all know what that means,' Hurst said darkly. 'So I tried Frank one more time — let the phone ring and ring, and when there was no answer I told myself I was being a silly bugger and took myself off to bed. Tried to get some sleep after that.'

'But you couldn't sleep?'

'No. It was no use at all. I just couldn't stop thinking about it. I lay there half the night thinking — what if it is him? It's not exactly a big place, Lower Quinton. So I made up my mind, got changed, got in the car and drove straight on out there.'

'And that's when you saw the smoke? Smoke coming from his house?'

'Yes. It was coming from round the back. There was one of your lot out front in his car. I knew then . . . well . . . thought it could be Frank they'd been talking about all day on the radio.'

Hurst raised his eyes. 'I knocked on the

car window, because the silly sod was fast asleep, and then I went straight round the side of the house. And it was on fire.' Hurst paused, stunned, as if reliving the shock. 'I thought I could somehow put it out — I ran in there without thinking — and got as far as that stairway. That's when the whole thing just seemed to come apart and fall on top of me. Your man had to pull me out.'

'And Frank inherited the house because he was the elder son?'

Hurst nodded slowly. 'The house has been in our family for generations. Nothing left of it now, so they tell me. I haven't been able to bring myself to go out there again.'

'And there was no other car? It was just the police car when you arrived?'

'Just me and sleeping beauty,' Hurst said bitterly.

'But what about his daughter?' I said. 'Rebecca. She still hasn't come forward, Mr Hurst, and we know Frank was looking for her. You said that she would write to him from time to time when we talked before, but where is she? Have you seen her?'

Suddenly the door swung open and Mrs Hurst came in with some tea things.

She put down the tray and sat down on the edge of a sofa. She was trim and neat-looking and far more elegant than her husband. She had very blue eyes and she gave her husband a look of ill-concealed annoyance that bordered on contempt. Hurst seemed not to notice it, or if he did he didn't care.

'They need to talk to Rebecca,' Hurst said.

'She's in London,' Mrs Hurst said. 'We already told you that. She'd be about twenty or twenty-one by now.'

Hurst sat back in his seat. Outside, their granddaughter was playing some game of her own invention and was running fitfully from place to place in the snow.

'He began to give up hope after she left him,' Mrs Hurst said. 'Got very absent-minded. Became fussy about certain things. Got rid of Nancy.'

'His housekeeper.'

'Yes, which I can tell you was not a good thing to do. She was very efficient. He let the whole house go, and when you asked him about it he shrugged you off. Actually, he became a bit of a bore.'

'He stopped talking about Rebecca altogether,' Hurst said. 'And we rarely saw him.'

'The house became a disaster. He went and bought that beastly dog of his. And he put those bars on the windows.'

'I couldn't believe it when I saw it,' Hurst said.

'I was furious,' Mrs Hurst said. 'He had absolutely no right.'

'But why did he do it?' I asked.

'He wouldn't tell me,' Hurst said. 'All he offered was a lot of bloody stupid nonsense.'

Hurst looked as if he had a mind to leave it there, but, seeing my expression of polite inquiry, he continued reluctantly. 'Well, he told me . . . he said he was sorry about what he had done to the house.'

Mrs Hurst looked surprised.

'He was sorry,' Hurst said. 'But it was a feeling he couldn't really explain. Of course, he knew the whole village hated him because of what had happened to Sarah. But he couldn't leave in case Rebecca came back. But he said that sometimes he'd be lying there, fast asleep in his bed, and he would wake up and be sure that someone was in the house with him. And he thought it might have been Rebecca. He thought she might have come back. But when he went downstairs there was never anything missing, although some things had been moved around.' Hurst looked up. 'He was losing his grip. I told him so as well. He didn't much like hearing it of course.'

'But how many times did this happen?' I

asked. 'How many times did he wake up like that and go downstairs?'

'Oh, I don't know — a few times, I suppose.'

'So he thought someone was trying to break in to the house. Even before that time he went to see her in London and she didn't show up?'

'That's right.'

'And when was that?'

'Oh, I don't know,' Hurst said. 'Around a year after she left maybe.'

'But what could they have been looking for? Did he have any kind of idea?'

Hurst placed his cup back on the table. 'I don't know. I tried to get him to move out of there and start anew. Told him he could move in with us for a while . . . while he looked for somewhere else. Somewhere a bit smaller if he liked. But of course it was no use.'

'But did you ever press him?' I said. 'Did you ever ask him what was really wrong?'

'Well, he started talking about Rebecca. None of it made much sense. He hadn't mentioned her in ages. But he said it didn't matter any more. None of it mattered any more. Because he knew for sure that she would never be coming back.'

'And did he say why? Did he say how he

knew this?'

'No. That's all he would say.'

I asked them for a photo of Rebecca. Mrs Hurst went upstairs and came back a few minutes later with a snapshot that I put in my pocket. Then I drove back to Dashwood Manor.

37

As Graves waited for Downes in front of
the ruins of the house, he remembered the
fire leaping up from the wreckage and
exploding into the air. It had been utter
pandemonium, and they had been sure that
the fire was going to spread into the forest.
And maybe into the village too. And then,
in the midst of all that chaos, he had
discovered that Downes had plunged himself into its raging centre. He'd been there
and then he wasn't. Like the house had
eaten him alive.

Downes arrived a few minutes later. He
got out of the car and, without a word,
beckoned towards what was left of the
house. Graves followed him down the path
to the garden and through the gate in the
black fence surrounding the swimming pool.

A plastic deckchair lay on its side amongst
a large pile of dried brown leaves. A plastic
pot had blown across the patio and now lay

wedged against the fence. There was a large umbrella, which was faded and folded shut. The water in the pool was dark, and there was a smell of rotting leaves.

'So Brad Hooper went to see Sarah,' Downes said, still hardly able to believe it. 'He went to see her on the day she died and he never said a bloody word about it.'

'Yes,' Graves said. 'He panicked. He thought she had told Frank about their affair and he wanted to know why. So he came round here to have it out with her. Then he saw Rebecca and was afraid she'd tell Hurst that he'd been snooping around, so he legged it.'

'And he was sure he saw Rebecca?'

'That's what he says. And so this is where it happened,' Graves said. 'This is where Mrs Hurst drowned.'

Downes nodded. 'It was Nancy's afternoon off, but she came back early. She spotted Sarah from the house. Ran down here and jumped in. Then she called an ambulance. It took them a while to get here — it was too late anyway. According to Nancy and to Frank Hurst, Sarah Hurst went swimming most days in the summer. The pool hadn't been used for years, but it was one of the first things she had repaired when she married him and moved in. She used to spend hours and hours sitting out here in the sun. And most days after her swim, she'd lie on one of those deckchairs over there, or on a towel by the side of the pool. And that's exactly what she was doing the day she died.'

Graves watched as Downes took a few steps away from the pool, while the wind picked up, swirling and rustling the leaves. The snow came in a sudden flurry, hard and sharp in their faces.

'An intruder could have done it,' Downes said. 'I wondered about that for a while — thought someone could have come round the back and tried to get into the house.' He turned and looked towards the ruins. 'You can just see the steps from here. She shouts out. Whoever it is comes through the gate and on to the patio. There's a struggle. She falls, hits her head and ends up in the water somehow.'

Downes ran his hand along his face. 'But what if I know all about Mrs Hurst's summer-time routine, how she likes to be out here all alone when it's hot? Hooper knew. She used to lie right here,' he said, drawing the tip of his shoe along the edge of the pool. 'That's where most of the blood was.'

Downes got down on his haunches and

looked, almost as if he half expected traces of the blood to still be there.

'Hurst?'

'Hurst knew that she'd been having an affair, but his alibi was unshakable.' Downes held his right hand wide open, as if he were holding something large and heavy inside it. Swiftly, he brought his hand down towards the tiles. Then he stopped abruptly, as if he were looking at Sarah Hurst's limp body lying by the side of the pool. 'All you'd have to do is roll her into the water and watch her drown.'

Graves looked out at the water, while Downes pressed his palms against his knees, thinking.

'Death by drowning,' Downes said. 'Because that's what killed her. It was the water that killed her, not the blow to the head.'

'That's what the autopsy said, is it?' Graves asked innocently.

Downes straightened up. 'According to Brewin, there was a single large contusion at the base of the skull,' he said, tapping hard at the side of the swimming pool with his knuckles, 'and there were several traces of stone embedded in her skull that matched the coping stones here.'

'So she fell,' Graves said simply. 'Sorry, sir, but it sounds pretty straightforward and you did say this kind of thing happens a lot.'

But Downes looked reluctant to let it go. 'I don't know,' he said a little weakly. 'It was just a feeling I had at the time, I suppose.'

'Maybe you're right, sir,' Graves said, giving in a little. 'Maybe Rebecca did see someone when she was up in her room. If Sarah Hurst's death wasn't an accident, I mean. And maybe that person found out later. Maybe Rebecca said something. Or hinted at something.'

'About Sarah Hurst, you mean?' Downes said.

'Yes.'

'All right, but why wait that long? Rebecca didn't go missing until she was older. It was two years at least after Sarah Hurst's accident.'

'Maybe she didn't really know what she had seen. She was too young. Couldn't piece it together until she was older, like Collinson said. Or maybe Hooper's lying through his teeth. Maybe he didn't run away when he saw Sarah lying there fast asleep. He could just as easily have picked up a rock, hit her with it and pushed her in. He admitted to me that he was furious with her.'

Downes fell silent for a while and then sighed loudly. 'You could be right,' he said.

'Could be that Rebecca's death is completely unrelated to that of the other two girls. Maybe it was an accident. Or maybe Hooper killed Sarah Hurst and then killed Rebecca later. But if that's the case, why did he admit that he came back here that afternoon when you talked to him? We could be chasing our tails in circles, you know.'

Downes caught his own dissatisfied and annoyed reflection in the surface of the water. He kicked a small stone and it skidded along the ground before making a mournful half-hearted splash. The stone became a pale white shadow in the darkness and then was gone.

'Come on. Let's get out of here,' he said.

38

'Doesn't really help us all that much, though,' Graves said, taking a gulp from his pint. 'Sounds like that housemistress sent you off on a wild goose chase, if you ask me.'

I lifted up my own pint glass, admired it for a while and then took a long swig. Well, one thing you could say about Graves was that he was direct. 'Unless Lang was wrong and the nightmares were about something else,' I ventured without much enthusiasm. 'Something that had nothing to do with the accident at all and he missed it. But you're probably right, Graves. It doesn't add to what we already know about her.'

'A quiet girl who preferred her own company,' Graves said.

I had chosen a bar in the upstairs rooms of the Royal British Legion near the train station in Moreton-in-Marsh. Or 'The Warmongers', as Powell had only half jokingly referred to it. 'And how about the village?' I said.

'There's hardly any talk about her and nothing concrete. A few people mentioned the accident on the pond. That's all they remember, or it's the thing they remember first anyway. You know about that, though.'

I nodded.

'We had a little more luck at her old school. But no boyfriends as far as we can tell and no close friends. She seems to have been a pretty, quiet girl right from the start or at least that's the feeling I got this afternoon,' Graves said. 'And she seems to have spent a lot of time at home. They seemed close. But when her stepmother died, he packed her off to that boarding school.'

'She didn't last long there,' I said. 'Apparently she stole some money from the bursar's office. She'd been seen but she refused to hand over the money.'

'How much?'

'Eight hundred pounds almost. It wasn't all that much money. Not for them of course. Just petty cash. They didn't want a scandal, so they kept the police out of it.'

Graves rubbed the side of his nose and sniffed and took another drink. 'Eight hundred pounds. You reckon she might have done it on purpose?'

'Got caught, you mean? Maybe. We know she wanted out of the school. Didn't seem to be very happy there. Maybe she didn't really care one way or the other if they caught her.'

Graves was not, I had been relieved to see, a teetotaller. In fact he was almost halfway through his first pint already. His hands, I noticed, had become rough from hauling all that rubble away from the house.

'So she stole the money, because she needed it to run away. But do you think she was running away on her own or was someone helping her? Someone who knew that she had stolen the money, been expelled for it, and was using it as a way of getting her on her own. Maybe it was just a trick all along,' Graves said. 'A trick to get her on her own.'

I put down my glass and turned it clockwise. 'Could be. Let's say for now that the person who killed Rebecca was the same person who made those two girls disappear. And let's assume that Sarah Hurst's death was simply an accident. We know Rebecca wanted to leave home anyway, so I'm not really sure that she would have needed all that much encouragement. She'd talked about it openly. Word gets round fast out there, so we can assume that it was common knowledge in the village.'

'And her killer knew that?'

'Maybe,' I said. 'I think it's a question of timing. They may have known that if Rebecca vanished with all her things, everyone would just assume she'd walked out. Her father included.'

'So no one would look for her?'

I fell silent briefly. Then I said, 'We don't know how they played it yet, but it probably began slowly. The one thing we know about our man is that he's patient. And when he acts he acts quickly and with no hesitation at all. That's his MO and it's a very unusual one. You look at the way he made those two little girls just disappear like that. Gail and Elise went missing seven years ago. And Rebecca apparently left home when she was around seventeen or eighteen. So that's around three years ago, and no one has actually seen her as far as we know in all that time. That's around four years between the time those girls went missing and when Rebecca disappeared off the face of the earth. The MO is the same in both cases, if it really was Rebecca down there, and it's looking increasingly likely that it is. He watches. He waits. And when the moment comes . . .' I stared across the table, grimaced and took another sip. A bigger one this time. 'He takes his time with her. Then kills her and buries her under that house.' For a moment longer I was silent. 'I think whoever it was,' I said finally, 'must have known she was going.'

'So they must have known the house well too — known about that space underneath it,' Graves said.

I nodded. 'And they've never left,' I said. 'That's the most incredible thing. They're still here somewhere. Maybe even in the village. Could be anyone.'

Graves drained his pint. 'Another one, sir?'

'Sure, why not,' I said, and finished what was left in my glass.

Graves took our glasses and, dangling them in his hand, headed across the old threadbare carpet to the bar.

'Get us some of those porky scratchings as well,' I called after him. I waited while the barman, who had years ago learnt that I was half Argentinian, eyed me suspiciously from time to time as he pulled my pint.

'So,' I said conversationally when Graves came back, 'how'd you end up out here? Pretty big station over there in Oxford. That's where you were, isn't it? I've been there a few times, you know.'

'My super said he saw you play rugger

once,' Graves said, deftly avoiding the question. 'Said you got sent off.'

'Did I?' I was not that surprised. I shrugged and tore open the pack of porky scratchings. 'Well, it was probably me if he says it was. Must have come against your lot in the league. I used to play a bit just to keep in shape more than anything else.' I shook my head. 'Christ, Graves, you've never seen such a dirty bunch of bastards in your life. You know, the first time I played, at half-time they opened a bottle of brandy and passed it around. I was expecting oranges.'

'What position, sir?' Graves said, genuinely interested.

'I used to be a flanker when I was younger, back home. Number 7. Of course, I was a lot quicker on my feet back then. And later I switched to Number 8. I never really enjoyed it as much after that, though. You ever play?'

'Oh, yes, at school all we ever did was play rugger. I was a winger. When I went to university I gave it up. I suppose I'd had enough of it by then. Got interested in other things.'

'Things like girls, you mean?' I said, and smiled broadly.

'Yes,' Graves said, and laughed, surprised.

'My father wasn't too happy about it, though, I can tell you. He had high hopes for me on that front and on other fronts as well. The school too. Let them down, I suppose.'

'Public school, you said.'

'Yes. I couldn't wait to get out of there, and to be perfectly honest I'd had enough of being half frozen to death in a soggy field. Didn't see much point in it.'

'I know what you mean,' I said. 'So why did they send you here? University graduate. Public school boy,' I said without malice. 'I thought you'd be right up their street.'

Graves didn't answer. He smiled and said carefully, 'You know I could ask you the same thing, sir.'

I had a huge weakness for porky scratchings, which were unheard of back home. I took a large one and swallowed it. I had brought the photo of Rebecca with me and I wiped my fingers before putting it carefully on the table. It had clearly been removed from a scrapbook, and there was some yellowish glue at the back. We looked at it. Rebecca was standing next to Frank in front of the house, and Sarah Hurst was standing on the other side of him. It was winter. Rebecca was smiling widely, showing two rows of very white teeth. Her hair was tied back in a bun. She was clinging to her father's arm. On Hurst's other side stood Sarah. She was taller than Frank, detached-looking and as beautiful as everyone had said she was. Her blonde hair lay loosely on her shoulders.

Graves took the photo, examined it and put it back again. 'She looks all in, doesn't she?' he said.

'Who?' I said.

'Sarah. Sarah Hurst.'

I picked up the photo. Sarah wasn't looking at the camera. She was looking away, towards the far side of the garden, with a neutral expression above a thin smile. I looked more closely. Her eyes were slightly sunken, and there was a haggard look to her, as if she had not slept very well for some time. And she seemed strangely cut off from the other two people in the photograph, bewildered, almost as if she couldn't quite figure out what she was doing there.

I slipped the photo into my pocket, not sure what to make of it. Graves shrugged. We sat for a little bit longer and finished our drinks. Then we trudged downstairs and stepped outside into the cold. I waved goodbye to Graves and walked towards my car, which was parked outside the station, thinking that Graves maybe wasn't so bad after all. Then felt guilty for thinking it and for taking him to one of Powell's old drinking holes.

I walked quickly to the car and tried to remember what Rebecca had really looked like when I had seen her. But I had seen her only that one time, staring at me from a high window.

Then I started to think about the crumbling graves and the thick vines clinging to the walls of the church in Lower Quinton. I remembered the flowers on the grave in the cemetery and the Hurst family plot out there.

Another image of her came to me as I remembered the black-and-white picture I had seen of her in the house. That school photo in the newspaper stuffed at the back of an old drawer. Her father had cut out the text but kept the photo. It was odd. In my mind I stared at the printed page, and from far off it was as if I could hear the crisp sound of ice cracking. I walked on. Already the memory of the photo was slipping away from me, becoming distorted.

I tried to bring it back. The dots in the picture once more joined together and contrived to form a face. Her hair was tied back behind her head in a bun, making the smooth curve of her jaw more pronounced. But then the image of her disappeared again and all that remained were dots.

39

I had a late dinner, which I cooked and ate with complete indifference. Then I phoned Powell and talked to him for a while. He started going on about some old wives' tale concerning the pond in Quinton. He wasn't able to focus, and his voice sounded ragged and almost incoherent.

These remote Cotswold hills had always held a fascination for him, and for years he had regaled me with innumerable stories and anecdotes about each of the villages. For Powell, this was his way of showing you who he was. When he reached out into the past it was as if he were seeing it. But on the phone it all seemed garbled and incomplete. He described how they used to drown witches in the pond; 'swimming a witch', they had called it. In the end Alex took the phone from him, apologized and hung up.

I was just about to go upstairs to bed when I heard a car drawing to a stop in my driveway. Seconds later the doorbell rang. It had actually been so long since someone had rung it that for a second I was sure that it must have been the television. Then it rang again. A hectoring bullying demand. Frowning, I walked quickly through the hallway, switched on the light and swung open the door. Warm light flowed on to the path of snow and on to the two people standing in front of me, shivering with cold. The woman in front of me smiled. And then a camera flashed behind her.

'Chief Inspector Downes?' the woman said. 'I was wondering if we could have a quick word. I know it's late. But we thought you might want to talk to us, as it's about Gail and Elise. We hear you've stopped searching out Hurst's house. And that you've still to make an arrest — is this true?'

'How the hell did you get this address?' I said, shocked.

'It's just a few questions,' the woman said. 'May we come in? You know, it's really freezing out here and poor old Bob's been stuck in the village all day, taking pictures.' She smiled. Behind her the roofs of the other cottages gleamed in the moonlight. 'We won't take much of your time. Maybe we can help.'

'Help?'

I turned around, went back into the hallway for my house keys, stepped outside and then slammed the door shut behind me. I took a quick step forward. The camera was raised once more, aimed at my face. I took another step and, catching the photographer off guard, snatched his camera from him.

'Hey,' the man said. 'You can't do that.'

The journalist, however, seemed unperturbed. 'It's Guillermo, right?' she said.

'What?'

'We were at Frank's house this afternoon. We were surprised to see that no one's out there any more, weren't we, Bobbie? Nobody's searching at all. Surely it must be a possibility that there are more victims out there? Victims you don't even know about yet. Why aren't you still looking?'

'Hey!' the man said. 'Give me back my camera.'

I was so stunned by the intrusion that I very nearly threw the camera into the bushes. 'I asked you how you got this address.'

The woman ignored me and took a step closer. 'What about Nancy Williams? Do you think she was an accomplice? And someone knew. Same way they knew about Hurst.'

'No, I do not, and don't go printing

anything about Nancy,' I said.

'Why not?'

'Because it's none of your damned business, that's why. Get the hell out of here.'

'But why? Frank was a suspect all along,' she said almost gleefully. 'We didn't know that. But you found a hairpin years ago in his swimming pool, didn't you? Apparently he wasn't even brought in and questioned when you found it. Which just seems incredible, really, seeing that the hairpin exactly matched one Gail Foster had been wearing the day she disappeared.'

I didn't even bother to answer. I just handed back the camera, went inside and slammed the door behind me. I closed the curtains. There were mutterings from outside. Then, later, the sound of steps crunching through the snow. I waited until I heard their car disappear down the drive, then went into my kitchen.

How had they got my address? God, they were relentless. It was the only way to describe them. They made the local journalists look like complete amateurs. Hard not to admire it in a way, though. The persistence.

But it was a different matter altogether when you were on the sharp end of it. Of course, it wasn't hard to know where they

379

had found out about the hairpin, now that I thought about it. They must have talked to Gail's mother and she must have told them and exaggerated its importance. Made it out to be a complete match. I couldn't say I blamed her for it. It was a good way to get their attention.

I refilled the kettle, put it on the hob and made myself a *mate.* It's best served at around 80°C, and it's easier to judge the temperature with a stove-top kettle than with an electric one, which boils too quickly. Then I slumped down into my armchair.

All was silent. Outside my window, the snow-covered fields stretched out under the moonlight. Bloody journalists. Coming out here in the middle of the night. I tried not to think about them and started to think about the pond instead. What had Powell been talking about on the phone? A witch they had drowned years ago in Quinton. No. Drowned was not the right word.

Swimming a witch. That was the phrase Powell had used. They had dragged the poor woman out of her cottage, stripped her, bound her hands to her ankles and thrown her into the pond to see if she would float. It was a known fact that water rejected those who had signed pacts with the devil. And so she had floated. But she hadn't floated for long.

Christ, what a nice little tale. I suddenly caught sight of my reflection in the window. A fierce look of worry crossed my face. But it wasn't Powell I was worried about this time.

I stared through my reflection at the hills rising into the distance and at the wide strip of trees beyond. I sat there for a while thinking of that old story. Why had Powell told me that one? My arms lay limply at my sides. I had left the kettle on for too long. It had begun to boil and steam rose up, leaving beads of moisture hanging on the ceiling above the stove.

I stood up, grabbed a cloth and absently took the kettle off the hob. I moved back to the window, pulled the curtain back farther and leant against the wall. Looking outside, I remembered staring at the pond from the silence of the graveyard after I had talked to Nancy. I remembered the pond staring back at me from the middle of the village like a black unblinking eye. And then I thought of Rebecca. For a moment, the unformed outline of something falling fast came into view. Rebecca burning in my arms.

40

I was waiting on the library steps in Stratford when the librarian came to open up the next morning. I spent hours searching through the newspaper archives and reading about the Taylor boys and their accident in the pond. The story had even made some of the national newspapers at the time.

It went very much as it had been described to me. The two boys had gone on to the ice along with Rebecca. They met at just after midnight on a school night in December, a few days before the Christmas holiday. Both boys, Ned, aged twelve, and Owen, aged thirteen, fell through the ice and drowned. Rebecca had been lucky. She had fallen in the water but managed to get out. Both boys were pronounced dead at the scene.

All of the accounts were the same. But one write-up in the local paper also ran a half-page photo. It was the same photo Hurst had had in the back of his drawer. I put down the paper, asked the librarian for a photocopy of the article and marched out into the cold. I got into my car and drove to Lower Quinton, where I sat inside my car, listening to the radio crackling on the dashboard. Then I stepped out, locked the door and walked alongside the village green.

I blinked and looked around, as if surprised to find myself back here in the village. Across the grass, on the other side of the green, I caught a glimpse of grey and then sudden light as the winter sun sparkled briefly on the pond's surface through the trees. I passed the old broken-down bench in the middle of the green. I took one quick backward glance at the village before making my way through the wall of trees that surrounded the pond.

There was a single gate at the far end of the chainlink fence that encircled the pond. Again, I was struck by the pond's size but more so now. The branches of some of the older trees reached all the way across the top of the fence and hung over the ice. The local kids had heaved a few rocks at the fence, trying to break it. The rocks now lay encrusted in the surface of the pond, along with arcs of hardened earth and pieces of torn grass.

I took a step forward and leant against the

fence. The water beneath the ice rippled with a strange urgency into the freezing rivulets of mud. There was a faded yellow sign that had been put up on a pole in the centre of the pond. It showed a silhouette of a man pitching forward into a sharply edged black hole. DANGER: THIN ICE.

I stared at the pond for quite some time. Then I decided to try the gate, and when that didn't budge, I took off my coat and placed it neatly in the crook of a branch. Then I climbed the fence and lowered myself to the ground on the other side.

I walked to the edge of the ice and with all my strength stamped at the edge of the water. Nothing happened. I tried again and again. A few moments later the first splintering crack went shooting along the surface. The water began to bubble beneath, ominous and slow. And then it began to pour through the crack. The crack opened wider as the edges fell and toppled beneath the surface. The water spread and brushed against the snow, which melted, revealing the dark clean ice.

From somewhere far off came another splintering crack. Another sound, louder this time, from somewhere near the centre. The water began to move, to push. Bubbles streamed upwards and broke against the roof of ice. I gazed at the gently lapping surface. I was very still for a moment. And suddenly I knew.

41

I spent the rest of the day finding out as much as I could about the accident on the pond. Everyone seemed to remember those two boys being dragged lifeless to the banks, and all the accounts were fundamentally the same as those that had appeared in the papers. But I kept on knocking on doors and asking about it. And all afternoon I kept on hearing the same story repeated over and over. It was getting dark by the time I decided to try the shopkeeper in the village shop.

She was wearing a drab housecoat, and she looked impatient and tired out. But her expression changed when I asked her about the pond. It was one that I had got to know well during the afternoon. I could almost hear her thinking, pond? What pond? It was as if she had forgotten it was there, though it was right across the road. It seemed that for the shopkeeper, like many others in the village, especially those who had been there for a number of years, the pond had slipped permanently out of view and remained invisible behind the wall of trees. That was until you brought up the accident. Now, looking at the pond through her dusty shop window, I couldn't help thinking there was something undeniably secretive about the way it almost seemed to be receding out of sight, as if the trees and shrubbery had conspired to shield it from prying eyes.

The single customer in the shop was already heading towards the counter, dragging a battered wicker basket behind her like a reluctant dog. She placed a bottle of milk along with some teabags next to the till and waited while the shopkeeper rang it all up.

'Billy Mathews,' the shopkeeper said without warning, as she handed over the change and waited with amusement for the customer's look of vague puzzlement to change to recognition. 'Thought you might remember,' she said quietly.

The customer looked up at me quizzically.

'He wants to know if I know anything about the pond,' the shopkeeper explained.

'Two lads died out there years back,' I said. 'I was wondering if you might remember it. Perhaps you even saw it.'

'Billy Mathews,' the other woman repeated slowly, putting away her purse, 'now there's a name I haven't heard in a while.'

Whatever errand she might have set out to do next could clearly wait; she shifted towards the counter and placed her bag in an alcove beneath the shop window. She smiled at the shopkeeper and said, 'Billy Mathews. My God.' Then she laughed. It came out like a bark, and the shopkeeper and I both jumped.

'Billy Mathews?' I said, confused. 'I want to know about two brothers . . . Ned and Owen Taylor. Who's Billy Mathews?'

But both of the women ignored me.

'God, he was a little sod, wasn't he?'

'Oh, I wouldn't go as far as that,' the shopkeeper said. 'He weren't that bad. High spirits, that were all it was. Anyway,' she added, 'must be thirty years now.'

'Try forty,' the customer said bluntly. 'Of course he was older than me, so I didn't know him as well as Helen,' she said, looking at me.

The shopkeeper managed another weak smile. 'Well, it was only two years — doesn't make much difference now, does it, Eleanor.'

Eleanor looked at her as if she had just said something absurd and then said, 'It was the council's fault those two boys died. That pond's a lot deeper than it looks.'

The colour in her already ruddy cheeks rose as she lapsed into thought about the village council. 'Oh, they had all kinds of wonderful plans as usual,' she said. 'They were going to restore the pond to its former glory as a kind of memorial to Billy Mathews. Those were their very words: "its former glory",' she said and gave another one of her barkish laughs. 'Though what for I'll never know — so we could all enjoy end-less picnics by its banks, I suppose, and feed the ducks. But of course, there weren't any ducks out there. There never have been.'

'So they weren't the first to drown out on the pond?' I said, shocked.

She looked at me very seriously and said, 'No, they weren't. After what happened to Billy, they were going to cut down all the trees and build a little wooden pier so you could go stand in the middle of it. And they were going to build a white fence all around it, so none of the kids could get near it again.

'They said it wouldn't take long — three weeks tops' — she drew out the words slowly — 'three weeks to drain it and pump out the silt, and then a few months for the rain to fill it. Nothing could have been simpler,' she said, letting out a long and exaggerated sigh. 'Took three weeks just to drain it.' Her face formed an expression of acute disgust. 'The stink of it was absolutely awful. There was no getting away from it for months. And it was deep, that pond. No one could believe just how deep. It seemed to go down for miles and miles — like a big black hole — which, when you come to think of it, is exactly what it is. The council lost enthusiasm for it after that, and were off to go and mess up something else.'

She moved forward to the counter. Her voice had taken on a solemn edge. 'That wasn't the worst of it, though. The thing is, they never got around to building a proper fence, which was about the only decent idea they ever had. That's how the Taylor boys managed to get in there much later.'

The shopkeeper shook her head. 'I watched him,' she said. 'We all did, didn't we, Eleanor? Load of us kids traipsed on over with Billy. To see if he were going to do it.'

'Did it for a dare.'

'He walked right into the middle of the pond,' the shopkeeper said. 'He wanted to walk across it only once — that's what he said he were going to do — but then of course he started showing off.' She laughed. 'Started doing these silly pirouettes on the ice. You remember that, Eleanor, how he kept on going round and round?'

Eleanor smiled grimly. 'Yes, Helen, I remember,' she said.

The shopkeeper nodded her head vigorously, as if she had just recalled something else. 'He used to wear those thick black glasses like Buddy Holly. And he was always breaking 'em or losing 'em.'

The shopkeeper's eyes had grown dim, I noticed, as if she were seeing herself once again as a child amongst the group of children gathered around the banks of the pond. And it wasn't hard for me to imagine myself amongst them too. For a moment, it was as if I had traipsed out in the cold with all the other children and was now craning my neck and staring at the boy on the ice.

'We'd all been banned, you see,' the shopkeeper said. 'The moment the pond froze over, they told us in assembly that we weren't to go anywhere near it. He probably wouldn't have done it if it hadn't been out of bounds. He was laughing and shouting and falling on his backside and us lot were all too, and he was daring us to do the same,' the shopkeeper went on. 'Though of course none of us would, even though the ice looked pretty thick.'

'God, I very nearly went on myself,' Eleanor said, shuddering.

'You weren't the only one. That's what they said later. Said it coulda been a lot worse. Most of the boys had half a mind to follow him. But none of 'em did go in the end. And then, just as he was about to come back, the ice broke and he was under.'

The shopkeeper put her hands in the pockets of her housecoat and said, 'He just disappeared. There was no warning.'

'Just a noise,' Eleanor said, looking straight at me, 'like a gun going off and that was that. One second he was there and the next he was gone. If he'd been a bit closer to the edge, we might have been able to reach him and pull him out, but as it was he was right in the middle when the ice broke. Took us a few moments to react. We were just children. Then we started to throw things out there — someone threw their coat, I think — towards the hole, and someone else threw a branch, I think it was. But we were so young we didn't really know what to do. And then we started to try and smash the ice, but it wouldn't shift. Of course, by then someone had gone running off for help. But it was far too late already.'

The shopkeeper folded her arms and looked once more across the green. 'He was dead by the time they dragged him out.'

I stared out of the window, across the road towards the green. The path leading to the thick wall of trees was nothing but a barely perceptible meandering line with thick leather leaves strewn in the snow all around it. But at that moment it was as if I were watching not Billy Mathews stepping on to the ice but the Taylor boys.

From above, it looked like they were playing in the jaws of some animal, its black endless throat rushing out of the cold hard darkness to envelop them. And all the while Rebecca Hurst, unable to help herself, laughed. Her laughter was loud in the sharp winter air; it echoed through the trees. And, revelling in the attention, they turned, and, like Billy Mathews, did a final pirouette, caught in the jaws of a trap that had already begun to close.

42

I slipped out of Lower Quinton in a matter of minutes, and before I knew it I was on the final stretch of road to Sam Griffin's house. His village was tucked away high in the Cotswold hills, and the road was covered here and there with patches of black ice. It had begun to snow again.

When my phone rang from the passenger seat of my car, I slowed down and picked it up.

'Looks like Brad Hooper was right,' Graves said.

'She was at home?'

'Yes. According to the school records she was anyway,' Graves said. 'Rebecca complained that she was feeling unwell just after 11.00 — that's when the kids have their first break. She went to see the school nurse. Then later, after lunch, she complained again that she was feeling sick. This time the nurse phoned her home. I've been asking around, and some of her old teachers think her stepmother Sarah might have come and picked her up just after lunch. Of course, no one's really sure about that. She could have gone home on her own. She lived close enough, so they might have just sent her off.'

'Are you sure it was the day Sarah Hurst died?'

'Yes,' Graves said. 'They chuck away the attendance records after a while, but the medical records are different. They have to keep them for five years. So they're all on the computer.'

'So she was there, then. She was in the house all along.'

'Well, I'm looking at a printout and that's what it says. So either she was faking it, or she was genuinely feeling ill.'

There was a brief pause. The snow had been ploughed high on either side of the road, forming a long tunnel. The village looked like a big smear of light at the end of it. 'I suppose you know you're in the paper, sir.'

'What?' I said quickly.

'It's some damned journo,' Graves said and sighed loudly. 'They've got a picture of you. It made the late edition.'

'Oh, Christ,' I said. 'What does it say?'

There was rustling in the background as Graves reached for the paper. ' "Brave Mum Breaks Silence in Missing Murder Case",' he read out loud. There was another pause. 'Gail's mother. Bit of a hatchet job, I'm afraid,' Graves said.

'Nothing about Rebecca?'

'No.'

'Good.'

A few kids on bikes were calling out to one another in the village. One stopped, packed a snowball and threw it at the car. It missed and went skittering to the other side of the road and disappeared down a drain.

'All right, go back and talk to Hooper,' I said finally. 'Or, better yet, try and get hold of him on the phone. It'll be quicker. I want you to find out if he saw anything else. And I want to know if things between him and Sarah Hurst were really as casual as he makes out. He says it was just a fling. But I want you to see if he's lying. Put the wind up him if you have to. You did a pretty good job of that last time. But I want to know exactly how serious it was and I want you to ask him if he's ever been out to the graveyard in Lower Quinton. Have you got that?'

'Yes,' Graves said. 'The graveyard in Lower Quinton.'

I shifted gear, my eyes straining, as I searched for the lane that led to Sam Griffin's house. 'And if he has been up there, ask him if he's ever visited the Hurst family plot. Right?'

'Right,' Graves said.

'And I want you to ask him — and it's important — I want you to ask him if he ever put flowers on Sarah Hurst's grave.'

43

Sam Griffin's thatched cottage was small, and had thick black beams that stood out unevenly within the white-washed walls. It lay beyond a series of dreary-looking cul-de-sacs at the edge of the village, and it was the last property at the end of a very narrow lane.

Griffin's wife ushered me in and led me through the cottage to the kitchen at the back of the house. Her husband, she told me, was out in the shed. I thanked her, slid open the back door and made my way across the lawn. I peered through the door of the shed. Griffin did not see me straight-away. He was busy cheerfully placing bulbs in pots on a broken-down kitchen table. A large plastic bag of potting soil stood open by his side, and a radio was playing softly in the background near an electric heater.

Griffin looked up, surprised when he saw me. He smiled a little sheepishly. He was wearing an old tweed jacket and a baseball cap. I stepped inside and shut the door behind me, while Griffin snapped off the radio. He was big and had to crouch a little as he walked around the table. He stretched out his hand, then, noting the earth on it, smiled again, wiped it roughly on the back of his coat and offered it again.

'So,' Griffin said, 'that's where you found old Frank. On the top of that hill?'

I nodded.

'Just like him to do his own labouring if it would save him a quid or two. Careful with his money, was old Frank.'

'You two fell out?'

'Oh, no, nothing like that. Just stopped seeing each other, really. He sold his share of the farm one day and 'a course I were out of a job. Didn't fancy working for his brother. They knocked down Frank's buildings, you know?' Griffin said incredulously. 'There's a bunch of offices over there now.'

'You must have been in and out of his house quite a few times,' I said, 'over the years.'

Griffin shrugged.

'What about his daughter? Rebecca,' I said carefully. 'Did you see her often?'

Griffin made a contemptuous snort. 'Not if I could help it,' he said.

'Why not?'

Griffin didn't answer. He was silent for a few moments longer. He seemed gloomy and tense. He stared down his long nose at his wellington boots. He took off the baseball cap and tapped it against his knees.

'I want to ask you something,' I said. 'When Sarah Hurst had her accident by the swimming pool, you were with Frank, weren't you? You were helping him pick out a pony for Rebecca. That's what Frank told us after the accident. He told us that's where he was when his wife drowned, and we talked to you later, if you remember.'

'Yes,' Griffin said. 'We'd gone to Launton village. Near Bicester. A fella I used to know had a new-born foal on his farm, and we went to look at it. Rebecca had been nagging at him about one for ages. And so Frank had given in. But he wanted me to have a look at it as well. We were out all day.'

'And you heard what happened when you were out there?'

'When they found Sarah, Nancy the housekeeper called here. She knew Frank was off with me, so the wife gave her the phone number of the farm. We were out there looking at the foal, and he gets the call. The next thing I know, and he's running, calling me over. We got into his old banger and drove straight back to his place.'

'And did he say anything on the drive back home?' I said.

Griffin was quiet for a moment. 'He said there had been some kind of accident. Sarah had been hurt.'

'And did you see Rebecca?'

'No,' Griffin said. 'I'd left my car at Frank's, and I just drove on home. I hung around for a while near the front gate. Talked to one of your men. He said I could go, but he took my address and phone number.'

'And when you two drove back to his house, did he say anything about Rebecca? Did he mention her at all?'

Griffin paused, remembering. 'No, I don't think so. Why would he?'

'No reason,' I said. 'But what do you know about her?'

Griffin moved around the table. 'This is about her, isn't it?'

'Yes,' I said. 'I think it is.'

Griffin laid his hands on the table and absently brushed away some more soil from the palms of his hands. 'Well, Frank spoilt her. But I expect you know that already.'

I nodded.

'And she could be a right bloody handful.

You probably know that too.'

'Well, we heard she could be difficult.'

'Difficult? Christ she was always in trouble,' Griffin said, putting the baseball cap back on his head. 'That boarding school . . . she didn't last long. Frank couldn't do a thing with her — never could. And you know what Frank was like. He was tough when he felt like it, and he had a temper on him an' all. And Christ help you if he had it in for you. But her,' Griffin said, 'Rebecca, she could do no wrong.' Griffin paused. 'She reminded him of her dead mother, you see. Diane. And when Diane died, it was just her and him for a while. And that suited Rebecca just fine. Oh, they were great pals. Went everywhere together. Did everything together. Anything she wanted, she just had to name it and Frank would get it for her. Then Sarah came along.'

Griffin paused again and pressed his body against the table. He folded his arms.

'And things changed then?' I said. 'When Sarah came on the scene?'

'She didn't like it,' Griffin said. 'She didn't like it one little bit. So she started being difficult again. Started playing up as soon as Sarah moved in.'

'You're saying,' I said, surprised, 'that she

wasn't happy about the marriage.'

'Yes. She didn't like it.'

'That's not what I heard,' I said.

'She wasn't happy about it at all. And when Sarah had her accident, she thought that things were going to be just like they were before. But they weren't. Things had changed, but she were too selfish even to see it. For one thing, Frank was mourning again. Because, despite what Sarah did to him, he'd forgiven her. And he'd got heartily sick of Rebecca acting up all the time. And so he sent her away to that school. She refused to go, but he packed her off in the Land Rover, dropped her inside the school gates and drove off. Left her there.' Griffin shook his finger in the air. 'And she never forgave him for it. Ever. And when she walked out on him . . . well, he kind of gave up after that. The life in him went out.'

Griffin stood up a little straighter and wandered around the side of the table. He reached into the bag of bulbs on the floor. He seemed unable to remain still or inactive for long. 'But you know what,' he said. 'I was damned pleased to see the back of her. And I was glad. Glad she'd gone. And I was glad when she never came back at all.'

Griffin delved into the bag and pulled out a bulb. He held it in the palm of his hand, threw it once into the air and then held it in his hand, as if sensing its potential.

'What about her accident?' I said. 'Out on the pond. Frank very nearly lost her. Maybe that's why he spoilt her.'

'That were just like her. You told her not to do something and she'd go right ahead and fucking well do it. Everyone in that village knew that pond was dangerous, and that was long before those two lads fell in. Of course, Frank said that was why she was like that — because of what happened to her out there. Load of rubbish. She was always a bloody pain in the arse. After the pond she just got worse. He were just making excuses for her as usual. He even got some bloke to try and sort her out. Didn't do her any good.'

'Victor,' I said. 'Victor Lang.'

Griffin shrugged and said dismissively, 'A shrink.' He put the bulb to one side and reached for another in the bag. He looked at me, contemplating me critically for a moment. 'I never told him, though,' Griffin said.

'Told who?' I said quickly.

'Frank.'

'Told him what?'

Griffin didn't answer. 'Thought he'd been through enough already,' he said. Griffin

404

reached for a much larger pot on the side of the shelf and began to pour in earth directly from the bag. 'Don't like thinking about it even now.'

I waited. Griffin shoved the top of his baseball cap higher on to his head. He reached into the bag again and saw my impatient eyes fixed on him in the gloom.

'When?' I said quietly.

'Winter,' Griffin said straightaway. 'Out by one of the old barns.' Griffin shifted slightly on his feet and sniffed loudly. He blinked and then nodded to himself, making up his mind. Then he told me.

44

'I didn't expect to see anyone,' Griffin said. 'But her bike was out there, leaning against one of the barns. There were no sign of Frank, which was odd, so I reckoned she must have come out alone. But I couldn't figure out why. But I could hear her,' Griffin said. 'She was in there all right. And she was talking. So 'a course I thought to begin with she must have been with someone else — some mate of hers from the village. But there was no other bike and I couldn't see anyone else.'

'She was alone?'

'Yes. But I could hear her going on and on. And when I went in it was just her. There was an old water trough on the other side of the barn. And she was standing in front of it with her back to me. Then she kind of stopped and started giggling to herself like a silly little girl. But she weren't a little girl no more.'

'How old was she?'

'Around fifteen or sixteen, I suppose,' Griffin said. 'Back for the holidays, I think this was.'

'So after her stepmother's accident?'

'Yes, it musta been. So I went in there. The barn was empty. We used to use it for storing feed, but we hadn't stored anything in it for donkey's years. But that didn't mean she had any business being there. So I were going to tell her to clear off and go on 'ome. But for some reason I stopped myself. I just watched her for a while, and then I took a few steps inside. I wanted to see what she was up to.

'There was this old sack with a piece of rope tied to the top of it next to her feet, and when I got closer I saw that the bag was kind of . . . moving. It were, like, squirming. She didn't even seem to notice it. And all the time, she just kept on talking. And suddenly, and I don't know why, I nearly turned back and left right there and then.' Griffin paused. 'I think I did stop for a while. Might have turned round, but I kind of made myself go on. I felt silly, I suppose. She were just a little kid, really, wasn't she? But there was something about that voice. And I suppose I knew . . . I knew that something was up and part of me already knew what she had in that bag.'

Griffin clutched the pot with both hands and stared across the table. 'So I kept on going. Wish I bloody hadn't now. I kept on walking towards her. And all the while she kept on talking. Then she reached towards the bag.

'First thing she does is she kneels down by the bag. And then she reaches for it. The bag starts moving straightaway, like they could sense her out there, and there was this damned awful wriggling. She seemed to think that was funny. So she keeps on doing it. Kind of reaching for it. Then she does it one more time and then quick as lightning she opens up the bag. I saw then that the rope was kind of tied in a loop at the top of it. She reached in. Then she closed the bag again. I saw she had something in her hands. It was big and thrashing about. I could see its tail. It reached almost halfway down her waist. She'd been bitten, but she didn't seem to care. It was a rat. It made this bloody horrible noise, and then she plunged it into the water and held it there. The bag next to her kept on moving.

'I suppose I froze. She started laughing again. My mind, well . . . for a second or two it kind of went completely empty. Like I was . . . I don't know, watching myself —

that it wasn't really me standing there at all. Then I felt this kind of numb feeling all over my body, and I couldn't make myself move. Then the next thing I knew I was marching right up to her and looking down into the water trough. The water.' Griffin paused and closed his eyes. 'The water, it were full of 'em. She must have filled the trough from the well just so she could do it. I didn't know what to say. Could hardly breathe. She must have been there for hours, and the one she was holding under the water was still thrashing about. The damned thing wouldn't die. The next thing I knew I'd grabbed her, and was spinning her around and her face . . . well, Rebecca's face, it looked different somehow.'

'Different?' I said. 'Different how?'

Griffin raised his eyes, so he was looking straight at me. 'It was like I were looking at someone else,' he said defiantly. 'It didn't look like her at all, and it was like she didn't know who I was either or even know where she was. But there was this sly look on her that I'd never seen before. She looked older somehow.' Griffin nodded to himself. 'Yes. It was like someone older was staring at me through a young girl's face. That's the only way I can think to describe it. But I wanted to slap that look right off her. I think I even raised my hand. I just couldn't bear to look at it any more. It was worse even than all that wet fur and the sound of that animal dying in the water. And then the expression was gone. And I was looking at her again. I was looking at Rebecca.'

Griffin stopped talking. He suddenly looked tired. He blinked. It was very quiet. Griffin pushed the pot away from him and started moving towards the door. I followed. He turned off the light. At the far end of the garden I could make out Mrs Griffin through the kitchen window, carrying a basket of laundry; she disappeared into another room. Griffin looked at the empty window for a moment and then started to walk back towards the house. Halfway there I stopped him.

'And this barn?' I said. 'Where is it?'

'Near Chippy.'

'Chipping Norton?'

'Yeah. Near Bliss Mill. Frank sold the whole lot — it's an estate now. Industrial estate.'

'And that barn?' I said anxiously. 'Is it still there?'

Griffin shrugged. 'Maybe.'

We walked on. 'I didn't know what to do,' Griffin said. 'I didn't know what I had seen. I couldn't really believe it, you see. And when it was all over I did my best to try and forget it. I was going to tell Frank. But she begged me. Begged me not to tell her old man. And after a while I agreed. Not for her sake, though. I did it for him. I did it for Frank.'

'But you told someone, didn't you?' I said.

Griffin nodded.

'Who?' I said. 'Who did you tell?'

45

My car sped through the gathering darkness towards Chipping Norton. Glimpses of trees and fences and fields became engulfed in frozen fog. The car shifted and wobbled as I took the small roundabout into town too fast.

I reached for my phone and called Graves. 'I think I might know where the body is,' I said as calmly as I could manage. 'Of one of the girls. Maybe both.'

'Where?' Graves said quickly. 'Where are they?'

'I think that they may have been hidden somewhere in an old barn. A barn on some land Hurst used to own. I'll explain everything later. Have you talked to Hooper yet?'

'I'm on my way to his house right now.'

'All right. You must talk to him. Then let me know what he says.' I hung up before Graves could ask me anything else. A few minutes later, I finally found the turning.

The small road began to slip downhill. The lead-covered dome of the old tweed mill stood on the crest of the hill. There was a car rental office. Beyond it stood a number of almost plastic-looking warehouses divided into units.

The road ended abruptly and was blocked with a metal beam suspended in the air like a checkpoint. Next to it was a long oblong trailer set down permanently in the concrete. I got out of the car, stepped into the cold and peered inside, where a young man was sitting with his boots propped up on a metal table.

I rapped hard on the door with the side of my fist and when the man still did not respond I pushed open the door. Startled, he stared up wildly. The chair began to slip and squeak beneath him, and at the last minute he made a desperate lunge for the table, jogged the edge and knocked his tea all over the newspaper in front of him.

He looked helplessly at the tea dripping on to the floor while I explained what I wanted. Then he politely introduced himself as Richard Rose, shook my hand and sponged up the worst of the spilt tea with paper towels. After that he grabbed his coat, keys and a torch, and we headed towards the buildings at the back.

'So it's still there, then?' I said. 'The barn's still there?'

'Yep. It's listed,' Rose said. 'Council won't let 'em knock it down, though we could do with the space. There's been some talk about converting it into flats, but you know what the bloody council are like. Take forever, that lot.'

We walked past locked buildings that were long and wide. Spread out neatly in front of us were parking spaces.

'Sure I'm not going to get you into trouble?' I said.

'No, you're all right.'

Rose led me towards the back of the furthest one and strode towards a chainlink fence. Set within it, so small that you could hardly see it, was a gate.

'For the gardeners when they come round in the summer,' Rose said as he searched for the keys. 'Strimming.'

He snapped open the padlock, and we had to crouch to get through. Rose seemed content to come along with me, and, looking up at the stone barn rising on the top of the hill, I was content to let him.

We strode quickly across the field, leaning into the wind, which rose as we moved closer to the top of the hill. The barn stood almost exactly in the field's centre, and from the bottom of the hill it looked like a slab of black in the moonlight. A faint sound came from the edge of the field — a stream.

We walked around to the doors at the front. Pieces of broken stone were scattered throughout the long grass and snow; brown leaves had piled up between the fragments. At the front, leaves had clustered and frozen around the barn's broken doors. The doors were hanging off their hinges, and we squeezed through them to get inside. There was a smell of damp and closed-in dankness. At the far end was the water trough. Something big rustled and fled into the darkness.

'So what are we looking for?' Rose said loudly.

'I'm not really sure,' I said. 'But water. I think water.'

Rose shone the torch upwards. At one point the entire roof had collapsed, and it had been replaced with corrugated iron, which had rusted almost completely away. The walls were whitewashed inside, and the stalls had collapsed and fallen in on themselves, while some of the huge central beams had cracked and lay in broken mounds on the floor. I paused, listening. Somewhere, down from the other end, was a faint sound of trickling water.

I took Rose's torch and flashed the strong beam ahead of me along the broken walls, stepping over the disintegrating pieces of wood and broken stones. Halfway along another piece of timber blocked my way. We stepped over it and peered into the darkness.

The beam of the torch danced along the floor. Old coils of rope. Large empty bags of fertilizer or feed. Briars and weeds grew wildly through the cracks in the ancient cobbled floor. I took another couple of steps towards the back. A large pile of toppling firewood had been set by one wall and forgotten about, and on top of it was a white broken window frame lying on its side, covered in cobwebs and dusty earth. I took another few steps and shone the torch closer to the ground, hearing the water more clearly now. I moved closer to the far corner of the barn. The moonlight fell through a small window and faded at my feet. More pale light shone through the broken roof. I could smell the stone-infused water down below now. I shifted a couple of old pallets and bags out of the way, hurling them roughly to one side.

'What is it?' Rose said from behind me.

'A well,' I said.

A long time ago there must have been

bricks built into a tall circle. A pump of some kind. But they were gone now. All that remained was a pit that had been bored deep into the ground. I knelt down and reached in. I could just touch the surface of the water with my fingertips. It was very cold, and there seemed to be a current pushing against my fingers as the water coursed its way beneath the earth.

I looked at the water for some time. Uncertain. 'Must be a natural spring running beneath us,' I said finally. 'Probably that's why they built the barn here in the first place.'

Rose shifted impatiently behind me and sneezed. He didn't seem at all interested. 'You know, I should be getting back,' he said.

'Just one second,' I said.

I stared at the water, thinking. I could phone and get some people out here first thing in the morning. Or I could know. I could know right now before sending anyone on a wild goose chase. So was I going to do it?

For a few moments I couldn't decide. I'd probably come down with a bout of pneumonia if I went ahead and did it. I sighed. I always end up going ahead and doing stupid things.

I thought of Gail Foster's mother and the promise I had made to her. Fire and now water. It was like some kind of test. I laughed at myself as I stared at the well. I found that I was already unloosing my tie. I stood up, took off my coat and handed the torch back to Rose. If I was going to do it I would have to do it now, before I changed my mind.

'I want you to help me out a bit more, Richard,' I said, 'if you don't mind.'

Rose, having seen me take off my tie and undo my shirt, suddenly looked nervous.

'It's not what you think, big boy,' I laughed in spite of myself. 'I want you to keep that torch on the water. I'm going to go in there and have a quick peek. It'll be a minute, no more than that. It's important.'

'All right,' Rose said, looking highly relieved.

I stripped and passed my clothes to Rose, feeling like an idiot in my boxer shorts. Then ever so slowly I lowered myself into the well.

46

Even before I touched the water, the cold air rising from its surface began to burn above my knees and then my waist. I lowered myself in farther. My breath sounded harsh and uneven. For a moment, I remained balanced above the well — then I took a deep breath and let go.

Any kind of preparation for the water had been utterly futile. My entire body went into a spasm. The freezing cold pounced, grabbed hold of my momentarily inert body and began to push me until I almost leapt with shock. I scrabbled at the sides and tried to push myself back up. But the bricks at the sides fell in white powdery clumps and cascaded down, landing in small splashes in the water next to me.

Rose, seeing me thrashing about and floundering, placed the bundle of clothes on the top of my coat and laid the bundle on the floor. Then he knelt down and stretched out his hand. I gratefully took it, and I pushed my way up, panting, so that I was wedged once more just above the water. I stayed there, shivering helplessly. My teeth chattered in my mouth so loudly that they seemed to echo all around the barn. I tried to gather up enough courage to go back in.

The surface of the bricks on either side seemed, after the intense cold, almost warm. Up close, I saw that they were slippery, and covered everywhere with an unpleasant green and brownish type of slime. Here and there, especially in the crags and crevices, were large clumps of a thick and sinewy vegetation.

'You all right down there?' Rose said, shining the torch on the water and looking highly amused.

'No,' I said. 'I'm not.' I gasped once and then went in again.

The second time was almost as bad. But I forced myself. I took a deep breath and slipped beneath the surface. I began to claw my way down, holding firmly to the side of the well with one hand, using my other to feel along the walls. I didn't know how deep the well was, but somehow I'd have to try to reach the bottom, if that was possible.

Slime, a crevice and nothing. I reached farther down. More slime, another bigger, wider crevice. I searched for as long as I could, then I pulled myself up. I drew air into my lungs and then pushed myself down again. Deeper this time.

The deeper I went, the more the water seethed and churned beneath me. My arm reached out, my fingers rapidly searched the surface, feeling for anything that could be wedged or tied down there. Weighed down. But there was nothing. I pushed myself back up, gasping, to the surface.

I waited a whole minute before I went down again, counting down the seconds on my watch. Rose was still kneeling by the side of the well. The water trickled and his voice echoed, bouncing off the walls.

'What are you looking for?' Rose asked. 'What's down there?'

'Probably nothing,' I said.

Not wanting to think of what might be there, I thought about the time I had ended up in a fairground when I was a kid. Mickey Mouse and Dumbo and spinning teacups. I breathed in deeply. Once, twice, and then disappeared beneath the surface. Bubbles rushed past my face. This was the last try.

Down below, it was pitch black, but for some reason the vegetation seemed to grow even more thickly along the well's walls. Long fronds of some weed, which I could not see, reached out and brushed against my face. I fumbled blindly in the dark. Now deep beneath the surface, I could feel the current of the water rolling around my legs.

My lungs began to burn and ache. I felt the first beginnings of a rising panic as I sensed the terrible solidity of the bricks around me. But I kept searching. The tips of my fingers ripped through the weeds and slime as I pushed myself farther and farther down. The pressure deep in my lungs rose. My mouth began to fill with water. I had to go back up now. But for a few seconds longer I refused.

Suddenly, I felt the muddy bottom of the well brush against the soles of my feet. I reached up, came upon a sharp shelf of rock and began to push with my feet. Then I pushed myself further down, around the base of the rock. My arms reached out, searching with one hand while I kept myself as immobile as I could with the other. From what looked like miles away, the orange light of Rose's torch shone through the water.

I reached out. My eyes widened in the darkness as I felt something that was smoother than the sides of the well. Blindly, my hands ran along it. A rope, or at least that's what it felt like. There was something attached to it. I felt it. It was soft and somehow even colder than the water.

Colder than the water.

Instinctively, I knew what it was. The shock gave me a mouthful of water as I recoiled. But the mud clung to my feet and to my ankles. Fear held me, and for a few terrible seconds I swung my arms in the water in circles and stayed put. But the movement of my arms had caused something to shift in front of me in the water. And suddenly something cold brushed against my face, moved along my lips and from there to the tip of my nose. It moved lovingly up along my forehead and into my hair. Reaching for me in the darkness.

Desperately, I pushed deep into the mud with my feet, but it was too soft. I twisted my whole body, writhing in vain to push myself free. Panic enveloped me along with the rising, whirling darkness. The black mud had now risen above my ankles, and the more I pushed the higher the mud rose. I thrashed about helplessly in the water, while the current suddenly seemed to pound beneath me, as if the water had sensed my presence and wished to drag me beneath the earth.

More water entered my mouth. I tried to cough it out, but only another larger mouthful of water slipped down my throat and pushed its way into my lungs. I twisted my head from side to side, aware, but only faintly, that I was screaming.

I reached forward, not caring now what I touched or tore in the darkness. My fingers dug into something very soft. With my other hand I grabbed at the rock, straining with every muscle. But none of it was any use. The mud's clutching resistance held me ever more tightly at the bottom of the well. I became dimly conscious of some sound coming from far above me. A suppressed yell or scream. The single orange light from above had gone. There was a sudden tightness in my throat, and a coldness coursed through my entire body. Numbing fear. My back emitted a single shudder in a spasm and then went limp. I struggled weakly, and for a few moments my hands reached for the narrow sides of the well.

There were a few more moments of a desperate and wild panic. Then, unspectacularly, it ended. My head tilted back. My heart rate slowed. My mouth opened. My eyes rolled back, glassy and empty. The blood rushed from my limbs towards my chest. And the burning searing pain in my whole body seemed to ease. My head began to loll forward, and then my arms drifted to my sides. I fell backwards so that my back bumped and rested against the ancient walls of the well. A moment of languid peace.

It came to me then with perfect clarity that I had never made it out of the Ford Falcon at all. I was still there, dying in Buenos Aires all those years ago. All the rest of it — my other life in England — had been an elaborate illusion. The illusion of a drowning man. I was still in the car, trapped with the other men. Soon my body would roll twisting into the brown waters of the river delta. It would float and be carried along, drifting ever outwards to the sea.

And I knew something else. I had found her at last. Not Gail Foster or Elise Pennington. They had never existed. They were just illusions that I had tried to grasp as the water filled my lungs and the current of the river began to take me away from the diminishing lights of the Ford Falcon. Pilar, I thought. Pilar. It's you Pilar, isn't it? I knew I would find you. But what have they done to you? Your poor face. What have those animals gone and done to you? I wanted to reach out and touch her face in the darkness before me one last time. I tried to lift my arms. But now they were as heavy as lead. And when I tried to move closer, the mud around my feet caressed my toes and held me, while the pounding of the

425

water subsided into a murmur. Oh, Pilar, I thought, you've been down here all this time and I never knew it. But how could I have known?

And in that moment I remembered her. I remembered the smell of her hair. With my hand outstretched, I touched the base of her neck with the very tips of my fingers. Her skin was stone cold, but I didn't care. I had found her.

47

Buenos Aires, January 1982

We never knew how *los militares* had found out where we were staying, but I hadn't expected them to come for me so quickly, and my brother and I had both been in a kind of daze since Pilar had disappeared. I had been asleep when I heard that loud, unmistakable banging on my front door. I had run bounding down the stairs towards the back porch, but one of them was waiting for me with his shotgun raised lazily at my chest.

He ordered me to go back to the house and unlatch the front door, where his partner was waiting for us. My brother thankfully had been out somewhere. They pushed me inside. A stifling Buenos Aires morning. Thunder and lightning rumbling far off in the distance. But no rain and no relief from the remorseless heat. Fans blowing everywhere in that strange chintzy old house.

The two men were similarly dressed in a near-parody of a civilian uniform. Shirts a little open at the chest and out-of-date slightly flared trousers. One of them, the bigger of the two, was wearing a thin leather jacket. It was the meticulously polished shoes that gave them away — that, and the shotguns hanging by their sides. They pushed their way in, asked if I was alone, then looked around the house. Obviously, they were casing it for later, when they or other members of their battalion would come back and steal everything inside it. I did not recognize them. But no doubt the blond man *el rubio,* along with his companions, was eagerly waiting for me somewhere and had sent these two to come and get me.

They seemed to be experts at it, and both appeared bored by the whole routine. The smaller one poured himself a drink from a decanter on the table, draped himself on the sofa in the darkened living room, placed his shotgun on the wooden floor and closed his eyes. The other one followed me while I went upstairs to fetch my identity card.

I was wearing a River Plate football shirt. The big man seemed to approve. He closed the door. Suddenly he started talking about some of the players. He was very knowledgeable. The identity card should have been easy, as you had to carry it wherever you went, but I just couldn't find it in a house that was still unfamiliar to me. I rummaged everywhere for it. But it just wasn't in the room. All the while I could sense the man's mood darkening. I was running out of places to look for it. I searched once again in a drawer by the bed, muttering, and heard a few bounding heavy steps and then felt a savage kick at my side that was so hard that it sent me into a sprawling heap on the floor.

I managed to pick myself up and finally found it in a drawer in a small table on the landing. He let me put on some trousers over my boxer shorts and then we went downstairs. In the living room the decanter looked half empty and the smaller man was fast asleep. The big man reached into his leather jacket, pulled out some plastic cord, tied my hands tightly together in front of me and then placed one of my brother's sweaters over my hands.

He shook the other man awake. The small man grumbled, swore and picked up the shotgun. They led me into the street and shut the door behind them. I gazed up, wondering if I should call out for help. But the fear was already so great that I found that part of me had completely succumbed to their will. They hadn't even done any-thing to me. Yet I was, in seconds, already acting the role of the prisoner. It was as if I were shrinking.

They'd left the ignition on in the car and I heard the throaty rumble of the Ford Falcon before I even saw it. The polished metal grille shone out between the large oblong orange lights, and the Falcon's engine rumbled greedily as we approached. The car was clean and as impeccable as the soldiers' polished shoes.

The small man got in the car first. I was led to the back. The streets were dark. No one about at all. What happened to me after this was of absolutely no interest to the men now sitting in the front of the car. These two soldiers in civilian uniform were just one small cog in a much larger machine that lay unseen all around the city. Somewhere my name was written out in black type along with an address. A docket perhaps or a file lying on a desk. Perhaps just a name on a long list.

As I sat in the back, all I could think about was the ad that they had run all summer in the cinemas and on the TV. An excited slightly effeminate male voice repeated a slogan. It banged idiotically in my head. 'Ford Ford Falcon. Falcon Falcon Ford.

Ford Ford Falcon. Falcon Falcon Ford. Ford Ford Falcon. Falcon Falcon Ford. Ford Ford Falcon . . .'

The images of the ad played out in my mind in almost minute detail. A child sleeping peacefully in the back. Silence! Four smiley faces at a petrol pump. Economic! A beautiful woman in a fur coat. Air conditioning! A disco packed with more sexy women. A tape deck! 'Four speakers!' A magician in a top hat popped open the boot. Hundreds of white rabbits and doves. The rabbits spilled out and flopped around on the floor. The doves flew out. Plenty of room!

It was dark down there in the back of the Ford Falcon. I knew that. And they were big too. Falcons had been a favourite with Argentinian middle-class families because they rarely broke down, were cheap and had a nice big boot. They were a favourite with the military police for exactly the same reasons. But the military always painted theirs a signature shimmering green. *Los Falcons Verdes* — a phrase that had quickly become synonymous with terror, torture and death.

48

Suddenly a lot of things seemed to happen at once. There was commotion around me. A muffled, dripping echo. I felt something tugging hard at a point just below my elbow. It lost purchase, then grabbed harder beneath my armpit, and this time it didn't let go. Seconds later, I felt myself rising. The mud shifted at my feet and then, almost with a reluctant sigh, the mud let go. I surged forward, gaining speed, and was being dragged, scrambling, through the water and towards the end of a tunnel that seemed to have no end.

After a shower, I warmed up back in the trailer and drank two hot cups of very sweet tea in front of the heater, while Rose showered and got changed in a small annexe. When my teeth stopped chattering in my head to the extent that I could actually talk, I phoned the station and called it in. Rose came back just as I put the phone down.

He gave me a long, critical look before he closed the door behind him and shook his head. He walked over to the kettle and put it on. He still seemed rather resentful and put out that he had been forced to save my life.

'There's going to be quite a lot of people here fairly soon,' I said. 'Would you mind taking them there? Back to the well?'

Rose shrugged. 'Sure, why not? As long as I don't have to go in there again. What's down there anyway?' he said.

I didn't say anything straightaway. 'You'll find out soon enough,' I said, looking at the stranger who had pulled me out of there and by some miracle had known what to do afterwards.

As if reading my mind, Rose said, 'They make us do a course. First Aid. 'Elf 'n' safety. Thought it was a waste of time . . . at the time.' He let that hang in the air and shrugged before reaching for a cup. 'Got us to practise on some dummy,' he said, looking at me. 'You know that you weren't speaking English just now when I pulled you out of there?'

'I wasn't?' I said, surprised.

'Yeah. You were going on in Italian or something. French maybe.'

433

'Spanish,' I said.

'Spanish. Right. And you kept on repeating something — a word, a place, or something. Over and over. Pilah or Piluh or something like that. I was wondering what it meant.'

'Pilar,' I said. 'I was saying that, was I?'

'Yes,' Rose said brightly. 'That's it. Pilar.'

'Well,' I said shortly. 'It doesn't really mean anything. Pilar's not a place or even a word. It's a name.'

'A girl's name?' Rose said, immediately interested.

'Yes,' I said.

I took a deep breath. It was the first time I had heard myself saying the name out loud for years. I raised my cup closer to my lips. 'So you'll be here when they come,' I said.

Rose nodded.

There was still some half-dissolved sugar in the bottom of the cup. I swigged it, licked my lips and placed the cup on the table. 'Thank you,' I said.

'Don't mention it. But you sure you'll be all right?'

'Yes,' I said. But I still felt light-headed and weak, and my brain was pounding like the water against the ancient walls of the well. For a moment, I thought of what was down there and shivered. I looked across the brightly lit room, glad of the warmth and of the company, reluctant to leave all of a sudden. I made myself stand up.

I looked hard at the young man standing by the old kettle, feeling a bit sorry for him. He was wasted here in this dead-end job. Maybe, it was because he had saved my life, or maybe it was because I knew that I would probably never see him again, but I found myself saying in a very offhand way, 'Actually, it almost happened to me before, you know.'

'What, you got yourself stuck in a well before?' Rose said.

'No, no. I nearly drowned before.'

'You did?' Rose did not look all that surprised or interested.

'Yes, it happened a very long time ago. There wasn't anyone back then to pull me out, like you did just now. So if you ever feel like ditching this job, you let me know. I can help you out on that. And thanks,' I said. 'Thanks for pulling me out of there.'

My car was waiting for me on the tarmac near the trailer. I stared fixedly in front of me, trying to bring some memory of Pilar into the light as I walked. But I had buried all of it deeply, and over the years the memory, of its own accord and with a definite purpose, seemed to have burrowed itself even more deeply into my mind. So that now, when I actually wanted to think about her, I could not.

For a moment there was nothing there at all, and I stood helpless in the cold trying to remember her. Then finally a splinter of memory came to me. My hands began to tremble. An image of her stood sharp and clear in my mind: her profile against the setting sun.

I stood in the cold for a while, remembering. Then I moved quickly to the car, opened the door and sat inside. I simply could not bear to think about Pilar any more. There was no point in it, and it just made my mind roam in endless circles. And the conclusion was always the same. I would never know. No one would ever know what had happened to her.

The phone was ringing deep in my pocket. I had the feeling that it had been ringing for some time. Still in a daze, I reached for it and answered it.

'Did you find them, sir?' Graves said.

'What?' I said.

'The girls, sir? Were they there where you thought they were? In that barn?'

'Girls?' I said. I just couldn't understand what Graves was talking about. 'Who?' I said stupidly.

'Elise and Gail. Were they there? Did you find them?' Graves said impatiently.

'I'm not sure. One of them maybe,' I said.

'Do you want me to come over?' Graves said. 'Where are you? I'm sorry but you sound awful.'

'No, I'm fine, Graves,' I said, snapping out of it. 'Did you speak to Hooper?'

'The arrogant sod burst out laughing when I asked him about the flowers. Said he didn't even know she was buried there. And didn't really care. Not exactly sentimental,' Graves added. 'But he did say something else.'

I paused and reached for the ignition. 'Go on,' I said.

'It looks like Sarah Hurst was putting it about a bit. Hooper said there was someone else. Something more serious, and that it was over between him and her a long time before Hurst got wind of it.'

'Over with him? With Hooper?'

'Yes.'

'And she ended it because of this other man?'

'Yes, that's what he said. But of course he didn't mention that before. That would have given him a motive and he figured he was in enough trouble already.'

'Did he say who?'

'No,' Graves said. 'But it sounded like it was pretty serious. He said that Sarah Hurst told him that she was going to leave her husband. Her and this other guy were going to run off together and never come back. They were just waiting for the right moment. That's why she broke it off with Hooper. Hooper said he didn't care all that much. A case of wounded pride more than anything else.'

'And you believe him?'

Graves didn't answer straightaway. 'Yes,' he said. 'I do.'

I started to reverse with the phone wedged between my jaw and my shoulder. 'All right,' I said. 'Where are you?'

'On the way back to the station,' Graves said.

'I'm on my way there now. Wait for me out near the front in twenty minutes and I'll pick you up.'

49

Once we had left Moreton behind us, I picked up speed, despite the snow. I had been calm after leaving the industrial estate. But now I was nervous and tense.

'So Nancy did know something,' Graves said. 'That's what you think, sir?'

'Yes, she had business here. I thought it was a damned long trip to make just for Frank Hurst.' I switched off the radio. 'But Nancy wasn't here for his funeral at all. Couldn't have cared less. She was here the whole time for something else.'

'But what?' Graves said, shifting in his seat to look at me and surreptitiously checking his seatbelt. 'What did Nancy come back to the Cotswolds for? What was she really after?'

I peered into the darkness ahead, really picking up speed now. 'We know whoever killed Hurst was after something. And they'd been after it for some time. It was something in that big old house, and Hurst knew it. The problem was he didn't know what it was. He didn't know what they were looking for. But somebody was trying to get in. So whatever they were looking for was important. It must have been important for them to take that chance.'

'So that's why he put the bars in. He did it to keep them out?' Graves said.

I nodded.

'And so he wasn't losing the plot at all.'

'No, he wasn't. Actually, he was right. Someone was watching him and waiting. So he put in all the bars to keep them out and then, just to be on the safe side, he got that big old dog and trained it to go after anyone snooping round his property. He kept watch too, and he reduced the space of where he lived to just a few rooms. And he fixed it so that whoever came looking would have to go round the back, where he'd be ready and waiting for them.'

'With a gun.'

'Exactly. I imagine it must have been a kind of hard monastic life. But the stubborn bastard probably quite enjoyed it in his own way. Also it fits. We know it wasn't Elise or Gail down there. The DNA you collected from Simon Hurst will prove that it was Rebecca, I'm sure of that now. But

Frank Hurst didn't know that his daughter was dead and buried right there under the house. And because he never knew, he waited for her. He waited for her to come back. So the question is: who was trying to get into the house and what were they after? We know that whoever it was also faked those postcards, and that whoever sent those postcards killed Rebecca Hurst.'

'And the postcards could be used to lure him out of the house.'

'Yes,' I said. 'But the trick could be pulled off only once. And whoever it was didn't look around the house. They searched in a very specific place, and they did it very thoroughly.'

'Her room. They looked in Rebecca's bedroom,' Graves said.

'They were looking for her diary,' I said. 'Her friend Alice said she was pretty attached to it. Went everywhere with it. And it always bothered me that it wasn't with her things. Why didn't she pack her diary when she left? And if she didn't pack it, where is it?'

Graves folded his arms. 'But that's what they were looking for?'

'I think so,' I said. 'But I don't think they ever found it.'

'But why?'

'Because somebody else already had it.' I paused and shifted in my seat. 'This is how I think it might have happened,' I said. 'Let's say Rebecca Hurst's killer murdered her just as she was about to leave home. That's why she had all her stuff ready to go. They walked in, and there she was, almost out the door. And when it was all over they buried her body under the house and her rucksack too. And when Hurst came back, she was gone and all her stuff along with her. So he just assumed she'd gone and done what she'd been threatening to do for years.

'But whoever killed her knew that they had to go back. Because after they'd buried Rebecca they realized they'd made a mistake. Something was missing from her things. They might have had a quick look for it, but with Hurst on his way home at any minute of course they couldn't hang about for long.

'Maybe she hadn't had time to pack the diary. Maybe it was still up in her room somewhere. But the problem with diaries is that they're secret, and because they're secret they're hidden very carefully. So whoever killed her knew that they were going to have to return and search for it. But what if the diary wasn't there? What if someone else had found it? Someone who spent a lot of time up in that room.'

'Oh, Christ. You reckon she could have been that stupid?' Graves said.

'Looks that way,' I said. 'Or desperate. Nancy told me she had a guest house up in Brighton, but her sister said she worked in a hotel. I checked. She was a chambermaid. Things weren't working out for her. And we know Hurst kept that room clean. What if Nancy found it while she was cleaning?'

'But why now?' Graves said. 'Why did Nancy wait all that time before coming back here? Why did she wait until Hurst was dead? And if she found it, why keep it? It was probably just an old schoolbook full of her writing.'

'I don't think she cared about Rebecca's diary,' I said. 'But I think she cared about what was in it.'

'Money,' Graves said. 'It was full of money. The money you said she'd stolen from school.'

'Yes, I think so. We know Rebecca stole some money. It wasn't all that much. But enough to get her to London and pay her way there for a few weeks at least. And she refused to give it back. Denied it was her, of course. I think it was the money she planned on using to go away.'

443

'And she hid the money along with her diary?'

'I think she must have.'

'So Nancy took the diary as well.'

I nodded. 'Her sister sent all of Nancy's belongings up to Brighton. I imagine that Nancy took the diary with her when she found the cash. Nancy probably forgot she even had it.'

'Until she heard there was a body beneath Frank's house.'

'Yes, and that's when she thought it might be worth having a look. And after that she must have set up a time to meet Rebecca's killer. From what we know, they didn't even show up at the café. But they were waiting for her down that lane.'

50

I parked the car up the street, away from the house and near the pub. We walked on past a small cottage. Below us were houses strung along narrow twisting lanes. Another pub and a church, an empty school and the occasional lorry or car trundled far down below. In the darkness a grimace spread across Graves's features as we got closer to the house.

We walked along the side of the wall and through the gate. We approached the front door very slowly. We didn't knock straight-away. Instead, both of us paused and watched. We could see Lang through a side kitchen window. He was sitting very still under the warm glow of overhead lights. He was cradling a glass of red wine in his hands, and as I looked he suddenly gripped it and brought it quickly towards his mouth. His wife, a dour-looking woman with streaks of grey hair, was loading dishes into the dishwasher and talking to him over her shoulder. Suddenly she turned around so that she was looking at him and pursed her lips. A look of disapproval crossed her face. Lang smiled wanly and put down the glass. He seemed to apologize and then stood up and helped her for a while. She spoke to him and he nodded from time to time.

When they finished, her features softened, and she wrapped her arm around his shoulders and kissed him fondly on the cheek. Then she padded away from him and slipped up the stairs. He looked relieved to see her go. He turned away from the sink, drained his glass, stood up and walked to the sideboard. He slipped out a bottle of wine from the rack above the fridge, examined the label and opened it. Then he poured himself a glass. A big one. He sat down. The dog was curled up fast asleep in a corner. He took off his glasses and pressed the bridge of his nose with his forefinger, and every so often he would look across at the dog sleeping by the stove.

From behind the thick oak door came muffled voices and then raucous laughter from the television. Lang sat a little straighter in the chair, brushed his trousers, shifted on his seat. I watched him and let him finish his drink. It would be his last for a very long time.

I took another step forward, sure that he would see us. But he stared at the wall in front of him for a while longer. You could almost feel the panic rushing towards him now that he was alone in his kitchen. He took another drink. He clutched at the base of the glass as if he were resisting the urge to hurl it across the kitchen. He looked sick to his stomach, and there was an expression of bewildered terror on his face, like a man waking from a nightmare. With a huge effort of will he remained still, restraining himself. He nodded to himself once. Standing in the shadows of the trees, I looked at him, wondering how many times Lang had been through this. I was sure I was looking at a man living in hell. Then I walked along the path and knocked on the front door.

It was answered by Mrs Lang. She was taking an earring out of her left ear and getting ready to go to bed no doubt, and she looked immensely put out when we told her who we were. Without saying another word, she turned around and headed off down the hall, leaving the door wide open as we waited on the doorstep.

There were boots and scarves and coats in a stand beside the door, and a bag stuffed full of old golf clubs was propped against the wall. We didn't wait for long. Graves went in first, and I followed straight into the kitchen.

I hadn't really expected Lang to try to run. It seemed undignified somehow, and there really wasn't anywhere for him to go. But the back door was wide open, and his wife was standing in the sudden cold of the kitchen, looking utterly bewildered. Lang was already halfway across the lawn. I nodded and Graves went straight after him, while the dog bounded around them both as if it were all a big game. I took a few steps into the kitchen and watched as Graves executed a perfect rugby tackle, tapping Lang at the base of his ankles so that he went flying. There was a loud crunch as he went head first into the snow. He tried to get up and run again, but Graves roughly picked him up and brought him back into the kitchen.

Mrs Lang looked at her husband and then at me. It looked like she wanted to say something but couldn't quite manage it. Her husband was covered in snow and mud. He wiped snow out of his eyes. The dog had followed them in and was wagging its tail furiously. Within seconds, the whole kitchen had become a mess of half-melted snow and muddy footprints. Lang wouldn't look at his wife as I read him his rights and arrested him for murder. I told him that we were going to take him to the station, and that she had better come along too.

51

I let Graves interview Mrs Lang back at the station and let Victor Lang stew for a while on his own.

Graves came out of the interrogation room and gently shut the door behind him.

'Yes,' he said. 'It was her. She was walking the dog up on Meon Hill, and she saw Frank Hurst up there. Victor was working at home with one of his patients. She was the one who told him.'

'So she told him that she'd seen one of his old friends out there when she got back home?'

'No, she didn't know who he was. She'd never met Frank Hurst. She walks the dog out there sometimes. When she got back home she told Victor that a strange man was working on the field as she was walking the dog. And that he just stood there glaring at her, and she didn't know why or who he was or what he wanted.'

'So Victor must have guessed that she had seen Hurst,' I said.

Graves nodded. 'But we still don't really have anything. She went out again after that and left Victor on his own. And she didn't come back until later, when he was there preparing dinner.'

'And how did he seem?'

'Perfectly normal, she says. He cooked her dinner, and they watched a bit of television and went to bed. So there's still nothing to prove he was out on the field. No one saw him there. Or saw a car. There's nothing to tie him to it or to any of it. I mean, I know he looked pretty out of it when we saw him at home, but he seems in control right now. And when he ran, I think he just panicked. And, sir, if he did kill Hurst, he rammed a pitchfork in his throat, went home for supper and then to bed by the sounds of it.'

'And he's waived his right to counsel,' I said. 'He says he doesn't need it and is demanding to know what all this is about.'

'But he ran.'

'I know. But he says he didn't hear the doorbell and had decided to let the dog out in the garden and was following it around to make sure it didn't get through into the neighbour's garden.' I pushed myself off the wall and shook my head. 'And what about the night Nancy was killed?'

'She said she went out and didn't come back until later. Victor was out when she came back in. Around 7.00. Or 7.30. When she asked him where he had been, he said he'd been for a drive over to Evesham, where he'd bought a paper and a few other bits and pieces. Then driven around for a while. Again, he seemed perfectly calm. She could be covering for him, but that's what she says. She seems totally baffled by the whole thing.'

Graves took a step forward. 'It was his dog, though, wasn't it, sir?' he said. 'That big old dog of his gave him away. It had to be someone with a dog, and who didn't live too far from Meon Hill. And we knew it had to be someone who knew Hurst was up there and who knew him. Someone who came back later.'

'Yes,' I said. 'That, and the stuff he left out. When I talked to him about Rebecca and her stepmother, he said they got along fine. But that's not what I heard when I talked to Hurst's foreman from the farm, and it's not the impression I got from that picture I showed you. So why would he lie about something like that if it wasn't important? It didn't make sense unless he had something to hide.'

'But it's more than that, isn't it?' Graves said.

'Yes, Lang was the only one who knew. He was the only one who spent a lot of time with her on his own and could have seen what Rebecca was because of his job.' I looked at Graves. 'I suppose you have a good idea of what that is now?'

Graves was silent for a moment. 'Yes. I think so. And Lang saw it too?'

I nodded. 'Well, if he clams up now, we're going to have a hell of a time proving any of it. There were no fingerprints on the pitchfork. So he probably wore gloves. And I've just been talking to Irwin and he says that the calls to Nancy's phone were all made from a call-box in Chipping Norton right in the town centre. Anyone could have made them. And, when it comes to Rebecca, we're talking about stuff that happened years ago. We don't even know when or how she died. And we still don't know how long she'd been down there and we probably never will unless he tells us.'

I started walking along the corridor. 'We're going to have to throw him off balance somehow,' I said. 'I've been thinking. There's one thing he had to leave completely to chance. He met Nancy in Cheltenham because of the diary. He wanted it because he knew something was in there that put him in the frame. So he arranged to meet her in a café and then followed her when she got fed up with waiting. Or he knew that she was leaving by train and banked on her taking the shortcut. So he's got the diary hidden somewhere or he's destroyed it. He killed Nancy because he couldn't take the chance that she wouldn't tell anyone, or because she would undoubtedly ask him for more money, or because she'd go to the police with it.'

'Yes, sir,' Graves said quickly. 'But how did he know that Nancy didn't make a copy, or have some kind of backup plan if things went wrong? There was no way he could have known for sure.'

'No. None whatsoever.'

'And he only had her word for it. The word of a blackmailer,' Graves said.

I nodded. 'Look, we're probably going to get one crack at this, so let's do it now, before he changes his mind and starts screaming for his lawyer.'

We stepped inside the interview room. I had hoped that Lang would have been sickened by what he had done. But he hadn't given up just yet.

'I want to see my wife,' he said. 'What do you think you're doing, bringing us here at this time of night? What's this all about?'

'You know why you're here, Lang,' Graves said wearily.

Lang looked away from him and at me. He had insisted that we let him change. And now he was wearing a dark well-worn suit and a striped cotton shirt. He sat straight in his chair with his hands in his lap.

Graves switched on the tape recorder at his side. The cassette made a click. For a moment I paused, thinking. Then I leant back in my chair, giving Lang plenty of room.

'So,' I said finally, 'perhaps it would be best if we started with Frank Hurst's daughter — Rebecca. Rebecca Hurst. Let's go over what I think I know, and we'll go on from there. All right with you, Lang?'

'Rebecca? I've already told you everything I know about her. You've dragged me all the way out here just to talk about Rebecca. Is that what this is all about?'

'You began to treat Rebecca when she was quite young, that's what you told me when I went to your house. She became one of your patients.'

'Yes,' Lang said. 'That's right. I've already told you that.'

'And this treatment started at her home when she was fourteen or fifteen and then

continued after her father sent her to boarding school. Is that right?'

'Yes.'

'And initially you thought she was suffer-
ing from post-traumatic stress because of
the incident at the pond. She nearly died
and watched two of her friends go under
the ice and drown, and it resulted in bad
dreams and negative behaviour.'

'Well, it was a bit more complicated than
that. But, put simply, yes,' Lang said.

'But,' I said, 'it was something else. It
wasn't what had happened to her on the
pond at all. But you didn't see it straightaway. And when I phoned you and told you
that I was going to get a court order so you
could talk about Rebecca, you had already
made up your mind that you were going to
lie. You told me that you hadn't had the op-
portunity to reach another conclusion. But
at some point you must have realized that
you'd made a mistake — a serious mistake
in your assessment of her?'

'I don't know what you're talking about,'
Lang said. 'I didn't lie to you. Why on earth
would I lie about a patient I hadn't seen in
years? I already told you what was wrong
with Rebecca. What do you mean another
diagnosis?'

'Was it when you saw her at home or later,

456

when she went away to school? Was it something you saw? Something she told you during one of her sessions?'

Lang paused. He was still sitting rigidly in his chair. 'Listen. There was nothing wrong with Rebecca. She was having some bad dreams. And she could be a bit destructive around the house, when she felt like it. She acted up sometimes. But that was all. I treated her, and she was making good progress. I told you that when you came to see me. The bad dreams were simply a response to a deep-seated trauma. I was very happy with the way she was progressing. Frank was too. And Sarah.'

'So you're saying that you cured her?'

'Cured her? Well, to the extent that that's possible, yes.'

'And there was nothing wrong with her? Beyond that? That's what you're saying? Rebecca was simply a normal teenage girl when you met her.'

'Yes.'

I motioned to Graves.

'All right, tell us about two nights ago,' Graves said. 'Your wife just told me that when she arrived back from work, you weren't there. You arrived late. And when she asked you where you'd been, you told her that you'd been for a drive.'

'Yes, that's right.'

'Did you see anyone when you were driving? Stop off at a pub? Anyone who can verify your story? Stop off for petrol somewhere? Where did you go?'

Lang paused. 'I had had a long day with my patients and needed some fresh air. I went for a long drive and stopped off in Evesham and wandered around for a while. I went to a shop and bought a few things. Drove around for a while. Then I went home.'

'And when was that?'

'I don't know. Around 10.00.'

'So quite late in the evening,' I said. 'And Evesham's on the way home — on the way back from Cheltenham.'

Lang shrugged. 'I suppose so, yes. So what?'

'So how long were you gone, would you say?' Graves said.

'Not long. Half an hour. An hour maybe.'

'And when you came back your wife was at home, waiting for you?'

'Yes, I think so, yes. If that's what she says, then yes.'

'And what about the day Frank Hurst died?' Graves said. 'Your wife told you he was on that hill, didn't she? She came back and described a man to you. She said she had seen a man up there, and he'd been staring at her and she didn't like it. You knew who it was, though. You knew it was Frank Hurst.'

'Well, no. Not straightaway. It was only afterwards, when I heard what had happened to him, that I assumed she must have been talking about Frank.

'I had no idea it was him at the time. I hadn't had any contact with him for years. Hadn't even thought of him until this all started. Look, I've asked you once already — what's this all about?'

'All right, Lang,' I said. 'Why don't you drop the act and think about where you are for a minute? How do you think we got to you so quickly? Aren't you wondering how we knew? Aren't you wondering why we've got your wife in an interrogation room right now? You must have known this could happen. That's why you ran just now when we came knocking on your door and made a fool of yourself.'

'But I told you I was —'

'Shut up, Lang,' Graves said.

'And that's what you were looking so worried about when you were sitting in your kitchen,' I said, 'and you didn't know anyone else was there. You must have known that this was a possibility. Nancy has been dead for less than forty-eight hours, and now here you are, sitting in a police station.'

'I'm sorry. Nancy. Nancy who? Who are you talking about?'

'Hurst's housekeeper,' Graves snapped. 'The one you beat to death and left lying in that back alley in Cheltenham. You know dammed well who she was.'

'What? I haven't been to Cheltenham for ages. I'm sorry, I do remember that Hurst had a housekeeper, but how am I supposed to remember her name? I didn't even know her, let alone that she'd been killed. What am I doing here?' Lang moved forward in his chair. 'What are you charging me with? I think I need to speak to someone. I've changed my mind. I want to call my lawyer. I want him here right now.'

'Lang,' I said, 'you honestly don't think Nancy was that stupid, do you? You must have thought that she might have made a copy in case something happened to her.'

Lang tensed and then immediately tried to hide it. 'Copy,' he said. 'A copy of what?'

'It was a risk you had to take,' I said. 'But there was no way you could have known for sure that she didn't make a copy. A copy of Rebecca's diary.'

'We found it this afternoon, Lang,' Graves said. 'We had someone check her place in

Brighton. She sent a copy to her own address. And it was still lying there on the doorstep. And she left another copy for safekeeping with her sister in case anything happened to her. She was going to milk you for every single penny you had, Lang.'

Lang closed his eyes. For a moment I thought that the whole thing had backfired. That he knew something that we didn't, and that he was going to insist again that we should get his lawyer. But then suddenly his entire expression changed. He looked far less indignant. The muscles in his face became less tight. In fact he looked almost relieved that it was all over. I had seen this many times before, but never quite as strongly as I saw it in Lang.

'She kept copies?' he said quietly.

'Yes,' Graves said. 'Every page. Photocopied and in two files. Rebecca's handwriting.'

Lang looked up. 'I'd like a glass of water, please.'

I nodded. Graves went out of the room and came back with a plastic cup. Lang took a large gulp.

Both of us waited and watched him, neither of us daring to say a word. Incredibly, Lang managed a half-laugh and I knew right then that it was over. 'That damned diary,' he said. 'It was about the only bloody thing I told Rebecca to do that she actually went ahead and did. Ever. In everything else she just ignored me. But that diary . . . So Nancy kept a copy, then?'

I nodded and, without giving him time to think, said, almost sympathetically, 'Must have been a bit of a shock. When you found out that Nancy had it. Nancy had found it when she was cleaning Rebecca's room. She had it with her when you were supposed to meet her in Cheltenham. You took the chance that she would have it with her and that you could trust her. Am I right?'

'Well, I couldn't take the chance she'd tell.'

'So what happened?'

'You already know, I suppose,' Lang said. 'If you've read the diary you know everything already.'

I nodded. 'We know. But I want to hear it from you. You got a call from Nancy. Or she came to see you, right?'

Lang took a deep breath. After another long moment he seemed to make up his mind. He took off his glasses, looked at his own reflection briefly in the lenses and then said, 'All right. Yes. She came to see me one afternoon. After Hurst's funeral. She told me she had the diary.'

'And she wanted cash for it?'

'Yes.'

'How much?'

'Twenty thousand pounds. I told her it would take me some time to get that.'

'And she hadn't read it before? It was only after Hurst was murdered that she read it?'

'Yes, she thought there might have been something in it.'

'She found it in Rebecca's room?'

Lang nodded. 'Yes. Rebecca had hidden it behind some old tiles in the bathroom. And one day, when Nancy was cleaning, it fell out.'

'So she took the diary and the money but forgot about the diary?'

'Yes. She told me that she put the diary in an old bookcase and forgot all about it.'

'Until she heard about what happened to Hurst?'

'Yes.'

'So she had a look through it?'

'Yes.'

'And did she ever mention taking it to the police?'

'She said that she needed the money. That things weren't going well for her in Brighton, and if she hadn't needed the money she would have taken it straight to the police.'

'Twenty thousand pounds. That's a lot of money,' Graves said.

'It was more than my life savings,' Lang said in a matter-of-fact voice. 'My wife would have noticed that it was missing straightaway. I didn't really know what to do. Told her I needed time to think. We arranged to meet in town before she left for Brighton, and I told her that I would bring her the money then.'

'So you knew she was living in Brighton and you took the chance that she was heading home by train after she met you?'

Lang nodded. 'I checked the train times. Knew that there were trains to London. If I didn't show up she'd probably take the shortcut and then try to phone me again once she was back home. I waited for her in that lane and suddenly there she was. Well, you know what happened next. You must have seen her.'

'Yes, we saw her,' Graves said.

'I didn't have long after that.'

'You searched her?'

'It was in her bag.'

'So you thought she had lived up to her side of the bargain?'

'Yes.'

'But you killed her?' I said. 'You are saying that you killed her, Dr Lang?'

Lang looked up and put his glasses back on. 'Yes,' he said. 'I suppose I am.'

'You hit her with something,' Graves said. Lang nodded.

'With what? What did you hit her with?'

'A bar. It was in the back of the car. In the boot.'

'A tyre iron,' Graves said coldly. 'Is that what you used?'

'Yes. I put it in a plastic bag and took it with me to Cheltenham.'

'What did you do with it afterwards?' Graves said.

'I took it home, washed it and threw it away in an old skip.'

'Where?'

'In Tewkesbury. Early the next morning.'

There was a pause. 'And the diary?' I said. 'You read it?'

'Later, when I got home.'

'All right,' I said. 'We'll come back to Nancy and the diary later. Because it was really all about Rebecca. Everything has been about her right from the beginning.'

Lang bit down on his lip. Then he looked up. 'Yes,' he said.

52

'Let's go back to her, then. What was it about Rebecca?' I said. 'When did you start to notice that there was something wrong with her?'

'Actually, I might not have identified it at all if it hadn't been for one of her teachers.'

'At the boarding school?'

'Yes. Her housemistress.'

'Ms Walker?'

'Yes.' Lang pulled on the creases of his trousers. Perhaps because he was on professional ground, he seemed a little calmer now, almost as if he were simply recounting a case history of one of his patients.

'She had noticed something herself?'

'She called me aside before one of my sessions with Rebecca one evening,' he said. 'I needed somebody else to see it too — for the idea really to take hold.'

'How long had she been there by then — at the school?'

'Oh, I don't know . . . not long, I think. I used to see Rebecca in a classroom over in the quad while the girls were in their houses doing their prep. Not very often. Once a month. I felt that we needed to see each other much more, but Rebecca wouldn't hear of it. She didn't want the other girls to know, you see.'

'But why? Why did you need to see more of her?'

'Because nothing seemed to be working. At school she was still essentially isolated. And, to be perfectly frank, the school didn't seem to be helping her either.'

'So there was something wrong with her?' I said. 'It was worse than you had first thought.'

'Yes.'

'So you'd realized by then that you might have been wrong? That the behaviour was not to do with her accident on the pond at all?' I said. 'You couldn't let me know that when I saw you. But, as far as she was concerned, it was of no consequence?'

'It was of consequence, but I began to feel that it wasn't the issue. But I couldn't understand where I could have gone wrong. In fact, I'd told Frank that we might well have to seek a second opinion. But then her housemistress drew me aside and said she wanted to talk to me about Rebecca. So when the session was over we had a chat in her office.'

'So what did she say?' I said.

'She seemed a bit upset. It took her a while to actually come out with it. She said there was something about Rebecca — something that she couldn't quite explain. She found she was avoiding her. Didn't even want to be in the same room with her. She'd asked one of the other girls to watch her and look after her. And she felt wretched about it, because she felt like she was letting the girl down.'

'Letting her down how?' I said.

'She told me that Rebecca wore her out. It could be exhausting to be in the same room as her for any extended period of time. And this feeling . . . well, she found that it could come over her very quickly, and that it wasn't entirely rational.'

'And she couldn't remember experiencing anything like it with the other girls?'

'Never.' Lang rested his hands on the table. 'And that's what really worried her. To begin with, I didn't think anything of it. Thought she was probably overreacting. But something had clicked in my mind, though at the time I didn't know what it was.'

'You mean that the symptoms were familiar? You'd seen something like it before?'

'No, I'd never seen it. Not up close. Not personally. But I'd read about it. As soon as she told me how Rebecca made her feel, I began to realize that she might just be right. There was something . . . there *was* something tiring about her, and sometimes when I left her I was pretty damned glad to see the back of her and I didn't know why. But, like Ms Walker, I didn't really like admitting it to myself. It seemed . . . I don't know, a bit mean-spirited to think of a child in those terms. And so I suppose I'd tried to ignore it. But, as I drove home that night, I couldn't help thinking about what she had said.'

'And you started to watch her?'

'Yes. And I began to notice other things about her. There was something ever so slightly off-key about her. Gestures made slightly too late or not at all. An emotional emphasis omitted or exaggerated. The right facial expression formed too soon. Her voice rising at the wrong time or not rising at all. I didn't really know what to make of it. Wasn't really sure what I was seeing, if anything.'

'I'm not sure I'm with you,' I said. 'But it was some kind of illness that she had? Is that what you are saying?'

'Yes, she was ill. Very, very ill. But I didn't

know how ill to begin with. But everything she said seemed rehearsed somehow. And after a while I got the impression that somehow I was being deceived. But I didn't know how or why, and I didn't understand what it meant. And then, soon afterwards, over the Christmas holiday, I heard some rather distressing news over at Frank's house.'

'About Rebecca?'

'Yes.'

'From Frank's foreman? Sam Griffin?'

'I never knew his name. A farm worker or labourer. Big man. Always wore a cap.'

'That's him. He came to see you in your house?'

'No. Not at the house. He must have spotted my car parked out front. And so he was waiting for me outside, at the end of the lane by the gate. He came at me from out of the trees and motioned for me to pull over. It was pouring with rain so I let him in the car to dry off.'

'And that's when he told you?'

'He said he'd seen Rebecca in one of the old barns. Said he'd caught her doing something. He'd caught her drowning animals. Vermin. He didn't know what it meant, but he didn't like it, and he thought I should know about it. And by the way he described it to me it sounded like she'd done it before.'

'So what did it mean? It was important, wasn't it?'

'I was deeply shocked because if true it was extremely serious,' Lang said. 'Very serious indeed. And so I confronted her with it straightaway during our next session.'

'And how'd she take it? I don't suppose she liked it,' I said.

'She was absolutely furious,' Lang said. 'She said he was lying. Said that he'd always had it in for her ever since she was a little girl. She said he was just trying to get her into trouble.'

'And did you believe her?'

'No. No, I didn't. Why would he lie about something like that? So we had a fight. She couldn't understand why I was taking his side. She started shouting. She told me to get out. Said she didn't want to see me any more. And anyway, so what? So what if she was killing them? They were only vermin on the farm. They had to be got rid of one way or another.'

'So she admitted it in the end?'

'In the end, yes. And the way he described it, she was getting something out of it.' Lang suddenly appeared a little cautious. 'So it changed things immediately.'

'But how?'

Lang ran his hands through his hair. 'Well, it pointed very clearly to something I hadn't seen before: sadism. And it was an aspect of her personality that she was clearly extremely adept at hiding. And that was the most worrying part of all. It was the first time I'd ever been given a glimpse of it. And I couldn't understand how I could have missed it. And he told me something else as well.' Lang lapsed into silence.

'Told you what?' I said loudly.

Lang seemed to snap out of it. 'He couldn't explain it, but he said that for a moment he felt as if he were looking at someone else. "Looking at someone else." Those were his words. And I started thinking that maybe he was right. And after that I just couldn't get it out of my head. I told myself that I was being a damned fool.'

'So that's when you started to suspect,' I said slowly. 'But you didn't want to admit it to yourself because she was so young. But you had an idea. And you kept on watching her after that?'

'Yes, far more closely. And then one day I saw what he meant.'

'So you two made up after the argument?'

'Yes.'

Lang sat back in his chair. He folded his arms.

'Come on, Lang, let's get this over with. When was it? When did you see it?' Graves said.

'It was near the end of the summer term,' Lang said. 'We met where we always did, in the classroom at the top of the school, overlooking the quad. The rest of the class-rooms were deserted, so we had the whole place to ourselves.

'I asked her to sit down. We talked for a while. She was looking forward to the sum-mer holidays. Her father had promised to take her away to France or Spain for a few weeks. I can't remember where. I asked her how she was getting on with the other girls at school, and she said much better. After we'd talked about that, I asked her to please talk it through with me again. I asked her to tell me what had happened. I hadn't planned on asking her. It just kind of came out. It would be the last time, I promised her.'

'Go through what again?'

'What had happened to her on the pond.'

'And did she?'

'Yes. Her voice, as she described the incident, was strangely toneless. Monoto-nous and even. I'd noticed that before. It meant something, I was sure of it.

'They had met on the green. Got there on their bikes. It was Ned's idea to go to the pond. They'd discussed it during the lunchtime break at school. They left the bikes in the trees. They didn't want anyone else to see them.

'But she didn't want to go on the ice. The other two had teased her, but she didn't care. She was cold and she wanted to go home. The ice looked dangerous. The boys went on first. Ned, the elder brother, and then Owen. She watched them. She called for them to come back, but quietly, because she didn't want to get them into trouble. They ignored her. She took a few steps on to the ice. And it began to crack. Then, suddenly, there it was. I sensed it. The faintest edge of something else in her voice. There was another emotion buried deep beneath the horror. Her eyes were bright. I sat very still, watching her. It had been like glimpsing a figure that was very far off. She kept on talking about Ned and Owen in that low, flat voice of hers.

'She managed to scramble to the bank and she had tried to help them. But they went under so quickly. The noise of the breaking ice had seemed quiet at first, but now the ice was breaking all over the pond. She was sure they must have woken the entire village and that someone would come to help them. But no one came. The two boys had been there, and then suddenly they weren't any more. She couldn't understand what had happened. But now she could see them. Struggling in the water. She didn't know what to do.

'She thought I was looking out of the window. But I was watching her reflection very closely. For a moment the tone of her voice changed. And her face had changed too. A look of, I don't know, slyness appeared as she stared at my back, and then she looked away into the distance. I gazed at her reflection, and suddenly all the thousands of little lies and half-truths she had told me over the years merged into one big and continuous deception so huge that it seemed to suck the very air out of the room. And I very much wanted her to just shut up, because being there — being anywhere near her — was unbearable. Because nothing that she had said was real.'

'But did you say anything to her at the time?' I said. 'Did you confront her with it?'

'No. Not then. I pretended that I hadn't seen it.'

'But why?' Graves said.

'I'm not sure. It was over so quickly. Her

475

expression had gone back to one of neutrality. She was still talking about Ned and Owen. I turned around and cut her off in mid-sentence. I made some excuse, I think. Said I was sorry but we had to finish the session early. We walked down the stairs without saying a word, and then I watched her take the path across the grass. A pretty girl wearing a pretty dress. Then she stopped and waved goodbye. And I remember thinking, it just can't be. The whole thing suddenly seemed impossible. Monstrous and unthinkable. I didn't even want to think about it. I tried to forget it.'

'But of course you couldn't,' I said.

'No, I couldn't sleep that night,' Lang said. 'Couldn't concentrate on my other patients the next day either. The days on which I had to see her again were the worst. I started avoiding her,' Lang said. 'Cancelled a few appointments. Tried to get someone else for her, but Frank wouldn't hear of it. And it didn't get any better. Every night, as soon as I closed my eyes, I seemed to see those two boys on the ice and I saw Rebecca watching from the bank. And sometimes, when I finally did fall asleep, in my dreams I became the one struggling in the icy water, unable to get out.'

53

'But there was no real way of knowing,' I said. 'No way you could be sure. That's why you waited.'

'Yes. I didn't see her after she was expelled from school, and I had my other patients, so I tried my best to forget her. Then I heard something. It was completely by chance — just an overheard conversation in a pub. I heard that those two brothers hadn't been the first. Another boy had drowned in the pond a long time ago and in exactly the same way. Fell through the ice. I'm not from Quinton, but apparently it's common knowledge round there.'

'But really you still had nothing,' I said. 'No proof. And then you started to think of someone else. You started thinking about Sarah Hurst.'

'No,' Lang said sharply. 'Not to begin with. Not Sarah.' Lang squeezed the bridge of his nose with his fingertips. 'I thought about the symptoms . . . the tiredness is a well-known reaction when someone is in close contact with a person like Rebecca. The emotional response is always the same: an overwhelming tiredness and lethargy in the face of a concealed personality disorder.'

'I'm sorry, what do you mean?' Graves said. 'We don't have your background, Lang. You'll have to try to be a bit clearer.'

Lang paused, thinking. 'It's well documented and I looked it up again after I began to suspect. An American psychiatrist described the psychopathic personality as a mimic, imitating a normally functioning individual. Later came the work by researchers in the field of criminal psychology. They began to develop a checklist of shared traits, but the idea is broadly speaking the same. Simply put, Rebecca was faking her emotions. And criminologists, those who have spent time with known psychopaths, have reported the same reaction — the same tiredness when in their presence.'

'So Rebecca was faking her emotions,' I said.

Lang sighed. 'As I said, I had noticed that her expressions and her way of expressing herself could be slightly off-key — that they could somehow come across as exaggerated and insincere. Or the things she said came too late, like afterthoughts. Or an emotional response didn't come at all. That was because the emotions weren't hers.'

'Not hers?' Graves said.

'She was replicating them because she simply couldn't feel them. Something was missing. A fundamental aspect of Rebecca's psychological make-up wasn't there. Pity. Love. Friendship. Empathy. She knew what they were. She knew how she was supposed to feel. She could recognize and name the terms. And she knew that other people felt these emotions. But she recognized them as a concept only. She could never really know what they meant because she was unable to feel them for herself.'

Lang sat back and reached for the cup of water. He took a sip and then a large gulp.

'So now that you knew what you were dealing with, it became easier to interpret what she told you?'

Lang sniffed and put the cup down on the table. 'Yes. When I talked to her, she was saying what she had learnt was expected of her — and it was the same with everyone else she met. She was copying your feelings even as you spoke to her. That's why it was so tiring to be with her, because all of her energy was fixed so completely and intently on you.'

'But why?'

'So she could survive,' Lang said, as if it were the most obvious thing in the world. 'So we couldn't see what she really was. She was hiding. And I knew it made her dangerous. Because if she could feel no empathy, she could feel no pity. Like the others afflicted with her condition, for Rebecca there were no boundaries. No moral limitations. She was not restricted by any type of code. And many of her other symptoms pretty much fit as well.'

Lang counted them off on his fingers. 'She was manipulative. She had her father wrapped round her little finger. Destructive, prone to lying and didn't seem to be bothered when caught out in a lie. Almost constantly in trouble. Glib. Superficially charming when she had a mind to be, but found it hard to develop long-term relationships. Impulsive and could act on whims. She was unreliable and as a person quite superficial.'

Lang looked down at his cup. 'And now that I had an idea of what she might be, every single event in her life, no matter how trivial, had to be re-examined. And if it were true, I had to look at what she had left in her wake so far.'

'Two dead boys,' Graves said quietly. 'The

Taylor brothers. And maybe not just them either.'

Lang nodded. 'Quite,' he said.

'And so that's when you started wondering about Sarah Hurst?' I said.

'When she had her accident, I didn't know. Didn't even suspect.'

'But she drowned. She drowned like the two boys,' I said. 'And she had a motive for this one. Rebecca hated her stepmother. Started acting up as soon as Sarah moved in. That's why she told Hurst about Sarah's affair with Brad Hooper. She wanted her gone. But Hurst forgave Sarah.'

'Yes,' Lang said.

'And so what happened then?' I said. 'You weren't treating her any more. But what? You decided to confront her?'

'I had to know. I really needed a lot more time with her, but I knew I wasn't going to get it.'

'But you couldn't stop thinking about her, could you?' I said.

'No. I couldn't stop thinking about Sarah and about what had happened to her that day by the swimming pool. Rebecca was supposed to have been at school. But she could easily have got to the house on her bike, or she could have cut class. And it was always water. She seemed to have some kind

481

of obsession with it. Nancy had found her by that pond, just staring at it, and it had taken her and Frank to drag her away from there. The animals — she had drowned them and watched them die. The Taylor boys drowned.'

Lang stopped for a moment. He reached for his half-empty cup and began to absently pinch the rim with his thumb and forefinger. 'It just got worse and worse. I couldn't stop thinking about it.'

'But that wasn't really what bothered you, was it? It wasn't Ned and Owen. It was Sarah Hurst you cared about. You needed to know about her. You needed to know what happened to her, didn't you, Victor?'

'Yes.'

'And you convinced yourself that it might not have been an accident at all?'

'I don't know. I was confused. I don't know what I was expecting. But I needed to see Rebecca one last time. So I phoned the house and asked if I could see her.'

'She answered the phone?'

'Yes. It was as if she'd been expecting me. She said I could come round the next day, early the next morning.'

'To the house?'

'Yes.'

'And when you arrived she was on her

way out?'

'Almost. She let me in and led me up to her room.'

'She was packing,' I said. 'She was packing and getting ready to go for good when you came.'

'Yes. She had a big rucksack on her bed. She said she was leaving, and she wanted to be gone early, before Frank came home from the farm. She'd have a whole day's start on him that way. She was old enough to leave home by then — seventeen or eighteen — and legally there wasn't anything he could do to stop her, but she wanted to be gone so he wouldn't make a fuss. And I think she was pleased that I'd called. But deep down nervous too. Of course, I know now that she'd come to the decision even before I'd called.'

'She wanted to show someone what she really was, didn't she?' I said.

Lang closed his eyes briefly and turned away. He looked very tired now. Crumpled and uncertain, he blinked in the light, as if he was not quite sure how he'd arrived in this small dull room. His chest rose and fell beneath his cotton shirt.

I was watching him very closely. The pace of my own heartbeat had quickened. My hand by my side had formed a tight fist.

Slowly, I unclenched it and put both hands in my pockets. The chair squeaked as I leant even farther back in my chair. Come on, I thought. Come on, Lang. Keep talking. Don't stop now. I looked across at Graves. He was waiting very patiently, or so it appeared, for Lang to go on.

'Of course, we'll never be sure exactly why,' Lang said finally. 'There's no way of knowing now. But for some reason, she needed someone to see who she was before she left for good. And she'd decided it would be me. For just a moment, she wanted to show her face. Her true face.'

54

'All right, so let's get this straight,' I said. 'You phoned Rebecca at home. This was when? After you had stopped treating her, right?'

'Yes. Around a year after our last session at her school.'

'And she said that you could see her at her home? She agreed to it? And she took you upstairs to her room? Her room in that big attic? And that's when she told you? So exactly when was this?'

'Fifteenth of August 1999,' Lang said without any hesitation at all. 'A hot summer's day. I parked the car and knocked on the front door. She came down straightaway. She was slightly breathless. As I said, I hadn't seen her for over a year. She had just been hanging around the house ever since she'd been excluded from school. The last time I had seen her she'd been a pretty girl, but in a year she had turned into a beautiful young woman. In fact, she was stunning. It came as a shock. Frank was out. The housekeeper off somewhere for the day. She looked pleased to see me. She said we could talk while she finished packing.

'So I followed her upstairs to her room. She was very matter-of-fact about it. She said she was leaving. She had to get the bus from Quinton to Moreton-in-Marsh and then the London train straight to Paddington. I asked her what she was planning to do when she got there. She told me that she didn't really know. She had some money — enough to keep her going for a while. She'd booked herself a cheap room somewhere in Bloomsbury for a few days. After that, who knew?'

'But you thought it could be your last chance? That you might never see her again?' I said.

'I hadn't really known what I was going to do until I got there,' Lang said. 'But I'd decided that I'd tell her what I had come to believe about her. I began slowly at first.'

Lang slipped down in his chair a little and placed his glasses on the table. He stared at them for a moment and put them back on. 'It was strange, because my voice didn't sound quite like my own. Her room was high up at the top of the house.' Lang drummed his fingers on the table.

I looked at him. It was now or never. I felt tempted to push him, and I could feel Graves at my side, tensing, ready. Lang finally focused and became very still. 'There was a wasp in there,' he said. 'The damned thing had got stuck on the window in the roof. And it kept on buzzing against the windowpane. It just got louder and louder. And as I talked I couldn't look at her, so I stared at the wasp. And I remember thinking, its face. The markings on its face — they looked just like a skull.

'And all the while the buzzing got louder and louder. And the damned silly thing kept on bashing itself against the window. I wondered why it couldn't find its way out. She seemed not to be listening to me. She kept on packing her things. It was as if what I was saying didn't matter. As if nothing I'd ever said to her made any difference.' Again, Lang stopped, a vacant expression on his face.

'And what did you tell her?' I said.

'I told her what I thought she was. I told her that she had led those two boys on to the ice that day. That it had been her idea, not theirs, to fool around on the ice, because she had known it was dangerous. I said she had chosen a time when she knew everyone

487

else would be asleep, so no one in the village would hear them.'

'And what did she say while you were telling her all this?' I said.

'Not a word. She just let me talk. Then she suddenly turned around. It looked like she had finished packing. She tied up the cord at the top and left the bag on the bed. She stood silent for a moment beneath the window. The wasp was still trying to find its way out.

'And then she told me. And the more she talked, the more animated she became. There was that same look I had seen back at the school, but now it was worse somehow.'

'And so she admitted it to you?' I said. 'She told you all the things she had done?'

'Yes. She said it was true about Ned and Owen. It had been her idea. She had heard about another boy who had drowned on the pond. And she wanted to know. She wanted to know what it looked like to see someone drown. That's all it was. Curiosity.' Lang looked up helplessly. 'She wanted to see what it was *like*.'

'And so she watched them step out on to the ice?' I said.

'Yes. Ned first and then his younger brother, Owen. She could hardly believe they were doing it. They kept on urging her to do the same thing. They seemed to be having a good time. But she refused. Said she'd be with them in a minute. And then she stamped on the ice. And in seconds they were under. Gone. She climbed into the water from the side of the bank, so she was wet, and then she started to call for help.

'Then she moved on to the girls — the girls who had gone missing. I wasn't sure what she was talking about to begin with. And of course, when I realized . . .' Lang fell silent and the blood seemed to drain away from his cheeks. Again, he ran his hands through his hair but almost frantically this time.

'So you hadn't suspected,' I said. 'You had no idea about the girls until that moment.'

'No, I had no idea. Of course, I'd known about the girls. But I'd only been suspicious about Ned and Owen until then. I think she assumed that I'd guessed about the girls as well.'

'But you hadn't?'

'No. Not at all. But when I knew . . . when she actually confirmed that I had been right all along about Ned and Owen, then, yes, of course, it all fit.'

'So you kept your mouth shut and kept listening,' Graves said. 'But you'd already got more than you'd bargained for, hadn't you?'

Lang blinked and breathed in very deeply. 'Yes. She was very precise. Very calm. She'd been riding her bike in Chipping Norton, near the outskirts of town. That's when she saw the first girl. She was playing in the garden. She asked her if she wanted to see a new foal on the farm. And the girl agreed.'

'They went together?'

'Yes. She took her the back way, along the fields, so no one would see them. She led her to an old barn and then . . . then she drowned her in the water trough.'

'And did she tell you what she had done with the body?'

'No,' Lang said. 'Only that no one would ever find it.'

'And the other — the second one. Gail Foster,' I said. 'She told you about her too?'

'Yes, she had already made friends with Gail. They went to the same school in Quinton.

'She decided on Gail because she was a nice girl, easy to make friends with. Gail already had lots of friends and she was pleased — pleased that Rebecca, who was a year older, seemed to like her. So when Rebecca knew that Frank was going to be out, she waited for Gail at the end of the lane near her house after school. All of the other children were under orders to go straight home and so no one saw them. She motioned for Gail to follow her.

'Rebecca asked if she wanted to go for a swim in the pool. She said that she had already talked to Gail's mother, who'd said it was all right. So they went straight across the fields, towards the house. She lent her one of her old bathing costumes, and they got changed downstairs in the living room.'

'So she made sure that they were completely alone?' I said.

'Yes. She wanted this one to last longer. Gail went in first and Rebecca watched. Watched her swimming, and then she jumped in too. It got cold, and Gail started to complain. Wanted to go home. It made Rebecca angry. Gail was strong for her age and she nearly got away, but Rebecca held her under the water. It was all over very quickly, though. Like the boys. She sounded disappointed.'

Lang was silent for a moment longer.

'What then?' I said.

'She had already dug a grave for Gail under the trees. She threw her in. Gail was still in her swimming costume. Then she threw in her school uniform on top of her. But Gail woke up, coughing. So Rebecca buried her. Then she packed the earth tightly and covered it with sticks and leaves.'

'She buried her alive?' Graves said quietly. I could see Graves trying to mask his horror. I did the same as best I could.

Lang nodded. 'She got back late. Dinner had been on the table. Frank asked her where she'd been. She told him she'd been out in the woods, exploring. Then she had her supper.'

'And did she say anything at all about a hairpin? The hairpin that we found later?'

'Yes. She said the police asked if it was hers. She almost said it was. But she knew that if it was ever proved that it was definitely Gail's, it would be obvious that she'd been lying. So she had said she wasn't sure — it was safer that way.'

Lang stopped. He seemed for a moment as if he were unable to go on. He looked dazed and a little unsteady. His Adam's apple rose as he swallowed. He seemed out of breath. Graves pushed the cup of water towards him. Without seeming to see it, Lang reached for it, took a large gulp and held the empty cup to his chest. His chest was rising and falling now. The hand gripping the cup was like a claw.

'And did she tell you about Sarah?' I said. 'Sarah,' Lang said. 'Yes.'

For a moment I was sure that that was it. That he'd had enough for one night, and that we would never hear the rest of it. But he seemed to rally. He nodded, urging himself to go on.

'She told me how much she had hated her,' he said. 'How she and her dad had been perfectly fine until Sarah had come along. So she'd pretended she was sick one day. It was hot and she knew Sarah would be lying by the pool. She watched her from her bedroom window for a while. And then she walked out round the back. Sarah was fast asleep.

'Rebecca found a coping stone that had been wedged beneath the gate. And she hit Sarah with it. Once was enough. Then she pushed her into the swimming pool. She took the rock with her and later cleaned it and threw it away.'

Lang lapsed into silence. 'The buzzing of the wasp had got even louder,' he went on finally. 'I kept on thinking: why not open the window and let it out? But I couldn't move. My hands were shaking. And when I looked at her, she seemed unreal somehow. Like something seen from far off. She kept on talking. I couldn't breathe. I kept on thinking about poor Sarah. About her grave out there in the church.'

'But she didn't know, did she?' I said quickly and leaning forward. 'Rebecca didn't know about you and Sarah. She didn't know that you'd been having an affair. That you'd met her while you'd been treating Rebecca. She didn't know that you were going to run away together and start a new life. No one else knew about it, did they?'

'No. No one knew,' Lang said quietly. 'But she kept on talking about her. The look on Rebecca's face was empty again. Already she was retreating. I took a step towards her. I think I meant to open the window to let in some air and to let the wasp out. She was standing by the door. She took a step forward and reached for her bag.'

'And that's when you knew that you couldn't prove a thing,' I said. 'She was taunting you with it. That's why she wanted to talk to you. It was part of her sadism. She couldn't resist. And you knew that you had to act quickly.'

'Yes. She started talking about how there was nothing anyone could do to prove any of it. That no one would believe that a young girl could have done something like that. Gail Foster was buried in a place where no one would ever find her, and they would never find Elise Pennington either.

And as for the others, they were just accidents: no one could ever prove otherwise. I suppose I took another step towards her. I was still thinking about Sarah. About standing over her grave, flowers in my hand. The flowers I still put there every so often when I can.

'And I realized of course it was true. There was nothing — nothing I could do to prove it. No one would ever believe me. Rebecca reached for the bag. There was something she had forgotten, or that she hadn't packed, because she brushed past me, on her way to the bathroom. And then I was moving. I knew that I couldn't let her leave. I think I might have slapped her. I'm not sure now. I might have done.' Lang paused. 'I remember her standing there in front of me. And then I think for a moment she knew. She knew and tried to run.

'She got as far as the stairs leading up to her bedroom. I grabbed her and held her facing me. She was strong. Her hands reached for me. My hands . . . my hands were on her throat. We fell and landed at the bottom of the stairs. She was still struggling. There was a curtain at the bottom, and she was reaching for it, trying to pull herself up and away from me. And then the curtain fell over her face, and I was glad because it meant I didn't have to look at her. And my hands were tightening and tightening around her neck . . . and then . . . she stopped struggling and she was still and I knew that I had killed her.'

55

The room was silent for a while. Lang pushed the cup of water away from him. He rested his arms on the table. He didn't seem to be able to look at us. I looked at him resisting the urge to say something. I let the silence continue.

'I just sat there,' Lang said finally. 'I'm not sure for how long. Just sat there. I went up to her room and sat on the edge of her bed and listened to her clock ticking on the table. I didn't want to look at her.'

'But you knew that you had time before Hurst came back. Rebecca had told you that already,' I said.

'Yes. After a while I found myself back on my feet and staring at her on the stairs. The curtain was still covering her face. Knew I had to get rid of her somehow. Hide her. But where? They'd look for her, and they'd find her. But then I took in her bag and the empty cupboards. All her stuff. Gone. She'd been threatening to leave home for ages.'

'So you thought you might have caught a break?' I said. 'If you could call it that. You thought they might not look for her if Hurst thought she'd run off.'

'Yes, so I picked her up and carried her downstairs and out into the garden. There was an old groundsheet on the lawn by a wheelbarrow. I wrapped her in it then went round the back of the house. There was an entrance there that the builders used.'

'You'd noticed it when you treated Rebecca at home?'

'Yes. I took her down the steps. There were some old crates there. A rusty bike. Cans of paint and a few broken tools. I cleared away a space in the middle, and then I began to dig, and as I dug I thought about those poor girls. Believe me, it helped. Then I went back up for her bag.

'But then halfway down the stairs I stopped and opened it up. I panicked when I saw it wasn't there. I was sure it would be there with her stuff. That she'd taken it with her.'

'Her diary.'

'Yes,' Lang said. 'It should have been with her things. She was very strict about it. Wrote in it every night. But it wasn't there.'

'And you'd phoned the previous afternoon. You were afraid she might have mentioned it in the diary. So if someone found the body they'd know you'd been at the house that morning. That you were the last person to see her alive. Or, even if they didn't find the body, they might get suspicious. Might think it strange that you never mentioned seeing her just before she left home for good. Especially if Hurst was the one who found it.'

'Yes. So I searched for it in her room, but I couldn't find it anywhere. I found a drawer full of her copy books from school, but her diary wasn't amongst them, so I went back downstairs with the rucksack. I put it near the groundsheet. Then I buried all of it. I didn't have much time, so I couldn't bury it that deeply. But it was deep enough. I didn't go home straightaway. I went upstairs and searched for a while longer in her room, but it was already getting late. I put the curtain back on the rail and tidied up. I had to think. I needed Frank to believe that she had gone away. So I took one of her textbooks with me.'

'So you had samples of her writing. And whenever you were in London you would send Hurst a postcard supposedly from Rebecca. So he would think she was all right. But you knew you'd have to come back,' I said. 'You knew that if Hurst ever found the diary he might put two and two together.'

'Yes.'

'And you broke in and tried to find it when he'd had a few too many. And you used the postcards to draw him away to London that one time, so you could have a proper look.'

'Yes, and the thing wasn't there. I couldn't believe it. And after that I couldn't get anywhere near it because of all those bars and then he bought that dog.'

'And after that you knew there was no way you could ever get back in?'

'Yes.'

'But you thought he'd found it, didn't you? That's why you went out there to see him after your wife told you that she'd seen him on the hill.'

Lang stared at the table. 'Yes. I was afraid. He kept on coming to the house. He just showed up one afternoon. I saw his Land Rover parked on the other side of the road. And when I went outside, he drove off. And on the weekends he'd be there, just sitting, watching the house for hours and hours. And he wouldn't say a single word.'

'So you thought he knew?' I said. 'You thought he'd found the diary?'

'Yes.'

'So when you heard he was up in the field, alone, you decided to go to have it out with him? Because if he knew, you had no choice. You had to try to make him see reason?'

'Yes. I didn't know what the diary said. My wife went out after her walk. I parked the car outside his house by the lane and went round the back. I walked across his garden, over the wall and then over the fields, towards the top of the hill. His dog started barking. I waited by some bushes. There was some old boy out there walking his dog, and he seemed to be taking forever about it, and I didn't want him to hear what I would be saying to Frank.

'Hurst was up there, bent over, fixing some barbed wire. He'd dumped his other tools behind him. The dog kept barking and barking. And I thought, if he knows — well, that's it, I'm done for. I thought: how can I ever make him understand? How can I explain to him what Rebecca has done? How can I make him believe me?

'The dog seemed to sense I was there, and it was really going berserk, so Frank went and gave it a whack. Then he came back. He was talking to himself — mumbling. I hadn't seen him up close for a while. And, as I watched him, I thought, he's just an old man. An old man with nothing to lose. A lonely old man mumbling to himself at the top of a hill. What's he got? Nothing.

'I was going to explain it all to him. I was going to try to make him see reason. I was going to tell him that I hadn't had a choice. But deep down I knew it was hopeless. And then —'

'You saw the pitchfork?'

'Yes, it was stuck in the ground next to an old tree trunk. It was almost dark. The whole place was completely deserted. I kind of watched myself leaving the trees, reaching for it. The dog started barking again, and this time I was glad, because it meant Frank wouldn't hear me when I came up behind him. I pushed him. Hard. He stumbled and fell over. Landed by some tree. He put his hand up and then . . .'

Lang looked up. 'Well, the dog just kept on barking. It was still tied up to the tree branch. I was sure someone was going to come out and see what all the noise was about. So I tried to calm it down a bit. But it was no use, of course. It just kept barking more and more loudly, and I thought, my God, the whole village can probably hear it. Someone's going to come up here any second and see me. So I . . . well, it was already tied up, so I just pulled on the lead. Didn't look. Just kept pulling. I couldn't let

it go. It would have gone for me straightaway. I didn't have a choice.'

'And you went home?'

'Yes, I went back the way I had come. I
was in a state. Couldn't think clearly. Wasn't
sure how it had really happened. Seemed as
if it hadn't happened to me at all. My wife
was still out. So I knew I had some time to
get myself together. I changed out of my
clothes and had a shower, and then I started
to think. If he has the diary, it must be
somewhere in the house. It's going to be
found. I panicked for a while. Thought
about going out there immediately — even
got in the car. Had to stop myself. Went
back into the house. Had another drink.
Tried to think it over. Someone could have
found his body up there, so the police might
already be at the house. I'd have to wait. So
I waited.'

'Until the next night?'

'Yes. I waited until my wife was asleep. I
parked in the village. And then I walked
over the fields and went back to the house.
There was a police car out the front, but
the man in it was fast asleep, so I went
round to the sheds. The back doors were
wide open.'

'So you thought you'd destroy the diary?'

'Yes, and Rebecca's body too. It would be

buried beneath all that rubble forever.'

'And you'd be in the clear. But we got her out. And then you got the call from Nancy. Hurst hadn't found her diary after all. Nancy had it. She'd found it when she was cleaning. So Hurst had no proof,' I said. 'But he'd begun to suspect. He didn't believe in the postcards any more. Not after you used them to lure him away and search her room.' I put my hands behind my head. 'You know, I always had a feeling after Sarah Hurst was killed that Frank was lying about something, or covering up something, or not telling me something. I kept on at him — kept on going back to his house, but he wouldn't give. Obstinate bastard,' I said almost fondly. 'He was trying to draw you out, Lang. He didn't know, but he suspected. I think deep down he knew what she was, and what she might have done, but he couldn't face it. But if anyone else could have seen what she was, it would have been you, and Hurst damned well knew it. He was trying to scare you to see how you'd react.' I leant forward. 'And then, when you thought it was all over and you were in the clear, you got a call from Nancy.'

'Yes,' Lang said. He looked utterly ex-hausted.

'But you read the diary.'

'Yes.'

'Did it say?' I said quickly. 'Did it say where Rebecca buried Gail?'

Lang looked up at me very sharply. 'Well, no, of course it didn't. Not directly. But . . .' Then slowly it dawned on him. 'But you told me you'd read it. You've got a copy. Why do you need me to . . .' He stopped. 'You don't have a copy at all, do you?' he said, and closed his eyes.

I shook my head. 'Nancy kept her side of the bargain as far we know, Lang.'

'So you were lying?' Lang said in a flat voice.

I shrugged.

He looked at me long and hard, but in fact he did not seem that surprised. The room was silent. There wasn't much fight left in him. 'All right,' he said. 'God. I don't know how much longer I could have kept it up anyway. Not after Nancy. Not after that.'

'Did Rebecca make any mention of where she buried Gail in the diary?' Graves said. 'Come on, help us out here, Lang. Come on.'

'Yes. She mentioned looking at her. Looking at her before she went to sleep sometimes.'

'So she could see it from her window, you mean,' I said.

Lang nodded. 'She mentioned some trees, I think. Out in the fields, or on the hill.'

Lang was staring up at me. He seemed to have collapsed in on himself. His shoulders were hunched in. He looked smaller somehow. He'd killed three people. One out of anger, and two just to save his own skin. Yet I couldn't help but feel a trace of pity for him. Then it was gone.

Lang looked up and stared wildly across the table. He looked at Graves first and then at me. His voice sounded ragged. 'You must understand,' he said. 'If it hadn't been for me, Rebecca would have kept on doing it. If I'd let her go, she would have kept on killing. There would have been others.'

I pushed back my chair. 'Yes,' I said. 'I think you're right about that. But I don't think that's going to help you all that much, I'm afraid.' I stood up to leave, and Graves followed. I looked back at Lang, staring across the room. He hadn't reacted to what I'd said. Or maybe he just hadn't heard me.

56

It was early morning when we finally left the featureless walls of the station behind us. It had been a very long night, and I had decided to give Graves the rest of the day off. He deserved it. We strolled out the front door and down the gritted steps.

'So you think Hurst knew, then?' Graves said.

I shrugged. 'Maybe. Not all of it. But he probably knew that she'd been home the afternoon her stepmother had had her accident. Or maybe suspected. That was what he was covering up when I tried to talk to him years ago.'

'But how did you know, sir? When did you begin to suspect that it could have been Rebecca who made those two girls disappear?'

'The night before last. I was thinking about the pond in the village and how it had been used before as . . . as a murder weapon.'

'A murder weapon?'

'Yes, the locals used to drown witches in it,' I said. 'Well, old women they thought were witches. Powell, my old partner, told me. And then I started to think about one of Rebecca's friends as well. Her friend Alice, her only friend at school, said the girls gave Rebecca a wide berth right from the start. Alice thought it was because Rebecca was new. But I think it was more than that. I think the girls felt an instinctive aversion to her. Could maybe sense something about her, much as her housemistress did later on. And then there was something else. Rebecca didn't know Alice all that well and seemed perfectly happy on her own. So why did she invite Alice over to her house? I think she wanted to prove how clever she had been, just like she did with Lang. Alice knew about Sarah's accident in the swimming pool, so Rebecca must have told her. I'm going to have a talk with her later, but I think that Rebecca probably told her about the pond as well. She might even have taken Alice into those woods Lang was talking about.'

We walked on. 'So what now?' I said.

Graves tightened his scarf round his neck. 'I'm going to get some breakfast,' he said, as if he had decided on that some time ago.

'A big fry-up at a greasy spoon. And then I suppose I'm going to have to do some Christmas shopping over in Cheltenham before it gets mobbed — just like it was the last time we were there.'

'All right,' I said. 'I'll see you tomorrow.'

I waved and watched Graves walk towards the street, his shadow trailing behind him and his shoes crunching loudly in the snow. I was secretly very pleased with my new sergeant. A wave of exhaustion suddenly came over me. I breathed in the crisp air and let the coldness of the morning seep under the collar of my coat. I wondered vaguely if Lang was finally asleep in his cell.

I plucked the keys out of my pocket, threw them in the air and caught them in the palm of my hand, although I wasn't going home just yet. Abruptly, I turned around and began to walk back to the station. I had to phone Elise's parents and tell them that I was on my way to see them. Then I would have to drive out there and tell them in person. But before that I had to talk to Gail's mother.

I would lie to them as much as I could. I would tell them that for Elise and Gail, it had been mercifully quick and that they had both gone in peace to their graves.

■ ■ ■ ■

In the end it didn't take us long to find Gail. Rebecca had buried her in a shallow grave in a small copse of trees just where the hill began to rise gently on the other side of the garden wall. When I glanced back at where the house had been, I realized with a shudder that Lang had been right: Rebecca would have been able to see the grave from her bedroom window. For a moment, it was as if the cold shadow of Dashwood Manor rose behind us. And staring out of the window was Rebecca. Smiling perhaps. Her face pressed against the glass and looking down on us all.

We had been there for a few hours when one of the men turned round and gave me a curt nod, and we knew that it was nearly over. I phoned Brewin, and we waited. He had been expecting the call and arrived half an hour later. Still, I didn't give the order to continue.

I hesitated because I suppose a part of me wanted to leave her there a moment longer in that remote spot. Gail had been part of the very earth itself, and she had been far away from the enclosed darkness of a cemetery. She had been out here amongst these ancient hills. The ground beyond her un-marked grave was covered in a fresh layer of snow. Bright in the late-afternoon sun. A few leaves fell. Others were already gathered together in the cold, lying amongst the scattered branches.

But I was aware of the men waiting, and Brewin shifting impatiently beside me, so I gave the order. Gail had been out here for too long amongst the whispering trees, and I couldn't let her stay.

ABOUT THE AUTHOR

James Marrison is a journalist with a Master's degree in history, specializing in American Secret Intelligence, from the University of Edinburgh in England. Marrison was a regular contributor to *Bizarre* magazine in the UK, where he wrote about true crime, and he also wrote for an English language newspaper in Buenos Aires, Argentina, where he now lives. *The Drowning Ground* is his first novel.